CATALYST

RACHEL GRANT

JANUS PUBLISHING

Books by Rachel Grant

PRAISE FOR
TINDERBOX
FLASHPOINT #1

"This first novel in Grant's Flashpoint series offers a multilayered, suspenseful plot that's strengthened by its appealing characters, strong attention to detail, and a healthy dose of romance. The story kicks off with a bang, literally and figuratively, and Grant keeps the momentum going through a series of plot twists and well-staged action sequences that plunge the heroes into the path of a vicious warlord who'll stop at nothing to consolidate his power in the region."

- Kirkus Reviews (starred review)

PRAISE FOR
CATALYST
FLASHPOINT #2

"The second novel in Grant's Flashpoint series offers intelligent romantic suspense that moves with the urgency of a thriller. The well-researched and timely plot finds the heroes confronting the realities of famine in South Sudan while unraveling a complex scheme to secure oil rights in the region."

- Kirkus Reviews (starred review)

This one is for my mom.

Glenda Stallings
1934–2017

She married three husbands, birthed seven children, and helped mother an additional seven stepchildren. An English teacher before going to dental hygiene school, she also started a business, closed the business, and cleaned thousands of teeth.

Her mind left this world long before her body did. Alzheimer's is cruel.

Chapter One

Camp Citron, Djibouti
March

Sebastian Ford scanned the club, his gaze landing on the woman he was searching for. He'd recognized her the moment he spotted her in Savannah James's office. What the hell was Princess Prime doing at Camp Citron hanging out with the base spook?

He'd questioned James, but she was her usual secretive self and refused to even confirm the woman's name, but an internet search confirmed Bastian's initial suspicion. Not that he'd doubted his own memory. He would never forget those pretty lips that had spewed terrible lies. Or those wide mocha eyes that feigned sympathy all while she calculated how to cheat people of their land rights.

He felt stares as he crossed the room and wondered who in the club had been here last night when he'd stupidly triggered a fight with Pax, a member of his own A-Team. It had been a dumbass move, and he would have happily stayed away from Barely North for the rest of this deployment, but instead he'd returned to the scene of his idiocy to pick a fight with an oil company shill whose daddy was one of the richest men in the world.

His XO was going to flip, but he wanted to know what the hell Gabriella Prime was doing in Djibouti. What atrocity did she intend to inflict on people who had even less than the tribal members on the reservation she'd attempted to screw over ten years ago?

He dropped onto the empty barstool next to her and ordered a beer while he figured out how to open the conversation.

The ten years that had passed since he last saw her looked good on her. She had a maturity about her that had been missing before. But then, she couldn't be much older than he was, meaning she must've been all of twenty-two or twenty-three when she'd been made Vice President of Screwing Indian Tribes for Prime Energy.

He cleared his throat to speak.

"I'm not here to get laid," she said before he could get a word out. "So you can save your breath."

"Don't worry, Ms. Prime, I'm not interested."

She startled at his use of her name and studied him. She raised an eyebrow. "I think you have me mistaken for somebody else."

"Not at all. Gabriella Stewart Prime. Only child of Tatiana Stewart and Jeffery Prime. With two older half brothers, you're the youngest of Prime's three children. Your daddy is the CEO of Prime Energy, and your great-granddaddy was the founder of the company. I'm good with names and faces, and I'd never forget you." His gaze swept her from head to toe. She *was* memorable, and not just because she was a Prime. She'd even done some modeling when she was really young, but that had been before she was on his radar.

"And you are?"

"Princess Prime, I'm your worst nightmare."

Her eyes narrowed. "Don't call me that."

"Fine, I'll call you Gabriella."

She scanned his body with the same degree of assessment he'd just given her. She paused on his face, her brow furrowed. "Did we have sex or something a long time ago?" She bit her lip, then said with a wince, "If so, I'm sorry, I don't remember you."

That startled a laugh out of him. Unexpected and strangely pleasing. "Sweetheart, if we'd had sex, you'd remember it."

She snickered. "One would hope." She picked up her drink and took a slow sip, completely unfazed by him. She set the glass down and smiled. "So if you aren't here to rehash or initiate a night of passion, why *are* you pestering me?"

"I want to know what you're doing in Djibouti."

"I don't believe that's any of your business. You haven't even told me your name."

"Chief Warrant Officer Sebastian Ford. Bastian to my friends."

"I think it's safe to assume I'm not one of those. What do your enemies call you?"

"Bastian the Bastard, but that's usually behind my back."

"And what do they call you to your face?"

"Asshole."

She smiled. "I like the straightforwardness of your enemies. Cuts right through the bullshit. But my dear granddaddy would be distressed at my using such foul language, so we'll have to come up with something else."

"We wouldn't want to have the old oil baron rolling over in his grave."

"Oh, not him—Grandpa Prime was a foul-mouthed sonofabitch. I was talking about Grandpa Stewart."

Bastian shook his head at how she was controlling this

conversation. Plus, she still hadn't answered his question. "Those who are neither friends nor enemies but who must tolerate me nonetheless call me Mr. Ford or Chief Ford. Mister is the official address for a warrant officer, but chief is acceptable."

"Chief Ford it is, then. Friends call me Brie. You may call me Ms. Stewart."

"Stewart? Not Prime?"

She shrugged. "I legally changed my last name to my mother's maiden name."

"Like Prime Petroleum changed to Prime Energy a dozen years ago? Obvious and unconvincing greenwashing."

"I wasn't greenwashing, I simply no longer wished to be associated with Prime Energy, and the decision to change my last name sent a clear message to Jeffery Senior."

"You call your father by his first name?"

"He insisted upon it when I worked for the company. Plus, it fit him more." She paused, then smiled. "But mostly, I called him asshole to his face."

Bastian couldn't help but laugh. She *still* hadn't come close to answering his burning question, and yet he couldn't resist a follow-up. "And your granddaddy wasn't bothered by your language?"

"Grandpa Stewart made an exception for Jeffery. He called my dad names that would make a sailor squirm."

"Why are you here at Camp Citron?" he repeated.

"Why are *you* here?"

Fair enough. He'd even get specific if it would elicit an answer from her. "I'm US Army Special Forces. My A-Team is teaching Djiboutians to be guerilla fighters."

"Special Forces. I'm impressed." Her gaze swept down

his body again. "I shouldn't have been so quick to say I'm not here to get laid." She ran her fingertip around the rim of her glass. "But then, it's not like you're a SEAL."

He snorted, irritated his body had responded to her perusal. She was a viper, even if she did amuse him.

He wasn't interested.

He nodded toward a table in the middle of the room, where Lieutenant Fallon and a few other SEALs were gathered. A glance showed they—not surprisingly— were checking her out. She was pretty, in Djibouti, and likely leaving in a few days—the perfect prospect for a no-strings screw. "If you're looking for a hookup, a few SEALs are over there."

"I'll keep that in mind after I ditch you." She took another sip, then asked, "How did you recognize me? It's not like I flaunt who I am. It's been years since someone recognized me."

He would imagine anonymity was important, given that her father was CEO of one of the world's largest oil companies and ransom payments made up a large percentage of the economy of Somalia, which was just ten miles away.

It was insane for her to be here, really. Her dad was a *billionaire*. She probably had her own millions—even billions—tucked away. Alarm registered. It would be foolish for her to be in this part of the world without a subdermal tracker. He took her hand and slid up her sleeve to study her arm, looking for a cut or bandage indicating she'd been chipped. But what he saw were track marks. Very old track marks.

She jerked her arm back and pulled down her sleeve. "I've been clean for eight years," she said, defensive. Angry.

"I wasn't looking for that." Guilt trickled down his spine. He'd invaded her privacy without meaning to. "I was looking to see if you'd been chipped by Savannah James."

"No. It would be a waste of resources."

She knew exactly what he was talking about, which was telling in itself. Trackers were top-secret technology, and Savannah James wouldn't have told Gabriella about her favorite spy gadget if she didn't think it was warranted, which meant Gabriella had refused the chip.

"How so?" he asked. "You're a prime target." The pun wasn't intended. He grimaced and let it stand without comment.

"One, because I've been in South Sudan for over six months and there hasn't been an issue because no one there knows who my dad is—changing my name to Stewart had multiple benefits. Two, I'll be there for at least another six months, which is far past the tracker's expiration date, and I can't fly back to Camp Citron every two months to get a new tracker. Three, there aren't any cell towers where I am, rendering a tracker useless. And lastly, there is no way in hell Jeffery would pay any sort of ransom for me, so why bother?"

Bastian's brain froze the moment she said "South Sudan." Princess Prime was hanging out in South Sudan? What kind of con was she pulling here? There was no reason for an oil baron's daughter to be in the war-torn country unless her plan was to steal their oil.

⌒

B rie grimaced as she confessed to a total stranger that her dad didn't give a crap about her. But hell, he'd just seen the scars that were her greatest shame, so it wasn't like she could go any lower in his estimation. She picked up her soda and sipped from the straw until it made a loud slurping noise, then caught the bartender's eye and ordered another ginger ale.

She'd changed. She'd pulled herself back from the brink. Chief Bastard could judge her all he wanted, but *she* knew who she was now, and she was proud of herself. Lord knew she had to take pride in her accomplishments, because no one in her family had kind words for her.

"What the hell are you doing in South Sudan?" Chief Bastard asked, his voice angrier now than it had been earlier. Where did his anger come from?

Maybe she really had slept with him back when she'd been using. He could have denied it simply because she didn't remember him. The male ego was more fragile than a soap bubble.

But damn, it was a shame if she didn't remember that body. Or that face. Eyes so dark they were almost black, slightly hooded, indicating Asian or Native American heritage. Given his other features, she'd bet Native American. She studied his mouth. His lips looked just right for kissing and other pleasures.

Seated as he was, she couldn't be certain of his height, but guessed he was an inch or two shy of six feet. His build was perfectly proportioned, muscular, with broad shoulders and narrow hips. He wore a T-shirt that hugged his pecs, and she'd be sure to check out his ass in those jeans when he walked away.

He was the Goldilocks of men. *Just right.* Or was he Baby Bear? It was Baby Bear's things that were just right. Goldilocks was the entitled white thief. But then, he probably wouldn't appreciate being called Baby Bear anymore than he'd like Goldilocks.

"What are you hiding, Princess Prime?"

The hated nickname pulled her out of her whimsy and rooted her firmly in the here and now, facing down a badass Special Forces operator who didn't like her very much. And it was entirely probable she'd earned his animosity in her Princess Prime days.

"I said don't call me that, Chief Bastard." The bartender set a fresh ginger ale in front of her, and she took a sip. "I'm not hiding anything. I work for the US Agency for International Development, better known as USAID. I'm an aid worker. I've been helping South Sudanese people who've returned to their villages after being displaced by the civil war prepare for the rainy season, which, by all accounts, is going to suck elephant dicks this year."

She dreaded the coming rainy season. She'd thought the last six months had been tough? That was nothing compared to what was around the corner.

"You're an *aid worker*?" He said the words with an unflattering amount of incredulity.

"Yes, Chief Ford. You can run a background check if you'd like. Tell Savvy I gave you permission to see my file. Brie Stewart is my name. And when you're done, let me know what intel she's gathered on me. I'm curious to know if she found out what happened in Denmark twelve years ago." Not that anything bad had happened—at least she didn't think so—Brie just didn't remember.

His shock that she had a real job was rather insulting given that she'd always been a hard worker, even when she made a few minor headlines for the exploits of Princess Prime. She'd worked sixteen-hour days for Prime Energy back then. She'd self-medicated over the soul-sucking job with drugs and sex, but no one could call her a slacker.

She regretted the drugs but missed the sex. Hell, she'd take up sex as a hobby again, if South Sudan wasn't such a terrible place for it. The three men she worked with were great guys—she'd most definitely be interested in them in the first world—but she wouldn't screw around with a coworker, not when the job was one hundred percent stress. It was a recipe for disaster.

She cast her gaze in the direction of the SEALs. Maybe she should try to get laid while she was at Camp Citron.

"Oh, I'd love to know what Savannah James has on you," Bastian said, pulling her attention back to him. "I bet she has the same suspicions I do."

Brie rolled her eyes. "And what would that be?"

"You were sent there by your father to ensure Prime Energy locks down the oil rights. You're the closer for a deal certain to screw starving people out of the only valuable resource they have."

She sighed. "Your Google skills are weak if you think I still work for my father. I quit my job at Prime Energy when I started grad school over nine years ago." She cocked her head. "How the hell did you recognize me?"

"Ten years ago, I attended a community meeting for an oil pipeline proposal PE was ramming through the environmental impact process in eastern Washington. I sat in the front row as you defended PE's plan to destroy an important Traditional Cultural Property to build a pipeline that would bisect the state from the Canadian border to the Columbia River. You had no respect for the sovereignty of tribes over their land. Your plan lacked even basic environmental protection for air and water, but you defended it because you didn't give a fuck about air Indians breathe or water Indians drink."

Well, that answered her question about his ethnic background, and it also explained why he hated her. Plus, she had no defense, because he was right. It was projects like that one that had set her on the merry path of self-medicating.

How ironic that it was that very project that triggered the decision for her to go to grad school to study cultural anthropology. After the National Historic Preservation Act and National Environmental Policy Act had been used to kill yet another major pipeline project, her father had deemed it necessary to show that someone at the top of the company hierarchy had the credentials to address NHPA and NEPA compliance in-house. He wanted her to find ways to skirt doing the necessary remediation, to be an expert witness who could refute evidence of Traditional Cultural Properties. He'd wanted her to be the cultural resources version of a climate change denier.

But in the end, her father had gotten more than he bargained for. Graduate school had been her escape route.

Her fellow grad students had helped her clean up and find the strength to turn her back on her family and Prime Energy. In grad school, she'd found purpose and a path to redemption.

But none of this could be shared with a stranger in a club on a US military base in Africa. While she knew she owed Bastian an apology for her actions as Princess Prime, she also knew nothing she could say would mean a damn thing to him. His goal here was to shame her, not find a reason to forgive her.

"PE lost that battle. The Corps of Engineers never granted our permit. You won." She dropped a twenty on the bar to pay for her two sodas, leaving a far bigger tip than she could afford, but she didn't want to wait for change. "Now, as lovely as it's been strolling down memory lane with you, I have an early flight back to the mud pit I call home. Good luck and have a good life, Chief Ford."

Bastian watched her leave, utterly confused as to why he felt like a shit for hurting her feelings, when she'd been the one who'd tried to undermine a Washington tribe's treaty rights so her daddy could add to his billions.

The Kalahwamish Reservation, his tribe's land, was on the Olympic Peninsula. Their land hadn't been in jeopardy, but tribes from across the state had all come together, much like tribes across the country had rallied to stop the Dakota Access Pipeline.

His belly churned, as it always did when he thought of DAPL. He was in Djibouti, serving his country, and that same country he loved and risked his life for had screwed over the Standing Rock Sioux Tribe. For months now, he'd been asking himself if it was time to get out of the Army and go home to take up the fight to preserve freedom for his tribe and all Native Americans. How could he continue to risk his life for a country that didn't give a crap about his people?

But damn, he loved being a Special Forces operator. After Cece burrowed her way into his family until there was no room left for him, his A-Team had become his family. Who would he be without the uniform? Without his brothers?

He loved his country. He loved his tribe. And sometimes it felt like they were still at war with each other.

He paid the bartender for the beer he'd barely touched and left the club. Night had descended while he spoke with Gabriella, or Brie, or whatever her name was now. It was full dark. The air was muggy and hot, and escaping into his air-conditioned Containerized Living Unit—CLU—held no appeal. He was restless. Antsy. Pissed off.

He walked out, beyond the buildings that clustered around the club, beyond the rows of containers that made up CLUville. They couldn't see the Gulf of Tadjoura from this part of the base, but there was an open area that offered prime stargazing.

He'd been stupid last night in attempting to hit on the woman Pax clearly wanted for himself. Pax was on his team, one of his brothers. But it hadn't felt that way since Yemen, and Bastian knew his own pride was the major issue. Just like with Gabriella, he'd held a grudge against Pax. But unlike with Gabriella, both he and Pax had made mistakes.

Princess Prime had crumpled under the shame he'd applied, while his attempts to shame Pax only made the soldier stand taller. But then, Pax knew he wasn't alone in the guilt department. Bastian shared equal blame.

He was such a bastard.

Ahead of him, he could see the silhouette of a woman. She stood in the open with her face toward the night sky, her long dark hair glinting in the yellow glow of a nearby light post. He stepped closer and caught the shine of tears on her cheek.

He shouldn't feel guilty for calling Gabriella Prime—or Brie Stewart—on what she'd done, but somehow, he did.

She was the embodiment of everything he despised.

But damn, that body. She wore simple clothes that hugged her slight curves.

The jeans and long-sleeved T-shirt were nothing like the tailored suit she'd worn all those years ago. He'd been a senior in college and had known nothing about women's clothing, and yet he could tell her suit had cost big bucks, as had her hair and makeup. Ten years ago, she'd looked like a glossy business fashion ad in the flesh. From his front-row seat, he could practically smell the money on her and it had never occurred to him that money could smell so damn good.

Cece had noticed his fixation and called him on it, claiming he had white-girl fantasies, and that he wanted to fuck the daughter of big oil.

He'd been trying to break up with Cece for nearly a year at that point and had wanted to tell her, no, he wasn't having white-girl fantasies, he was having anyone-but-Cece fantasies, and the women he dreamed about came in all colors.

Gabriella Prime just so happened to be the latest and whitest.

When he finally managed the breakup a month later, Cece accused him of wanting to track down the bitch from the oil company and become her Indian boy toy. Gabriella had made a strong impression on Cece too, apparently.

Staring now at the woman who'd played a role in some rather hot relationship escape fantasies, it was amazing he'd recognized her. Brie Stewart bore only the slightest resemblance to the polished Gabriella Prime, but she was every bit as compelling. More so now, because she looked real.

She wasn't Oil Company Barbie anymore.

She was a little thin—likely due to living in South Sudan, not because she'd relapsed into heroin addiction. He believed her when she said she'd been clean for years. If she'd been using in South Sudan, she'd look like a junkie. Drugs combined with the place would've hollowed her out.

He'd witnessed the combination of poverty and addiction first-hand. Princess Prime might've been able to maintain a polished façade while supporting a heroin addiction, but there was no way that could be done in a place like South Sudan. He'd also seen enough to recognize when someone was an addict, when they were recovering, and when they relapsed, and he was certain Gabriella Stewart Prime had gotten her shit together.

"Are you just going to stand there and stare at me, Chief Ford, or did you follow me out here to tell me more about why you suspect me of wanting to harm the people I work my ass off to help?"

"I didn't follow you. But if those are the only choices, I guess I'll go with continuing to stare at you."

"I'm flattered."

"You're a beautiful woman, it's a simple fact."

She laughed softly. "No, I'm not. I mean, I clean up well—I'm not being falsely modest—but you don't live in my world and get to maintain the illusion you're anything special, not when everyone is so eager to point out that my eyes are too wide, my face too round, and that I should have a surgeon take care of my unfortunate nose."

"Unfortunate nose?" He'd never even noticed her nose. It was just a nose. "What's wrong with it?"

"It's giant, obviously."

"White people are weird."

"I'm sure that's true, but in this case, you might mean rich people."

"They're the weirdest white people of all." He cocked his head. "So, you still rich? I mean, should I make a play for you because you're loaded?"

She pressed her hand to her heart. "You'd be willing to overlook my unfortunate nose?"

He shrugged. "If you've got money, sure. I can work around the beak."

Her laugh was genuine, and she wiped her cheek, erasing her tears. "Thank you. I needed that." Then she approached him, stepping farther from the streetlight and into the darkness that separated them. She came to a stop in front of him and placed her hand on his chest.

He knew this was nothing more than a tease, and yet his heart rate kicked up, which was insane. Worse, she could feel the rapid beat, and there was just enough light to see her smile.

Damn, she had a smile. Sweet, sexy. He didn't notice her unfortunate nose because he was too busy looking at her perfect lips.

She placed her other hand on his chest and rose on her toes, sliding both hands over his pecs, giving every sign she was impressed by what she felt through the thin layer of his T-shirt. She brought her mouth to within an inch of his. "Do you want to kiss me, Bastian?"

"Strangely, I do."

"You'll end up disappointed."

"Why is that? Are you a terrible kisser?"

"Oh no. I take kissing very seriously. Like everything I do, I give it my full hundred and ten percent. I'm a magnificent kisser."

He laughed. She had a certain crazy appeal. "Then

why would I be disappointed?"

"Because then, of course, you'll want to have sex with me. And you'll probably fall in love with me, because I'm also very good at sex."

"I could be willing to take that risk. I don't fall in love easily."

"But in the end, you'll be terribly disappointed to learn that I am completely and thoroughly cut off from my family. I live paycheck to paycheck on my USAID salary."

That was the most appealing thing she'd said so far. As if mesmerized, he found himself leaning down and pressing his mouth to hers, unsure if she'd really intended things to go this far. But even that edge of uncertainty turned him on.

Forbidden fruit had always been an aphrodisiac for him, and she represented the ultimate enemy in his world.

Her lips opened under his, and the sweltering night grew hotter as their tongues mingled. She tasted sweet, and she hadn't been kidding about her kissing skills. The bold stroke of her tongue announced she'd absolutely intended this, and the soft sounds she made told him she enjoyed it as much as he did.

Her fingers gripped his T-shirt. His hand slid around the back of her neck. He could get lost in her mouth. He wished there was a wall to back her up against. He wanted to pin her and grind his erection against her spread legs.

His lips left hers to trail along her jaw and neck. He reached her collarbone and licked the salt from her skin, sweat put there by the humid night. He paused, closing his eyes, breathing her in.

Even her sweat smelled good. He wanted to take her

back to his CLU and fuck her against the container wall, just like he'd imagined all those years ago, when he'd fantasized about banging Oil Company Barbie.

All at once, the shock of what he was doing came to him. He was making out with Gabriella Prime.

Some spank bank fantasies were never meant to become real. He'd lusted after Gabriella when he was twenty-one because she was the ultimate taboo. His parents would never approve of her in the way they did Cece. At twenty-one, it had been mental rebellion. At thirty-one? It was just stupid.

He pulled back and fixed a smile on his face. "Well, I think I survived that without suffering great disappointment. But I'm sorry to say I don't want to have sex with you and won't be falling in love with you. But thanks for giving me the chance to find out. Nice seeing you again, Gabriella." With that, he turned his back on her and walked away.

Chapter Two

South Sudan
One month later

By all accounts, the rains had started early this year. The roads were still passable, but in a few more days, they might disappear. Brie lay on her cot and stared up at the metal roof, listening to the musical tap of the mild storm. The roof magnified the sound. A slight sprinkle sounded like a deluge. Was it the rain that had woken her at—she hit the button to illuminate her wristwatch—just after three a.m.?

She was lucky to have a metal roof and walls. The locals only had thatched-roof huts. The storm was light right now, but they'd get worse.

Who would've thought it could feel hotter when it rained? This close to the equator, it was hot to begin with, but now, with the need to close the windows against the storm, it was sweltering. The thatched-roof huts breathed, at least. But they also let in water and mud.

Every time she adjusted to the...*uniqueness* of living here, the conditions changed. At least now she could use more than six cups of water to wash her entire body every few days. Maybe she'd grow her hair long again. She'd chopped it all off the day after she returned from Camp Citron, giving herself a super-short cut in a fit of depression.

Chief Bastard never would have recognized her as Princess Prime without the long dark hair she'd been known for. Cutting her hair had been a stupid rebellion, directed at a man she'd never see again.

Not that she wanted to see him again.

That was a definite no. He'd reminded her of the person she'd been. The woman who'd hurt people for company gain. Business first, humanity second. He believed she still was that person.

Then he'd kissed her. Soft and sensual and hot at the same time. He kissed like a man devoted to the art form, only to turn and walk away in cold, flagrant rejection.

What had she been thinking to let it get that far? What had she been trying to prove to him? To herself?

If she'd wanted to prove she wasn't the woman she used to be, it would have been smarter to point out she'd worked in several developing countries over the last five years, South Sudan being only the most recent and most dangerous. She had no part in what her family did. She gave back to the world instead of taking. Not that he'd have believed her.

Kissing him had been very much the old Gabriella. His harsh reminder that she couldn't atone for her past had her throwing herself at him to convince him to like her, to see her as something other than Jeffery Prime's daughter and first-class oil industry shill.

But life didn't work that way. *Men* didn't work that way. Screwing him wouldn't improve his opinion of her, and she damn well knew it. But still, in a fit of insecurity, she'd gone for the ego boost but crashed and burned on liftoff.

Pathetic to realize four weeks had passed and she was

still thinking about Chief Warrant Officer Sebastian Ford and that kiss. There was something wrong with her that one conversation, one kiss, could set her so far back in her self-esteem.

But then, it probably wasn't her self-esteem that obsessed over him. It was her body. It had been a year since she'd gotten laid, and he was a fine male specimen with his thick biceps and dark eyes.

She wondered what he looked like in his uniform, sweaty and dirty after a day of training locals in the desert sun. She'd peel off his clothing, layer by layer, and then things would get *really* dirty…

The crack of a bullet sounded, jolting her from her ridiculous fantasy. *What the hell?*

A second burst of fire sounded, then a third. Three shots in each burst.

Shit.

It was the signal. Invaders had breached the outer perimeter. They didn't have much in the way of security at this facility. Just two guards whose job was to sound the alarm, because they lacked the ability to take on an assault force.

The list of suspects for this was endless. Boko Haram? Troops representing the current president? The former vice president's rebel forces?

Any and all of them could be after the food stored here, and only a fool would stick around to find out the answer. She slipped on her boots and grabbed the backpack that she always kept within arm's reach.

She raced to the storage room with the crudely disguised escape route as she heard glass breaking at the front of the facility. As expected, security hadn't been able to hold them off for long.

She hoped the guards were okay. They'd done their job in providing the warning shots. They weren't expected to put up resistance in the face of certain defeat.

The supplies in this building could be all that prevented this area of South Sudan from reaching a magnitude of four on the Integrated Phase Classification scale for measuring food insecurity. IPC 1 indicated food insecurity was minimal, while IPC 5 meant famine.

With the ongoing civil war, there hadn't been much planting this year, meaning harvest yields would be low. Now the rainy season was upon them and they were already at IPC 3, making the food stored here valuable. When the roads became swampland in the coming days, this grain would be all that stood between the locals and starvation.

She arrived in the storage room in unison with her three coworkers. Like her, they were breathless and carried their own emergency packs. Alan lifted the panel that covered their exit. It wasn't so much a door as a hole in the aluminum wall hidden by a slightly larger sheet of aluminum. There was no hinge on the sheet, no attachment to the structure, just a piece of flimsy metal. The hole was disguised by debris on the outside of the building and usually blocked by crates on the inside.

The exit wasn't far from a line of trees that gave way to grassy swampland that edged the river. They were just a few miles from the Ethiopian border.

Ezra had grabbed the satellite phone and was attempting to call UN security, based in the capital. His eyes were bleak as they met hers. "Even if I get through, Juba is too far away."

"If we all escape, they will search for us," Jaali, the lone South Sudanese USAID employee, said. "Brie must get away. I will stay and tell them you are all long gone, back to America."

She knew why he made the offer. Odds were, the men at the front of the building were just after the food. While it wasn't unheard of for male aid workers to be raped in this situation, female aid workers were raped ninety-nine percent of the time.

"I'll stay with Jaali," Alan said. "Ezra, Brie, head to the UN in Juba—"

The door to the storage room cracked as it was battered from the other side. Jaali shoved Brie through the small opening, and she forced her way through the pile of garbage on the outside. Before she made it through, the panel slid back into place behind her.

She was outside. Alone. There hadn't even been time for Ezra to follow.

She ran toward the swamp. She would hide there until it was safe to head into the village. If she was lucky, she'd be able to locate someone with a truck and catch a ride to where she could find help.

~⌒~

Bastian sat at the table in Special Operations Command headquarters with the rest of his A-Team, braced for the coming briefing. The moment he'd heard the words "South Sudan" combined with "USAID," he'd felt sick to his stomach.

The head of SOCOM stood and addressed the room. "Five hours ago, a USAID facility in eastern South Sudan was attacked." The commander clicked on a laptop touchpad, and a map of the South Sudan border with Ethiopia was projected onto a large screen.

"Our nearest estimate is a dozen men attacked the

facility. All four USAID workers have been taken hostage."

There were multiple USAID facilities in South Sudan. Gabriella could be stationed at any one of them. He met Savannah James's steady gaze. She gave nothing away.

The commander tapped the computer again, and the projected image changed. Official USAID portraits of four aid workers were laid out in a square. Pretty brown eyes and a not even remotely unfortunate nose were on the bottom right.

His vision dimmed, but he pulled up before anyone could see his reaction. The name under her portrait—Brie Stewart—gave him hope no one in South Sudan knew who her father was.

"The UN compound in Juba received a distress call from one of the aid workers moments before they were taken," the commander continued. "Peacekeepers arrived at the village, which is about twenty-five miles southwest of Akobo, at oh-five hundred, where they found the facility in flames and hostages gone." A moment passed as he let that statement sink in. "It was assumed the facility was attacked for the food aid stored there, but according to locals, the building was torched before a single bag of grain was removed. The local Ciro clansmen attempted to put out the fire but were fired upon by the assailants. Three locals were killed. The survivors fled into the swamp, returning only when they saw the militants' truck leaving the village. They spotted at least three USAID workers in the back of the truck."

"So they burned the food, shot at locals, and took USAID workers hostage," Lieutenant Randall Fallon, leader of the SEAL team, said. "The aid workers were the target all along?"

The commander nodded. "That appears to be the case."

"Have they made demands?" Bastian's XO, Captain Oswald, asked.

"None as yet. We intend to rescue the hostages before they have a chance."

Bastian sat up straight. "We know where they're being held?"

The commander tapped the pad on the laptop again. A cluster of cylindrical, thatched-roof huts appeared on the screen. "The truck was spotted by several individuals entering this small village about ten miles from the USAID facility. One informant said he saw three hostages being moved into this hut." With a laser pointer, the commander indicated a hut in the middle of the screen.

"Only three?" Pax asked.

"We haven't been able to confirm if the woman, Brie Stewart, is with her male coworkers," the commander said.

Bastian did his best to keep his face blank, even as he found it hard to breathe.

Was this about her? Did the abduction have to do with Prime Energy? Or had they separated Brie from the men in order to rape her? Last year, a USAID facility in Juba had been hit, and all the women had been rounded up and gang-raped by rebel forces. But government forces were no better; they were known to rape women and children when ransacking villages.

His chest constricted.

"How confident are we in the intel?" Lieutenant Fallon asked.

All eyes in the room turned to Savannah James. Her

specific title was unknown, but Bastian had long suspected she was more than a CIA analyst. He believed she was Special Activities Division, making her a field agent who was as well trained as any military special forces operator. SAD was the super-secretive department within an already intensely secretive agency. It was said Savvy's work was so classified, not even she knew her real name. "Assets I have in the area have heard rumblings about a Boko Haram strike, potentially targeting US citizens."

"And you did nothing?" Bastian said, then snapped his jaw shut. He was out of line, but at least she was CIA and not in his chain of command.

"Warnings were issued to all US citizens in the area, including USAID personnel," James said in a clipped tone, her cold eyes unflinching. "If the aid workers chose to ignore the warnings, it's on them." She gave him a tight smile. "The US military can hardly mobilize in response to every whispered threat in the region, Chief Ford."

"What about the intel on the hostage location?" Lieutenant Fallon prompted.

"We have multiple identical accounts from different witnesses on the location of the truck. One eyewitness gave the hut location. We're certain they're in that village, less certain of which hut they're being held in," James said. "But once they move, we're likely to lose them. Boko Haram has gotten very good at hiding hostages."

"And we're certain this is Boko Haram?" Pax asked.

"We're reasonably sure they're affiliated with the terrorist organization," James said, "but they might not be card-carrying members."

A detailed map of the surrounding area filled the screen. The Pibor River ran to the east; the Nanaam River was farther to the west. There were plenty of trees and swampland, but it wasn't thick forest cover, it was more grassland, which could be just as concealing in places. There was open space around the hut where the hostages might be held.

"We're planning a joint operation, SEALs and A-Team?" Captain Oswald asked.

"Yes," the SOCOM commander said. "We want the A-Team in the swamp and grasslands, neutralizing scouts while SEALs go for the hostages."

"How long until wheels up?" Fallon asked.

"At seventeen hundred hours, both teams will take a transport flight to our Forward Operating Base in western Ethiopia, where we have two silent birds waiting to take you to South Sudan at twenty-one hundred."

"That early? Shouldn't this be a deep-night op?" Fallon asked.

"We don't want to risk them moving the hostages," the commander said. "It's only May first but the rainy season started early. In a matter of days, the roads in the area could be impassable. Another storm is expected tomorrow. We're monitoring the area with satellites. If they move the hostages while you're en route, we'll adjust accordingly."

Bastian fixed Savannah James with a hard stare. Someone had to explain who Brie Stewart was. It would be irresponsible to send in SEALs and an A-Team, all of whom would risk their lives to rescue the hostages, without advance warning that this might have nothing to do with USAID and everything to do with the fact that one of the hostages was heir to one of the richest men in the world. Bastian would speak, but he didn't want to reveal he'd met Gabriella Stewart Prime or they might pull him from the op.

Finally, Savvy gave him a slight nod and stood. "What I'm about to tell you doesn't leave this room. It's not classified per se, but secrecy is the best protection for Brie Stewart." She went on to reveal Brie's full name and family connections, never once meeting Bastian's gaze as she did so. It appeared Savvy wanted him on this op too.

Interesting. She always had an agenda, but he had no clue what it could be in this instance.

"So it's possible," Lieutenant Fallon said, "that they attacked the facility and torched the place because they were after Gabriella Prime. Whose bright idea was it to send an oil heiress to fucking South Sudan?"

"Only a handful of people know who she is," James said. "She was safe because she hid her identity. Also worth noting, she is estranged from her family and is no longer one of the heirs of the Prime family fortune. She earned the job on her own merit—she has a master's degree in cultural anthropology—and USAID has a hard time retaining women employees in places like South Sudan. With the ongoing attacks on women and children, many locals are afraid to speak with male aid workers. They're afraid of all men. Brie has worked for USAID for nearly five years and has been stationed in several developing countries. She took the job on the condition that no one would know who she is."

"Sounds like somebody figured it out," Captain Oswald said.

"We don't know that," Savvy said. "Intel indicates this is Boko Haram. It may have nothing to do with Brie Stewart."

"Why wasn't she chipped?" Pax asked. "You mentioned she was here at the end of March. You could've implanted a subdermal tracker in her then."

"As you know, trackers have big limitations. One of which is battery life. The other is viability after a certain amount of time. Their maximum reliability is sixty days. We'd have to fly her back here every two months to replace the chip. That's a lot of expense just to keep an aid worker in place."

"Make her pay for it, then," Carlos Espinosa, a sergeant on Bastian's A-Team, said. "She's loaded, and she's the one at risk."

"We discussed that," James said. "But as I mentioned, she's estranged from her family. She's not a wealthy heiress anymore. And her USAID salary is probably less than any of us makes per year."

"Bullshit. People like that have trust funds." This came from Sergeant Cassius Callahan, another A-Team member and one of Bastian's closest friends.

Bastian admitted to himself that he'd had the same thought. Once upon a time, Brie had an expensive drug habit, but given the amount of money she must've had in her trust fund, it was hard to believe she'd injected it all.

Savvy shrugged. "I ran a full check on her. She and her family parted ways before her trust matured when she turned thirty. There's a property in Morocco she owns along with her two half brothers, but nothing she can liquidate. Besides, it's a moot point; the other limitation is trackers need an active cell phone signal to piggyback on. Cell towers are few and far between in South Sudan outside of Juba or the oil drilling operations. We're talking about a country where they don't have water or electricity in most areas. War has decimated what little infrastructure South Sudan had. Djibouti is rich with resources in comparison."

"Why was she here—at Camp Citron—to begin with?" asked Lieutenant Fallon.

"That's need-to-know only and has no bearing on your mission," Savvy said. "Brie Stewart is to be treated like any other hostage. This could be Boko Haram or a by-blow of the civil war, and we can't let on to the locals that she has wealthy family members." James placed her fists on the desk, knuckles down. "We are not in the business of ranking hostages based on their bank accounts, and she is no more important than the three men who were also taken."

With that they all turned their attention to planning the rescue operation. Bastian dialed in his focus as they formulated a plan, giving no outward sign this mission was different for him. And it shouldn't be different. As Savvy had said, Brie was no more important than the others.

But to him, in spite of everything, she was.

⁓

Brie crouched behind branches, ass-deep in muck. She'd managed to evade the searchers in the dark, but daylight was a different story.

The fact that they'd continued to search for her only raised questions. But then, there was no end to her list of questions. Minutes after her escape, she'd seen Ezra, Jaali, and Alan as they were marched toward the truck, backlit by the burning building.

Thousands of pounds of food that would've fed entire villages for months, destroyed.

If they didn't want the food, why storm the

compound? How did destroying food serve a strategic goal?

This couldn't be about her. No one—not even her coworkers—knew who she was. Chief Warrant Officer Sebastian Ford and CIA agent—or whatever she was—Savannah James were the only people for thousands of miles who knew about her family.

Could Bastian have betrayed her?

She would never believe that. He might hate her, but she couldn't believe he was a monster. He was a Special Forces operator. He wouldn't risk the people of the village. He wouldn't jeopardize other USAID workers.

People had died in the village last night. Shot by the men who'd stormed the facility. Were Ezra, Jaali, and Alan hurt? Jaali had limped as he crossed the dirt road. Had he been beaten while the others were spared, because he was South Sudanese? He served his country by ensuring food aid was given to all in need, and for that he was considered by some to be a traitor. His work aided everyone—including enemy tribes. Both rebel and government militias would've been fed by the food in storage.

If this was another battle in South Sudan's ongoing civil war, the wanton destruction of food would only make the locals more desperate. They'd hardly be eager to fight for the side that had just ensured their children would starve.

After watching her coworkers' forced evacuation and the horrifying gunning down of those who sought to save the food, she'd fled into the swamp and made her way south. If Ezra's call to the UN went through, help would arrive, but she hadn't stuck around to wait for them, because it was only a matter of time before they began searching for her. She had to put distance between herself and the village.

Plus, if Ezra's call hadn't gone through, it was up to her to find help.

The options were limited. Kemet Oil had a rig operation to the north, near the Upper Nile. The head of the operation used to work for her father. He'd recognize her. Plus, Prime Energy was in the process of trying to secure the rights to build a pipeline to deliver oil from South Sudan to the Atlantic, removing the need to pay Sudan for use of their pipeline. It was a billion dollar project meaning that at any given time, representatives from Prime Energy could be at Kemet Oil headquarters. Her brothers might even make an appearance.

To make matters worse, the Russian-based oil company, Druneft, was also vying for the pipeline concession. The last thing she needed was for someone from Druneft to recognize her.

She'd suck it up, though, and go to them if she believed Kemet Oil would lift a finger to help aid workers. But they wouldn't. Many of their workers were children—slave laborers.

She pulled herself from the marsh and trudged up to the road, staying low and out of sight, as she'd been doing for the last several hours. She'd been heading toward Juba on instinct even as she mentally debated the only other option, the UN camp a hundred miles to the northwest.

Her USAID facility had been located here in an attempt to get people to return to their villages and out of the overloaded UN camps where malaria was rampant and food supplies low.

A year ago, this area had been a stronghold of the

rebels, but the fighting had moved north, creating a no-man's-land of burned-out villages in the eastern region of the country. With the camps at critical mass, USAID determined that placing food reserves in the old villages might convince the women and children to return home. Most of the men had been killed during village raids. Most of the boys who'd survived had been impressed into service.

The population of Brie's village had tripled in the months she'd been there, but now that the food they'd relied on to see them through the rainy season was gone, many would likely head back to the camp.

The camp couldn't spare peacekeepers to help her. Most of the UN personnel were medically trained aid workers and the few peacekeepers needed to protect the camp's thousands of residents from both rebel and government forces. Plus the road to the camp would flood soon, while the road south should last for several more weeks.

She might as well go south, where she'd come across several villages just off the main road to Juba. Someone was bound to have a radio, or if she was lucky, a satellite phone. Lacking those, they might have a truck and she could catch a ride. She wouldn't have to walk all two hundred and fifty miles to the capital.

With a dugout palm tree canoe, she could paddle upstream, but fighting the flow would wear her out. And the river meant risking river blindness and other fun diseases and parasites. She had her malaria pills in her pack, but they only protected her against the one disease.

Following the road to Juba was the most promising direction. She zigzagged from swamp to road, seeking signs of friends or foes, and walking through the muck to hide her tracks. Her skin itched where mud had dried on her face. She scooped up another handful and rubbed it across her cheeks. It worked as both camouflage and sunblock.

She sweltered in the early afternoon heat. Mosquitoes nipped at her, reminding her to take the day's antimalarial dose. She washed it down with a few bites of beef jerky and a few sips of water.

Venturing alone into the bush held risks greater than facing down cheetahs, tiang, giraffes, and jackals. The men who'd attacked the USAID outpost weren't the only threat Brie might face. Government soldiers were known to rape women when they left their village to collect firewood or food. For that reason, she'd never ventured into the bush alone. Her pack had a knife, but she didn't know how to fight with a knife. She didn't know how to fight, period.

She began to shake with exhaustion and fear, and forced herself to take a deep breath, think about her coworkers, and keep walking. They'd sacrificed themselves to protect her. They needed her to keep her shit together and find help.

She came to an intersection where a muddy track split from the main road, heading west around the wetland. She knew if she went far enough, the westward road would give way to savannah, but this road must be avoided at all costs. Deep within the marshlands, there was a market where none of the factions that were destroying South Sudan reigned supreme, but where they all came together to buy and sell. At the market, men could buy anything—artifacts, drugs, weapons, but mostly they trafficked in children for labor or sex.

Situated in territory held by neither the president nor

the opposing vice president in South Sudan's civil war, it was believed the market had formed a few months ago. The market had been the primary reason for her visit to Camp Citron, to report what she knew about it to Savannah James. But it wasn't like the US could or would take action to shut down the operation. After all, Americans weren't being threatened by this human trafficking.

South Sudan's oil was spoken for—claimed by Chinese and British oil companies with American Prime Energy and Russian Druneft vying for the pipeline construction contract. Closing down the slave market wouldn't help PE's bid for the pipeline, so there was no strategic reason for the US military to get involved in a minor thing like child trafficking in South Sudan.

Nothing to see here. Move along.

It was that heartless attitude she'd had to tolerate while working for Prime Energy that had led her to self-medicate in the first place. It was a stain on her soul that she'd ever averted her gaze from the truth of the damage her family did to the world in a quest for power and ever more wealth.

The rumble of an engine in the distance warned her of an approaching vehicle, and she jumped off the road and waded into the swamp just as fat drops of rain began to fall again. If it was a friend, she could be wasting an opportunity to hitch a ride. But waiting by the road to find out was a risk she couldn't afford to take.

The rain would be good for hiding her tracks, but if it turned into a real storm, she'd be in trouble. As it was, she couldn't cross the wetland—it was too deep and boggy. Even if she could, she'd find herself in the middle of a wide, flowing river that would be even harder to cross.

Still, she considered it, because if she could cross the river, she'd lose anyone who was hunting her, plus, after hiking a few more miles, she'd reach the border with Ethiopia.

She took a step into the deeper muck, and promptly slipped.

Nope.

She considered all the wildlife that likely made this wetland home as she swatted at mosquitoes.

Nope. Nope. Nope.

She regained her footing and continued to walk just inside the edge of the marsh, hoping the showers wouldn't turn into a storm. At least the muck swallowed her footsteps. When she ventured up to the road, there was no disguising her tracks.

She'd been told that during the height of the rainy season, sometimes the Sudd—the vast swamp that was one of the major geographical features of South Sudan—extended this far east. Roads would vanish. It was one of the reasons USAID had selected this area for food storage. At least by foot, the location served areas cut off when the roads flooded.

The rumble of yet another engine had her stepping deep into the vegetation that protruded from the swamp. She wouldn't think about swamp-dwelling critters, wouldn't imagine water snakes residing in the muck.

She tucked herself into the greenery of a shrub that thrived in the wetland. Between the mud on her face and dirty clothes, she was camouflaged.

She held still, careful not to rustle branches or splash. Even her breathing was shallow, but that was due to fear.

A car door slammed, then she heard two men arguing

in Arabic. They were looking for her. They must be from different tribes with their common language being Arabic, because they both had local accents.

Had they been sent by the rebels? The government? Why were they after her? They'd already destroyed the food and they had her coworkers.

She didn't dare move. Breathing was no longer an involuntary act.

Minutes ticked by. Birds chirped. A warm breeze filtered through the stiflingly hot day. Eight degrees above the equator, every day was hot, the air always thick, even when it rained.

Eventually she heard the sound of retreating footsteps, followed by car doors slamming.

Tires kicked up rocks on the muddy track.

She took a shallow, silent breath.

They'd moved on.

She waited five minutes, debating if she was safer heading back the way she'd already come—after all, they'd already searched there—or if she should continue south.

But help wouldn't be found behind her. There was only forward, even if she had to walk all two hundred and fifty miles to Juba.

Slowly, she emerged from her hiding place. She scrambled up the low bank and tucked herself behind a tree so she could peek down the narrow road, to see how far ahead the searchers had gone. No sooner had she settled in than she heard the sound of a shotgun being cocked behind her.

Chapter Three

The pickup truck bounced along the dirt track, bruising Brie, who lay in the open back, with every pothole and rut they hit. She still didn't know who had taken her, or why, but beyond binding her hands and feet and taking her pack, the man hadn't touched her, which was a relief.

Her abductor bore the six parallel lines across his forehead—ritual scarring that indicated he was Nuer. The vice president of South Sudan, who was the leader of the rebels, was Nuer. The president was Dinka. The country had dozens of ethnic groups, and Dinka and Nuer were the two largest. Combined, they equaled only about twenty-five percent of the population.

Was this Nuer man aligned with the rebels? The only thing she was certain of, he wasn't one of the two men who'd been searching for her. This man spoke one of the many local languages, but didn't speak much Arabic. While English was the official working language of the Republic of South Sudan, Arabic had once shared that title, and it remained the *lingua franca* of the country. Her Arabic was passable—better than her captor's.

The rain had stopped before he took her, and she'd done her best to leave as many footprints by the side of the road as she could.

If Ezra's call had gone through, then surely the US military would send a team to liberate her colleagues. If so, hopefully they'd search for her and see those footprints—if another rain didn't wash them away.

The truck hit a particularly deep pothole. Brie's body floated in the air before slamming down on the truck bed. With her hands bound to a tie-down, she couldn't protect her head. Her temple hit the uneven surface with enough force to see stars.

Nausea rose. Eyes closed against the bright sun, she breathed slowly and managed to keep the bile down.

Would the US send a team from Camp Citron? That would be the logical choice.

She thought about the implausible kiss and wondered if Bastian knew of the attack on the USAID facility. And if he did, would he think the pampered princess had gotten what she deserved?

L ess than an hour after they arrived in South Sudan, seven scouts had been quietly dispatched from their positions in the marsh by Bastian's team, ensuring they didn't tip off the hostage guards. The signal was given, and the SEALs moved in. Shots sounded.

Bastian waited from his position in the marsh, ready to move, wishing he'd been in on the raid to free the hostages. Minutes later, a SEAL announced the hostages were safe and that four of the five guards had been killed. The remaining man could look forward to a long, uncomfortable interrogation back at Camp Citron.

For now, they could be satisfied that all twelve tangos were accounted for. These men had been no match for the combined training of a Special Forces A-Team and a

SEAL team.

Boko Haram or the government or rebel fighters had to know the US military would crush them when they'd attacked a US government aid organization. So why destroy the USAID facility? What had they expected to gain?

Unease slid down Bastian's spine. Maybe they did know who Brie was.

"How many hostages?" he asked over the radio.

"Three. Brie Stewart isn't here."

He made a beeline for the hut where the SEALs remained with the freed hostages. Several of his teammates followed.

Inside, Bastian scanned the three USAID employees. "Where's Brie Stewart?"

Ezra Johnson, an American aid worker with skin so dark he could pass for South Sudanese if it weren't for the lack of tribal scarring, studied him, his gaze landing on Bastian's name tape. "You're the asshole from Camp Citron."

Interesting. What had Brie told the man? Savannah James said Brie's coworkers didn't know who she was.

"He's an asshole who just helped save your life," one of the SEALs said.

"Yes, but I'm still an asshole." Bastian turned to Ezra. "Where. The fuck. Is Brie?"

"We don't know," Ezra said.

"She escaped before the fire," said the other American hostage, Alan. "We stayed behind so she could get away." He cleared his throat. "It doesn't go well for the women."

He was talking about rape. These men had sacrificed themselves so Brie could escape. Bastian gave a nod of respect.

"The men were looking for her," the South Sudanese aid worker, Jaali, added. "They spoke of it, in a local dialect on their radios. I listened. They were searching, but not finding."

"Where would she go?" Bastian asked all three men.

"There aren't a lot of people she could turn to." Alan's face darkened. "She had three choices. Go to the Kemet Oil operation that's about twenty miles to the north, the UN camp to the northwest, or follow the road south toward Juba."

"What do you think she'd do?" Bastian asked.

"She'd choose Juba over Kemet Oil," Ezra said firmly. "The company uses child labor and aren't likely to help us."

"Why wouldn't she go to the UN camp?" Pax asked. "It's closer than the capital."

"She might, but it's still pretty far, and the road will disappear in rain in the coming days," Jaali said. "The main road to Juba is her best bet. The road is higher ground and lasts the longest when all the others flood."

Bastian turned to his detachment commander, Captain Durant, who'd entered the hut along with the rest of their A-Team. "Permission to split the team in two and go after Brie Stewart, sir."

The captain nodded for the team to step outside the hut where they could speak without being overheard by the USAID employees. Bastian followed the tall African American commander who'd been at the top spot on their team since the Yemen mission over a year ago. Outside, Captain Durant said, "Given who she is, we should consider using the full team in addition to several SEALs."

"Too many people on this and we risk exposing her secret," Bastian said. "Send half the team to check out Kemet Oil and the UN camp, while six of us search the route to Juba. Two teams of six can keep a lower profile. Any more than that, and whoever took her might start to wonder just how valuable she is."

"They may already know," Lieutenant Fallon said.

Bastian tipped his head in a slight nod. "But if they don't, why make it obvious?" A-Teams were designed for this type of operation; splitting into two teams was a common practice. The only unusual aspect was that Bastian was determined to be the one leading the team that searched the Juba road.

Durant studied him for a long moment. "You didn't disclose to SOCOM you know the woman."

"We met briefly when she was at Camp Citron a month ago."

"Long enough for her to know you're an asshole," Fallon said.

Bastian shrugged. "What can I say? My charm comes naturally."

The captain held his gaze. "Did you fuck her?"

"No, sir." He'd never quite figured out if he regretted that or not.

Durant gave a sharp nod. "Take Blanchard, Callahan, Ripley, Goldberg, and Espinosa."

"We'll search in the south, along the Juba road." He held his breath, hoping the captain wouldn't argue and send him to the UN camp.

Durant nodded. "Two days, Chief Ford." He looked over Bastian's shoulder and addressed the team assembled there who would accompany Bastian on this mission. "You need to find her within forty-eight hours.

If you don't, the US military will have no choice but to go all in. Gabriella Prime cannot become a reason for the US to become embroiled in South Sudan's civil war. Be discreet. And fast."

The members of his team nodded, and Bastian felt a surge of pride. His men were the best. Just weeks ago, he and Pax had been at odds, but after his encounter with Brie, he'd pulled his head out of his ass and salvaged what had once been an important friendship. And he had Brie to thank, in a roundabout way, for his mental extraction.

Back inside the hut, Bastian pulled out a map and spread it on the table. He grilled the three USAID workers on the route she was likely to attempt and the risks she'd face along the way.

Alan cleared his throat as Bastian rolled up the map. "Mr. Ford, you need to know about the market. If someone found her, they might have taken her there."

"Market?" Bastian asked, spreading the map again.

"I'm not sure where it is—no one is, exactly. It's not a place any of us could go and expect to return from. Somewhere deep in the marsh to the west, there's a slave market. We think it formed sometime in the last few months, or at least, that's when there was an uptick in children disappearing—more than usual. They sell other things at the market too—weapons, drugs, artifacts, anything that supports war and terror—but mostly they sell children."

"And you think they'd take her there?"

He nodded. "It's one of the reasons we made sure she escaped. Months ago, we noticed a decrease in the number of women and children who'd been raped and released. The slaughtering stopped too—we thought the war was winding down—but then we started hearing rumors of the market, and it became clear the economy had shifted and slavers were taking women and children who were returning home after taking refuge in the camps—for a while, no one realized they were missing, because no one knew they were coming home."

"Why hasn't this been reported?" Captain Durant demanded.

"It was. It's why Brie went to Camp Citron a month ago. She told some woman there everything she knew about the market."

Sonofabitch. Savvy knew all along, and she didn't say a fucking word.

Need-to-know my ass.

They had needed to know. This might have nothing to do with USAID, nothing to do with the fact that Brie was a Prime. It could be about the market.

The rain clouds had dissipated, leaving a celestial canopy visible through the branches of the tree Brie was tied to. Something tickled the back of her neck. She squirmed against the rope that secured her hands to her waist. It must be an insect of some sort.

She should be sleeping, but that was impossible, trussed up as she was. She closed her eyes. And a different sky came to mind…

She sank back into the moment when she'd been trying to regain her composure and Bastian had found her staring at the stars.

It was too much to hope his or another Special Forces team would be sent to South Sudan to find her. But hope she did, because she had to hold on to something.

Not far away, her captor snored loudly as he slept on

the hard ground. She still had no idea who he was or if he was associated with the men who'd invaded the USAID facility.

Nothing about working in South Sudan had been comfortable, but this was a new lesson in how good she'd had it in her aluminum-walled living quarters. For starters, she'd had a cot, and when the generator had fuel, they'd had electricity.

Tonight she lay on rocky ground, bound to a tree. No pillow, no blanket, no water, no food. Tied at wrists and ankles.

And she was utterly terrified.

A sinking feeling had settled in her gut when her captor had turned his truck around and headed west. The rough roads meant they were driving through the marsh, on tracks that had never been smoothed by any type of machinery.

They were in the no-man's-land, heading toward the market. And she knew with a certainty that chilled her on a humid night that tomorrow she would be sold to the highest bidder.

Chapter Four

Bastian took stock of their gear. Night vision goggles, weapons, ammunition, water, food, a hefty amount of cash. Just what everyone in this war-torn country needed. Add to that radios, maps, and a satellite phone and they were ready for a few fun-filled days sightseeing in South Sudan.

UN peacekeepers provided his A-Team with four battered SUVs. Two would search to the north and northeast. Two would go south under Bastian's command.

Ezra approached Bastian as he climbed into the vehicle. "Find her," the aid worker said. "Promise me you'll find Brie."

Bastian gave Ezra a sharp nod, wondering if he was in love with her. If she loved him back, then Bastian would deliver her into Ezra's arms. All he cared about was that she survived.

Two hours after dawn had broken across the central African country, they alternated between driving and searching the side of the road on foot, finding traces of what they believed was Brie Stewart's passage at regular intervals.

Even though the swamp didn't show footsteps, her trail was easy to follow. Broken reeds, ripped lily pads, snapped branches lit her path. Easy tracking for a Special

Forces team. Hell, they taught foreign soldiers how to do this type of tracking.

Ripley, Espinosa, and Goldberg were mucking about the swamp's edge while Cal, Pax, and Bastian searched along the higher ground. Pax let out a whistle indicating he found something. Cal and Bastian joined him at the side of the dirt track that passed for a road.

"Boot print," Pax said, pointing to the tread mark that had become familiar in the hours since they'd been following her steps. "She stepped up to scout. From the angle, she returned to the swamp, going that way." He pointed, and Bastian saw the faint depression where reeds had been crushed.

Bastian nodded, his gaze to the north, following the path she'd taken. "We're ten miles from the USAID building." He was strangely proud she'd made it this far while men hunted her. She was smart. Determined. Even if she did leave a trail. Most people would.

"What's the deal with her, Bas?" Pax asked. His breaking protocol by using Bastian's first name was a signal that this was an off-the-record sort of query.

"Nothing," he said brusquely.

"Bullshit," Cal said. "You told Cap you didn't fuck her. Was that a lie?"

"No lie." He took a deep breath. He owed these men the truth, not that there was much to tell, but they were risking their lives to save Brie Stewart. "I recognized her. When I saw her with Savvy at Camp Citron, I knew exactly who she was. And I—" He paused. *Own it.* "I hated her for the things she did when she worked for Prime Energy and let her know it."

"If you dislike her, then why insist on leading the team to find her?" Pax asked.

Espinosa, Goldberg, and Ripley climbed the bank to join the conversation. Fair enough. They deserved the truth too.

He shook his head. "That's the thing. Something about her got to me. We didn't even talk all that long. But in the end, I felt like a shit. Like she really has changed, and I was kicking an aid worker—who's providing relief to starving people in fucking South Sudan of all places—in the face.

"I mean, who does that? She could live anywhere in the world, eat off golden plates, and binge on truffles and caviar. Yet she's living and working *here*?" He spread his arms wide to encompass the humid, mosquito-filled swampy landscape. "After we met, I did some research, and learned fun facts about her work here. For instance, she only had electricity when the fuel truck arrived to fill the tank for their generator—which happened maybe once a month. During the rainy season, the truck can't get there at all. Water is scarce in the dry season because the streams might have the cholera bacteria, and mosquitoes carrying the malaria parasite thrive around water sources.

"And I haven't even mentioned the number of rapes committed by government and rebel forces, or the special risks to aid workers. Some have been abducted—*by government forces*—and large ransoms demanded. When foreign governments refuse to pay, they demand money from the oil companies, who are trying to restart their drilling operations in the midst of war." He gazed down the narrow road, not seeing the trees or ruts. In his mind, he saw too-wide brown eyes and a flawless unfortunate nose.

He let out a slow breath. "She's been here seven

months now, and by all accounts intends to stay through the rainy season. As far as I can tell, she's the real deal."

"She could be trying to generate positive PR for Prime Energy," Espinosa said.

"If that were the case, wouldn't Prime Energy have her splashed all over their website?" Ripley asked.

"Not if they wanted to keep her safe," Cal said. "They could be waiting until she's home again and then promote the hell out of her charity work."

Bastian shrugged. "Hell, it's possible this whole fucking abduction was arranged by PE. But what if they didn't? What if she's genuine? Savvy said she's been working for USAID for five years. This isn't her first deployment, it's just the most dangerous, and PE never promoted her work before."

"Won't she be surprised you're the man leading her rescue," Cal said.

Bastian forced a smile and aimed for jocular. "I'm sure she'd prefer a SEAL like Lieutenant Fallon."

"Don't they all, though," Espinosa said.

Pax grinned. "The smart ones prefer Special Forces." He nodded toward the road ahead. "Speaking of, I promised Morgan we'd rendezvous in Rome before she leaves Europe. SOCOM approved my leave request for next week—which means I need to get my ass back to Camp Citron so I don't miss my vacation. Let's find Brie Stewart and get the hell out of South Sudan."

With that, the best damn half A-team that had ever served in the US Army resumed tracking the reformed, quirky aid worker Bastian was desperate to find.

Chapter Five

Even though she'd expected it, Brie still couldn't quite believe her situation. She was in a slave market. A real, honest-to-fucking-Satan *slave* market.

How could a place like this exist in the twenty-first century?

Children were gathered in small clusters, connected by rope. Some girls wore bright-colored, traditional Sudanese tobes, while others wore nothing at all. Flies gathered around their eyes, and they wore the dazed look of starvation and shock.

Bile rose in Brie's throat. The girls were as young as nine and likely faced sexual slavery. The boys were maybe a year or two older, and those who escaped sexual slavery were destined to work in diamond mines in the Central African Republic or work for the oil companies here in South Sudan.

Children—of both genders—might be sent to Qatar to work as domestic servants, to Poland for sexual servitude, or Saudi Arabia and Yemen for forced begging. She'd known this market existed, but seeing the children was still shocking. Horrifying.

There were no adult women. Where were the mothers? Slaughtered by the slavers before their children's eyes?

Or were mothers frantically searching the bush and Sudd for their babies?

Brie wanted to save every child here. Children who should be home with their families. In school. At the park trying to catch Pokémon. Or being told by their parents that they couldn't wear a sexy vampire costume on Halloween because dammit, nine-year-olds shouldn't be sexualized.

But these children had never heard of Pokémon or Halloween. They'd never known the joy of dressing up as a superhero and demanding candy from strangers.

Really, there was nothing better than Halloween. It combined the joy of pretending to be something greater than one's self and chocolate. She wished every child on the planet could experience Halloween at least once. These kids had likely never even had candy.

Horrifying that they'd only known war and famine, and now they would know slavery.

Once upon a time, she'd naïvely gone to grad school so she could understand the perspective of the indigenous groups that were being harmed by Prime Energy practices all over the world. Her fellow students had rightly scoffed that, coming from the ultimate privilege as she did, she would *never* understand. Not really.

Now, here she was, at a slave market, to be sold to the highest bidder. The anthropologist in her recognized she *was* being presented with an opportunity to understand. The terrified part of her told the academic to fuck off.

This shit was getting real.

Upon arriving at the market, she was searched by a guard—a white man who only grunted his commands, giving no hint as to his native language or accent—then fitted with a metal collar with a six-foot chain. After obtaining her leash, the Nuer man who'd captured her led her across the sweltering market, heading toward a series of thatched-roof huts in the market center.

Dozens of children sat in clusters of three and four as men shouted their attributes in Arabic and English. Some slavers were white; others were dark and bore scars that indicated a dozen different ethnic groups.

At least a dozen buyers milled through the market, looking over the children. These men were of different ethnic backgrounds, with every shade of skin represented. None bore tribal scars. Were they Europeans and Americans who ran the diamond mines and oil companies, or were they in the market for sex workers?

Foreigners looted the continent of both resources and citizens. They took the oil, diamonds, gold, and other precious metals from Africa, knowing full well that nothing trickled down to the citizens of the countries they raped.

Rape was an apt word. These men violently took what they wanted. Government leaders profited. Their armies were well funded, but not by tax dollars. The rulers of most of the resource-rich countries of Africa didn't need the consent of the people to govern, because they didn't need tax dollars. They got their money—and therefore their armies—from oil, diamond, and other mineral revenues.

With citizens removed from the governing equation, there was no need to give a crap what the masses needed. So the people of Africa lived far below the poverty line, while their dictators enjoyed lavish wealth.

These children would suffer so their dictator could entertain men like her father at their dinner table. Men like Viktor Drugov and his son, Nikolai, the Russian oligarchs her father had sold his soul to years ago.

Today, she would suffer with the children. A fitting justice—to have a Prime pay this price, except her father wouldn't give a damn if he knew. So all the horror would be hers, and hers alone.

Was she to be a worker or sex slave?

Who was she kidding? She would be a sex slave. There was no hope she'd be anything less horrible.

Damn, she wanted to talk with the children who'd been ripped from their families. She wanted to hold them and tell them what they faced wasn't sex. Sex was something shared. A joining. A joy.

Rape was something taken. Even if they—and she—acquiesced to avoid further pain, it was rape. There was no shame in not fighting. Whatever it takes to survive. Even if the only option was to submit.

Survival was paramount.

She stumbled, and the Nuer yanked on the chain, jerking her forward.

She wanted to save all the children she passed, but the truth was, she couldn't even save herself.

B astian rolled his shoulders, looking at the road ahead and behind, then finally down again. There on the ground in front of him were Brie's footprints. They faded into drag marks, then disappeared next to fresh tire tracks on the muddy road.

They'd suspected it, but here was the proof. She'd been caught.

The tire tracks turned in a U, heading north again. There were no paths to the east that weren't cut off by swamp and river. The other half of his team was searching north of the burned USAID facility. That left west. There'd been precious few roads that trailed west toward the savannah, which narrowed their search area considerably.

West, deep into the marshy grasslands that concealed a slave market.

"We need better intel on the market," he said to Ripley, who had the satellite phone. "Is it controlled by rebel or government forces? What tribe holds the power here?" Alan had said neither Dinka nor Nuer controlled the area, but he was an aid worker, not privy to intel gathered by intelligence agencies. "Get Savannah James on the phone."

A moment later, they had Savvy on speaker. "Both rebel and government forces have been driven out of the area. SIGINT indicates there could be Russian players." SIGINT was signal intelligence—data gathered by intercepting signals.

"How are you getting SIGINT out here?" Ripley asked. A fine point, considering that only satellite phones worked in this electronic dead zone.

"I'm not. The intercepts are elsewhere, but we think the communications pertain to the market."

"What about human intelligence?" Espinosa asked. "Has the Russian connection been supported by personal accounts?"

"Brie Stewart was my best hope for HUMINT on the market."

The idea that Brie could right now be taking in the mother lode of intel twisted Bastian's gut. He knew this was Savvy's job—and Brie must've been game or she wouldn't have been at Camp Citron—but Savvy never should have asked someone untrained in espionage to report on a black market that trafficked in weapons, drugs, and children.

"So it's possible Russians are backing the market, providing security, laundering money, and who knows what else," Cal said.

"Yes," Savvy said.

"Wasn't there some sort of alliance between Prime Energy and Russia's Druneft?" Bastian asked, again wondering if her abductors had known she was a Prime.

"The alliance fell through about six months ago," Savvy said. "Now the two companies are competing for the same pipeline concession."

"So this could be about Brie's family connections and a business rivalry."

"We can't rule anything out. But if someone found out Brie is a Prime, she never suspected. And she was careful. After you recognized her, she considered not going back because she was compromised. I convinced her you would keep her secret."

He appreciated that there was no question in Savvy's tone.

"We need the coordinates for the market, ASAP," Cal said.

"Satellites are searching as we speak. We *will* find it."

"Why the hell didn't you find it before?" Bastian asked. "You've had, what, a month?"

"It wasn't high priority. We have no role in the market and had no reason to believe an American would end up on the auction block. And you might recall we spent a week of that time searching for Morgan Adler." Savvy's tone was defensive. But then, she'd just admitted that while she was gathering intel on the market, there'd been no plans for the US to *do* anything about it.

"Hurry and find it," Bastian said and ended the call.

He studied his team. If they were going into the market, they needed to get out of their military gear. None of them could pass for Sudanese, but they could conceal their US Army affiliation. Fortunately, blending with locals was one of the skills Army Special Forces excelled at.

Once they had the coordinates, Bastian would enter the market alone. His features were ethnic enough to not be obviously American, plus Special Forces were given leeway on shaving, allowing them to fit in with the locals they trained, and he'd taken advantage of that for the last few weeks. He rubbed his thick beard, grateful, not for the first time, that men from Pacific Northwest tribes tended to have more facial hair than other indigenous Americans. Between his beard and Arabic fluency, he'd be able to navigate the market with ease.

The others would be in position outside the market and ready to move when he located Brie. All that was left was to pray she hadn't already been sold.

———

As both adult and white, Brie was a rarity in the market. A fact made clear when the man holding her leash dragged her toward one of the thatched-roof huts in the center.

The common language here was Arabic, and she understood enough to know the transactions that took place inside the huts were different from the wholesale marketing of children outside.

She was to be auctioned separately, out of view of the regular market crowd. Inside the hut, her chain was attached to a bolt embedded in a concrete block at the center of the round structure.

The Nuer man who'd abducted her received payment from the man who locked her chain to the bolt. The Nuer left the hut, his part in capturing and selling her complete.

The slaver pocketed the key as his gaze scanned her from head to toe. This must be his hut. Was the whole market his, or was this the equivalent of a booth in a farmer's market?

Wouldn't Savvy love Brie's observations on the market now?

The slave trader had facial scars, but Brie couldn't identify a particular tribe from the pattern. Without preamble, he produced a sharp knife, pulled her shirt collar away from her throat, and sliced downward, splitting the cloth from collar to hem.

Instinctively, she covered her bare breasts—she hadn't spared a moment to don a bra when she fled the USAID building—but he waved the knife in front of her face and she dropped her hands.

Next he reached for her waistband. The blade nicked her skin, drawing a bead of blood. He signaled with the knife that she would undress herself or risk being cut.

I will survive this.

She mentally chanted the words as she removed her clothes.

I will survive this.

She had to believe in something, and she chose survival. She didn't dare hope to be unscathed. Rape was a certainty. But she would live. She would find a way to escape. She was thirty-three years old and spoke English, French, and some Arabic. She wasn't a starving child. These men usually preyed on the young and weak. Kids who spoke only their tribal language. Children who knew nothing of life beyond their war-torn villages.

I will survive.

Whoever her buyer turned out to be, he would make a mistake somewhere.

If fighting back is too dangerous, I will be meek to protect myself. There is no shame in not fighting. There is no shame in survival.

She removed her boots, then dropped her pants and underwear to the floor. She stepped out of the pile.

No shame in stripping when threatened with a knife.

Once upon a time, she'd learned to stand regally and present speeches to sell a toxic development plan to people who didn't want it. If she could do that, she could handle this.

Fully nude, she faced her abductor without flinching. The man had dead eyes. He scooped her clothes from the floor and tossed them out the door.

I will escape. I will come back to this place. I will help the children here. And I will kill you with your own knife.

The last vow caught her off guard.

Could she kill a man?

The metal collar around her neck chafed in the heat.

Yes. Absolutely.

An hour after they received the coordinates from SOCOM, Bastian entered the market. He was unarmed except for a knife, and wore civilian clothes that signaled Western and buyer. This was to be a quick recon mission. He would only act now if Brie's sale was imminent.

She had to be in one of the three huts near the center of

the market. Even though the market operated without fear of reprisals, they wouldn't conduct the transaction of selling an American woman in the open. That was the sort of thing the US military couldn't ignore.

Assuming, of course, that they knew Brie was American.

Bastian studied the layout of the market. Six guards patrolled the edges, keeping parents or other would-be rescuers out and the children in. Proof the market operators weren't fearless.

He counted the clusters of children who were lined up in the sweltering heat. At least fifty children. Some cried, but most sat silent with a thousand-yard stare as flies vied for the moisture in their eyes.

Bastian hardened his jaw, thankful for the cover of his beard. Today, he was a buyer. He couldn't react to the sight of starving children offered up as chattel.

If he returned here with a full twelve-man A-Team and a squad of SEALs, they could take out the slavers and free the kids. End this atrocity in one sweep.

But he couldn't do that today. Today, he was only authorized to save one American adult, meaning this op would fuel nightmares for years to come.

SOCOM had been clear: retrieve Brie Stewart and no one else. Otherwise they risked alerting the South Sudanese government that the US military had conducted a rescue operation within their sovereign borders. The US could not get drawn into South Sudan's civil war.

The US military had played that game too many times, with sometimes disastrous results.

But still, his gaze took in the beautiful ebony-skinned children. Malnourished. Emaciated. They faced slave labor or sexual exploitation. He'd have to be a monster to walk away.

He *could* save some of these kids. Now. Today. But that risked his mission objective—to rescue Brie Stewart.

Weeks ago, he'd gone AWOL with Pax and Cal to save Morgan Adler, and they had managed to save a bunch of girls who'd been rounded up by a warlord to fund his private army. He'd thought that place was bad, but this market brought atrocity to a whole new level.

He cut through the market, inspecting the "wares" while keeping his revulsion from his face. He had a hidden mic in his collar and a tiny earpiece, keeping him in touch with his team.

Ripley and Espinosa spoke Arabic and could translate Bastian's conversations with merchants for the others. The easiest way to spring Brie without revealing he was a soldier was to buy her. He had money. The question was, did he have enough?

Could he buy all the children?

Doubtful.

Plus it would be noticed if he suddenly bought out the market. And the slavers would just be encouraged to round up more children.

No. These assholes had to bleed.

He reached the huts at the center and circled the first one. Made of grass-thatched mud, the structure had plenty of gaps for him to peek inside. He whispered to his team without moving his lips, "Southeast hut is the arms depot. AKs, grenades, and a shoulder-fired rocket launcher."

"Relaying the intel to Savannah James," Ripley said.

Bastian moved on to the next hut. He couldn't quite make out what was inside but suspected some of the items were artifacts. Probably drugs too. Both funded terrorism. Did Boko Haram or ISIS use this market? He passed the intel on to Ripley and then moved on to circle the third hut.

The mud filled the gaps better on the structure than the others and a curtain covered the open doorway. He thought he saw a woman inside but couldn't confirm it was Brie.

From the chatter, he learned potential buyers would get to view the goods one at a time before the auction began. Some cynically speculated that they were stalling, waiting for a special buyer to arrive and the previews were just to drive up the price before the man got here.

A special buyer meant auction was fixed. It had to be Brie.

He'd just have to line up with the other previews and try to buy her before the auction even began. With enough money, it might work, but he would need every dollar they'd taken from the Blackhawk.

He headed back toward the market entrance to grab the money and confer with his team. He heard a piercing shriek and turned to see the source. A girl who couldn't be more than ten lay huddled on the ground, her arms covering her head as she sobbed.

A man three times her size kicked her in the side and yelled at her to get up and take her place on the block.

Bastian wanted to puke.

Instinct urged him to lunge for the man and gut him.

But his mission required him to keep on walking.

Chapter Six

"**N**o fucking way can we rescue Brie and leave the kids behind." Bastian paced in front of his team, his entire body shaking from what he'd witnessed in the market.

He had to get his shit together and get back there. He looked to Ripley, who had the satellite phone. "Call Cap. Get the rest of the team here."

"We aren't authorized to save anyone but Stewart," Espinosa said.

"Fuck SOCOM and their orders. This market needs to be wiped off the map. *Jesus*. Savannah James knew about it, and no one did anything?"

"No Americans were in jeopardy," Goldberg said.

"Well, an American is now. We're here. We're armed. We can take these assholes. They don't expect Special Forces to come calling."

He met Pax's gaze, then turned to Cal. They'd understand. They were at Desta's compound last month. They'd helped rescue the girls and smuggled them out of Somaliland. They'd caught shit for making the girls the US embassy's problem, but the women who worked at the embassy had quietly thanked them for doing the right thing.

"We can rescue the children and get them across the river, into Ethiopia. Sort it out there. Drop them in one of the refugee camps," Bastian suggested.

"No way. The Ethiopian government will freak if we dump refugees on them. We could lose our Forward Operating Base," Ripley said.

The stability of the FOB in Ethiopia was tenuous at best. They'd all be booted from Special Forces if they caused a troop withdrawal.

"Maybe we can get Jeffery Prime to drop a wad of cash on the Ethiopian government, as thanks for helping out in the rescue of his daughter," Cal said.

"They're estranged," Bastian said.

"So what? Do you think it would look good if he didn't make a donation as thanks after his daughter—who's an aid worker—was rescued?" Cal responded. "The guy shits money. Plus they need good PR after those documents were leaked that showed how they've been suppressing global warming data for the last decade. Brie is his ticket to PR heaven."

"There's another possibility that wouldn't risk our FOB and wouldn't require Prime's cooperation," Pax said.

Everyone turned to the master sergeant. "What if the kids escaped...on their own? With a little help from an A-Team. We can lead them to the river. If we can round up some boats for them, they can hide out in the islands that dot the marsh and maybe make their way into Ethiopia."

"We'd need a bunch of boats," Bastian said. But the kids were small and far too thin. He'd bet they could fit ten in a dugout palm canoe. "Five at least."

"There were several stacked in the village where the hostages were held. The rest of the team can grab them on their way south."

"It would take time to get them in place. Brie could be auctioned any minute."

"You'll go in and buy Brie," Pax said. "Cal and Espinosa will enter the market a few minutes after you to secure the kids. By the time they reach the river, the others will be there with the canoes."

Cal and Espi were the logical choices. Black and Hispanic respectively, and both sporting decent beards, they were less likely to draw attention than if Pax, Ripley, or Goldberg attempted to blend. Pax's skin might have a darker, southern European tone, but it was still obvious he was white, and the fact that his beard was only about two days old didn't help matters.

"With Cal and Espi in position, after Brie is clear, they can trigger an 'accident' in the arms hut," Pax said. "The kids can escape in the melee that follows. Then Espi can lead the kids like the Pied Piper down to the river, Cal covering their flank. The rest of us can move in and mop up, make it look like the kids did all the damage and orchestrated their own escape, taking out anyone who sees us. It'll take at least two hours to get to the river, plenty of time to get the boats in place."

"We'd need to draw some of the guards away," Cal said, "so Espi has a chance to talk to the kids, tell them what to do." The kids might not speak Arabic or English, but it was their best option.

"Cause a scene with Brie. Get all eyes on her," Espinosa suggested. "Odds are, they'll be watching her anyway. I don't imagine she's typical merchandise."

Bastian's nod was uneasy. It wasn't a great plan— there were far too many variables that were beyond their control, but it was their best option. Worse came to worst, they'd gun down the slavers and set the kids free.

At least with this plan, there was a chance they could make it to the relative safety of the islands hidden in the swamp. Maybe some would find their parents there, or make it into Ethiopia as refugees.

No matter what they did, his A-Team was going to be in a shitload of trouble with the US Army and SOCOM, but in the end, they were all in. Fuck the job if they had to turn their back on these kids. The dishonorable discharge would be worth it.

O ne by one, men entered the hut and circled Brie. They spoke in Arabic to the man who'd chained her, either assuming she didn't understand or not caring.

They complained about her body to lower the price. Tits too small. Ass too big. Fat. Skinny. Ugly. It wasn't like these monsters could hurt her feelings. She hoped they all found her as repulsive as she found them.

A few men spoke directly to her, asking questions in Arabic, which she pretended she didn't understand. They switched to English, and she answered with a French accent.

She stared each potential buyer in the face. Memorizing his features. When she escaped—and she would—she would describe these men to the US military. They would be hunted down.

At least, she wanted to believe that. The truth was, the US military would probably avoid antagonizing South Sudan. No one knew who would win the civil war, and so the US continued to play neutral.

She clenched her fingers into a fist, the nails biting into her palms, making her glad she hadn't trimmed them in two weeks. Her nails were her only weapon, and they were sharp.

She gathered from the words exchanged between potential buyers and the seller that the bidding would take place soon after all the private previews had been completed.

A Saudi man circled her. He touched her ass, and she flinched. The man laughed and grabbed again, this time pinching her.

She was chained at the throat, but her arms weren't bound. She jabbed the man in the eye with a sharp nail, using a move Ezra had taught her. The Saudi howled with pain and lunged for her. His hands closed on her throat, above the metal collar.

An instant later, searing pain shot down her side. The man attempting to choke her recoiled with another yelp of pain.

The slaver had lashed out with a whip, hitting both the Saudi and her. Punishment for striking a potential buyer, or punishment for touching the merchandise?

The man was tossed from the hut, and she gathered from the shouts that followed, he wasn't permitted to join the bidding.

Both, then.

Her left biceps throbbed. A welt formed along her arm and trailed down, curling around her side just reaching the top of her left buttock. She was certain to end up with a nasty bruise, but at least the skin hadn't broken.

She was studying her wound when footsteps sounded on the dirt floor, and she looked up to see the next buyer. A jolt of recognition went through her. To hide it, she turned back to studying her welts.

This man worked for Druneft now, but once upon a time, he'd worked for her father.

All she could do was hope he wouldn't recognize her. She was covered in mud, naked, bruised, with hair shorter than she'd ever worn it before. She doubted her best friend from high school could pick her out of a lineup.

She kept her face averted, attempting to look cowed, which wasn't hard after being whipped. He asked questions in Arabic with a bogus British accent. He then addressed her directly, in English. "Where are you from, my dear?"

It was possible he was here to help her, although the odds of that were miniscule.

She cleared her throat, her brain blanking on how to conjure the French accent. Her hip and arm throbbed. Terror had been slowly creeping up on her, and now she found she couldn't speak.

The whip lashed out again, snapping before her nose, a warning.

She let out a yelp and answered, "Madagascar," she said, naming her last USAID assignment. She knew the country and the French language to fake her way through this.

The man circled her slowly, tutting as he viewed her from behind.

She was naked and chained by the throat and was being threatened with a whip. As if she gave a fuck what this man thought upon viewing her ass.

He left. Her guard held the whip in front of her face. "You answer the questions, or you get more of this." He spat into the dirt.

"Whip me, and you'll drive down the price."

He looked like he wanted to argue, but he wasn't stupid. Badly injured, she'd sell for next to nothing.

Another man stepped into the hut, and Brie lifted her gaze to memorize another face. The man's eyes flicked to hers, then dropped down, dismissive as he studied her naked form, then slowly he raised his gaze to hers again.

She wobbled on her feet as shock radiated down her body.

Chief Warrant Officer Sebastian Ford.

~⌒~

Bastian turned cold at the sight of Brie stripped and chained.

Jesus. He'd walked past a line of starving children to enter this hut, and in the hut next door, there was a guy selling an assortment of weapons.

This fucking country.

And South Sudan was only one of several African countries that trafficked in children.

This fucking continent.

But the truth was the US and other countries with power knew exactly what went on here, and did nothing to stop it.

This fucking world.

He'd witnessed atrocities in many places and forms. Hell, he'd grown up on a poor reservation and had seen crap go down there that had the power to make him cry even now. Yet humans could still shock him with their inhumanity.

But right now, he had to be a soldier.

No. Not a soldier. Right now, he was in the market for a sex slave, and the woman before him was just what he was looking for.

"Is she a good fuck?" Bastian asked the seller in Arabic. He was good at this, the blending. It was what

Special Forces did. They infiltrated. Became one with the community. He could pass for a soulless slave trader who belonged here without breaking a sweat.

"Excellent fuck," the slaver said. "Very tight pussy."

Bastian used the anger the words triggered to feed his character. He wouldn't consider what the answer indicated. His gaze swept down Brie's naked body with cold indifference. "Does she fight?" he asked.

"No. No fight in her. She's well broken."

If he had a heart left, it would have seized. Outwardly, he shrugged and turned for the door. "Too bad. I like a woman who fights."

Haggling over human flesh. An old Army jingle flashed through his mind. *"Be all that you can be…"*

"Wait!" her keeper said. "She fights. She blinded a man just minutes ago for touching her ass."

Bastian turned back, and his gaze swept her body again. He gave no sign of recognition. No wink, no nothing to put her mind at ease, while inwardly he cheered that she'd fought back. The welt on her arm was likely the price she'd paid.

Savvy said Brie spoke Arabic, not fluent, but enough. He wondered if she'd hidden this from her captors.

He touched the welt, his fingers lightly tracing the raised skin. He wanted to find the man who'd touched her and do worse than blind him. But instead he needed to be just like that man. He grabbed her ass and squeezed.

She flinched but didn't strike him. Her gaze met his. Her eyes burned with anger and unshed tears.

The guard snapped the whip. "No touching before the auction!"

Bastian raised his hands in surrender. "Fine. But I'll pay more if I can have a taste first."

The whip snapped again, this time dangerously close to Brie's face. She yelped and jumped back, tripping over her own chain.

Bastian caught her by the shoulder, preventing her fall. His gaze met hers, and for a brief moment, his guard slipped. Her eyes widened in silent communication.

Fuck. If anyone caught the exchange, they were screwed.

He shut down his reaction and grunted. "Clumsy bitch." To the guard, he said in Arabic, "You got any other women? I like bigger tits."

The man reached out and grabbed her breasts, lifting them and squeezing. "There's enough here."

Brie swung out with her right fist, knocking the man's head toward her, then she jerked her head as if she intended to head-butt him, but checked herself, muting the blow. Clearly, she wasn't trained in fighting.

The slaver dropped back, hurt, but not as badly as he could have been. He lashed out with the whip.

She screamed, and blood sprouted on her chest; a thin line of liquid red crossed her right breast and curled over her shoulder.

In a flash, Bastian had the man pinned to the dirt floor with his knife at his throat. "You're damaging my property," he said in a low voice.

"She's mine! You haven't paid."

"You will sell her to me, or you will die." He shaved a chunk of beard from the man's throat.

"You will pay—and pay well—or *you* will die."

Bastian lifted the man from the floor, keeping his knife at his throat. He kicked open his duffel bag, revealing the stacks of hundred dollar bills. "That enough for you?"

The man nodded.

Bastian needed to seal this deal while the man was afraid and before he remembered his special buyer. "But you only get this if you give her to me now. No auction." If this failed, he'd take out the slaver and make a break with Brie. "No one else will pay you this much."

The man stared into the duffel. He hesitated a moment, then reached into the pouch on his hip and pulled out a key and handed it to Bastian.

"Take her."

Chapter Seven

B rie could hardly breathe from the moment she'd recognized Bastian. He was here to save her, making him the most beautiful man she'd ever seen.

At least, she hoped he was here to rescue her. He was a little too convincing in his role of buyer.

He looked different. Scruffy and mean. Fierce. Dark. Hostile. But then, weren't Green Berets trained to blend, to fit in with the locals? If she hadn't recognized him, she'd be utterly terrified.

Frankly, she was still terrified.

Bastian sheathed his knife and quickly unlocked her chain from the floor bolt. The key didn't work on the collar. He looked to the slaver, who was busy counting his money. "Unlock the collar."

The man waved him off. "They'll do that when you leave the market."

His eyes darkened, and she wondered if this screwed with his plans. "Unlock her now." His stance was threatening, but all he had was his sheathed knife.

She braced herself for walking through the market nude with a metal collar around her neck. As far as degradations go, it was the least of what she'd expected but was a humiliation just the same. She crossed her arms over her chest, unable to help herself. Some reactions were instinctual.

Bastian's nostrils flared, and a moment later, he used his knife to cut the cloth from the doorway and presented her with the covering in an indifferent manner. Master to slave. "Cover yourself."

He frowned when she took the item gratefully. A reminder that she was supposed to fear him. Or at least be angry.

"Master has given Dobby clothes!" she said in her French accent, adding bitterness to the tone.

His expression didn't change, but his eyes…something happened there. He read her loud and clear.

The cloth was dirty and thin, but she was grateful for it just the same. Twisting the cloth at her throat like a sarong, she tied it around her neck. The fabric cradled her breasts, but at least she was covered. Tears came to her eyes. She'd tried to ignore the horror of being stripped and on display, but it had bothered her on a deeper level than she could process in the moment.

Covered, she straightened her spine and walked through the opening into the bright sunlight. Bastian leaned close and whispered, "Fight me."

She jerked away from him. He yanked her back to his side. He said something she didn't understand in Arabic, and the men who'd gathered around the hut—the ones who'd been waiting for the auction that now wouldn't happen—laughed.

A few angry eyes pierced her and Bastian, probably for being denied the chance to bid. She glared at them as she yanked her chain from Bastian's grip, swinging the end so it hit him on the shoulder.

Bastian reacted accordingly, taking back the chain and yanking her toward him. His eyes glittered, his expression fierce. True fear shot through her, tempering the relief that had yet to fully register in her system.

"I like them feisty," he said, his tone all hard edges, "because then they scream more when they break." He slipped a hand between the split in her sarong and pinched her breast.

She yelped and jumped back, her nipple aching at the assault. Her attempt to escape wasn't faked.

She wasn't just scared. She was terrified.

Weeks ago, he'd made it clear he didn't like her. What if he *wasn't* here for a rescue? What if he was involved in some dirty deals and now he was here to make sure she didn't get away?

After all, he was one of only two people who knew exactly who she was. He could be responsible for her abduction.

She bolted for the market entrance, only to be brought up short by the chain. She choked like she'd been clotheslined and fell back against Bastian's hard chest. He let out a mean laugh even as he whispered into her ear. "Perfect. Sorry. Fight me."

She believed him and she didn't.

The world was too surreal, too cruel to make absolute sense.

He then scooped her up and flung her over his shoulder. The cut from the whip burned as she brushed against him before settling into place with his shoulder at her diaphragm.

He slapped her ass and marched for the exit. She pounded on his back.

"Scream," he murmured.

She let out a shriek that put her other cries to shame.

They reached the perimeter of the market, and he set

her down. She pushed at his chest, but he held her in place. His eyes were lit with an unholy light. "Hold still, hellcat, unless you want to remain leashed."

She stiffened. He was too damn convincing. He could take his game to Hollywood and make a fortune.

The same guard who'd collared her before now unlocked the metal band. She yanked it off and tossed it down. It landed with a thunk, and she took what seemed like her first deep breath in days.

She lifted her gaze to Bastian's. His eyes held an intensity that was different. He grabbed her arm and leaned down and whispered, "Run," then released her.

She was barefoot on uneven ground, but she did her best, terrified and confused at the same time. Why wasn't he running too? Where was she supposed to go?

Did he have no plan beyond releasing her from the market?

A moment later, he tackled her and rolled with her across the hard, sharp pebbles that filled the muddy track that passed for a road.

He pinned her beneath him and shouted to the market guards. "This bitch tried to escape."

Two guards came running as Bastian got to his feet.

The guards reached them and yanked her arms, as if they would drag her back to the market. She kicked and screamed.

Behind them—back in the market—an explosion sounded.

Before she could take in what was happening, Bastian's blade flashed, and one guard dropped to the ground. The second reached for his gun, but Bastian was faster.

Blood spurted from his neck, and he flopped down onto Brie.

She pushed at him, scrambling to get out from under the dead man. Bastian shoved the fallen guard aside and pulled her to her feet.

"Go for the trees," he said, propelling her forward.

She dove for the thick vegetation that crowded the road. He remained at her heels.

"This way," he said in a low, urgent voice, pushing a branch aside.

She stepped on something sharp and recoiled.

"Keep going," he said. "If you can't, I'll carry you."

She shook her head. Her brain scrambled for purchase with the same frenetic urgency as her feet sought a path through the thick vegetation. Both brain and feet failed, and she tripped, pitching forward into tangled vines.

Before she could let out a yelp, Bastian's hand slapped over her mouth. He pulled her to his chest, his large hand muzzling her.

She was trapped against his body and silenced by his hand. No longer bound by chains, but still a prisoner.

Tears did fall now. There was nothing she could do about them.

He removed his hand and cradled her head to his chest. His touch transformed from harsh to tender. "Shhhh. I need to hear what's going on in the market."

She ceased struggling and strained to hear over her racing heart. She should have realized he wasn't restraining her. He'd killed two guards—slavers. That put them on the same team.

She took a slow, silent breath and listened. Shouts. High-pitched children's voices. Men cursing in Arabic.

"She's hurt. Whipped by the slaver and battered by our escape," Bastian said. "I'm going to grab my pack and make for the truck. Over."

She looked at him in confusion, then realized he must be speaking into a hidden radio. She canted her head and saw a flesh-toned object tucked into his ear canal. The receiver.

"I killed the two at the south entrance. They had guns. Shoot the other guards with the dead guards' AKs. Give the weapons to the oldest children if they want them— but only if they're old enough to understand what they're doing."

He paused, and she wished she could hear the other end of the conversation when his eyes hardened even as his lips curved in a chilling smile. "Good."

Another pause followed by, "After we get the truck, we'll go north to the rendezvous point. Check in at thirty. And thanks." His gaze met hers. "She's free and her injuries look minor. Over."

"Your team?" she whispered.

He nodded.

She leaned toward him and directed her voice to his collar, where the microphone must be hidden. "Thank you."

She had no clue if they heard her, or even who they were. But her words were inadequate to the emotion that flooded her.

"We need to get moving. There's always a chance the guy who sold you had guards ready to follow us to bring you back. Slavers aren't the most honorable of men, and selling you twice would double his take. My team is going to lead the kids east, to the river, so we need to go the other way."

"They're saving the children?"

"As many as they can."

She threw her arms around Bastian and squeezed.

"Thank you." If being stripped naked and whipped meant even a few children were saved from slavery, it was worth it. Every horrific moment. Every painful, shredded nerve ending.

His arms closed around her for just a moment, then he released her. "I've got a truck hidden about a mile from here."

She followed, moving as fast as her sore foot and the vegetation would allow, finding it hard to believe this was really happening, that she'd been rescued.

"Sorry about tackling you," he said. "We needed a distraction to draw the guards away so Espi could move the kids away from the hut before the explosion. It's why I needed you to fight me when we left the hut. So all eyes would be on us."

"I figured that when you said they're saving the kids."

"There was no way I could tell you."

"I know. I'm just grateful it worked."

"We hope," Bastian said. "They still need to get the kids to the river, without anyone knowing we helped them."

"The Army didn't authorize this?"

"They sent us in to get you. Only you."

She understood, but still, it triggered an ache. "Thank you for disregarding orders."

"None of us would have been able to live with ourselves if we'd let those kids be sold."

He stopped and scanned the woods. He must've spotted what he was looking for, because his mouth curved in a wide smile and he made a beeline for a downed tree. There, he moved aside some broadleaves and pulled out a large pack. He plucked a protein bar from a side pocket and handed it to her. "I would imagine you're starving."

After working in South Sudan for seven months, she'd long since stopped using words like "starving" lightly. But now wasn't the time to say that to the man who'd just killed on her behalf. Instead, she gratefully accepted the food and said, "Thanks."

And she was intensely hungry. The last thing she'd eaten had been the beef jerky she'd had the day before. Her abductor had claimed all the food in her pack and hadn't shared the trail mix he'd had for breakfast.

She downed the bar so quickly, she risked choking. Bastian handed her a water bottle when she was done. She wanted to rinse the mud from her face and blood from her chest, but water was too precious to waste in that way.

While she ate and drank, he donned his pack and retrieved his rifle. She'd never been so happy to see a gun in her life. She wasn't home free yet, but their odds were improving by the moment.

They set out again, the vegetation thickening and offering no clear path. He came to an abrupt stop and raised his arm, his hand in a fist. She'd been taught that and a few other military hand signals. That one meant freeze. So she did.

She didn't know his next hand signal but guessed he wanted her to drop and hide, which she also did.

A second later, he fired his rifle, then dropped down beside her.

"Got one," he whispered. At least she thought it was a whisper. Her ears rang from the report of the bullet.

"How many are there?" she asked.

"Three." His gaze darted to the right. "I'm going to circle around. Get behind them. Stay here."

She nodded, even though she hated the plan. She wanted to stay with Bastian and his big gun, and that wasn't a euphemism.

He crawled around her like he was some sort of cat—quick and nimble, a creature of the forest.

Several big cats had habitat in South Sudan, including lions and cheetahs, but they would be found on the savannah, not here. No, here they faced more dangerous creatures.

Sweat pooled between her breasts as she sat in a dank hole in the flooded grasslands and listened for movement. Bastian was quiet like a cat too. Her heart beat louder than he moved through the damp leaves. Brie pulled herself into a tight ball and held her breath so she wouldn't make a noise.

She closed her eyes and again saw the guard's face, right before Bastian slit his throat.

The image had been assaulting her brain from the moment it happened. Not surprising, given the gruesome nature and that she could still smell the man's blood on the cloth she wore.

But with sudden clarity, she realized that wasn't the reason she couldn't let the image go. She'd seen him before.

Three shots broke the silence. What if the shots were fired *at* Bastian? Was he injured? Dead? If anything happened to him, it would be her fault.

She was the reason he wasn't with his team. She was the reason he'd come to South Sudan. Everything was her fault.

Was it simple happenstance that she ended up at the slave market? Or was it possible the USAID facility had been attacked because of her?

Chapter Eight

Bastian waited in silence until he was certain the remaining two men were dead. One had been a headshot—no question there—but the other had been hit in the chest. He'd made low noises as the blood drained from his body. When no sounds issued for a full ten minutes, Bastian inched forward silently.

The long wait had to be excruciating to Brie, but he gave her props for holding silent. He searched the bodies of all three men, snapped a photo of the one whose face wasn't destroyed, tucked his phone away, then traced their footsteps through the vegetation, making certain there weren't more who'd retreated.

The dead men were white and their clothing generic camo that could be purchased in any military surplus store. Their weapons were AKs, which told him nothing. Kalashnikovs were the most available weapon in Africa.

Odds were they were mercenaries. Market security. Did they have orders to bring Brie back to the market for a second sale? It was telling that they went after her even after the explosion. They could have gone after the escaping children, who represented lost revenue.

Who bankrolled market security? Russians? Could these mercs be representatives of the special buyer?

One thing he was certain of: the market had been far too organized—right down to the collars and keys—to be a no-man's-land. Someone controlled it.

Bastian returned to Brie's side, where he found her curled in a ball. She gazed up at him, not speaking, her eyes wide with pain and fear. "I'm sorry," he said. "I had to be certain they were dead and no others were hiding in wait." He pulled her to her feet. "Let's go."

"Where are we going?" she asked.

"I've got a truck this way." Rain started to fall. Fat drops filtered through the leafy canopy. The road had been slippery coming in, and he'd parked the truck well off the narrow trail that twisted through the grassland. "We better hurry if we're going to get out of here before the road becomes impassible—we've got a long drive ahead of us."

"Are we heading to Juba?"

"No. We've got a rendezvous point where a Blackhawk will pick us up. By oh-two-hundred tonight, you'll be headed home."

Brie said the first thing that came to mind. "Home? Where is that supposed to be?" She glanced around the thicket of woods that surrounded the market, effectively hiding it in the swath of flooded grasslands. South Sudan was the only home she had right now.

"That's for you to decide," Bastian said. "Where did you live before you came here?"

It felt like decades ago, given how time had stretched in the months she'd been here. "I was in Madagascar for a while, and a few other places before that. When I was stateside last year between assignments, I had a sweet little spot on a friend's couch in Seattle."

Bastian marched ahead of her through the grass. "You

mean to tell me you're homeless? That's hard to believe."

So he still thought she was only in South Sudan to close an oil deal? Anger rose, but she tamped it down. This man had just saved her life and killed five men to do it. "Believe me, don't believe me. That's really up to you. But for the record, I gave up lying when I quit booze, drugs, and my family."

The thicket gradually thinned until only sparse trees separated them from open grassland. Bastian held up a hand, the signal to halt, and studied the area.

"Where's your vehicle?" she asked.

"The other side of that rise."

The rain was gradually increasing, and a glance at the now-visible sky showed it was only going to get worse. There were no roads here, just tracks through the grasslands. A hard storm could make the drive to reach the road impossible.

"How far is the rendezvous point? Can we walk it?"

"We wouldn't make it in time."

"Can you change the location?"

"If we need to, but right now my team is scattered, so that would require coordinating using long-range radios—communication that can be intercepted." He flicked his collar, where the microphone must be hidden. "We're already beyond the range of this. For now we need to stick to the plan."

She understood. In South Sudan, where cell towers— and electricity—were a rarity, radio communications were vital and heavily monitored. "We'd better hurry, then, before the road washes out."

Bastian nodded. "We're going to run low and fast across the grass to the other side of the rise," he said. "Can you do it?"

"Yes." Her foot throbbed and her side ached from the whipping, but she could power through. She could do anything as long as it meant she wasn't going to be a sex slave to some deviant asshole.

He gave a hand signal, and she crouched and ran. An ankle twisted in the muck, but she kept going, pushing herself to keep up with him. They reached the SUV, and he circled it, doing a quick check to determine if it had been tampered with. He unlocked her door, and she slipped inside.

In moments, they were underway. The sky opened up and rain pummeled the windshield as he cut across the grassland, aiming for, she hoped, an actual road. The tires slipped but then gained traction, and they lurched forward in jerky starts and stops, reminding her of the Indiana Jones ride at Disneyland.

Oh Indy, you have no idea.

She spied the road fifty yards ahead. It wouldn't be much better, but at least it would take them to the main road that cut through the flooded grasslands and went all the way to Juba.

Bastian steered with skill that hinted at a history of mudding. Had he spent his youth in trucks with giant tires cutting up wilderness areas? Or did the Army train their Special Forces for everything, including a South Sudan rainy season exfiltration?

Once on the dirt—or rather mud—road, the SUV lurched as they hit a pothole hidden in the muck. Brie bounced, and her head hit the roof, in spite of her seat belt.

With one hand, Bastian grabbed the radio from his pack in the backseat and tried to raise his team, but received only static in reply. "Must be the rain," he said and slid the radio back into the side pocket, keeping his eyes on the sloppy track ahead of them. "I'll try again when we get to the main road."

She nodded, feeling almost dazed to be in the truck, sheltered from the pounding rain. How long ago was it that she'd been lying on her cot, listening to the rain on the metal roof, and thinking about Bastian the Bastard Green Beret?

"You okay?" he asked.

She wasn't sure how to answer. Did he mean her head? Her foot? That she'd witnessed two men having their throats slit to save her? That she'd been whipped? Or the fact that he'd just bought her in a market?

"Sorry," he said when she didn't answer. "That was a dumb question."

She rubbed her head and cut him some slack. "No. It's okay. I think I ache everywhere, but I'm okay. I think?"

She winced as she inspected her bare foot. It was coated in mud, so she couldn't be certain, but she had a feeling the cut was deep. Plus her ankle… It wasn't doing great. She'd probably twisted it when she ran. But she was alive. "I'm better than I would be, thanks to you and your team. Thank you."

He flashed a cocky, flippant smile. "Just doing my job, ma'am."

His light tone caused an ache. She was just a job to him. Not that she should be anything more. It was just— she was probably rather fragile at the moment. Her brain wasn't really keeping up with her emotions.

She cleared her throat. "Well, thank you just the same. I hope you will pass on my thanks to your commander."

"The mission was ordered by SOCOM, but I'm the one who insisted on searching for you after your coworkers were rescued."

She jolted and twisted to face him, gripping his knee. "They're okay?"

"Yes. Sorry, I should have told you that sooner."

"Today...hasn't exactly been normal." She gingerly lifted her hand from his leg.

Jesus. She'd been *sold* to this man. She knew he'd been acting in the market, but he'd been chillingly good in the role. Her brain was scattered between impressions of him. The slave buyer. The angry man she met at Camp Citron. The soldier who'd killed five men to protect her and help rescue dozens of children.

Suck it up, buttercup. He despises you, but he saved you nonetheless, which makes him pretty damn heroic.

"Shit. I suck at this," Bastian said. "The truth is, I wasn't going to leave South Sudan without you, Brie. Orders or no orders. No bullshit."

"It's okay. I understand how you feel about me. It doesn't matter. I'm grateful just the same. More grateful, actually."

"No, you don't understand. I was wrong about you. When we first met, I—"

She cut him off with a swipe of her hand. "Please. Can we not talk about that *now*?" She let out a pained laugh. "I'm having a rough day."

Bastian swallowed and his knuckles whitened on the steering wheel, but he gave a sharp nod.

The rain continued to fall, showing all the earmarks of a significant storm. They reached a fork in the road, and Bastian swore.

"What's wrong?"

"We're supposed to go left."

The left fork was flooded. Completely wiped away.

"That's not going to happen."

"You know this area?"

"Only vaguely. I was warned to stay away—too far off the main road, things get dicey." She lowered her voice and muttered. "That might be the mother of all understatements."

He grabbed a map from his pack and tossed it in her lap. "Find us a route out of here." He put the truck in gear and took the right fork.

Fortunately, the map was a printout of high-resolution satellite images. "When were these photos taken?" she asked.

"Yesterday," he said. "Before we left Camp Citron."

She glanced out the window at the cascade of rain. "Lucky break in the rain."

"Very lucky. Without satellite, we'd never have pinpointed the market."

They came upon fork after fork in the mazelike flooded grassland, and she directed him on which road to take. They were going in the wrong direction for the rendezvous point, but eventually they'd get to the main road. At least an hour—maybe two given how slow they were moving—would be added to their driving time, but it wasn't like they had a choice. According to the locals, the main road to Juba would be the last to give way in the rainy season.

But they hadn't made it to the main road yet, and the four-wheel-drive SUV slipped and slid on the narrow track. Bastian handled it with ease, comfortable behind the wheel.

Brie kept her focus on the map because watching the road was too alarming. At least the flooded grasslands were relatively flat—if she had to face a drop-off on either side of the vehicle, she'd be losing her lunch. "We're adding miles to our driving distance," she said.

"I hope we don't run out of fuel. We've only got two jerry cans."

"Ironic that Kemet Oil has an oil rig to the north, yet actual gas stations are nonexistent here. There's a village to the south where we can probably buy gas from one of the locals." She knew everywhere they could find gas for a fifty-mile radius and was glad she could use that knowledge to aid in her rescue.

Several kilometers to go before they reached the main road, the gas gauge dropped below the red zone. Bastian stopped in the middle of the muddy track. "Stay inside—keep dry. This should only take a few minutes."

He climbed out of the cab and grabbed the jerry can from the back. He'd been driving nearly two hours, and his back and shoulders were tight from the tension of trying to keep the SUV on the road. He rolled his shoulders, then hooked the funnel to the spout and poured in the gas, careful not to spill a precious drop as rain drenched his back.

He tossed the empty can in the back of the SUV and turned to circle around but paused as he passed the passenger door. There was Brie, huddled in the seat with her knees pulled to her chest, tears sliding down her cheeks.

Hours ago, he'd purchased her from a slave market. Then she'd watched as he killed two men with a knife. One of them had bled out all over her.

And he could only imagine what hell she'd been through prior to that.

Without thinking, he opened the door, reached in and unlatched her seat belt, then pulled her into his arms.

His team had rescued women before, and he'd never touched the victim more than necessary. But this time, he knew her. And dammit, she probably needed to be held. Even if she hated him, she needed comfort.

She pressed against him, burrowing into his chest as his arms closed around her. A low sob escaped from her throat, and he stroked her back. He wanted to tell her everything would be okay, but what happened to her wasn't okay, and it wasn't over until they were on the Blackhawk and headed back to Camp Citron. So he just held her as she cried. "I'm so sorry. So fucking sorry."

She was under his protection now. He'd get her the hell out of South Sudan, and someday, this would be just a bad memory.

He pulled back and pressed his lips to her forehead. "We need to hit the road."

She nodded. "Sorry I fell apart."

"That was falling apart? Honey, you should see me when I lose at pool."

She gave him a weak smile, which was the best he could hope for. He circled the truck and climbed back in the driver's seat, and they were on their way again.

"Cal killed the man who sold you," he said, keeping his gaze on the sorry excuse for a road ahead. "He told me over the radio right after we left the market. He retrieved the bag of money. No money exchanged for you will feed the terror and war machine."

"Thank you. That's good to know."

The truck slipped, and he pumped the brakes. They'd be lucky to make it to the main road in this mess. The track was nothing more than a raised mud slick that cut through a rapidly expanding swamp.

He'd call out the universe for hating him, but he didn't believe the cosmos was in charge of his fate. Plus it irritated the hell out of him when people assumed he believed everything was spiritual simply because he was Indian.

But then, he was frequently irritated by the assumptions people made when they learned his native heritage. Some dipshits said they expected more woo.

He didn't do woo.

He rounded a bend in the track, and the road ahead completely disappeared.

He kept going straight. There was no other choice.

Too late, he realized the other choice was to stop and get out and walk.

All at once, the nose of the truck dove down, buried to the windshield in the muck. He'd driven off the higher track that served as a road, into the deep swamp.

Brie screamed at the sudden lurch as the vehicle sank toward her side, listing as if it might flip. Mud covered the lower half of her window. She pushed against the door as gravity pulled them deeper into the muck.

Bastian pushed open his door. Mud slithered into the cab through the opening. "Shit!"

How deep was this swamp? Could they be swallowed whole? There was nothing to use to prop the door open, and the angle of the vehicle worked against him. The door slammed shut, cutting off the flow of mud but trapping them in a sinking vehicle. He shoved it open again and wedged his ankle in the opening. It pinched like hell but didn't close.

"Climb over me," he said to Brie.

She did as instructed, pushing the door wider as she

crawled across his chest, using him as a ladder as the truck shifted to an eighty-degree angle.

"There's nowhere to go," she said as she slipped through the door.

Her weight shifted them to a full ninety degrees—and they were still sinking. Mud poured in on him.

"Crawl onto the side," he said needlessly, as she was already moving to the rear panel of the SUV.

Once she cleared the opening, the door pinched his ankle again. She lifted the door, relieving the pressure. "I've got it. Move your foot."

His foot tingled with the lack of blood flow. He was trained for working through injury, and this was no different, even though the cause was weather, not enemy combatants. Right now, the rain and mud were the enemy, and he'd conquer them as surely as his team had beaten a warlord's army.

He twisted, pulling his torso through the muddy opening, sliding onto the side of the truck next to Brie.

Freed, he rested for a moment on the rear cab door. Their combined weight on the side of the sinking vehicle gave gravity the edge, and the entire vehicle disappeared under the mud.

Shit. His pack. The second pack full of supplies for Brie. Their gear was in the backseat.

He ordered Brie to move to the rear quarter and wrenched open the passenger door he'd been sitting on, burying his arm in the mud-filled cabin as he groped for his pack. His fingers closed on a strap. His M4 rifle? It had been next to his pack. He took a deep breath and plunged his head and shoulders into the mud so he could reach deeper. He twisted the M4 strap around his wrist and kept groping until his fingers closed on a pack. He hoped it was his, because that one contained the bulk of the supplies.

Thank God.

With his free hand, he shoved on the driver's headrest to leverage himself free, pulling out both the rifle and fifty-pound pack from the mud with his other arm. He crawled backward to again slide free from the interior.

He swiped the mud from his nose and mouth and took a deep breath as he settled back on the rear panel. His breathing was heavy after the suffocation of the thick muck.

No time to catch his breath. He slipped his arms through the pack straps and draped the rifle across his back before he wiped the mud from his eyes.

Eyes cleared, he glanced around. Were they sinking deeper? Any thought of going back in for the second pack was squelched. With the pouring rain, it was hard to see exactly where the high ground of the road was.

As it was, they could step off the vehicle into the deep muck and drown.

How far had they veered from the road?

He met Brie's gaze. Her beautiful brown eyes were wide with fear.

One of the stereotypes he faced on a daily basis was that he was supposed to be in tune with the earth. As a Native American, he was supposed to be able to hear the whispers of the mother and find his way, or some bullshit like that.

Well, if he'd ever needed woo, it was now.

Sadly, he'd have to rely on his Special Forces skills instead.

Chapter Nine

Brie wobbled as the truck shifted. She gripped Bastian's shoulder to keep her balance. *Holy crap.* The swamp had swallowed the truck whole, like it was some sort of monster with an appetite for beat-up utility vehicles.

This couldn't be happening. She'd already been abducted, chained, stripped, whipped, and *sold*. Truck-eating bogs was one ordeal too many.

She tightened her jaw and looked up into the downpour. Ahh, fuck. She'd have to save the angsty breakdown for later.

The angle of the truck hinted at where they'd gone off the road, and she could see a slight rise where the road must be. Four feet away. From there, they could wade to higher ground.

"We're going to have to jump," Bastian said, confirming her thoughts.

She took a deep breath and launched herself from the truck before she could lose her nerve. But the mud gripped her feet, and she didn't spring up like she'd hoped. She sank deep into the muck a foot shy of her goal.

She grappled for purchase, all while sinking deeper. She tried not to panic as the mud weighed down her arms and her feet tried to find firm ground beneath her.

She was going to drown in mud.

Panic kills.

She slowed her movements, fanning out her arms as if she were swimming to propel herself toward the firmer ground that supported the road.

There must be roots, vegetation that stabilized the roadway, or it would have succumbed to the swamp sooner.

Hands shoved at her from behind, pushing her upward, giving her the leverage to reach firmer ground. She scrambled up the soft bank and flopped onto the road, discovering it was only covered in three inches of mud. She flipped over and grabbed Bastian's wrists. He grabbed hers, locking their grip. With her butt planted on the road, she pulled, leaning back, pulling him from the swamp.

She didn't have the strength to lift him, but his feet must've found purchase, because he emerged, birthed from the bog, one slow step at a time, as she dragged him forward.

She lay flat on her back in the shallow mud by the time Bastian's body was completely free. He lay on top of her. They were chest to chest, still gripping each other's wrists as rain poured down on them.

Water swirled around her head and flowed toward the swamp. They should get up. Follow the road. Get to higher ground. But right now all she wanted to do was lie in the middle of the flooded road with the Green Beret who'd just saved her life again.

He started to rise from her chest, and she gripped his filthy, muddy shirt, holding him in place. She imagined how they would look to a stranger coming upon them, coated in mud, embracing. Hysterical laughter bubbled inside her chest. Insane didn't begin to describe this day.

Bastian's body quaked before the rumble of his own laugh erupted.

She was alive, coated in muck, and above her, Bastian's equally coated face was lit with a warm, wild light. She wrapped her muddy hands around his muddy, bearded cheeks and pulled his face to hers. She pressed her muddy lips to his. They kissed, openmouthed and exuberant, a celebration that tasted of earth and rain and joy. They'd cheated the bog god of his sacrifice.

Who would've thought *rain* would be the most dangerous thing she faced today?

The kiss ended, and he peeled his body from hers, climbing to his feet. He reached down and pulled her upright. Standing, she faced him and wiped a streak of muck from his face, but it was a lost cause. They were both hopelessly, endlessly drenched in mud.

"We need to get to higher ground," he said. He nodded toward a low rise back in the direction they'd just driven through.

She turned to where the vehicle had disappeared in the muck. "The map," she said. She'd left it in the cab. It was destroyed now. She closed her eyes. "I stared at it enough. I remember—I hope." She studied the road. "The road jogged left for half a klick, then there was a fork where we'd go right. Several more twists and turns, and we'll reach the main road. From there, ten miles south is a village—one I know. I make weekly rounds to monitor food and other supply levels. The village is on my rotation. They might be able to help us there."

"Is there a way to get there without taking the main road?"

She closed her eyes, pictured the map. "Maybe. But it's probably as flooded as this road is."

"Then we'll go to the road." They started walking, following the line of the high ground as best they could. After they'd gone about a hundred yards, Bastian patted the side of his pack, then cursed.

"What's wrong?" she asked. "Aside from everything, that is."

"My radio is gone. Sonofafucking bitch. It must've slipped from the side pocket in the mud. It could be in the cab, or in the swamp next to the road."

He glanced back, toward where the vehicle had been lost to the swamp, not saying what they both knew: there was no going back for the radio.

They'd never find it. Hell, they probably wouldn't be able to find the SUV at this point.

They walked side by side, following the line of the road as best they could discern it. It was slow going and she stepped tentatively, in case the road disappeared again under her feet. Her ankle screamed with each step, but she didn't complain. Walking was the only option.

At one point, she did accidently step off the road, but lacking the weight of the truck, she wasn't sucked out into the swamp. Bastian caught her and pulled her back to the firmer ground.

Gray sky and relentless rain made it hard to judge the time of day. As near as she could guess, it had been mid-afternoon when they left the market and the rain started. Several hours had passed since then, given the trek through the woods, the drive slowed by mud, rain, and twisted route, and now they'd been walking for well over an hour. The sun would set soon, and they'd lose even the ambiguous gray light.

She couldn't keep walking in the dark. Bastian might have night vision goggles, but she didn't, and she'd already stepped off the road once. Plus her ankle hurt like hell, every step sent pain shooting up her leg. "What are we going to do?" she asked, a little afraid of his answer.

"We need to find high ground. Rest. Regroup." He pointed to a rise in the distance. Trees surrounded the low hill. "We're going there."

It was the swampy version of an oasis in the desert.

"We'll take a break. Figure out our next move."

The storm lightened by slow degrees. By the time they reached the hill, it was reduced to a sprinkle. Night fell as if a switch were flipped on the sun, telling her it was about seven p.m. This close to the equator, sunrise and sunset were consistent and fast.

Adrenaline had kept her going, but with a destination in sight, the pain in her ankle became all-consuming. By the time they reached the hill, she could no longer hide her limp. Between the cut on her foot and twisted ankle, she could barely put weight on it.

Bastian cursed and scooped her into his arms. "Why didn't you say something?"

She draped her arms around his neck. "Because you'd do something like this. You can't carry me ten miles."

"Instead of resting for only an hour, we'll stop here for the night. Take care of your foot. Maybe you can walk tomorrow."

"We'll miss the rendezvous."

"That was going to happen anyway once we lost the truck."

She leaned her cheek against his shoulder as he carried her up the rise. At the top, he set her down and spread a plastic sheet over the tall grass. A wasted effort, considering how wet and muddy she was, but it would be more comfortable than soaking into the mucky ground.

He sat on the sheet, and she dropped down beside him. Now that the adrenaline that had seen her through the worst of the day had faded, she began to tremble with pain and fatigue.

"Let's take a look at that foot," he said as he pulled a first aid kit from his pack.

"Mud didn't get inside the pack," she said as he laid out items from the kit on the plastic sheet.

"The main pocket was cinched tight. We lost the radio because it was on the outside." He washed her foot with a damp towel. "Sorry I didn't have shoes or clothes for you. We had to pull together the rescue fast."

She tugged at the muddy, bloody cloth she wore. "This works." She wasn't feeling particularly picky in that moment.

He used sanitizer to clean the cut on the arch of her right foot, and she sucked in air through her teeth at the sting.

With the mud removed, it started to bleed, a fresh flow of bright red blood. He wrapped it tightly with gauze, then shifted to her ankle, which he probed with gentle fingers. "A little swelling. Does this hurt?" he asked.

"No. Only when I put weight on it."

He pulled out a cold pack and snapped it to release the icing chemical. "Keep this on it tonight. No walking unless absolutely necessary."

She nodded and frowned. "I need to pee."

He inclined his head toward a tree that was only a few feet away. "I'll turn around."

She did and he did, and she grimaced at the thought that they'd progressed rapidly to the peeing-with-the-door-open stage. Living in South Sudan had cured her of inhibitions around bathroom habits—one couldn't be squeamish and live here—but it was different being around an American she didn't really know.

She adjusted her sarong and settled back on the plastic sheet and put the ice pack on her ankle. He pulled a protein bar from his pack and handed it to her. "Dinner is served."

She gave a short laugh. Even though she'd had the snack earlier, her stomach was collapsing in on itself from hunger. She opened the bar and broke it in half. One thing she'd learned working in a famine-struck country, they needed to ration. There was no telling how long they'd be stuck out here, and there weren't any crops to be found in the grasslands. No edible berries. Nothing. In South Sudan, all available food resources were picked clean. Uninhabited areas like this one had nothing to offer, or people would have settled here.

He took his portion without argument. They both needed strength if they were going to get out of this situation. "I have several more bars, some MREs and jerky. Enough for two or three days if we're careful."

She looked toward rain dripping from the leaves. "At least water won't be a problem. It'll take a few hours to walk to the village tomorrow."

"If you can walk."

"I will walk." She would because she had to.

He finished his miniscule dinner and stretched out on the sheet. "You need to sleep."

"I don't know if I can," she admitted. She was wet and muddy and maybe just a tad bit freaked out.

He pulled her down so the back of her head rested on his chest. "I'll be your pillow," he said. His arm draped over her chest. He found her wrist and trailed along her skin until his fingers entwined with hers.

The reminder she needed that she wasn't alone.

Stars peeked in small clusters as the clouds dissipated. "So, your friends call you Bastian. Your enemies call you asshole. What do lovers call you?"

"Why do you want to know?"

She smiled up at the stars. "Future reference."

He chuckled. "Bastard mostly. I don't tend to stick around."

"Good to know. I've been called bitch for the same reason."

"What's wrong with people that they don't understand a simple hookup?" he asked. "It's not like I ever promised it would be anything more."

"Right? I mean, you bang a guy in an elevator, and he gets mad because there's no need to invite him into your penthouse after that."

"That's just efficient right there. He loses points for being fast, but still, efficient. Doesn't even mess up the sheets."

"In his defense, it was a tall building."

"I'll keep that in mind."

"For future reference," she repeated. "I mean, right now, you smell like swamp. And I'm guessing your junk is coated in mud."

She felt his body shake with laughter as his fingers threaded through her muddy hair. "This might be where the term 'rain check' comes from."

After the day she'd just endured, it was crazy to realize she was stretched out on a grassy hilltop with Chief Bastard, *laughing*. But it felt right.

Plus, it was so much better than crying. "So. It's

been…quite a day."

"Yep." He plucked something from her hair—a twig, probably. Then combed out the short strands with his fingers. "You chopped off your hair," he said idly, as if this was normal conversation after rescuing a woman from slavery and swamps.

"It's easier to wash." She wasn't about to admit it had anything to do with him. She'd cut off a foot of hair because that was her usual reaction to rejection. No need to feed his ego, which was probably inflated enough as it was.

"I like it."

She sighed as his fingers scraped her scalp. She was a sucker for scalp massages.

"If anyone told me ten years ago," he said, "we'd end up on a hilltop stargazing together in South Sudan, coated in mud after having escaped a slave market, I'd have told them they were nuts."

She laughed. "I think it's a nutty scenario for any two Americans, but admit we might be a more unlikely pair than most."

"Princess Prime and an Indian? No one could predict that."

"Hey, I'll have you know not all Native Americans hate me. I do have a master's degree in cultural anthropology, you know."

"Yeah, but you must know what Indians think of cultural anthropologists."

She nodded. When she first started graduate school, she'd assumed she was hated for her family name and oil company connections; it had been a surprise to learn the reputation ethnologists had with some tribes. But the feeling wasn't universal thanks to the efforts of anthropologists and tribal members to bridge the chasm and work together to protect cultural heritage.

"The discipline is changing. We work together more than we divide."

"I know. But it's still there for some of us, the feeling that anthropologists and archaeologists want to tell us our past and our culture, study us like we're lab rats, then appropriate some parts of our culture and denigrate the rest."

It was true. Many had done that. Some cultural anthropologists still did.

"What tribe are you from?" She rolled to her side, so she could see his face, still resting her head on his ribs.

He brushed flecks of dried mud from her forehead. "Kalahwamish. We're on the Olympic Peninsula of Washington."

"I know of it. I went to grad school in Portland. That's the tribe that inherited the sawmill properties about fifteen years ago, right?"

"Yep."

"I believe both an archaeologist and a cultural anthropologist had something to do with that."

He smiled. "True. And I never said *I* don't like anthropologists. I helped rescue one from a warlord last month."

She laughed. "Ah, the old *I have anthropologist friends* defense."

He laughed too. "Hey, it's true." He cupped the back of her head and pulled her mouth to his. His lips were a scant centimeter from hers when he said, "I'm going to make an exception for you. If you want to study me—every inch of me—I'm willing to be your lab rat."

"Well, I'd need to have research questions if it's going

to be a valid scientific endeavor."

His lips brushed hers, soft and sweet, then he released her, and she lowered her head to use his chest as a pillow again. "We'll have plenty of time to come up with questions, because the study can't happen now. Aside from the fact that you smell like moldy bog, I need to stay alert."

"*Moldy* bog? Bog wasn't bad enough?"

"I call 'em like I smell 'em."

She made a show of smelling her underarm, then said, "Fair enough." She studied the sky, her head gently rising with each inhalation of Bastian's. "What happens now?"

"You sleep. In the morning, we'll walk to your village. See if we can find someone there with a radio. If not, we'll try to buy a ride to Juba."

It wasn't an impossible scenario, which gave her hope.

"We should take turns sleeping. You need to sleep too."

"We will, but you need to sleep first. You sleep for six to eight hours. You need it. After you've gotten decent rest, I'll wake you to keep watch and grab two hours. I'm trained for this and can go longer, but I'll be more effective if I sleep when I can."

She nodded, glad he was being reasonable, not macho. Clearly, Special Forces were smart and practical.

She wanted to do her part, but had to admit, right now she was desperately tired. "Sounds fair." She turned so she could see his eyes in the starlight. "Thank you. For coming to my rescue."

He traced her eyebrow. "You're welcome, Brie. Now get some sleep. I've got your back."

She closed her eyes, figuring sleep would be

impossible in spite of her exhaustion, but Bastian's rhythmic breathing, gentle touch, and promise of protection overrode her fear, and she slipped into much-needed oblivion.

Chapter Ten

Bastian waited until Brie was in a deep sleep before carefully sliding out from beneath her. He pulled his combat uniform shirt from his pack—he hadn't worn his ACU in the market—and slipped it under her head. She stirred but didn't wake.

He circled the clearing at the top of the rise, scouting for danger. Their situation was so fucked. In a few hours, a Blackhawk would land at the rendezvous point, and they would be nowhere to be found.

He'd fucked up and lost the vehicle and the radio. This was all his own damn fault.

He paced and circled their hilltop refuge. Thank goodness the rain had stopped. He had a rain shelter but would only break it out when necessary. He had to conserve their supplies because getting to the village probably wouldn't be simple, and if they had to go all the way to Juba, that could take days.

He pulled his knife from his pack and turned to the cluster of trees that ringed the hill. He needed to make a cane for Brie if she was going to be able to make the trek. He would also make sandals for her, using paracord and the insoles from his boots.

He found a sturdy branch and set to work.

As he whittled, his gaze repeatedly flicked to the woman who lay sleeping on the thin plastic sheet. He shouldn't have kissed her as they lay in the muddy road.

He wasn't even entirely certain who'd initiated the kiss, but there was no doubt it was not standard operating procedure for a Special Forces operator. The fact that she'd been stripped naked and sold to him just hours before made his actions even worse. Reprehensible.

Then he'd compounded his mistake by flirting with her, offering to let her study him anthropologically. He'd mentally justified it by telling himself she needed comfort after the horrors she'd been through. And that was true, but it was also self-serving justification.

He'd enjoyed flirting with her. Making her laugh.

And the truth was, he hadn't been thinking about what she'd just been through when he kissed her. He hadn't been thinking at all. There was no justification.

He should have recused himself from this mission so someone objective, who wouldn't take advantage of her, was sent in to save her.

Ten years ago, she'd been queen of his fantasies. That alone disqualified him from being her rescuer. Then a month ago, he'd kissed her.

An outside observer might think he was taking advantage of a vulnerable woman, and he couldn't deny it.

He wasn't a nice guy when it came to relationships. He had sex and was out the door, but he was always upfront about it. There were those who felt his behavior was synonymous with asshole, but even he'd never imagined he was this far gone, that he could want a woman because she was the ultimate forbidden fruit, and act on the impulse when she was at her most vulnerable.

That was what this was about, right? She was forbidden because she represented the very things that attacked the fabric of his culture. Oil companies. Anthropologists.

Hell, she was a recovering addict just like his uncle, making her a risk he couldn't afford.

If someone made a list of the worst possible women for him, Gabriella Stewart Prime would top it.

But the flirting had come so naturally. If he listed all the things she'd been through in the last forty-eight hours, flirting with her was just about the most inappropriate thing he could imagine. Except getting a hard-on was even worse.

He was so fucked. If his XO found out about any of this shit, he'd catch hell. Brie was the daughter of one of the richest men in the world. His CO, XO—hell, probably all of SOCOM—would believe he'd hit on her for that reason alone.

The idea made his skin crawl. Who her father was made his skin crawl. Everything about this situation could make him a spokesperson for eczema cream.

He scanned the horizon. With starlight undiminished by light pollution, he could see a fair distance. To the north were the oil fields that were grinding back into production in spite of the civil war. Some believed the oil companies supported keeping the war going because it meant less oversight, and more concessions. They paid smaller fees to the government because they had to provide their own hired army to protect their operation.

Armies that could protect a slave market?

A basic truth: countries in Africa were being used and abused by foreign corporations as much today as when slave ships had transported people to the New World.

He needed to keep his anger at Prime Energy front and center. Brie might not be part of the company—or even her family—anymore, but she was still a Prime. No matter what name she called herself these days. If he held on to that, it might prevent him from doing something stupid—like kissing her again.

Like caring for her.

***

"Bastian?" Brie whispered into the darkness, uneasy that she'd woken and found herself alone.

A moment later, he was at her side. "You okay?"

Relief flooded her. "Yes." She sat up. "How long did I sleep?"

He glanced at his watch. "Nearly six hours. Go back to sleep."

She rubbed her eyes. "No. I'm good. You should sleep now. You can get four hours, instead of only two." Clouds had rolled back in, and the night was deep and dark. "We missed the rendezvous." She'd known they would, but somehow, having the appointed time come and go felt more final.

"Yeah. But that's not a bad thing. It means they'll send a team to search for us."

"Do you think...we should stay here? Wait for them to find us?"

He dropped onto the plastic beside her. "Fuck if I know. We had to take a different route through the grassland. We're miles away from where they'll start searching."

"But they'll see the flooded road..."

"All the roads are flooded now. They won't know when we went off course. And they won't find our truck. Won't see our tracks. There was too much rain." He looked up at the sky. "And there's more to come."

He was silent a long moment. "I think they'll expect us to make our way to the main road. They'll search for us along the corridor."

"They won't…assume we're dead, will they?"

He shook his head. "No way would my team let anyone write me off."

She smiled at his conviction. "I'm glad to hear that, because I'm pretty sure my family would happily declare me dead." She was thankful for the darkness that hid the expression she couldn't control in the raw wee hours of the morning. She didn't want him to know that the knowledge that her half brothers didn't care about her still hurt.

She didn't want anyone to know she still longed for a family connection. There had been good times with Rafe and Jeffery Junior. When she was eight, she'd been certain she had the best big brothers in the world.

Unable to put weight on her foot, she abandoned the sheet for Bastian's use and sat with her back against a tree. From there, she could see him stretched out on the tarp and keep an eye on a full one hundred and eighty degrees of hillside and swamp.

She was impressed by his ability to lie down, close his eyes, and instantly go to sleep. She couldn't imagine the sort of training a person went through to be able to do that. That was some serious control.

She watched the even rise and fall of his chest as she attempted to process what had transpired over the last two days.

Watching Bastian sleep was a pleasure she hadn't expected. His handsome face relaxed and didn't look upon her with the disdain he'd shown at Camp Citron, or the pity he'd shown after he saved her. Best of all, he didn't resemble the brutal façade he'd shown as a slave buyer.

More than anything, she'd like to forget how he looked in that role. But the image was burned into her brain. It hadn't been him. It wasn't his nature. She knew that. But still, he'd terrified her.

So instead she thought about the soldier she'd flirted with just before going to sleep. She'd guessed he was a player from the moment they met. And now from their conversation tonight, he'd confirmed her assessment, meaning they had a player history in common.

She'd always avoided serious relationships, even before she'd so badly used Micah and then found she'd begun to care for him. After Micah, she'd built a wall around her heart. She wouldn't risk caring for a man ever again. It was too dangerous.

Four hours after Bastian lay down on the mat, his eyes popped open in an impressive display of the same body mastery he'd demonstrated in going to sleep. Dawn was breaking across the sky, which had clouded over with thick, dark storm clouds, casting the morning in gray light. They shared an MRE for breakfast, and then she tentatively tested her ankle, using a cane Bastian had fashioned for her in the middle of the night. The pain had eased somewhat, and with the cane for leverage, she could walk at a decent pace.

It would work.

But then, it had to.

They set out within fifteen minutes of Bastian's waking, continuing down the muddy road on the path Brie had memorized while staring at the map. The road had drained somewhat after the storm abated, and only an inch or so of muck covered the slick surface. In addition to the cane, Bastian had also made sandals for her using the insoles from his boots, broadleaves, and paracord. The makeshift sandals worked well enough to protect her feet from sharp pebbles and other debris buried in the muck.

"We need to talk about the market," Bastian said. "It's important we go over it so you remember the details. The longer we wait, the more muddled your memory will become."

She knew he was right, and saying it aloud would help set the memories. But damn, she didn't *want* to talk about it. Didn't *want* to remember. But who knew what was important, what piece of information would help the CIA figure out who ran the market?

"How long were you inside the market before I showed up?" he asked.

"Two hours? Maybe three?" The time was hard to judge, because every minute had felt like a lifetime.

"We should probably go back to the beginning—like who grabbed you, for starters."

She told him about the Nuer man who'd initially found and abducted her and sold her to the market. She went on to describe the men who examined her in the tent and told him about the one who worked for Druneft, who had worked for Prime Energy years ago.

"Did he recognize you?"

"I don't think so. But maybe. I was a little shaken up in general. My impressions could be off." She frowned. "But he's not the only person in the market I recognized. One of the guards—the guy who fell on me after you slit his throat—his face was familiar. I think he was a toady for a former South Sudanese general named Lawiri. General Lawiri showed up at our facility about two months ago, full of bluster, trying to claim the food supplies to feed his army."

"Whose side is he on, the president's or the vice president's?" Bastian asked, naming the two major factions in the civil war.

"That's the thing. Neither. He's trying to raise his own army. I heard his band was beaten back by rebel fighters and he fled the country."

"Where did he go?"

"No idea. But I'm almost certain the guard whose throat you slit was one of Lawiri's bodyguards."

Chapter Eleven

Savannah James paced the main room of the temporary building that housed SOCOM headquarters at Camp Citron. The mission had gone to shit the moment Bastian got Brie out of the market. Now they'd lost Bastian and the oil tycoon's daughter, and it looked like an entire A-Team had gone rogue and opted to save the children in the market. At least, she assumed that was why they'd missed their rendezvous and they'd been cryptic about the reason.

She couldn't blame the men for showing their humanity, but it seriously messed up the State Department's publicly stated position that they would not get involved in South Sudan's civil war. If it turned out government or rebel forces controlled that swath of land, then the US had just taken sides in the conflict.

Savvy's ass was the one on the line if the intel she'd been gathering was bad. She didn't give a fuck about her ass over the safety of children, but she'd been hoping to get assets in place in the market to determine the leadership structure and take covert action to destroy the people who were behind the operation, ending the practice for good. As it was, the market would probably spring up again elsewhere and more children would face the auction block.

It was a choice between saving fifty children or

thousands. Now, if this market had been destroyed, they might never know who was behind it.

Special Forces Operational Detachment Bravo, better known as the B-Team, was the headquarters element of the Operational Detachment Alpha—A-Team—currently deployed in South Sudan. Savvy watched as the B-Team worked frantically to coordinate with the A-Team to establish a new exfiltration point. But the team was scattered and claimed to be hampered by yesterday's storm.

Ripley had reported that weapons being auctioned in the arms hut had exploded, and in the ensuing chaos, the children had made a break for freedom. No one on the B-Team believed any weapons had miraculously exploded without aid from someone on the A-Team. Savvy's money was on Espinosa. He was the demolitions guy. But Cal was a weapons sergeant.

The team's silence in the aftermath had lasted several hours, likely because they couldn't be expected to follow orders they never received. But where the hell was Chief Ford? Savvy knew he wouldn't risk the primary objective of rescuing Brie Stewart. Aside from being a hundred percent team player, Bastian was wound tight when it came to the oil heiress.

Savvy had observed the two of them in Barely North, and she'd followed him outside the club and witnessed him kissing the woman in the dark. Two days ago, Savvy had watched his face as the identities of the USAID workers were revealed. For one instant, she'd seen stark fear in the Green Beret's eyes.

Bastian Ford might not have a clue how he felt about Brie Stewart, but Savvy was damn certain it wasn't anything approaching hate.

She had no doubt he'd give his all to rescue Brie, and had told his captain as much before they deployed. The man had given her the same disgusted, slightly appalled look she often received when she meddled in military affairs, but she'd been right on the money. Captain Durant had even admitted that Bastian had requested to lead the search mission.

She was damn good at reading people, and SOCOM loved the intel she provided, but hated it when she applied her insight to their soldiers and SEALs.

Tough shit.

She was here to do her job, no matter how uncomfortable it made the big boys with fancy and explosive toys.

Now she stared at one of those toys—a large screen filled with the satellite image map of the market and surrounding area. She willed it to reveal Bastian and Brie's location, but try as she might, sheer will had never produced intel on the spot like that.

They'd lost hours of surveillance yesterday in the rain, and today the landscape was different after the network of roads surrounding the market had flooded.

Where had Bastian and Brie gone? Were they on foot, or had they made it out of the marshland in time?

How long had Brie been in the market? What had she witnessed in the time she was there? If what Savvy suspected was true, Brie may have recognized people. Either locals she'd interacted with in her work for USAID, or the long-shot hope that she'd seen someone affiliated with Kemet Oil or Prime Energy.

But if Brie had recognized anyone, certain players would be all the more anxious to take her out before she could return to Camp Citron and share what she knew.

Savannah's cell phone rang, and she glanced at the ID. *What the hell?*

Why was the A-Team satellite phone calling her number?

She glanced around the room. Given SOCOM's general distrust of her and her methods, this call wasn't a mistake. The A-Team wanted to talk to her, and they didn't want their B-Team to know.

She stepped out of SOCOM headquarters and into the heat of the Djibouti morning to answer the call. "Why the hell are you calling me and not SOCOM?" she said without preamble.

Sergeant Cassius Callahan's deep, rich voice triggered a reaction she neither wanted nor would admit to. "We need your help, Savvy."

A slight jolt spread through her at hearing him use the nickname she'd been given by Morgan Adler a month ago. Pax and Bastian had started using the nickname, but this was Cal's first time calling her Savvy. It made no sense that Cal was under her skin. She didn't understand it. He disliked her as much as the rest of SOCOM. The only man who was friendly to her was Pax, and that was because of her role in aiding the search for Morgan last month.

The very fact that she felt any sort of reaction to Cal's voice was not good. She prided herself on maintaining a cold distance. Given her job, she didn't have friends. Sure, she created a false sense of security to get people to talk to her, but she kept her heart locked down tight so she didn't have to feel bad if—*when*—people got hurt.

People like Brie, who seemed nice enough but who was doing a risky job in a risky place and who had agreed to feed Savvy intel, making her job that much riskier.

"What's going on, Cal?"

"We managed to get most of the kids to the river, where they were lucky and found some boats they could take to islands in the swampland. But we've also got an orphaned girl and boy, both around fourteen. You need to find a way to get them out. Fast. They're starving and won't survive the swamp."

"The CIA isn't in the business of humanitarian aid." God, she sounded like the coldhearted bitch everyone believed her to be. But what he asked was impossible.

"They have intel you'll want to hear. They weren't up for auction; they're market slaves. They *worked* there—and have been there for months. They speak English, Arabic, and a few of the local languages."

Excitement trilled through her. "That changes things."

"Yeah. We figured."

His judgmental tone cut to the core. "I caught hell with my superiors and the American embassy because of the girls you saved from Desta last month. And not only did I not complain, I managed to find every one of those girls' families and came up with the budget to send them home. It's easy to make a decision to save someone in the moment when you don't have to deal with the fallout, Sergeant. Without my help, those girls would have been dumped back in Somalia to be preyed upon again."

Cal cleared his throat. "That's why we took most of the kids to the river. There were nearly fifty. The youngest couldn't have been more than eight."

Her eyes teared. She was glad she was outside and facing the building, where no one could see her reaction.

Not that anyone would believe her tears even if they saw them with their own eyes. No one believed she had a heart. Hell, everyone but Pax and Morgan would probably assume she'd taken the call in the midst of chopping onions.

She kept her reaction out of her voice. "You're sure the kids can provide actionable intel? You aren't lying to force my hand?"

"Of the two of us, Savvy"—he said the name with an emphasis that bordered on sarcastic—"I'm the one who never lies."

It's my job to lie. She wanted to say the words aloud but didn't. If he couldn't see it, it was his problem. Hell, half the time, she figured he didn't believe they were on the same side.

"Can you help us and get these kids out of here?" he asked.

"I'll see what I can do. Send me photos, names, tribe and clan affiliation. I'll also need dates—as near as they can guess—estimating how long they've been in the market." She could probably get them priority clearance so they could fly to Camp Citron with the team. "But Cal, we need Brie Stewart. Where are Brie and Bastian?"

"We don't know. They got out of the market. That's all I'm certain of."

"Could they be dead?" She had to ask the question.

"*Hell no.*" Cal grunted with annoyance. "Bastian's a damn tough soldier. There's a reason he's second-in-command. He won't fail."

"Then why the hell hasn't he checked in?"

"Fuck if I know. Something must've happened to his radio. But don't worry. We'll find him."

"Where would he go? Where would he take her?"

"Brie'll know how to find allies in the smaller villages. They'll aim for one of those and probably try to hitch a ride to Juba."

"We'll focus the satellites on the smaller villages and look for activity." They'd already been doing that, but still it was nice to have the theory confirmed.

"What about the kids?" Cal pressed.

"I need to make some calls. Send me the info, and I'll get back to you."

———

The sun burned through the clouds and turned the water from yesterday's rain into vapor, making the air thick and unbearably humid. In the heat, rain would be a welcome relief, no matter what it did to the roads. In spite of the cane, Brie's limp became more pronounced as she walked, but there was no helping it. She had to walk, and it had to hurt.

It was noon by the time they reached the outskirts of a small village Brie was familiar with. The population had averaged about fifty people, but if word had filtered south about the food stores being burned, it might have been abandoned. Locals, especially along this corridor, had counted on being able to receive food from USAID during the rainy season.

"I need to do reconnaissance to make sure the village is safe," Bastian said. "I don't like leaving you alone, but with your ankle—"

"I'll find a place to burrow in and hide." It was the only solution.

The village abutted a thick forest of trees that flourished in the flooded grassland. It wasn't hard to find a spot for her to tuck herself into viney roots and hide. It reminded her of yesterday when Bastian had gone off to shoot the men who'd tracked them through the woods. In spite of the completely groundless optimism she'd felt since waking that morning, she began to shake. She pulled her knees to her chest in her small well in the muck and met Bastian's gaze.

What if this was the last time she'd look into his eyes? What if something happened to him as he was trying to protect her? South Sudan was the kind of place where people were randomly shot simply for being in the wrong place.

Anything could happen, at any time. But having Bastian by her side had been a comfort, a relief. One she didn't want to give up. Ever.

"I'm coming back for you, Brie."

He said it with such conviction, she believed him. She had to believe him.

If she didn't, she'd slide into a panic attack, and frankly, it was a little late for that.

Chapter Twelve

The village had far fewer than the fifty occupants Brie had told him to expect. Bastian counted a dozen at best. The good news was, none appeared to be armed or dangerous. These weren't rebels or government forces. Boko Haram hadn't set up shop.

At least eight of the inhabitants were women and children. But unfortunately there wasn't a vehicle to be seen. If the people who lived here had taken off for one of the UN camps, they'd taken their vehicles with them. Perhaps someone was ferrying groups to the camp, and they would return, but Bastian couldn't count on that. This would be a rest stop to allow Brie's ankle time to heal, and nothing more.

He fetched her from her hiding place. She knew these people and could get information they wouldn't offer to a stranger. Best to enter the village with her by his side.

Together they approached a man who sat in the shade of a strung-up tarp. The village was littered with debris—broken vehicles, rotting timber from a construction project that never happened, rusted-out wheelbarrows, and brittle plastic of all kinds that hadn't withstood the test of sun and time.

It reminded him of poorer neighborhoods—on and off the reservation—back home. But really, the place mirrored the villages in Djibouti, with the exception of water. Here, water was in abundance, saturating the earth. Lush green plants sprung from the grassland. Animals flourished.

But thanks to civil war, humans did not.

The current famine, Bastian knew, was a man-made disaster. South Sudan had abundant fertile land. They also had oil. And, for those who lived close to the rivers, water. But decades of conflict had taken a toll. In 2011, the country separated from Sudan and became the world's youngest democracy. Peace lasted only two years before civil war broke out, and now, farmland remained fallow and citizens starved.

The man sitting in the shade by his garbage heap was emaciated and missing teeth. He bore scars along his face, neck, and arms—raised bumps he'd probably received when he was a boy. Marks of his tribe.

That too, reminded Bastian of home. Not the scars, but the concept. His tribe didn't have markings, but others did. When Bastian was young, he'd wanted to mark himself to show pride in his heritage. He'd had the long hair and the badass attitude. The military had cut one and taught him how to channel the other.

Giving up his hair had been…devastating in a way he hadn't expected. It was assimilation, but one he'd signed up for. His own doing. In response, he'd gotten a tattoo at the first opportunity. His hair belied his tribal connection, but his skin would wear the mark forever. The salmon motif tattoo identified his town—Coho—his tribe, and his culture.

He had that in common with this man, except his tattoo was hidden, while this man wore his tribal scars on his face.

Bastian couldn't begin to guess his age. Life was hard

in East Africa and aged men and women quickly. Famine took a particular toll. Were he to guess, he'd put the man in his fifties based on looks alone, but life expectancy here didn't go much beyond that. It was more likely he was in his thirties.

Brie knelt before the man and clasped his hands. "Kamal, where is everyone?" she asked.

Kamal smiled at her touch, but then his lips turned downward. "They have gone. Some went to the camps. Others went to Juba. They will not be back."

Brie squeezed his hands. "You heard what happened to our facility."

He nodded. "The food burned. The president burned our food."

His quickness to lay blame caught Bastian's attention. "What makes you say that?" he asked.

Kamal cocked his head and squinted up at Bastian, who had the sun at his back. "Only the president would be so cruel to burn our food. To keep us starving. So we must abandon the fight. If we starve, we cannot fight government forces."

This was entirely possible. Famine was a weapon of this war. But it was only speculation and could just as easily have been the rebel forces. Or another heretofore unannounced player.

"Is everyone going to leave?" Brie asked.

Kamal shook his head. "Abdo is too weak to make the journey. He and his mother stayed. Others didn't want to leave. Another airdrop comes in two days. Four have gone to the drop location to line up for the food. That's four bags of grain to share."

"How long does it take to get to the drop site?" Bastian asked.

"A day, at least," Brie said.

Kamal nodded. "Abdo only has to make it three more days."

These people were so close to starvation, surviving three days was questionable. Brie met Bastian's gaze. Her eyes beseeched him. He gave a sharp nod and pulled two MREs from his pack. "This is all we can spare."

B rie swiped away a tear and took the MREs from Bastian, whispering thanks as she stood. She crossed open space—in another world, it would be called Main Street, but here there was no such thing—between two rows of thatched-roof huts. She knelt before Abdo and his mother, June. She handed June the MREs. "These are for you and Abdo. Eat them slowly." This food would be a shock to the system, not what their bodies were used to digesting. Eating slowly was their only defense.

June nodded and held her son, who lay listlessly against her side. She stroked the five-year-old boy's cheek. Shooing away flies as she did so. "Thank you."

Abdo was heartbreakingly skinny. His bones looked like sticks covered with dark skin. It was hard to imagine his legs wouldn't snap if he tried to walk. The last time Brie had seen him, a month ago, he'd been dangerously thin, but this was end-stage starvation.

June's gaze flicked down Brie's battered, muddy, and bloody makeshift sarong, finally landing on the sandals that barely covered her feet. "You need clothes?" Her lip curled. "Soap?"

Brie nodded. It would be foolish to say no when clothing was one thing June could offer. They might have items to spare, and she needed shoes for the long walk to Juba. "I would be grateful for shoes, sandals, anything."

The woman nodded, signaling with her head to the inside of the hut behind her without disturbing her weakened son. "Inside. You will find my sister's clothes. She died months ago. Help yourself." And then June smiled, showing crooked, gapped teeth. Her smile was beautiful and something Brie had witnessed only once before. "And take soap too. You stink."

Brie laughed and stepped into the hut, where there was a woven container in which she found several cloths long enough to wear as a traditional tobe. Even though the cloth was old and worn, the colors remained bright. Beautiful. The next item she spotted were sandals that were made from strips of rubber cut from a tire's inner tube attached to the thick tread of the tire. They were perfect protection against thorns and other sharp items that covered this country, and she could cut the straps and tread to fit her feet if necessary.

But the most precious item had to be the homemade bar of soap. With the rainstorm, sparing water for bathing was not an issue. She'd noted several containers and barrels had collected gallons of water. More storms would hit in the coming days, meaning she could be luxurious in her bathing.

She gathered the bounty and asked Bastian for money to pay June for the items. He gave June four thousand South Sudanese pounds—about thirty US dollars. Then Bastian and Brie sat in the shade and split a single protein bar to discuss their next move.

"I'm worried being here will endanger these people," Brie said. "They don't have a car or radio. I think we should move on."

"You need to rest your ankle."

She shrugged. "I can walk a little farther if it means everyone is safer. I've been thinking…if we go deeper into the bush, there's another village. One that was abandoned not long after the civil war started. It was one of the places we'd hoped to repopulate, but it's fallow now. There are a handful of huts. The well is dry, but with the rain, there's probably a catchment system for water like they have here." She pointed to the barrels and other random debris that had been set out to gather the rain.

"Won't they be breeding ground for mosquitos?"

"I take antimalarials. Don't you?"

He nodded. "But you're behind."

"I've only missed two days. Do you have some in your pack?"

He nodded again and pulled out a vial with the tablets.

"Great. Then I'm only one day behind." She glanced up at the sky. "When we get there, we can dump the standing water if we see mosquito larvae. It'll rain again tonight. We can catch freshwater and use purification tablets for drinking."

"How far is it?"

"Three, maybe five miles? I've only been there once, months ago, when we were trying to decide if it was worth doing repair work. We opted to wait until next year, given that this village still had room for more people."

"It's possible that rebel or government forces have moved in."

"I don't think so. They'd have to pass through here by car. It's not on any other road. And everyone here would've fled if one side or the other was moving into the area."

"But they could walk there and bypass this village."

"True."

Bastian pursed his lips as he considered her proposal. Finally, he nodded. "It's probably the safest way to give you time to rest your foot. But damn, I was hoping we'd find a radio here."

"Fourth-world problem. Spend much time in South Sudan, and you get used to the lack of phones and radios."

"It really doesn't bother you, being out of touch?"

She shrugged. "I miss watching kitten videos on YouTube, but to be honest, life here sucks bad enough— taking a break from world news has been a relief."

"The news might be bad, but it can't be worse than this." He glanced around the impoverished village. "I grew up on an Indian reservation. I'll take rez poor over South Sudan poor ten days a week."

Brie's gaze fell on June as she coaxed her son to eat small, slow bites of food. "Me too," she said softly.

T he abandoned village was the perfect refuge. Bastian surveyed the cluster of huts. Tucked away and remote, it was easy to see why it had been deserted in the first place, but for their purposes, it was exactly what they needed. Shelter. Water. A safe place for Brie to mend.

She'd barely made it the last half mile, and he'd cursed her out once she'd settled down in the shade of a hut so he could take a look at her ankle. It was swollen, and the cut on her foot looked infected. "You should have told me. I could have carried you."

"It was faster to just walk."

Shit. There was no way she'd be better tomorrow for them to set out for Juba. They were going to be here for a few days at least.

He washed her wound and slathered it with antibiotic ointment, gave her an ice pack for her ankle, and then made her take an antibiotic pill to knock out the infection.

He then set about checking the various containers for drinkable freshwater, and managed to find a few gallons that were usable with purification tablets.

He dumped a few of the algae-covered galvanized bins and scrubbed them down, then rigged a tarp on an old frame to catch rainwater and pour down into the clean bin. The clouds were back, and, as Brie had predicted earlier, rain would begin to fall soon.

Medical and water needs attended to, Bastian set about inspecting the huts to find one that could shelter them from the coming storm.

There were eight to choose from, two of which were in decent shape but for a few gaps in the roof. He gathered thatched bundles from the structures in the worst shape and used them to patch the roof of the best one.

He ordered Brie to rest while he worked, but she insisted on going through the garbage that littered the village, to see what could be salvaged. When it was clear she wouldn't sit still, he asked her to find something to dig with and to gather every tarp and piece of plastic she could find from the abandoned huts. With the rain, plastic sheeting would be a precious commodity, and he wanted to dig out an easy hiding place for her in their one good hut.

The day was muggy, so he stripped off his shirt before he climbed a rickety ladder to make the roof repairs. Thank goodness the poles that framed the structure were sturdy and could support his weight. He paused in his labor to drink from his hydration pack, and caught Brie staring at him while he did so.

Her gaze was blatantly carnal as she paused in her tarp gathering to study his chest.

He couldn't help himself and sat back in his perch on the roof, knowing it would give her a better view.

She grinned. "What's the tat?"

He glanced down at the fish that swam across his right pec. "Salmon motif."

"Coast Salish?"

"Yes."

She smiled and said, "Nice," but her gaze wasn't on the tattoo when she said it.

That was all it took for his prick to wake up. He returned to his job of replacing bundles of thatching, trying not to imagine how it would feel to have her hands explore his body with the same heat her eyes had.

They would be here for days, as stranded as if they were on a deserted island. Hell, they even had the grass huts and tropical heat. It wasn't a good idea to let carnal fantasies take over.

They weren't playing house—no matter how domestic this moment felt. They were hiding from slavers and militants and possibly terrorists. His job was to protect her until she could walk again. That meant sleeping only when she kept watch, and being vigilant every other hour of the day.

Sex couldn't happen. Besides, it would be completely inappropriate. She was vulnerable.

She was also Princess Prime.

Although the last bit felt more and more like an excuse that didn't hold water anymore. She'd come a long way since her Princess Prime days, and he was a dick for not letting it go.

The truth was, keeping his hands off Brie these next few days was going to be a challenge to his willpower. Especially if she kept looking at him like that.

Chapter Thirteen

The rain came down in waves, and Brie was thankful for the repairs Bastian had made on the hut. At some point in the past, the roof interior had been lined with plastic sheeting. Bastian had used duct tape to repair gaps, and between the added thatching and mended sheet, the roof did a decent job of keeping the rain out.

Brie had insisted Bastian take the first sleep shift. He'd slept a scant four hours the previous night and needed it more than she did at this point. Plus, it was hard to imagine anyone would be out in this storm if they could avoid it. Given that no one knew where they were, this was as safe as they could possibly be.

As day slipped into night, she leaned against one of the thick wall posts, clutching his M4 rifle, which he'd showed her how to use, on guard duty for six hours while he slept.

She'd offered to guard for eight. They'd settled on six. Staying awake wasn't a problem for her, given the pain in her foot. She'd skipped the ibuprofen for just that reason. She'd take it at the start of her sleep shift.

She watched the rise and fall of his chest, glad he'd left his shirt off and she could get a closer look at his tattoo. It was the traditional red, black, and blue of Coast Salish art. A beautiful design on a beautiful body.

Watching him, she was grateful she hadn't met him ten

years ago. Back then, she'd have wanted to use him as she did Micah. Slipping him information that could be used against PE to kill the project.

Micah had never known the information he so conveniently found in her condo had been left where he'd be certain to find it, that she was feeding him the information because she wanted the oil pipeline to fail. Instead, he believed he'd seduced her and she was too much of a twit to guess he was committing corporate espionage. When, in fact, she was the seducer and spy.

In the end, she'd let him believe his version, and she'd played the part of the deceived woman. She'd cried real tears in their last fight, not because she felt duped, but because she'd grown to care for him, and it was over. It had to be over.

Had she met Bastian back then, she might have pulled the same stunt. Lord knows she'd have wanted to screw him. The guy could be a model, with his dark, hooded eyes and piercing looks. Even his beard was hot, and she'd never been a fan of beards.

She wanted to trace the lines of his tattoo with her tongue. To go from ink lines to the grooves that defined his muscles. She wanted to follow those grooves south with fingers, lips, and tongue.

He'd saved her. First in the market, then when they were pursued, and finally from the mud. She'd been attracted to him a month ago—before he'd been the least bit personally heroic—and now that attraction had magnified to epic proportions.

With the heavy rain, tomorrow they'd have enough water collected in the bins for washing, and she'd break out the precious bar of soap. For now, she fantasized about lathering his skin. Washing the sweat and dirt from his hard body.

She released a quiet breath. She had no doubt Bastian found her attractive, but there was no way he would ever see her as anything other than the embodiment of everything he hated. He might screw her, but he'd never respect her. And while she was a fan of the string-free lay, respect was a key component. She wouldn't share her body with a man who didn't respect her.

She might be the embodiment of corruption and greed, but to her, he was the embodiment of heroism and redemption. The very things she craved for herself.

Her mental take was obvious: if she could win the respect of this one man, she would prove to herself she'd changed. That she didn't have a black soul. That she wasn't the horrible thing she'd been raised to be. It was a ridiculous test to hinge her self-worth on. He was practically a stranger, and he had every reason to think she was a fraud.

But she couldn't help it. She wanted to win him over. She felt it like a craving. A compulsion. As a recovering addict, she knew about resisting cravings. She could resist this need.

Given their current situation, resistance was the only option.

B reakfast on their second morning together consisted of a handful of trail mix for each of them and as much water flavored with iodine they could drink. In the years she'd worked for USAID, Brie had gotten used to the taste of the purification tablets. She'd also adjusted to smaller meals. USAID provided enough for them, but she hadn't consumed more calories than needed.

Exceptions were made for birthdays and holidays, but otherwise, she and her coworkers had been careful, self-rationing to make their own supplies last.

Of course, even that food was gone now. Lost in the fire. Raising the question of whether or not it was aid workers in general who'd been targeted. Ezra, Alan, and Jaali couldn't work without food any more than the locals could survive without it.

This breakfast shared with Bastian was only slightly smaller than she was used to, and she'd be fine for several days on the low rations. Bastian was probably prepared for this sort of thing through training—like the way he could fall asleep at the drop of a dime—but given his muscular build, he needed far more calories than she did. She tried to get him to take more of her portion.

He was stubborn and refused.

The first half of the day was spent inside, avoiding the rain. Bastian taught her Arabic curse words, and she taught him a few words in the various local dialects she'd managed to pick up. He told her stories about the Army and she told him about her months in South Sudan.

They played the drinking game "quarters" using a South Sudan pound and an old cup. They didn't have beer for the penalty, which was fine because Brie didn't drink, so instead, whenever one of them managed to drop the coin into the cup, the other had to answer a question.

Fortunately, the coin didn't bounce well on the dirt floor, and there were more misses than hits until they both found their groove.

"Who did you lose your virginity to?" Brie asked after making her shot.

"My first girlfriend. Cece."

"How old were you?"

Bastian shook his head. "You don't get follow-up questions without sinking the coin." He took a shot and made it. "Who did you lose your virginity to?"

"Alejandro, the gardener's son."

"Isn't that a little cliché?"

She raised a brow. "No follow-up questions without sinking a coin."

He laughed. "Touché."

She sank another one. "How old were you?"

"Nineteen. I was a sophomore in college."

She cocked her head, surprised he hadn't been younger. But she refrained from asking. She had to earn it.

His next shot landed flat on the rim, wobbled, then dropped into the cup. "Yes!" He curled his fist and pumped his arm in the international teenage boy symbol for victory. "Why Alejandro, the Mexican gardener's son?"

She laughed. "Who said he was Mexican?"

"Gee, I don't know how I figured that out, Ms. Cliché."

"For your information, he was Costa Rican. And oh, so very perfect."

"I think I hate this dude."

"But not as perfect as you."

"That's more like it. But you still haven't answered my question."

"I was eighteen and"—she held up her fingers in air quotes—"'dating' the son of one of my dad's business associates who was ten years older than me. And by"—more air quotes—"'associate' I mean the dad was a Russian oligarch, and the son an oligarch-in-training. I was expected to make the young asshole son happy so our families would be joined in unholy kleptocracy."

"At eighteen, you were expected to marry the guy?"

"Not marriage, not yet. It was clear blowjobs were expected, though, to keep him on the hook. His family had a home near ours in Palm Beach and another next door to ours in Morocco. I was friends with his little sister when I was thirteen. Then when I was eighteen, things changed, and it was assumed I was cool with the arrangement.

"We were at the Palm Beach house one evening, and my dad and brothers were out for the night. I realized this was supposed to be *the night*, the one where I blew him or screwed him to seal the deal. But he was the kind of guy who tortures small animals—his little sister told me stuff when we were girls that freaked me out. There was no way I would ever put my mouth on his dick.

"I still had stupid romantic notions back then and believed sex could mean something. But at the very least, I wanted to *like* the first guy I let in my pants. I knew he might get violent, so I faked food poisoning. When he was in the bathroom, I stuck my fingers down my throat and vomited all over the bed. He was so grossed out, he couldn't get out of the house fast enough. As soon as he left, I crossed the yard to the gardener's apartment and jumped Alejandro, who'd been my friend for a while."

Bastian just stared at her, openmouthed, so she picked up the coin and dropped it in the cup. She didn't even bounce it in the dirt first, but he didn't seem to notice. "So, did you love her, when you had sex with your first girlfriend?"

Bastian's jaw snapped shut. "You cheated. There was no bounce."

She flashed an innocent smile and batted her eyes.

He laughed. "Does that always work for you?"

"Usually."

He plucked the coin from the cup. "Yes. I was in love. It took a long time for me to fall out of love with her, but once I did, love turned to resentment. Damn, your eyes are effective. If it wasn't for your unfortunate nose, you'd probably have my social security number already."

She licked her lips. "Your social security number isn't what I'm after."

Bastian's eyes flared with heat, and he shifted on the floor in a way that made her suspect his pants were binding at the crotch. "It's one thing to play a silly game to pass the time in a rainstorm, but sex would distract us both, and we can't afford that."

"I know. Plus you smell like moldy swamp."

He laughed. "*Moldy?* I'll have you know I only swim in the freshest of swamps."

She plucked at her sarong. She still wore the dirty one, because she hadn't wanted to don the clean cloth she'd gotten yesterday until after she'd washed. One of life's small pleasures. She glanced at the roof. "We should have more than enough water to bathe and drink now." He'd replaced the full galvanized bin with an empty one under the water-collecting tarp several times in the last hours. They had enough water to see them through days if needed.

"I'll set up one of the huts for you to bathe in once the storm lifts."

Her whole body lit at the prospect of being able to get clean again, and she smiled and resisted the urge to kiss his bearded cheek in thanks.

The rain was a double-edged sword. It erased their tracks—unless someone had followed them closely yesterday, there was no way they'd be found here now—and provided them with water to drink and bathe. But it also trapped them—inside, off the roads. Even walking to Juba would be impossible. Not that she could walk two hundred miles on her ankle anyway.

Fourth-world problems.

"The food drop is tomorrow. The plane might fly over us on the way to the drop site in the north. The pilot might see us if we're outside."

Bastian's gaze snapped to hers, all flirtation gone. "Who handles the food drop?"

"The UN provides the food, plane, and pilots. They have an agreement with the government so the plane isn't shot down, but the president has blocked other food aid, so it's not without risk. I wouldn't be surprised if government forces grilled the pilots after the run, demanding updates on the condition of rebel forces. Not that they'd reveal anything, but still, if they saw us, something could slip."

Bastian's gaze unfocused, telling her he was lost in thought. Then he leaned forward, wrapped a hand around her neck, and pulled her face to his. Right before his lips met hers, he said, "I know how we're going to phone home, without forcing you to walk on that ankle." Then he kissed her, hard and fast.

She closed her eyes as the kiss went on a beat longer than she suspected he intended, but not long enough. He released her and said, "Thank you," then relaxed back against the support post.

"For what? How are we going to make like ET?"

"That's just it. We're going to skip the radio and talk to the stars—or rather, satellites."

"And?" she asked, knowing he was drawing out his

answer on purpose, making her want to both jump him and strangle him.

"Crop circles. SOCOM must have satellites searching for us. I'm going to write a note big enough for the satellites to see, but we'll have to wait until after the food drop."

Chapter Fourteen

In the late afternoon after the rain had slowed to a drizzle, Bastian carried the galvanized bin into one of the roofless huts. It would make a decent bathing chamber. He couldn't forget how Brie's eyes had lit up when he told her he'd set up a place for her to bathe.

He was such a fucking sucker for her eyes.

He didn't have to wonder why she'd been successful as a model in her early teens. She could sell him a surfboard in the desert just by fluttering those long, dark lashes.

But it wasn't just her eyes. It was also her far from unfortunate nose.

And her ass.

He shook his head, thinking of the quarters game. He hadn't played a drinking game since he was twenty. And it had never been that fun. Or revealing.

Bin placed, he set out to find a stool for her to sit on, so she could wash without putting weight on her ankle. Helping her bathe was out of the question. Not if he wanted to stay sane. And celibate.

He found a light cloth in one of the huts and shook it out. It smelled musty, but it was intact. He could hang it over the door to give her privacy as she bathed. Another celibacy aid.

In the same hut, he found a folding chair that needed only a few screws to fix, which he salvaged from an old truck that was returning to nature. Repairs complete, he placed the chair in the bathing hut next to the bin full of water, then hung up the curtain.

He returned to their shared hut and scooped her from her seat on a tarp. She squealed in surprise, but then draped her arms around his neck. "What are you doing? I can walk."

He knew she could. But this was more fun. "No point in risking slipping in the mud." He was pathetic in his excuses but didn't care if she saw right through him.

He set her on the chair in the middle of the hut. "I'll be back with the soap."

"And the tobe cloth for me to change into."

He bowed. "And clean clothes. Anything else?"

"A loofah? And bath salts. Ohh...and conditioner. I would sell my left kidney for hair conditioner."

"Sorry. No loofahs, salts, or conditioner. But I might have some gauze you could use as a washcloth. And it'll only cost half a kidney."

"A bargain at any price." She ran her fingers over her short hair. "Good thing I went for the buzz cut. But I still miss conditioner."

"When you get back to the US, you can have a Costco-sized bottle. On me."

She pressed her hand over her heart. "You do know how to woo a girl."

He tweaked her nose. "Damn straight."

Minutes later, he was planted outside the hut, her vigilant guard, as she set to work scrubbing the dried swamp from her skin. Bathing was important. She could have more cuts hidden under the muck that needed to be cleaned. He'd forgotten about the stripe she'd received from the whip. He really should have considered that yesterday and insisted she bathe then in spite of the rain.

With the missing roof, sunlight poured into the hut at an angle. What he hadn't counted on was that the light would shine through the curtained doorway, offering up a titillating silhouette.

Holy fuck.

Brie stood on one leg, with her bad one kneeling on the chair. She used the jar he'd provided to pour water over her head and down her body.

In profile, he saw a silhouette of pert nipples jutting from small, high breasts, a flat belly, and a perfect round ass. She let out a soft sound of pleasure as she worked the soap into her short hair.

Bastian cleared his throat to stop his own groan.

Brie froze. She made no sound, not even water dripped. Hell, he could swear the birds stopped chirping.

How low could he be? He was being a voyeur—even if it was unintentional—and she knew it.

She began massaging her scalp again. "You can see me," she said. Her hands left her hair and slid down, over her breasts, which she then rubbed, as if soaping with enthusiasm.

"Yes," he said. No point denying it. "I didn't mean to." He turned his back to the hut. "I'm not looking now."

"You can look, but it's only fair that I get to watch you bathe next."

He kept his gaze averted. "Sweetheart, I'm Special Forces. I can go weeks without bathing."

She snorted. "Not if you want to share a hut with me."

"Given our situation, it would be smart to have me smell like a swamp thing."

"Screw smart. I refuse to share a hut with a guy who

smells like Sasquatch." He heard dripping water and the soft lap of cloth on skin. "I want you to watch, Bastian."

He didn't turn. He didn't need to. His imagination was vivid enough. In his mind, he saw water flowing in rivulets down her back and the cleft of her ass. She'd been so coated in dirt from their swim in the bog, water would leave trails through the silt, running down her breasts, across her belly, and around her hip to that rounded ass.

Fantasies from ten years ago had nothing on the image conjured now. He had to marvel at the situation. He was in the middle of a rescue op, stranded in South Sudan, and he had a massive fucking boner.

~⌒~

B rie didn't know if Bastian was watching or not, but the thought he might be turned her on. The mud had caked when it dried, and it was no act that she had to take her time lathering and scrubbing her skin. Knowing Bastian might be taking voyeuristic pleasure made the act of washing sensual. She slid her hands between her thighs and very thoroughly washed her clit. She gave a soft moan.

If he hadn't been watching, had he turned now?

She stroked and cleaned. Her body coiled tight with the building pleasure. She wished she could see him, but the sun entered the hut from above and behind her, making the sheet opaque from her perspective.

The moment was strangely intimate. Separated by a flimsy sheet, he was invisible to her, and she didn't know if he watched, yet she had no doubt he was as aroused as she was.

She scooped water from the bin with the jar and

poured it over her head. The lukewarm water cascaded down her body and splashed into the tub. The water caused her nipples to tighten, and she pinched them, calling them into peaks he would see in her silhouette if he watched. She imagined his mouth at her breast, sucking as his hands cupped her ass. He would pull her against him as he sucked her nipple, so she could press against his erection. She groaned.

From the other side of the sheet, Bastian let out a guttural sound. That answered the watching question. He grunted and said, "Fuck me."

She let out a throaty laugh. "Is that an offer?"

"Hell no. It's a description of my situation. I am so totally fucked."

"How so?"

"You're a beautiful woman, Brie, but right now, you are my mission. That's all. For your safety and mine, I can't let my guard down. I can't even sleep unless you're on guard duty. Sex is not an option. Not here."

She smiled. "See now, I told you if we kissed, you'd want to have sex with me. I'm a great kisser."

Bastian barked out a sharp laugh. "You win. I wanted to fuck you then. And I want to fuck you now."

She liked his honesty. He wasn't shy, and she was never coy. When they got out of South Sudan, they could have some serious fun together. But sadly, that was probably days away.

She picked up the soap again and resumed bathing. She wouldn't tease him or herself anymore and washed perfunctorily, getting the job done quickly so as not to prolong the temptation. She owed him that much after all he'd done for her.

Chapter Fifteen

B astian didn't know whether to be relieved or disappointed when Brie's bath turned all business. Relieved. He should definitely be relieved. But that didn't mean that was how he felt.

How the hell could the woman be so damn sexy even now, in this situation?

This was the most bizarre mission he'd ever been dropped in. He was guarding an oil heiress who wasn't an heiress anymore, and they were stranded like castaways in the middle of a brutal civil war.

Special Forces training really didn't cover this.

After she bathed, he scouted the area where he intended to write his note to SOCOM. He needed a big field to present a readable message. He didn't have bright orange signal panels—they'd been in the second pack in the back of the truck—so he had to work with materials at hand, which meant he'd have to come up with his own symbol or words. Something that could be seen by satellite and that would signal who had written it. He debated what would be the most effective, and in the end decided to use the same code that had rescued Morgan a month ago.

It was simple Morse code and would be easy to press into the flooded grasslands: three dots, three dashes, three dots. Better known as S-O-S.

He'd stack the symbols. Dots above dashes above dots. The whole message would be contained in one neat square.

Morse code would be easier to see via satellite than the curve of the letters, and his role in Morgan's rescue would be remembered by SOCOM. They'd know it was him.

He did the math to determine the area required to be visible, how large the dots had to be versus the dashes. Now he just needed to wait for the rain to abate. Satellites couldn't see through the thick cloud cover, and he didn't want to mark the field before the food drop flyover.

It went against his nature, but caution was the rule here. So he was stuck with Brie for a few more days at least, stranded in a remote village. Time stood still, and sex felt more inevitable with every moment, but it wouldn't happen here. Not while he was on duty.

He had honor to maintain, but more than that, he wasn't a dumbass to drop his guard.

He took his turn in the bathing hut, and if Brie watched, that was her own problem, because he was all business. Rinse, soap, scrub, rinse.

He emerged from the hut to find Brie with her back to the doorway, his M4 in her hands like he'd showed her. She took her guard duty seriously, but then, she knew what failing meant. Bastian would be killed, but Brie would be taken and sold again.

"I was thinking of heading out into the grasslands and seeing if I can shoot up some dinner. We're probably going to be here for several days if the rain keeps up."

"You can hunt?"

He nodded. "I'm Special Forces. Living off the land is part of our training. If I get something big, we can set up a smoker in one of the huts."

She nodded. "I can help with that. Locals showed me how to process game."

He smiled. He shouldn't be surprised, but he was. She was so not the princess he once thought she was. He took his M4. "Let's go."

She nodded and followed him, using the cane to help her walk. "What about the noise of the bullet?" she asked. "Someone might hear."

"I've got a suppressor."

They settled in the damp grass and waited in silence. Eventually, a stork took flight, and he dropped it with one shot. Tomorrow, he would set up snares to catch game, but that took more time with less guarantee of success, and he was hungry after days on low rations.

The bird was large with enough meat to last two days. He plucked the feathers while Brie built a fire and spit. They cooked in one of the decaying huts, so the flames wouldn't be seen in the dark.

While the bird roasted, Brie flipped through the playlists on his iPhone, which she'd found when she dug through his pack for matches. "You are such a Seattle boy. Nirvana. Pearl Jam. Soundgarden. Heart. Seriously, *Heart?*"

"Heart is kickass women singing kickass songs. I love Heart. Who doesn't love Heart? I think the problem here is you." He crossed his arms. "They were my first concert."

"How old were you?" she asked.

"Nine." He smiled at the memory. His mom had been a fan and had taken him to Seattle for the show. When he was sixteen, he'd gone to see them again with friends. "'Magic Man' is hot. And their version of 'Stairway to

Heaven' is a fucking religious experience."

She laughed. "I'm more of a 'Barracuda' person myself."

He couldn't help but smile. "I bet you are."

Goddamn, but he wanted her. Here. Now. With the phone playing Heart's greatest hits. Instead, he turned the spit and listened to the sizzle as fat from the skin dropped onto the coals.

She glanced down at his phone. "Nothing you have here fits South Sudan."

"What's the problem? Were you planning a dance party?"

"You, me, and the ibex."

"I'm not sure ibex dance."

"Not to Pearl Jam, anyway. They prefer a different beat. Where is the *Hamilton* soundtrack? Or Adele."

"You can't dance to Adele. But there are some danceable tunes on there." In a flash, he imagined putting on headphones and engaging in a different sort of dance.

Just like that, he had a new bucket list item. He wouldn't feel like he'd lived until he'd had sex with her to music.

A fter they finished their dinner of stork breast and iodine-flavored water, Brie dug out a cracked glass bowl in the garbage that littered the village. She washed it and dropped Bastian's iPhone in it to magnify the sound, then set it in the middle of the open area between the huts. "Let the dance party begin," she said as she queued up a mixed playlist and sat on the chair he'd repaired for her shower.

Even with the bowl, the music wasn't very loud and

was drowned out just a few feet away by the sound of crickets and frogs chirping the night away. South Sudan had its own soundtrack.

"You really want to dance?"

"*I'm* not dancing. You are." She pointed to her leg. "Ankle."

"So basically, you expect me to perform for you."

She rested her chin on her fist in anticipation. "If only I had popcorn."

He laughed and pulled her to her feet. "No way. You can at least sway."

"I'll fall."

"I'll hold you."

The first song was hip hop she was unfamiliar with, and Bastian planted a hand on her hip as he began to move, but as he got into the rhythm, he released her and grinned as he did a solid impersonation of Channing Tatum in *Magic Mike*. It was more performance than dance. A show just for her.

He had moves and rhythm and a sexy-as-hell body. She just wished he'd strip like Tatum did in the movie. His moves were uninhibited and unabashedly erotic in the sultry South Sudan darkness. If she blocked out everything beyond their tiny moonlit village, she could enjoy the buzz in her belly, the attraction that went both ways.

She'd always been a firm believer in chemistry, and she was convinced that she and Bastian would be a combustible combination.

The beat changed, and Bastian returned to her side, slipped a hand around her waist, and pulled her into some dance moves that didn't put stress on her ankle. She laughed and leaned into him, enjoying the humid night, and the firm body that held hers as they danced to "Radioactive" by Imagine Dragons.

The song ended and she started to pull away, but the next song was "Kissing a Fool" by George Michael, and Bastian pulled her tight against him.

Her body rocked with his, and he sang the words into her ear as they danced. His voice was smooth and sexy, just like George.

Jesus, was there anything this guy wasn't good at?

How had she missed the perfection of the song in the thirty-three years she'd lived on this earth? It was big band, jazzy smooth, and utterly mesmerizing on the muggy, starlit night.

She could be wearing an evening gown and four-inch heels and he could be in a tux, instead of her in an old tobe and him in the stained and dirty T-shirt and jeans he'd worn in the market.

It was probably the most romantic moment of her life, dancing with Bastian in the moonlight as George Michael sang to them in haunting, sexy tones.

The notes of the song wound down, and her lips found his, and she wasn't entirely sure which one of them was the fool, but they were definitely kissing, and she never wanted the stroke of his tongue against hers to end.

But eventually, it did, and he lifted his head to stare down at her, his eyes hot with desire, his breathing heavy. She'd made him breathless, and she could feel exactly how aroused he was against her belly.

After a long moment he said, "You'll take the first sleeping shift tonight."

She held his gaze, then nodded. He was right, and there was nothing else to say, really.

Chapter Sixteen

The rain put Bastian's resolve to the test. Day three in the abandoned village, and the deluge didn't let up, giving him no opportunity to create a message in grass already flattened by the storm. If the rain kept up like this, they could be here for weeks. And there was no way he'd last that long without screwing her.

On one level, he could trace the logic to conclude they were utterly safe, and passing the time with wild, intense sex was just plain common sense.

But he had a brain above his shoulders too, and that one reminded him anyone who might've survived the market could also know this abandoned village was the smartest hiding place and find them. And the rain wouldn't put off anyone desperate to find Brie.

Sex would have to wait until after they were rescued. Which meant it would never happen, because once she was safe, he'd never see her again.

But damn, this rain was a problem. The satellites wouldn't see his message. Hell, he couldn't *write* the message as long as the rain was beating down the grass. He really needed those orange signal panels that had been lost with the SUV.

But the rain couldn't stop him from his preparations, and he spent the day taking apart a collapsing hut. He'd use the posts and poles to press down the grass and form the dots and dashes. They'd be darker lines on the green grass and might be visible even if the grass was flat from the rain.

The unrelenting rain soaked him, which was good for his libido. It wasn't cold rain, but being soaked to the bone was never fun.

Brie was stretched out in their dry hut, napping or playing with his phone, he didn't know, because he was determined to avoid her today. Not easy when they were the only two people in the world, and he was guarding her.

He had the hut dismantled and the poles he needed stacked and ready. There was nothing left for him to do but return to their hut and dry off.

He pushed aside the tarp door and stepped inside, coming to a halt when he heard the song. "Kissing a Fool."

Shit. Dancing with her had been a major mistake.

She jolted and scrambled to turn off the music. "Sorry," she said. "It just came up on the playlist. I wasn't—"

He shook his head. "It's okay." But damn, it wasn't. He was hard again. It was rainy and miserable outside, and cozy in here.

This was a recipe for disaster.

"We can't, Brie. It's just not safe."

"I know."

He sighed and set his M4 down and grabbed a water bottle. He took a long slow drink, then sat as far from her as he could get and still be inside the hut. "We need to take a few steps back. We could be here several more days. Probably *will* be here several more days. No more playing quarters. No dancing. No flirting. We just need to work together."

She nodded. "Agreed."

"If there's a break in the rain tomorrow, I'll set up the message. I'll also hunt again, because the snares are empty thanks to the rain. In the meantime, we need to find a way to pass the time that doesn't invite…problems."

"There are some books on your phone. We can read to each other. But the batteries might die."

He shrugged. "I've got chargers that run off batteries. We carry so much electronics, we need to carry universal battery-powered chargers."

He divvied up their meal of leftover stork breast, and she began to read Sherman Alexie's *Reservation Blues*.

It was interesting hearing a Northwest Native American's words delivered in her white cadence, but she didn't do a bad job, reminding him that she'd studied cultural anthropology in Portland. Something that both irritated and impressed him.

Some anthropologists were condescending bastards. But he had to admit, Brie seemed to be one of the good ones. And she'd shown no sign of being a wannabe.

Wannabes were the worst.

After he finished eating, she handed him the phone and he read to her while she dined. Darkness fell, ending yet another day as castaways.

They took turns reading late into the night, finishing the short book and starting in on a suspense by Karen Rose. Finally, Brie's yawns grew pronounced, and he insisted she take the first sleep shift. After she drifted off, he set himself up outside the hut. He sat under a plastic sheet and watched the rain, one hand on his rifle as he kept guard.

Stranded, day four. How was it that the days had already begun to merge together? The drone of an aircraft engine had Bastian diving for cover in the middle of the muddy grasslands and calling out to Brie to do the same. The airdrop must've been delayed due to the rain. All he could do was hope the first row of dots he'd created in the swampy grass would go unnoticed by the pilots.

The plane buzzed past to the east, not straight overhead, but the pilots would have an oblique line of sight on the field. Would it pass this way after the cargo was dropped?

Could he afford to wait for another break in the rain?

The satellites could get a good image now. Today. Who knew how long until they had another window like this?

He had no choice and resumed laying out poles in the grass to form the dashes to make the O in S-O-S.

Brie stayed off her foot at the edge of the field, overseeing his work, making sure the dots and dashes were evenly placed. Watching his back.

He glanced up at the sky. It looked like another storm was coming. SOCOM might not see this today.

When they did see it, he wondered who would swoop in to the rescue. He hoped it would be his team, because the SEALs would have a grand time flipping him shit over the need to rescue a Special Forces operator.

Of course, Cal and Pax would probably razz him as well. He was basically screwed no matter who they sent. But damn, he couldn't wait to see his teammates' ugly mugs. He needed to know if anyone had been injured in the market fight. In the back of his mind, that fear was there.

It was always there.

He'd planned the extraction. If any of his brothers had been hurt, it would be his fault.

Savvy stared at the screen and cursed. After a short window, clouds once again covered frigging half of South Sudan.

Her cell phone buzzed. It better be Cal. Or even better, Bastian. She got her first wish. "Give me some good news, Cal."

"Um…the kids have escaped to the Sudd and White Nile?"

"I knew that already. Where is Bastian?"

"We don't know. There's no trace of them. The storm wiped away everything."

"Sonofabitch."

"No sign of them in the satellite images?"

"It's too cloudy."

"Keep looking."

"I am. Everyone is." It was what she'd been doing all day. On the computer in front of her, she had a slide show of the last images they'd been able to acquire, from yesterday evening, when the cloud cover had thinned. They weren't great shots, but they were at least recent.

Up on the big screen were the baseline images, ones that had been taken three days ago, as soon as they realized Chief Ford and Gabriella Prime were MIA.

"You're sure they went south?" she asked.

"No. But that's what her coworkers said they believe she'd do. She knows the area, the people. Bastian would listen to her if she said south is their best option."

"Is the team in Akobo?" she asked Cal.

"Yeah. The roads are too messed up for recon. We'll use the helo once we get a solid lead."

Savvy pulled up images of the closest village to the south. No changes in the images taken two days apart. She continued farther south, along the main road. Bastian would be searching for a radio. A truck. Fuel. Those were found along the main corridor.

But what would Brie do?

She'd been traumatized. For all they knew, she could be injured.

Brie would want to hide.

Savvy returned to the village image and caught a faint line that led west through the grasslands. Another village?

She found it and zoomed in. The image was hard to read. She pulled up the baseline from the clear day on the big screen, and could see what looked like circles—eight huts?

She sent yesterday's image to the big screen. Yes, eight huts. But one circle...looked different. The color had changed. That could be due to the rain.

"There's a village to the southwest that might be promising." She gave Cal the name as near as she could tell. "If it clears tomorrow, we'll focus the cameras there. Find out what you can about the place on your end."

"Will do. Thanks, Sav." Cal hung up.

That was one of the most civil conversations she'd ever had with the Green Beret, but then, in this they had the same goal. Of course, they always had the same goal, but sometimes the military guys didn't believe it. They didn't trust her because they knew she lied without compunction or remorse. She twisted and manipulated.

They were on the same team, but Savvy was willing to sacrifice eggs to make the omelet. She didn't have the luxury of being vegan.

She stared at the screen. Her gut told her that the change in color of the circle wasn't a trick of the light. It meant something. The question was, would it lead to Bastian and Brie?

B astian had removed his shirt in the heat, and Brie enjoyed the view as he used a compass to lay out his message in straight, even lines.

His waist was as impossibly narrow as his biceps were impossibly wide. He was like a sculpture, but instead of marble, he was flesh-and-blood perfection. She couldn't remember the last time she'd lusted after a man this much, but then, this was the first time she'd ever been stranded quite like this, and she'd been celibate for a year.

A girl had needs, and Chief Warrant Officer Sebastian Ford could fulfill every one.

As a recovering addict, she knew how to face temptation head-on. But she hadn't always won those battles.

Kissing Bastian had been the ultimate inebriant. His lips against hers, his tongue delving deep, taking, giving. Hot and sweet and sensual. It had been exactly like that first moment of a new high.

All rush and adrenaline. The sheer ecstasy of knowing in her soul that the next hit would take her even higher.

Except the next hit never delivered. There was no way to hit that high. It was the ultimate letdown, every high being lower than the one before, until eventually, there was nowhere left to go but a negative gain. A high so low, it was buried.

And yet, here she was again, watching Bastian and wanting that hit. Craving a pinnacle that didn't exist.

She knew better than that. Being with him made her into a junkie again. That it happened in South Sudan was both bitter and ironic. It was easy to deal with her addictions here: there was zero opportunity to use. In this war-torn, battle-weary, fledgling democracy, she hadn't needed to fight temptation at every moment.

But now she'd fixated on Bastian, and if she knew what was good for her, she'd let this craving go unfulfilled before she found herself in another destructive addiction spiral, this one leading to a devastated heart.

Chapter Seventeen

The sky had cleared, giving hope that satellites would see Bastian's message, but they had no way of knowing when the message was received and wouldn't know until a team arrived.

There was no "if" in this scenario. His plan would work. But Bastian had to admit it was time to consider a backup plan. Brie's ankle was better, and the infection in her foot was improving thanks to the antibiotics. Another two or three days, and she'd be able to walk for longer stretches.

This was their fifth day in this village. How long should they wait before moving to plan Bravo?

He completed a dozen push-ups, the hot sun shining down on his bare back. He'd had to ditch his body armor to enter the market, and it had been lost with the truck. It was strange to be without armor while on a mission, but he enjoyed the freedom from the weight and heat.

He flipped to his back and did a hundred sit-ups, then rose to his feet and grabbed the clothesline he'd cut to jump rope length and did a rotation of double unders. He couldn't do his daily five-mile run, so jump rope would have to do for cardio. The workout burned energy and kept him from losing his mind from boredom and sexual frustration.

He did five more reps of push-ups, sit-ups, and double

unders before dropping the rope and stretching for the warm-down. A noise behind him told him Brie had finished in the shower hut, and he turned to face her.

The sarong clung to her wet skin, adhering to her soft curves, and just like that, all the good the workout had done to dampen his libido was lost.

He knew she wasn't *trying* to be sexy and seduce him. She had two thin cloths to wear for clothing, and she washed and dried one while wearing the other. She didn't even have underwear.

He hoped to hell she didn't get her period while they were stranded, although given that she'd lived here for months, and was adept at improvising with the supplies they'd salvaged from the abandoned village, he had a feeling she could manage.

She was resourceful and strong in ways he'd never imagined. Women had to deal with so much crap that men could never endure—and he wasn't simply referring to menstrual cycles, but those were on the list.

"Is my sarong on backward, Chief Ford?"

He lifted his gaze to hers to see her raised eyebrow, and he realized he'd been staring.

He'd been frozen mid-stretch with his leg extended. He shifted to the other leg and shook his head. "No. It's just that with the dirt washed away, your unfortunate nose really stands out."

She laughed. "You were staring at my hips, not my face."

His gaze had dropped lower to avoid seeing the wet fabric clinging to her breasts, but he wouldn't offer up that excuse. They needed no more reminders of the attraction that wouldn't go away and couldn't be acted upon. Not here. Not now.

He met her gaze as he continued stretching. "I was wondering—what will you do if you get your period while we're stuck out here?" Might as well ask. It was stupid that the subject was taboo when it was a basic fact of life that half the world's population menstruated for a large portion of their lives. "In fact, what do women here *do*? The villagers have next to nothing."

She cocked her head, clearly surprised but not the least bothered by his question. "Actually, that's one of the reasons I was hired by USAID in the first place, and why aid organizations need to hire women to work abroad— because we address issues men don't even realize are a problem. Did you know that a large percentage of girls in sub-Saharan Africa drop out of school when they start menstruating, because there are no toilets and no running water at the schools?

"Water, sanitation, and education are all interconnected, and for decades, water and sanitation specialists were male engineers. It never occurred to them that girls were dropping out of school around the age of twelve because puberty meant periods. Many put it down to societal barriers to girls getting an education. But it was the girls making the choice, because there was no way for them to manage their monthly cycle in a sanitary way in the classroom."

From the light in her eyes, he could tell he'd stumbled onto her passion without even realizing it.

She spread her arms to indicate the abandoned village. "Famine is our core concern for the moment, but as you can see, South Sudan needs more than food. One of my jobs was distributing underwear to women and girls—it has a waterproof bottom under a crotch pocket that can be filled with cotton, torn-up fabric, grass. Anything absorbent."

He furrowed his brow. "But I thought anthropologists just studied Native Americans as if we're lab rats so they could pass on what they learned about our culture for white people to appropriate?"

She let out a soft laugh. "That's in the first-year grad curriculum. Second year, we delve deeper and look for ways to appropriate cultures on other continents." She settled on the ground, leaning her back against their hut wall. She pulled her knees to her chest, tucking the bottom of her sarong beneath her knees so she didn't flash him. "And to answer your initial question, my period isn't due for another week—but stress could bring it on sooner, or delay it. If it starts, I'll cut up one of the tarps and make myself a pair of panties and fill it with grass. If you don't have a needle and thread, I'll use an acacia thorn and fibers."

It was in moments like this that he found it hard to believe he was talking to Princess Prime. "I've got a needle in the first aid kit. But why don't you make underwear now?"

"Have you ever worn underwear made out of an old, dirty tarp? I'll wait and see if I need it, thanks."

He nodded. "Fair enough. And if you have a need, you can adapt my underwear."

"Awww. I'd finally get in your pants."

Her voice had taken on the soft, seductive quality it had held that first night they'd lain together on the hilltop. He shifted his position to both try to contain and hide his thickening penis. He reacted to her far too easily—but then, that had been true from the first moment he'd seen her when he was twenty-one.

At the time, Cece had accused him of lusting after

white girls, claiming he wanted to escape his Indian heritage. He'd known her logic was bullshit, but he'd felt guilty for his white-girl lust just the same.

Of course, after the breakup, he made it a goal to sleep with women of all races and colors and had been successful in that regard. One thing he'd learned about himself—he had no preference. Women—he liked them all.

And right now he liked Brie Stewart. A lot.

"I have a favor to ask," she said.

He cocked his head in question.

"Will you teach me how to fight?"

He frowned. "I don't think that's a good idea."

"That's what you do, isn't it? You were in Djibouti to teach locals how to be guerilla fighters. You're training soldiers."

"Guerilla tactics aren't just about hand-to-hand combat. We deal with weapons. We improvise. It's about a small force taking on a bigger army with surprise, targeted attacks on infrastructure." He was deflecting, he knew.

"But you do know how to fight hand-to-hand. And you teach others."

"Yes." So much for deflecting.

"Why won't you teach me? It's not like we're pressed for time."

"Because I can't hit you. Not even in practice."

"That's stupid. If you were sparring with Savvy, could you hit her?"

He *had* sparred with Savvy. Dammit. "Yes. But even with sparring, sometimes a real blow slips through. She's trained. You aren't. If I hurt you, I'd lose it."

"You can't possibly hurt me with a stray punch more

than the whip hurt. More than the degradation of being stripped and chained."

Aww. Hell. She had a point. "It will require us to get close to each other. You can't spar in a sarong."

"What if I have to fight in a sarong?"

"It'd probably split open."

"And in the moment—trying to defend myself, I wouldn't give a damn if I'm flashing my attacker."

He sighed. She was one hundred percent right, and he needed to get rid of his hang-ups. "Tell you what—you can wear my boxer briefs and T-shirt." He frowned, remembering her attempt to fight the slaver when she was chained. "We should probably work on tactics like head butting and other techniques that work when you're bound."

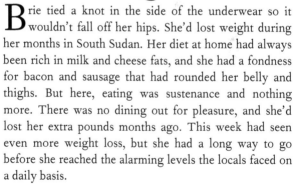

Brie tied a knot in the side of the underwear so it wouldn't fall off her hips. She'd lost weight during her months in South Sudan. Her diet at home had always been rich in milk and cheese fats, and she had a fondness for bacon and sausage that had rounded her belly and thighs. But here, eating was sustenance and nothing more. There was no dining out for pleasure, and she'd lost her extra pounds months ago. This week had seen even more weight loss, but she had a long way to go before she reached the alarming levels the locals faced on a daily basis.

She still had some curves, but she wasn't sculpted like the Green Beret who'd rescued her. Watching him do push-ups and jump rope shirtless had become her new favorite pastime.

What did Bastian think of her body? His gaze had

dropped from her breasts to her hips damn fast after she'd showered.

Even though nothing could happen between them, she wanted him to desire her, to believe that the lust between them flowed both ways. It would be disappointing to feel this intense pull and be alone in her desire.

She'd spent most of her life wanting the people she cared about to care about her in return. This was nothing new. Rejection hurt—whether it was her brothers not giving a damn about her unless she could seal a business deal by flirting with the creepy old guys, or simple unrequited lust.

In her work, she'd moved on and found her soul again. But she couldn't help but wonder if the attack on the facility had been about her. Was it her fault the food was lost?

Her fault people had died and would starve?

No wonder she wanted to escape into lust-filled fantasies. She was supposed to be here to help, but it was possible she'd made everything worse for a group of people who were already desperate.

And now Bastian was stranded with her. Separated from his team, who could have been injured—*or worse*— in her rescue.

Shit. She was spiraling. She could see it. Feel the vortex. Guilt pressed in on her. Her breathing turned shallow.

She had much to make up for in her life, but this *wasn't* her fault. She didn't ask for this, couldn't have guessed her family was so far gone, they'd come after her here. And she'd had no proof they'd come after her. The man she'd seen in the market worked for Druneft now and the other man she'd recognized had been a henchman for

General Lawiri. Lawiri's man couldn't have anything to do with her.

She took a deep breath. She'd learn how to fight. She and Bastian would be rescued. And when all this was over, she'd make sure the village was loaded with food and restored.

Her family would pay for it, or she'd make sure every nasty secret they had was exposed, starting with their dirty deals with Viktor and Nikolai Drugov. Price fixing was only the tip of that iceberg.

~⌒~

A determined light had entered Brie's eyes. In spite of the fact that she looked hot as hell in his T-shirt and boxer briefs, there was nothing about her that exuded sexuality. She stood before Bastian, feet spread and arms raised.

She was ready to learn how to kick ass.

Well, teaching that just so happened to be one of his specialties.

Guerilla fighting might be more about tactics than hand-to-hand, but that didn't mean he didn't know how to fight. The Army had honed his skills, but the truth was, he'd learned brawling on the reservation. His rez wasn't as tough as some—the Kalahwamish had new affluence once they'd gotten the sawmill property back. The tribe even ran tours that were similar to a West Coast version of Williamsburg. But when Bastian was a teen, they'd been as poor as any of the remote reservations. Poor meant there were some bastards on the rez who'd made sure the brats like him grew up just as tough as their predecessors.

On the rez, fights broke out for the slightest insult. It

wasn't about winning. It was about pride, and he'd known how to take a beating and still hold his head high. When his mom became tribal chairwoman, that meant fighting to defend his dad's honor. Indians were capable of being just as sexist as their white counterparts.

Bastian had been a shitty fighter, but when his mom became chairwoman, he got tired of getting his ass kicked. A Warren—the most powerful extended family in his tribe—with an ax to grind against the Fords, owned the only reservation gym, so he joined an off-reservation gym in the town of Coho. There, Bastian spent all his free time and learned how to fight. When his biceps thickened to near-superhero proportions, the boys on the rez stopped calling him a whitey-wannabe. They didn't dare. And later, when he joined the Army, they'd showed respect. In spite of the bad history between tribes and the US Army, most tribes were proud of their members who served.

Bastian loved both his countries—the Kalahwamish Tribal Nation and the United States of America. He fought for both. Bled for both. Would die for both.

Since he was fourteen, he'd pushed his muscles and honed his tactical skills. Now, seventeen years later, he was second-in-command of a Special Forces A-Team with an eye on the top spot. The ultimate warrior, who would bring honor to both his tribal ancestors and Army predecessors.

The end result: Bastian could fight, and he had no qualms about fighting dirty, which was exactly what Brie needed to learn.

He stood before her, bare-chested and primed for the coming lesson. "Ready?" he asked, no longer seeing her as anything other than his assignment. He was a soldier with a job to do.

She smiled and gave a sharp nod. "Bring it."

B astian came at her hard, fierce, and one hundred percent professional. He slammed her to the ground countless times, but he always managed to cushion her landing, both protecting her and showing her how to roll with the blows.

He showed her how to kick, punch, block, head-butt, and evade as the hot sun scorched their skin and dried the muddy ground. The heat and exertion worked together to exhaust Brie, and she missed a block. His leg swept hers, and she went down into the dirt, no cushion this time, just hard, painful ground.

"Shit! Sorry!" Bastian said as he dropped to her side, too late to roll and take the brunt of the fall.

She gasped, struggling to take a breath as the wind rushed from her lungs. She managed a shallow inhalation, followed by a slightly deeper one.

Bastian's face pinched with worry. "Shit. I never should have agreed." He cupped her face. "Breathe, sweetheart. Please. I'm so sorry."

She shook her head. Another puff of air managed to reach her lungs. "S'okay. My fault. Fine." A deeper breath. "Will be. Fine."

He stroked her cheeks, staring into her eyes. She focused on his dark irises, relaxing her esophagus and diaphragm. Finally, a slow but full breath filled her lungs.

His eyes no longer held the guarded gaze of a teacher. They were liquid black and full of heat that had nothing to do with the burning sun.

She smiled. She'd have a few choice bruises but was

otherwise okay. And she'd learned a lot from the private self-defense lesson. She'd been holding her own until exhaustion tripped her up. If stamina was her biggest problem, she'd be okay. It was unlikely any fight would ever last the ninety minutes or so they'd been sparring. She'd never be able to go that many rounds.

"You have the most beautiful smile." The words slipped from Bastian's mouth soft and low, like he didn't want to say them but they escaped on their own. "It was the first thing I noticed about you. Ten years ago. Your smile reached your eyes. It wasn't cold, like everyone else on the panel. It never made sense to me. How someone so warm, so vibrant, could do something so soulless."

"I was blindsided at that public meeting. I didn't know about the TCP," she said, referring to the Traditional Cultural Property that had rightly halted the project. "I really thought there would be no tribal issues, that what we were doing was a win-win for Washington, the tribes, and Prime Energy." Her smile had been real at the start of the community meeting, but by the end, she'd been screaming inside. She'd been set up and thrown to the wolves by her brothers. Again. She'd stepped into the project late in the game, when Jeffery Junior dropped it in her lap, claiming he had a meeting in Moscow he couldn't miss.

She'd always wondered if JJ really had gone to Moscow.

Bastian's lips flattened. "There is no such thing as win-win when it comes to tribes and Prime Energy."

She missed the warmth in his gaze and stroked his bearded jaw, hoping to bring it back. "I know that. I learned that night, and kept learning in grad school. I was…naïve then. Or hopeful. Probably just plain stupid."

"Don't call yourself stupid. Ever."

"But I was. Such a fool."

Bastian rolled to his back, pulling her up so she straddled him in the sun. His bronze, tanned skin and colorful salmon tattoo glistened with sweat. He smelled of earth and exertion, and between her thighs, his cock thickened, telling her his mind had gone the same direction as hers.

"A fool, maybe. But never stupid."

She leaned down, bringing her lips a scant centimeter from his. "Am I being stupid now?"

"A fool, maybe," he repeated. She felt the rumble of his deep voice as her breasts pressed against his chest.

She touched her mouth to his. The lyrics to "Kissing a Fool" floated through her mind as his lips parted and his tongue invaded her mouth. At least now they knew which one of them was the fool.

The kiss was deep and slow and sensual. There was nothing urgent about it even as her body coiled tight at the feel of his erection.

Taking him deep would feel so good. He'd make love to her slowly, languidly, just like this kiss. She reached down, between their bodies, and stroked his hard length over the top of his pants. She fumbled with his fly, then got her hand inside, and felt him shiver as he groaned when her hand wrapped around him and slid up the shaft.

His tongue stroked hers, still languid but deeper, as if he couldn't get enough of her mouth. Enough of her touch.

He rolled again, and she was on her back in the dirt, and he was cradled between her thighs, her hand between them, holding his cock. His hips rocked, and he thrust in her hand, pressing her thumb into her clit and—*oh God*—she wanted his hand there. His mouth.

His lips left hers, and he lifted the T-shirt, exposing her breast. As with the kiss, his tongue did a slow exploration of her skin before he sucked her nipple deep into his mouth.

She gasped and released his erection so his cock could slide along the boxer briefs over her clit.

Jesus. She was so hot for him, she could come with just a few more strokes. He chuckled as she rocked her hips, trying to do just that, and pulled away so his penis didn't touch her. "Oh no, sweetheart. We're going to take this nice and slow. Until you're aching so bad for it, you beg me."

"I'll beg now, if that's what you want. Fuck me, Bastian. Please, please, fuck me."

His mouth moved to her other breast. He licked her nipple, then scraped his teeth over the tip and blew a cool breath and watched it pucker. Then he licked her again, the tip of his tongue lapping at her before he finally sucked.

His methodical, slow touches were killing her. In the best way. His lips moved lower, kissing and licking his way down her belly.

This—*he*—was definitely going in the right direction.

He reached her belly button, and all at once he froze. It was only a moment, but she felt the change in him. A shift in his attention.

All at once, she remembered this wasn't safe. There was a reason they hadn't spent the last few days doing exactly this. Her body stiffened, and she pushed at his shoulders, intending to rise and make it easier for them both to walk away from this moment by separating their bodies.

But he resisted, and he dropped his full weight on her, trapping her. His lips again found her skin, but now they trailed upward, past her breasts, flowing north with tongue and lips.

He wants to continue?

He reached her ear, and nuzzled it as he whispered, "There's someone here. In the tall grass to the right." He traced the shell of her ear with his tongue as he continued, "I'm going to let you up. I want you walk to our hut, swinging your ass like you expect me to follow and fuck your brains out. Like you don't have a care in the world. Grab my Sig. Hide under the tarp. Shoot anyone who enters if they aren't me."

She'd gone cold at his first words, but she'd stroked his ass to cover her reaction, so anyone watching would think they were oblivious.

He dropped his forehead into the curve of her neck. "Before I let you up"—he cleared his throat—"can you put me back in my pants and zip me up in a way that's not obvious?"

She did as he asked, and he let out a groan as if they were still at foreplay. Once he was back in place, his weight shifted, but before he let her up, he kissed her— hard, deep, and fast. This wasn't part of the act, nor was it foreplay.

She suspected this kiss was good-bye.

Adrenaline shot through her at the realization that he believed this screwup—making out in the middle of the day, in the middle of the abandoned village—would be the death of him, and very probably her as well.

She gripped his skin. She couldn't get up. Couldn't

leave him. His eyes burned into hers. "Go, Brie." His lips dropped to hers again. "Don't worry about me. I've got my M4." One last kiss, and he rolled to the side.

She stood on shaking legs. "You coming?" she asked, loudly.

"Not yet," he said, giving her a leer. "Gotta take a leak. Get naked. I'll meet you inside." He slapped her ass. He was a soldier again, playing a part, and she was thankful he was on his game.

She kept her gaze on him, refusing to look toward the grassland that edged the village. "Hurry."

"Sweetheart, we've got all the time in the world."

She offered up a throaty laugh and made a beeline for their hut, swinging her ass as instructed. It took all her willpower not to break into a run.

Inside the hut, she grabbed his handgun, which he'd showed her how to use days ago. She made sure it was loaded, but her hands shook so badly, she was afraid she'd drop it. The small roll of duct tape in his pack gave her an idea. She grabbed it, then slipped into the body-length pit she'd helped him dig on the first day they were here. She covered herself with one of their tarps, making the round hut appear empty. With all the tarps that covered the floor, it would take an intruder precious seconds to realize where she was.

Those seconds could make all the difference.

Hidden, she ripped off a strip of tape. She gripped the gun with her right hand and used her left to wrap the tape around gun and hand. This way she wouldn't drop it, and it would be impossible for someone to take it from her.

Chapter Eighteen

Bastian casually scooped up his M4 and headed toward the latrine. Just a guy taking a piss before getting laid.

While he knew deep down he'd fucked up in letting things go as far as they had with Brie, he also knew that the make-out session was probably the best cover they had. It had meant they were close together and he could whisper instructions. If they'd still been sparring, or if they'd been separated with one of them in the shower or hut, it might be over already. He'd be dead and she'd be taken.

Who would have thought that having her hands in his pants was the one thing that bought them enough time to save her life?

Thank God he'd had enough brain cells left to hear the stumbled step followed by the all-too-human grunt of pain.

Whoever was in the grassland, they were clumsy and poorly trained. Definitely not his Special Forces team.

Bypassing the latrine, Bastian reached the spot where he was sure the guy had taken cover after twisting his ankle. He pulled out his dick and pissed, aiming for where the guy was hunkered in the thick shrubs. His M4 casually pointed at the same spot, index finger on the trigger. He shook off and tucked himself away, smiling as if he hadn't a care in the world.

There were at least two guys behind him, inching forward, but they were less likely to strike with his gun trained on their buddy. But he couldn't play this game for long before they would go for Brie in the hut.

He had no worries about her ability to shoot attackers. After her experience in the market, he didn't doubt her resolve. But still, he needed to take out these guys before they got to her. He'd fucked up in letting them get this close.

The man he'd pissed on shifted, lifting his gun, and Bastian fired. A clean shot that hit center mass. The guy slumped back, his gun still in a tight grip.

Not dead.

The crunch of a step behind him. *Fuck.*

He fired again at the man who was already bleeding out. Head shot. Bastian spun around without waiting to watch the gun fall from the guy's hand.

Two men, one black, one white, advanced on him from a hundred feet away. A third man stood in the doorway of the hut.

Bastian fired at the man going after Brie first. Before he could get off another shot, he was hit from behind, a blunt object across his temple.

The world swam as he tried to stay on his feet. Fuck. There'd been another guy in the shrubs.

"Don't kill him," one man said in Arabic. "We need him alive to parade before the cameras."

He elbowed the guy behind him in the throat as he raised his gun. His vision was blurry, giving him twice as many targets. He squeezed the trigger.

Another blow to the head came. As if a switch had been flipped, his vision turned black.

Brie held her breath against a scream after hearing the first gunshot.

Please let it be Bastian who fired the shot.

Pinprick holes in the old tarp showed a body blocking the sunlight of the doorway. A second, then third shot followed. The body dropped, replaced by unobstructed light.

Bastian must've shot him.

She stayed hidden, praying her shaking with fear wouldn't reveal her location.

Words in Arabic were followed by a fourth shot. *They want Bastian alive?*

Did they want to use him to prove the US was running ops in South Sudan? Was he to be beaten and put on the news as proof of US treachery?

"The girl is more important than the soldier," a second man said. Again, light from the doorway was blocked by a body. "Come out, Princess," he said in English. "We know you're in here."

Princess?

Who were these men? They'd spoken in Arabic to each other. Were they from Kemet Oil?

The man entered the hut and looked like he was scanning for hiding places. Bastian's pack and some blankets were piled up and big enough to hide her, distracting him for a moment, and then there were all the tarps on the floor.

She waited until he was above her before she pulled the trigger. Even her wildly shaking hands couldn't miss that target.

Through the holes in the tarp, she could see she'd hit

him in the forehead. He dropped on top of her, trapping her under the sheet, suffocating her with his weight.

She shoved at him, trying not to panic and scream—and failing.

Another man entered the hut and cursed, probably when he saw his dead associate. She worked her gun hand free, thankful she'd taped it to her, or she'd have dropped it once the body fell on her.

Bastian had warned her the first pull was harder—it acted as the safety—but now it took only the softest squeeze of her finger and the second man also dropped, landing at her feet.

Untrained as she was, the recoil required a two-handed grip, but with the tape, again she held on to the pistol.

How many men were there? Would she just lie here and wait for them, one by one?

She couldn't do that. Not when Bastian must've been injured—no way would he have allowed these men past him.

He could be dying. He could be dead.

A sob burst forth.

No.

She refused to believe that. To even think it. He needed her, just as she'd needed him in the market. It was her chance to return the favor.

She pulled the tarp from her face and kicked at the man at her feet. Her ankle screamed in protest, but she sucked in a deep breath and kicked again as she shoved the first man to the side as far as she could in the tight hole.

She kept her gaze on the door as she wriggled out from under the remainder of his weight. Freed at last, she approached the doorway cautiously.

"Come out, Princess Prime, or your boyfriend is

dead." Again the words were English. They probably didn't know she spoke some Arabic, which meant she'd never come into contact with them through USAID.

But then, he'd just called her Princess Prime, so the men were connected to her past, not her present.

"Prove he's still alive," she said in a choked voice.

"He's unconscious," the man said.

"What do you want?"

"What we've always wanted. You. My boss was unhappy when he didn't get you in the market. And he was livid when he learned an American soldier had you; that the greedy trader sold you before we got there. Now, come out, or I'll slit the soldier's throat."

She didn't have a choice. She couldn't let Bastian die, not when she could save him.

They wanted her alive. She'd suffer, but she wouldn't be killed. At least, not right away.

"If you hurt Bastian, I'll shoot you like I did your partners."

She glanced toward the two men. The one she'd shot in the head was definitely dead. The other man? She couldn't be certain. She thought she'd hit him in the chest. He could be dead, or could be biding his time. She'd have to turn her back on him to leave the hut.

She raised the gun-taped hand and stepped over the body that blocked the doorway. Outside, she saw Bastian slack in the arms of a white man who held a knife to his throat. Bastian's wide shoulders blocked the man's chest, leaving only part of his face visible. A sharpshooter could take out the man without hurting Bastian, but Brie had never fired a gun until today.

"Drop your gun," the man said. His accent held a hint of Russian.

"I can't. It's taped to my hand." She made a show of trying to drop it, praying the tape would hold against her sweaty skin. With the hair trigger, she was liable to shoot herself if it dropped.

"Untape it."

"I can't. My finger is on the hair trigger. Slightest twitch and it might fire. Bring your knife here. Cut the tape."

"How stupid do you think I am, Princess?"

"Are we talking IQ or street smarts?" She counted the bodies that littered the ground outside and in the hut. Four men had died for nothing. Not that she would mourn the loss of slavers and kidnappers. "Drop the knife," she said, pointing her wildly shaking hand at the man.

He laughed, and she realized her mistake. It was obvious she couldn't make the shot, not without risking Bastian.

Bastian could die, and it would be her fault.

She turned the gun toward her temple. At this close range, no matter how badly her hands shook, she'd make the shot. "You'll never get paid if I die right here."

"You wouldn't do it."

Her gaze hardened. This man had no idea what she was capable of. "I won't be a sex slave. May as well end it now."

All it would take was the slightest pressure from her finger, and the game was over. She could see it. Feel it. Embrace the end. At least it would be on her terms.

The man must've seen the truth in her eyes, because he shifted the knife away from Bastian's neck. He still held it, but at least he wasn't giving Bastian a shave.

Brie lowered the gun from her temple. She felt her

heartbeat all the way to her fingertips and worried the thumping pulse would cause her to twitch and fire the gun.

She took slow, even breaths, trying to calm herself before a stray spasm killed her or someone else.

Killing two people was enough for one day.

"Now what, Princess?"

"Tell me how you found me. How do you even know who I am?"

The slackness of Bastian's body scared her. She'd seen the slight rise of his chest. He was breathing. But that could change with a head injury, and from the blood on his temple, it was clear that was how he'd been incapacitated.

"We found you because the people in the nearest village decided they wanted to live more than they wanted to protect you."

Oh God. Had they hurt anyone?

She didn't bother to ask. She wouldn't trust his answer anyway. "And how did you know who I am?"

"My boss has been looking for you for some time. Can't say I blame him. I was one of thousands who jacked off to the cosmetics ads you did when you were thirteen. You were fuckable, even then."

The gun in her hand fired into the dirt inches from the guy's feet. She hadn't meant to do it. She'd flinched at his words.

"Guess I hit a nerve." The man laughed. "How I imagined shoving my cock into your mouth back then." His gaze flicked down the length of her. "And you're still skinny. I could close my eyes and pretend you're still a nubile thirteen-year-old."

She raised the gun. Her hand was steadied by rage. She

shot the dirt near his feet again, this time intentionally.

He recoiled, and Bastian sprang to life. He thrust his head backward, head-butting the guy in the nose. In a flash, Bastian seized the knife and slit the man's throat.

Brie watched in shock at Bastian's speed and lethal action. She stood rooted to the spot, when a bang sounded and searing pain tore through her thigh.

She whirled even as her leg crumpled beneath her. Behind her was a sixth man with a rifle. She raised her gun hand and fired as she fell. Her shot went wide.

His rifle jammed, but he charged toward her. She kept firing in a panic, until the gun was empty. None of her shots came near him.

More shots sounded. Blood sprouted in the charging man's chest. Another hit his throat. He dropped to the ground five feet in front of her.

She turned to look at Bastian, and was shocked to see he held only the bloody knife. He'd been going for his M4, but it was several feet away.

She scanned the trees as she clawed at the tape on her hand. She needed to get the empty gun off so she could stop the bleeding in her thigh. Pain threatened to drown out all other thoughts.

June, Abdo's mother, stepped from behind a tree, sporting a rifle. Tears sprang to Brie's eyes. June had fired the shots that saved her life.

Brie managed to break the tape and rid herself of the Sig, then she attempted to crawl to Bastian, but pain overwhelmed her.

June reached her side. "They came to our village."

Brie gasped against the pain. "Did they hurt you? Is everyone okay?"

The woman nodded. "Kamal was hurt, but he will

recover. We had to tell them where you are. I took Kamal's gun and followed. I was only one against six. I couldn't take them all."

Bastian dropped to Brie's other side, setting his pack down next to her. Blood dripped down his temple. "There were six men, total?" he asked as he pulled out his first aid kit.

"Yes. Six. I saw where they hid. Waited. Wanted to shoot the one before he hit you, but you were in the way."

"You saved us both," Bastian said. "Thank you."

She spat toward the body lying by the hut opening. "These men are worse than the soldiers who steal and rape. From what they said, I think the black men worked for General Lawiri. I don't know who the white man worked for."

Bastian probed at Brie's wound, and her vision dimmed. "Bullet's still in there."

"Can you remove it?" she asked.

"I'm not a medic. I've been trained, but…I'm sorry, Brie, but this is going to hurt like hell."

"We have alcohol in our village," June offered. "Just for this kind of thing."

"No. No alcohol." She gasped as Bastian hit a shattered nerve.

"It might help, Brie."

Tears spilled down her cheeks from the intensity of the pain, but she couldn't open that door. She knew herself. Knew her triggers. "No. I can't." She gripped his hand. "And Bastian—if we're rescued, and medics take over, no opiates. Promise me. No opiates."

He nodded and leaned down and kissed her. Blood from his temple dripped onto her cheek. "I promise."

June took up Bastian's M4 and acted as guard as Bastian performed the surgery in the middle of the abandoned village.

Fortunately for Brie, she passed out from the pain before the forceps grasped the bullet.

❧

Oh dark thirty, and Bastian paced in front of the hut where Brie lay sleeping. He'd wanted to leave the village but had no way to move her that didn't involve carrying her for miles, and still had hope his team would show up any time now. Abandoning the village at this point could be the biggest mistake he made during an op full of epic fuckups.

June had returned to her village to see to her family. He was alone as he paced in front of the hut, going over every minute of the last seven days in his mind as he tried to figure out what he could have done differently.

His brain was fuzzy. He was fairly certain he had a concussion, but there was nothing he could do about that.

Six men were dead. Hired help of an exiled general? He hoped to pass that theory on to Savvy, but right now he wobbled on his feet and his vision blurred. He was chilled to the bone on the hot night, and wanted to crawl into bed with Brie to get warm. He must have a fever.

Fuck. That wasn't good.

The whirr of a helicopter sounded in the distance. He turned toward the noise and rocked on his feet at the sudden movement.

In spite of his disoriented mind, his hope lifted. He knew that sound. Stealth Blackhawk.

His team.

He stood his ground, in front of the hut, as the hawk

passed overhead, kicking up mud and debris.

Next thing he knew, he was looking up into Goldberg's face. He must've blacked out?

Goldberg was the team medic. Bastian cracked a smile. At least, he hoped it was a smile. "About time you got here."

"Shit, Bas, you scared the hell out of us." This from Cal, who also hovered above.

He turned to Goldberg. "Forget about me. Brie. Shot. Check on her."

"Washington is taking care of her," Goldberg said, referring to the team's other medic.

Bastian gripped his arm. "Tell him, no opiates. She can't have opiates." Then he slipped into darkness.

Chapter Nineteen

Bastian grinned at the three men who filled his small room in the aircraft carrier's medical facility. "How the hell did you convince Captain Oswald to authorize this visit?" he asked Cal, Pax, and Espi.

"We told him we would do a rundown of every screwup you made on the mission," Espi said with a wink.

Bastian grimaced but still managed a laugh. "Don't worry, I've already compiled that list."

Cal dropped into the visitor's chair at his side. "Don't be hard on yourself, Bas. The mission was fucked up from the moment she was taken to that market. I refuse to feel guilty for saving the kids."

It was true that not rescuing the kids was pretty much the only thing they could have done differently. Well, he also could have not been engaged in a make-out session with Brie while six men took up positions around their camp, but Cal didn't know about that fuckup. And the truth was, that had likely saved their asses, so he refused to feel guilty for that one.

Pax dropped a duffel bag at the foot of his hospital bed. "Rumor has it you're going to be here for a few more days, so I grabbed your phone and a few other personal belongings we recovered from the hut."

"Thanks, man." He and Brie had been halfway

through a Karen Rose thriller he'd had on his phone—by tacit agreement, they'd stopped reading aloud before they reached the sex scene—and it looked like he'd have plenty of reading time while he was stuck here.

A nice guy would give the phone with unfinished book to Brie, but he hadn't seen her since they'd arrived on the USS *Dahlgren* three days ago. She'd been confined to her bed with her leg injury, and he…he hadn't gone to see her because he was a chickenshit.

They were back in the real world now—or as real as it got on a Navy aircraft carrier—and soon she would go back to the US and he would return to Camp Citron. There was no place for her in his world, and vice versa.

He couldn't even begin to imagine what his parents would think of her. Not that that mattered, because he didn't do relationships.

"So, we hear your brains were scrambled by mercs," Espi said with a grin. "Cheap-ass mercenaries? My hero worship of you is wavering, Chief."

"They were badass, probably superhuman," Bastian said. "I think Marvel is going to make them villains in the next Captain America movie. And there were at least two dozen of them."

"Three dozen," said a sexy, sweet voice he hadn't heard in days.

Bastian's gaze swung to the open door, and there was Brie, leaning on a cane. A real one, not the one he'd carved out of a branch eight days ago.

Holy fuck, but she was beautiful, even battered and wearing a garment that would steal another person's dignity. On her, the hospital gown looked like a fashion choice. She'd donned a second gown, wearing it like a robe over the first and covering the open backside. She'd cinched the waist with a strip of gauze, which she'd tied in a big, flowery bow with at least half a dozen loops.

Medical ward chic.

She wasn't Oil Company Barbie. She was Patient Barbie, and she made it look good, like being stuck in the medical ward on a Navy vessel was a desirable thing.

"Or at least, that's what I'll tell everyone, for the right price," she added with a slight smile, her confidence seeming to falter when she met his gaze.

She probably wondered why the hell he hadn't visited her. He smiled, covering the ache in his chest where his heart should be. He wasn't entirely sure he could answer that question himself.

"Brie, you're just in time to meet a few of the guys on my team."

He introduced his friends, who attempted to convince her to stay, but she refused. "I don't want to impose on your visit. The doc wanted me to start exercising my leg, and I heard your voice. Glad to see you're okay, I was worried." And then she left, moving fast enough to give him hope her injury was healing quickly.

"What the fuck, Bas? You haven't seen her? It's been three days." Cal's face was fierce. Angry. Pax mirrored the expression.

Espi's gaze was still fixed on the hallway where she'd hobbled away. "Damn, I didn't know a hospital gown could look so…*hot*."

"Come closer and say that," Bastian said, his fist clenched.

Pax had the nerve to *laugh*.

Then Espi flashed a grin.

Ahhh fuck. He was being taught a lesson.

Assholes.

But then, he had it coming. He'd been far worse with Morgan, Pax's girlfriend. He cleared his throat. "Message received. I'm a bastard."

Espi turned to him. "She's pretty, but I was more interested in your reaction. Why the hell are you playing dumbass games?"

"What happened in South Sudan?" Pax asked.

Bastian closed his eyes and willed his visitors to leave. Why had he been happy to see them? "Nothing."

Cal laughed. "You are so full of shit."

"You could do worse than banging an heiress," Espi said with a laugh. "No one would blame you."

"Fuck all y'all. I was on duty. We didn't screw."

"Ahh. So that's the problem," Pax said. "You aren't on duty now. You must've been hit extra hard if you're ignoring this opportunity. Maybe we should take a look at your X-rays."

"Captain Oswald is right, you do gossip like teenage girls." But he was laughing. Shit. He'd missed these guys and was glad everyone on his team had returned to Camp Citron without injury. They'd freed the hostages, rescued Brie, saved a few dozen children from slavery, all without embroiling the US in South Sudan's civil war.

By definition, it was a successful mission.

But it didn't feel like a success.

Brie had been shot, and it was his fault they'd even been there. If he'd pulled over before the road disappeared. If he hadn't lost the signal panels, if he hadn't lost the radio, none of that would have happened.

"You going to Rome with Morgan?" he asked Pax.

"No. Missed the window. She's coming here for a few days before heading back to the US. She needs to confer with her crew anyway and check a few new sites they found in the survey corridor."

Their deployment had been extended by a few weeks to make up for lost training time after Morgan had been abducted, and now they'd lost another week. It was likely more time would be added. Their trainees weren't ready for prime time, and another team wasn't scheduled to arrive until late June. "I'm sorry, man," Bastian said.

What else could he say?

Pax shrugged. "Saving the kids was more important."

They all nodded. Thinking about the market still felt surreal. He'd been so focused on Brie, he'd never really had a chance to process it. He'd seen some bad shit as a soldier, but the kids in the slave market ranked up there with the worst atrocities.

"Chief Ford, this appears to be a bad time." A woman's voice drew his attention. His gaze—along with the gazes of the three other men—swung to the open doorway.

Savannah James.

"Sav," Pax said, "we were just leaving. He's all yours."

Savvy's gaze flicked to Cal and then back to Pax so fast, Bastian wouldn't have noticed except he'd been looking for it. There was tension between those two, and Bastian had never been able to tell if it was the good kind or not.

Were they involved, or just circling like sharks, waiting for the other to break?

Either way, neither the CIA operator nor the soldier was happy with whatever it was that set them both on edge when they neared each other.

They should probably just screw and get it out of their systems, but he understood Cal's reluctance. Spooks were cold and calculating. That Savvy was probably Special Activities Division only made her more frightening. Never trust a person whose job title included the acronym SAD.

Pax and Espi said their goodbyes and filed out of the room. Cal stayed rooted to his spot next to Bastian's bed. He crossed his arms. "Where are the children?" he asked.

"That's classified, Sergeant Callahan."

"Considering my team got those kids out of the hellhole, you can make an exception."

She crossed the small space and ran a finger down Cal's chest, lowering her voice to a whisper. "It doesn't work that way, Cal. You know that."

"You two wanna be alone?" Bastian asked. "I mean, it's my hospital room, but I can drag myself out of bed and leave you."

Cal stood there, holding her gaze for several beats past normal. Finally, he said, "Get better, Bas," then stepped out of the room.

Yeah, those two needed to fuck. Sooner rather than later.

Savvy closed the door and faced him. "I want a full report," she said, dropping into the visitor's chair.

"I already debriefed with SOCOM."

She shrugged. "Pretend they didn't share it with me."

"Make them share. My head hurts, and I'm sick of going over the details."

"But I want to hear it all from you. The layout of the market, who was there, everything."

"There isn't much to tell. I was focused on Brie. My team can tell you more about the market."

She leaned forward. "But that's the thing. Brie is who I want to know about most of all. She's the key to this fiasco. You've just spent a week cozying up to a woman who's ninety percent porcupine, and yet you didn't get jabbed. My guess is you know her better than most men. Her coworkers, Ezra and Alan, were useless. They didn't even know she was a Prime."

"Ask her," Bastian said. Savvy's take on Brie surprised him. Porcupine? She was anything but.

"I want the stories that are buried. The ones about her brothers. She never talks about Rafe and Jeff Junior, but I think she'll talk to you."

"Bullshit."

"She will."

"Why would you believe that?"

"You make her feel safe."

"She was shot while she was with me. I doubt she'll ever feel safe around me again," Bastian said.

"Wrong. It's a different kind of safe. She can be herself with you—both the Prime because you know about that part of her, and the Stewart. She wants to screw you and needs someone to confide in. Whatever happened with her family was bad. She has it locked down tight and doesn't see the connection to South Sudan. The Russian merc mentioned the modeling she did when she was thirteen and implied his boss has been after her for some time. I think she knows who he is but doesn't realize it."

"You need to ask her. Not me."

"I have asked her. She said there were a lot of creeps who mailed her and stalked her when she was thirteen. Too many to begin to guess who it could be. But given everything else, I think this was someone close to the family. Otherwise, how did he find her?"

Bastian had been eleven when the cosmetic ads had run and had paid zero attention at the time. When he looked up Princess Prime nearly six weeks ago, he'd seen references to the ads, but because they'd been banned in the US, he hadn't crossed any firewalls for a refresher course.

"What's the deal with the ads? I don't remember them."

"The photos were borderline child pornography. She was made up to look like a sex kitten and given suggestive items like a popsicle to suck on. In one, she wore nothing but a towel, and you could see side boob and bare back, all the way down to the crack in her ass as she looked over her shoulder at the camera, her expression blatantly seductive."

Bastian grimaced. Brie had been a virgin then, so the photographer must've coaxed those looks out of her. Why the hell did her parents allow the shoot? And why hadn't they stopped the release of the images?

"I've asked Brie about the photo shoot and fallout at length. She regrets it, naturally. It was a lark for her. She did it to please her mom, who'd been a model prior to marrying Jeff Senior in the early eighties. It wasn't in the public documents related to the divorce, but Brie said she learned later the photographer was her mother's lover. Which is pretty sick when you think about it. The guy was banging the mother, but from the photos, it was clear he wanted the daughter."

"What happened to the photographer?"

"He'd done a series of ads for the same cosmetic company—all with underage girls. Brie's were the most explicit, but the others weren't much better. After the ads were banned, police got a warrant and raided his studio, where they found images that were full-on child porn. He died weeks before his trial was set to begin. Poisoned by a toxin that was never identified. Probably a Russian concoction—the photographer was Russian."

"Is there a connection between the Russian photographer and the Russian oil company?" The man Brie had seen in the market had worked for Prime Energy, but now he worked for Druneft. It was the only link that jumped out so far, but it was weak at best.

"None that I've uncovered, but the man died in the late nineties. Brie's maternal grandmother is Ukrainian, and Tatiana visited both Ukraine and Russia often after the Soviet Union broke up. She probably met the photographer on one of those trips. He moved to the US about a year before he photographed Brie."

Her story about losing her virginity had stuck with him, but this showed it wasn't just the men in Brie's life who were shits. Her mom hadn't protected her either. "Her mother passed away a few years ago, right?"

"Yes. Breast cancer."

"Were they close? Brie and her mother?"

"I have no idea. It's one of the things I want you to find out."

"Why the hell does this matter?" he asked.

"Because Brie is the catalyst for what happened in South Sudan."

The idea had crossed his mind too, but Savvy sounded certain. "Why do you think that?"

"She saw a man from Druneft—who used to work for her father—and a man who might be one of exiled General Lawiri's bodyguards in that market. If that indicates an alliance between Erfan Lawiri and the owner of Druneft, Nikolai Drugov, then we've got a serious problem. Brie is the connection between all these elements, and I don't believe it was a mistake she ended up in that market. If either Lawiri or Drugov is running that market, why were they so determined to capture and sell her?

"This is about her, her family, and oil. My job is to gather intel. South Sudan is on our radar because of the oil reserves and the opportunities for enemy states to seize power in the destabilized democracy. To Brie, it might be small and personal, but there are worldwide implications."

He closed his eyes, thinking of the woman who hid her vulnerabilities behind a dry, self-deprecating wit. "You want me to seduce her into opening up and telling me about her family."

"Yes."

"That's a shitty thing to ask of me, and a horrible thing to do to Brie."

Nary a ripple of remorse flickered across Savannah James's face. "So? You want her. That's been obvious from the start."

"If you know anything about me, it's that I don't hang out for postcoital chitchat." Shit. He never screwed around with anyone he might care about. Cece had taught him to avoid relationships, and he sure as hell couldn't open the door to feelings between him and Brie. Something had happened in South Sudan. He wouldn't be able to sleep with her and keep his heart locked down tight. It was why he'd avoided her from the moment they'd arrived on the aircraft carrier.

Using sex to get her to talk would be cruel to them both.

"You sleep around. She sleeps around. It's not like I'm asking you to do anything either of you are averse to."

"I don't fuck for the Army."

"Maybe it's time to start. Put your dick to good use."

"I'm Special Forces, not a spy. You can't force this on me."

Savvy leaned forward and held his gaze. "No. But if you don't, I'll find someone else. I've already got a list. Lieutenant Fallon would be perfect. Civilians just love Navy SEALs."

Jealousy like he'd never imagined filled a void in his chest. "You really are a bitch, you know that?"

"No, Bastian. I'm a patriot."

"Bullshit. You just like screwing with people's heads." No way would Fallon agree to her plan. This was manipulation, pure and simple.

Her eyes hardened, but she offered no excuses. "As long as Brie is on the *Dahlgren* recuperating, so are you. Your superiors at SOCOM know the situation and have agreed not to interfere. They don't like it, but they see the big picture. The staff here have their orders to leave you alone. It's why you've been given separate rooms instead of being assigned beds in the main ward. You'll have unfettered access to Ms. Stewart while she's here. The no-fraternization rules on an aircraft carrier won't apply to you." She gave him a tight smile. "Fuck her. Don't fuck her. That's up to you. The point is to get her talking, and report back to me once you learn anything that might be important."

B rie fiddled with the bow she'd tied at her waist, embarrassed she'd sought Bastian out in a moment of weakness, that she'd wanted him to see the silly outfit she'd made, after a week of wearing improvised clothing that included rubber tire sandals.

Here she was on a massive Navy vessel, still improvising. It was meant to be a silly, shared joke. Better quality than ratty old-tarp underwear.

Once upon a time, she'd lived a life that required high fashion. In that world, the rubber-tire sandals would have been perfectly acceptable, as long as they had a thousand-dollar price tag.

She knew more than a few of her friends from that era now wore diamond-encrusted "ally" safety pins. They weren't bad people, but they were clueless. White, shallow, and rich, they didn't see how white privilege had shaped the world and their place in it.

Brie was no saint, and she was aware she benefited from a great deal of white privilege even without her family's money—after all, an A-Team had been sent to rescue her in South Sudan. If that wasn't privilege at work, nothing was. She tried to be thankful for the gifts she was granted and to use them to give back, to be a force for change, instead of being defensive and full of denial. She still failed, and it wasn't like she'd renounced the house in Morocco once she'd learned she was one-third owner. But she tried to be aware and to correct her own actions when her unconscious exercise of privilege came to light.

Of course, she could do more good if she hadn't gotten herself cut off from the family billions. The money could have done far more for others than the questionable donation of her time and attention, such as it was.

In the long run, wasn't getting cut off the most selfish thing she could have done? Standing on principle had helped no one, least of all herself. Now her family operated without a conscience—not that they'd had one even when she was in the fold—and did more damage without her there to speak for the trees.

She was a shitty Lorax.

Selfish to the bitter end, she chose her pride over the trees. Her honor over environmental justice.

She'd left the money behind and helped no one.

When she looked back at her life, was there anything she could point to that she could be proud of? She'd thought that would be her work for USAID, but now it was likely her presence in South Sudan had only endangered the people she wanted to help.

She fiddled with her gauze belt. She'd been good at fashion. Clothing and makeup had been fun. She'd enjoyed the parties, the flash and glamour. It was why she'd wanted to model for that creep Grigory to begin with. The ultimate dress-up game where she got to be pretty and sexy, clueless that it would be a magnet for pedophiles.

Her mother had been a fashion model in her heyday and taught Brie tricks of the trade, like dressing up a boring outfit with a silly bow. Now the gauze flower felt pathetic. Like wearing a gaudy, diamond-encrusted safety pin.

No amount of accessories would make her an ally when her presence in South Sudan had brought pain and suffering.

Gabriella had been makeup, flowers, and diamonds. An accessory of Prime Energy, who could be had for the right price.

Brie was… She didn't know exactly who Brie was. She'd been trying to be someone else. Someone worthy to make up for the work she'd done for Prime Energy. But that woman was a fraud too. She wasn't selfless or magnanimous. She was merely seeking self-serving redemption.

A tear spilled down her cheek, and she realized she was in a self-pity spiral. The kind that once upon a time had led to drinking and drugs. The kind that could lead her there again if she wasn't careful.

All because Bastian hadn't come to see her in the three days they'd been in the medical ward together. She was pathetic, pinning her self-worth on a man.

Jesus. This was why she'd avoided relationships. Emotional attachment always led to this. The bleak spiral. The self-loathing. The desire to use.

A drink would soothe the ache. A pill would take away the pain. A needle would deliver her to bliss.

No.

Fuck. No.

I am better than this.

She stood and paced her small room, leaning on the cane. Dr. Crane wanted her to walk, to work her leg muscles. She'd get her wish, because walking was how Brie always faced the pull of craving. The ache for escape.

She preferred running, but she was days—weeks?— from being able to run any distance. So she paced her small room, not daring to leave the confined space because she might run into Bastian or the men on his team.

Men who'd risked their lives for her unworthy ass. The cane slipped on the floor, and her leg nearly buckled.

Pain shot up her hip.

Shit. Shit. Shit.

Deep breath. Slow down. Plant the cane. Walk. One foot in front of the other.

"The kids escaped."

The deep male voice came from the doorway. She turned to see one of the soldiers who'd been in Bastian's room. He was tall with wide shoulders. Utterly imposing. "The ones in the market?" she asked.

"Yes." He stepped into the room. "Master Sergeant Pax Blanchard," he said, holding out a hand.

Her right hand gripped the cane, so she offered her left. "Brie Stewart."

"Sorry," he said, switching to his left.

"Are they still in South Sudan, the kids?"

"Most of them escaped into the White Nile or the Sudd—they told us that's where their parents were, on the islands, hidden in the swamp. We got two out with Savvy's help, but she's being secretive about where they are."

"She does enjoy keeping her secrets."

Blanchard nodded. "The market—it was destroyed. I thought you'd want to know. No kids will ever be sold there again."

Emotion swamped her. She covered her mouth as she sucked in a breath. "Thank you. It means a lot to know something good came out of…what happened."

"Bastian insisted we save the kids. It was his plan."

She understood what he didn't say. Because they'd saved the kids, the rest of the A-Team hadn't been there to back up her extraction, leaving her and Bastian stranded. They'd been on their own when the team could have swooped in, rescued her, and left.

As if she needed another reason to respect Chief Warrant Officer Sebastian Ford. "I wouldn't have it any other way."

The soldier nodded. "Glad to see you're recovering."

"Thank you, Sergeant—and please share my thanks

with everyone on your team."

"If you visit Camp Citron before you leave, you can thank the team yourself."

"I have no idea where I'll go from here, but I hope I'll get that chance."

He nodded. "It was nice meeting you, Ms. Stewart." With that he turned and left, and she was once again alone, waiting and wondering.

Waiting for the man who'd saved her in South Sudan. Wondering why he hadn't visited her in the last three days. And hating herself for wanting to see him. For valuing his opinion of her more than she valued her own.

H e was a coward, plain and simple. He should have gone to see Brie the moment Savvy left. But Bastian had stayed in his room like the chickenshit he was.

Now it was two a.m., and he couldn't sleep. He wanted to see her. Read aloud to her. Talk to her. Play quarters with her. Do everything Savvy had ordered him to do with her.

But it was Savvy's orders that also held him back. He couldn't use her like that. He couldn't get involved.

He also couldn't walk away.

His head ached, and it had nothing to do with the concussion.

He tossed aside the bedcovers. No way was he sleeping tonight. His room was too small. He stepped out and nodded to the hospital corpsman who monitored the ward overnight. He was just going to pace. That was all.

He wasn't going to see Brie.

Just because he stood outside her room didn't mean he

was going inside. But the same compulsion had him turning the knob on her door and silently entering her room. There were enough lights on the medical monitors that he could see her sleeping form on the bed.

There. He'd confirmed she was here. Time to go before he woke her.

He settled into her visitor's chair, because clearly, his brain no longer controlled his body. He watched the rise and fall of her chest and tried to figure out why he was here.

"This is a little creepy," she whispered.

He startled, bumping her rolling meal table and knocking it into the wall with a loud bang.

She laughed. "Smooth, Chief."

He ran a hand down his face and shook his head. "That's me. *Smooth*."

"What are you doing here at..." Her voice trailed off as she looked at the clock. "Two in the morning?"

"I missed you," he blurted, like the fool he was. "I wanted to see you."

"Bullshit. You could've seen me any time in the last few days, but you waited until the dead of night."

He reached out, took her hand, and cradled it in his. "It's true. I've missed you. And true I could have come sooner. I'm sorry I didn't."

"Why didn't you?"

He threaded his fingers through hers. Her hands were smooth but not soft, the fingers slender and warm. He'd forgotten the pleasure of simply holding hands. Forgotten how the touch could be laden with anticipation and trigger a spread of warmth.

Just as he'd entered her room without conscious thought, he pulled her fingers to his mouth and nipped at the tips. Then he sucked her index finger and enjoyed her soft gasp of surprise.

"What do you think you're doing?" she asked.

"Holding your hand."

"With your mouth?"

He smiled and moved to suck on her middle finger.

She touched his chin. "You look good without the beard."

"Which do you like better? Bearded or without?"

"I don't know. I only saw you without for a minute, and it's dark in here. I'll tell you tomorrow."

He turned her hand palm up and began to massage, applying pressure to the muscle between thumb and index finger. "I need to thank this hand, for saving my life."

"Just the hand?"

"And the brain it's connected to." He massaged up her arm. "How is the leg?"

"Getting better. It still hurts, but I can walk if I don't put too much weight on it. The ankle sprain is almost gone too. How's your head?"

"Better. Vision isn't blurry anymore. Headache is mild. But I can't sleep."

"So you figured if you can't sleep, I might as well be awake too?" Her voice was soft and sleepy but held humor.

"Scoot over."

"What?"

He stood. "Scoot over. So I can lie down. I think I'll be able to sleep if I'm with you."

She did as instructed, and he settled in next to her, raising the railing at his back to keep himself from falling off the narrow bed. It was too small for two people.

"You might be able to sleep, but I don't think I will," she said.

He pulled up the railing on her side as well, trapping her in with him. "There. Now we can pretend this is a pillow fort." He pulled her snug against him, so they were chest to chest, hip to hip. She smelled of a flowery soap, and he wanted to nibble on her neck to see if she tasted as sweet as she smelled.

"Aren't you going to get in trouble for this?"

Savvy had cleared that path for him, but he couldn't admit that to her. "I'll sneak out early."

"The person on duty at the desk might see you."

"He did. He didn't say anything. Honestly, I don't think he cares." That was certainly true.

"Why were you avoiding me, Bastian?"

He ran his fingers through her short hair. "Because I'm a bastard." *Also true.* He leaned into her and kissed her nose. "I'm here now." He traced her eyebrows and cheekbones with a fingertip. "Go to sleep, Brie. You're safe. I promise, you're safe."

Far too late, but the truest thing he'd ever said.

Chapter Twenty

Sleeping pressed against Bastian's side wasn't the most comfortable Brie had ever been. This was why she'd had a strict policy of never spending the night. It was sweet to try to sleep cuddled up to a guy, but sleep in those situations was usually elusive.

She turned on her side, putting her weight on her left—and uninjured leg. In a sleepy haze, he draped his arm over her, spooning his knees behind hers, his crotch pressed to her ass.

Okay. That wasn't so bad.

It was kinda nice, actually, the feel of his firm thighs against hers, his arm cuddling her, making her feel safe.

She closed her eyes.

Bastian was in bed with her. Holding her. It was a fantasy come true, having the big, warm Green Beret wrapped around her as he slept.

The comfort lulled her to sleep, and she dreamed vivid, awful dreams that escaped her conscious mind when the loud snoring of the man at her back intruded into her somnolent abyss.

Not only was he snoring, but he'd rolled to his back and was taking up three-quarters of the narrow bed.

He was the worst sort of slumber party guest, a loud bed hog.

She elbowed him gently. "Bastian. You're snoring."

He rolled to his side, cupping her breast as he burrowed his mouth into her neck. "Sorry," he murmured and promptly dropped back into a deep sleep.

She smiled, enjoying the embrace. They'd spent days together, yet they'd never dared to sleep at the same time.

Sex was one thing, but simultaneous sleeping… It brought intimacy to a whole new level.

She covered the hand that cupped her breast, smiling at the casual contact, and drifted back into a deep sleep.

B astian woke, his arms full of woman. And not just any woman, but the one he wanted more than sun and air and food combined. Her gorgeous, rounded ass was cradled against his rock-hard erection in what had to be the smallest bed that had ever accommodated two people.

Suddenly, he was grateful all beds weren't king-sized. He'd take a narrow bunk with Brie any day. But this wasn't his bunk, it was a hospital bed, and all at once he remembered he had to keep up the charade, to vacate her bed before dawn lit the sky.

He'd never been more reluctant to leave a woman's bed, and this after an adulthood spent escaping at the very first opportunity.

But then, he hadn't been inside Brie's body—not yet. This wasn't a post-sex cuddle session. This had been sleep and comfort and basically asking for trouble. He never shared a bed for sleep after sex, so this begged the question: what did it mean to sleep with a woman without sex?

Even worse, he didn't want to leave her. He'd slept deeper in the last four hours than he had in weeks—

maybe months.

Damn. This could be habit forming. Like a sleeping pill.

He kissed her neck as he scooted back to extract himself from her side.

"Bastian?" she said in a sleepy voice.

"I need to go back to my own room, sweetheart."

She rolled to her back and faced him. "Are you going to ignore me when the sun rises? Like before?"

"No." He kissed her eyebrow. "I'm done being a bastard."

"Promise?"

"Cross my heart."

She offered him a faint smile. "Kiss me?"

He cupped her face between his palms and gave her what she asked for. His tongue slid between her lips and claimed her mouth.

Kissing her was the best thing in his screwed-up world. Her tongue met his, a sweet, hot stroke that weakened his defenses.

He should keep his distance. Keep this physical. Only physical.

Impossible.

She sucked on his tongue and reached down between them, stroking his erection. He groaned into her mouth.

He found the strength to pull back. "Your leg is bound to get hurt if we take this any further now."

"I could go down on you." He could hear the grin in her voice. "And you could go down on me."

Damn. He wanted to do that for her and so much more. And he loved the fact that she wasn't shy about stating what she wanted. But the intimacy of oral sex, now, was too soon. Not if he wanted Brie to open up to him about her family. For that, he had to take things slow, not treat her like this was quick, convenient sex.

The problem was...he didn't know how to conduct a slow seduction. He'd prided himself on his honesty with the women he had sex with. No false promises, no commitment. Sex today, goodbye tomorrow.

This had to be different.

Crawling into bed with her had been an impulse—and a good one. Not having any kind of sex with her now felt similarly right.

He'd follow his gut when it came to seducing Brie.

"Sweetheart, no way can I taste you and stop there. It's gonna happen but not until you can enjoy it without risking injury." He kissed her neck again, then lowered the rail and slipped from the bed. With one last kiss on her lips, he said, "Go back to sleep. I'll see you in a few hours."

Bastian showed up at Brie's door after she'd finished her morning shower and the nurse had changed the bandage around her leg.

She was more than sponge-bath clean, and, for the first time in nearly two weeks, she had real clothes to wear, thanks to Savvy, who'd dropped several items off when she'd visited yesterday.

The clothes had been purchased at Camp Citron's store and carried different messages about Djibouti, playing with the "ja-booty" pronunciation of the country's name. She didn't care about the tired jokes, she was just grateful to have more than a stained cloth or hospital gown to wear.

"Nice to see you dressed," Bastian said as his gaze

swept her appreciatively.

She stood and twirled, as if the sweatpants and T-shirt were a fancy gown. She wobbled mid-spin. She'd forgotten to grab the cane.

He caught her and pulled her to him.

She leaned against his chest, liking the feel of him and liking even more that there were no rules here. This wasn't forbidden or dangerous. Just fun.

She *needed* fun.

"Saved me again," she said.

A corner of his mouth curled upward. "I should start charging a toll."

She played with the collar of his shirt. "I can think of ways to repay you."

His laugh was warm and deep, and, pressed against him as she was, she felt it in her solar plexus. "I like the way you think, Ms. Stewart." He brushed his lips over hers in a sweet, quick kiss, then released her. He held up his phone. "I was thinking we could finish the book we started to pass the time."

"I'd like that. I've been going out of my mind with boredom." It had been a mixture of boredom and anxiety as she wondered why Bastian hadn't come to see her. She'd been bedridden the first two days, so going to see him hadn't been an option. "I need to walk for a bit. Join me in the hallway? Then we can read."

After ten minutes of pacing the hall, they returned to her room and settled in. She sat up in her bed and read to him. The crime scene investigation scenes were easy to read aloud, but eventually, Brie reached a sex scene. She smiled and glanced sideways at Bastian, then continued reading, adding more emotion to her voice as she read the dialogue, adding in a little breathy panting, even if it wasn't on the page.

Bastian cleared his throat. "Maybe you should skip that scene."

She raised a brow, noting his erection as he sat in the chair next to her bed. "But it's just getting good."

He shook his head. "I'm in pain enough as it is. Show some mercy, woman."

The cell phone in her hands chose that moment to ring. "Saved by the bell," she said, handing the phone to him, noting Savvy was his caller.

"Chief Ford," he said as he answered. His expression went blank as he gave the CIA officer yes and no answers. Several curses were followed by, "Fine," and then, "I'll tell her." He hung up.

"What's going on?"

"Prime Energy leaked the story of your abduction and rescue in South Sudan. It's all over the news. South Sudan's president is demanding answers for why he wasn't informed the US military conducted a covert operation in his country."

"Uh, maybe because it was covert?" Brie said, to cover the sinking feeling in her gut. "Who told PE about my abduction? I left strict instructions for USAID to never contact my family. No matter what."

"Senator Albert Jackson spilled the beans about the op to your family. I take it you know him?"

Shit. "Uncle Al," she said softly. Then she met Bastian's gaze. "He's not really my uncle." Albert Jackson was a Texas oilman, and an associate of her father's. She'd known him since she was a baby and had been uncomfortable around the man ever since that stupid photo shoot when she was thirteen. Every time he saw her after that, he offered her a lollipop—he always had one in his pocket, just for her. It had taken her until she was fifteen to figure out why.

She'd been surprisingly naïve for someone who'd been so publicly sexualized at thirteen—but that was part of how it happened, that naïveté made it impossible for her to understand the innuendo of the photos.

At fifteen, one of Rafe's friends had cornered her and spelled it all out for her. Told her what was being said behind her back, told her to stop taking the damn lollipops from Uncle Al. That it was her cluelessness and innocence that turned the asshole on. Rafe's friend had been one of the few good guys in her life, someone who looked out for her, like a big brother.

Once her eyes had been opened, it had hurt that her actual brothers hadn't shown the same concern, but they were their father's sons.

After that, she'd picked up on Uncle Al's other advances, which included "accidental" groping until the time she "accidently" kneed him in the balls.

"So what does this mean?" she asked Bastian. "Besides I'll never be able to work for USAID in a developing country again?" She'd expected that and honestly didn't know if she wanted to return to aid work after everything that had happened, but still, having the choice taken from her triggered an ache.

But then, she didn't have to be in the developing world to personally pass out reusable menstruation underwear to adolescent girls. She could raise money for the project of her heart. Girls wouldn't be held back from going to school simply because they hit puberty. She could— would—make a difference even if she never set foot inside the third world again.

"The DoD is scrambling to make it clear the US hasn't

chosen sides in the war, and part of that is putting on a show of the military action being personal—Senator Jackson is on his way to Camp Citron now and tomorrow there will be a 'surprise' ceremony with a large press corps on *Dahlgren*'s flight deck—celebrating the safe exfiltration of the daughter of a close personal friend who also happens to be as close as we get to American royalty."

"I am *not* a princess. My dad is a billionaire, but that doesn't make me a princess." Oh, hell. The press would bring up the cosmetic ads again. Given that they'd been banned due to her age, at least most news outlets wouldn't show the images. They'd move on from her short-lived modeling career to rehashing the handful of incidents when she was drunk or high and made an ass of herself. She had no doubt they'd make snide remarks about her work for USAID, questioning her motives, brains, and sincerity. To top it off, her anonymity would be gone forever.

"I don't suppose I can refuse to be a part of the ceremony?" she asked with a grimace.

Bastian's look was sympathetic as he shook his head. "The ceremony will also honor the anonymous Special Forces and SEAL teams that rescued you. I'll be on deck for the ceremony but won't be identified."

"Lucky," she said, trying to make light of the fact that she felt like her entire world was crashing in. "Uncle" Al made her skin crawl. Just thinking of him, she needed to move. To walk. She climbed from the bed. "I need air."

"The flight deck is restricted."

"There's got to be another deck…someplace I can go." She could feel panic crowding in and took a slow, deep breath. *Get a grip, girl. It's just a dog-and-pony show.*

Back in the day, you fronted dozens of those without breaking a sweat.

Yeah, but then she'd been a high-functioning addict, and her ability to pull off big media events while using had been part of the rush.

Bastian stared at her for a long moment. He must've seen the desperation on her face, because he said, "I'll check with the doc," and left the room.

He left his phone on his seat, and she picked it up. She would call Savvy. She needed details. She entered his passcode and unlocked it as a message from Savvy popped up. In hitting the button to open the call log, she accidently opened the message, which read: *Need answers, ASAP.*

Brie snorted. *Yeah. Don't we all.*

What answers Savvy expected Bastian to provide while cooped up on an aircraft carrier, Brie couldn't begin to guess, but it probably had something to do with the market. Savvy had been after Brie to remember every last detail, and was probably hounding Bastian just as hard.

From the log screen, she called Savvy's number. The woman answered immediately. "Can you talk now?"

"Yeah. But this isn't Bastian." Unease settled in her gut. She wanted to talk to Bastian when he was alone? Well, she could hardly judge that. The woman was CIA and Bastian was Special Forces—and Brie knew SOCOM missions were classified, even from the people who'd been the focus of the op.

"I take it Bastian told you about Senator Jackson."

"Yes." She steeled her spine. "I don't want to be part of anyone's photo op—least of all Albert Jackson's."

"You don't have a choice."

"I disagree. This is just a PR stunt for him—a cool photo op he can use to raise campaign funds in the future, and I don't want to be a part of that. It's not like the South Sudan government has any real reason to complain about a SOCOM op to save US citizens."

"While that's true, you still need to be part of the ceremony. Jackson sits on the Armed Services Committee—that's how he learned of the op. I shouldn't have to remind you you're being given medical care on a Navy aircraft carrier after an A-Team and SEALs risked their lives to save you. You can't snub the military that just saved your ass."

"I'm grateful to the military, but Albert Jackson is a creeper."

"Be glad he isn't bringing your brother with him. Jeffery Junior was pushing for a visit. I worked my ass off to crush that plan, pointing out that this is an ongoing investigation and Jeffery Junior has zero security clearance or vetting."

The idea of seeing JJ on *Dahlgren* gave her heartburn. Well, "Uncle" Al had one thing going for him—he wasn't a Prime.

She was in a corner. But that didn't mean she couldn't call the shots.

"Here are my terms: Jackson will not touch me—not even for a handshake. I'll read a written statement. I won't answer any questions or speak with the senator on or off camera. Any of these terms are violated, and I'll tell the world about how he groped me when I was fifteen. If he balks at these terms, tell him I'll mention the lollipops."

"Navy brass will want to review your statement first."

"Agreed." She looked down at the clothes she had on.

Should she face the cameras as Brie or Gabriella? She sighed. This would be easier with the armor of makeup, and she really wanted to keep Brie to herself. It was time to resurrect Gabriella Prime. "And Savvy, I'm going to need makeup. Commercial grade, camera ready. And clothes fitting an American princess."

Bastian took Brie to an upper deck to walk and get fresh air, which seemed to calm her, but her tension returned once they were back inside her small, windowless room. He coaxed her into talking about the senator, and rage burned in his gut when she described the lollipops and how her brother's twenty-year-old friend had to explain the subtext of what Jackson was doing.

"I'm so sorry, Brie. I hate it that the men in your life never looked out for you. I want to kick Jackson's, your dad's, and your brothers' asses."

Savvy wanted to know more about her brothers; here was his chance.

"At least Rafe had a decent friend. I had a crush on him for a time—probably because he didn't look at me like a piece of meat." She smiled. "He married a friend of mine about five years ago. Rafe was best man. They invited me to the wedding, but I didn't go. It was their day, and while Rafe isn't as bad as JJ, there were no guarantees there wouldn't be tension."

And here he had an opening. "When was the last time you saw your brothers?"

She wrinkled her nose, telling him just thinking about it made her uncomfortable. "Eight years ago."

"What happened?"

"I left the business and refused to be their puppet," she said in a stiff tone. There was more to the story.

"What did they want you to do? What—"

She held up a hand. "My thigh is really throbbing right now. I think I want to close my eyes a bit."

He knew she wouldn't take anything stronger than ibuprofen for pain, so her request was reasonable, but the way she said it told him she was deflecting. "If you ever want to talk, Brie—"

"I think you should go and let me rest."

He stood, leaned over her, and pressed his lips to her forehead. "Can I come back tonight? To sleep?" He realized as soon as the words slipped from his mouth, he had no ulterior motive for the request. He just wanted to hold her.

"Better not. I need to get a decent night's sleep if I'm going to be ready for tomorrow afternoon's circus."

Bastian was certain of one thing as he left her room. The direct approach wouldn't work. No wonder Savvy wanted him to seduce her.

Chapter Twenty-One

Bastian showed up at Brie's room midmorning the following day. He'd already had breakfast, met with the doctor for morning rounds, and had a lengthy phone conversation with Savvy. But all he'd wanted was to see Brie, knowing she'd be tense today.

He smiled, seeing her in a tight T-shirt and yoga pants that cupped her gorgeous ass as she bent forward, sorting through items in a shopping bag that rested on the guest chair. "Mornin', beautiful," he said.

She startled, bolting upright and turning. Then she smiled, a broad grin that showed some of yesterday's tension had left her. She plucked the bag from the chair, clearing the seat for him, and said, "Morning." Her gaze swept him from head to toe, then she added, "Handsome?"

He laughed. "We only get three minutes of shower water. I'm not going to clean up until before the stupid deck ceremony." He dropped into the vacated visitor's chair. "Until then, this is what you get." Twenty-four-hour stubble and a sleepless night meant he looked like he had a hangover.

"Bad night?" she asked.

He gave a tight nod. His head hurt like a bitch. A reminder that he might be hanging out in the medical ward to seduce her, but the concussion was real. Guilt had contributed to his sleepless night. He didn't want deception in their relationship, but Savvy had a point. Brie was holding back a painful event that could be relevant.

But then again, it might not be. It could just be ugly family dynamics.

She walked up to him and placed her fingers in his hair, and slowly, gently, began to massage, avoiding the cut above his ear.

He let out a soft groan. Her touch was just right, raking her nails sweetly across his scalp, massaging in small circles that released tension. He leaned forward, planting his forehead against her belly. "God, that feels good."

She worked her way forward and back, giving his whole head the gentle treatment. "I don't think I've ever properly thanked you for rescuing me," she murmured. Her lips brushed the bandage over the cut where he'd taken the concussive blow as her fingers moved lower on his neck and shoulders, where she dug in deeper, and he realized just how stiff his neck and shoulders were.

He groaned again.

She worked his shoulder muscles, and his tension melted in gradual degrees. He let out a slow breath and raised his head. Her breasts were level with his mouth, and all he wanted was to lick her and make her feel good too. No ulterior motive. Just healing touch. He cupped her hips and pulled her forward, being gentle with her wounded leg as he pulled her to straddle him on the chair.

She settled in place over his erection. She let out a soft "Oh," and scooted forward, rocking against him as he placed a hand on the back of her neck and pulled her mouth to his.

The kiss was hot and slow and deep, and he cursed himself for leaving the door wide open, limiting how far it could go. He released her mouth and said, "You're welcome."

B rie wanted this sweet, sexy moment to last forever...except her foot couldn't touch the floor while she straddled him on the chair, putting stress on her thigh and causing it to ache. She pressed a kiss to his lips, then said, "Leg," and scooted from his lap.

"Sorry," he said. He stood and placed his hand at the small of her back for the two steps it took to get to her bed.

"It's okay." She settled on her bed and raised the back to a sitting position and propped a pillow beneath her right knee like the doctor had suggested. She leaned back and smiled at him, taking in the concern in his eyes. "It's fine once pressure is off the wound."

"Can I do anything?"

"Just keep me company. We've got an hour before I need to start getting ready."

He scooted the visitor's chair close to the side of her bed and took her hand in both of his. "You got it." He kissed her knuckles.

She swept her hand to the shopping bag. "Savvy sent me makeup. And clothes." She didn't know how she felt about Bastian seeing her as Gabriella again. He didn't like Gabriella, but he liked Brie. And she *was* Brie.

But there was a part of her that had loved Gabriella's power. Gabriella was strong and smart and regal. If she could be Gabriella without chemical boosters, would she return to the role?

Now that Brie couldn't be an aid worker, she might have to. Gabriella knew how to fund-raise and cut deals. Gabriella had all the money contacts who could make her project happen. Brie didn't.

Whether she wanted Bastian to see her as Gabriella or not was moot. It would happen. In just a few hours. She bit her lip and cast about for something to talk about. "Have you told your parents you're going to be on the news today?"

His mouth tightened, but he nodded. "Actually, yes. I wasn't going to, but some of the guys on the rez will get a kick out of seeing me wearing my green beret, so I sent them an email."

"Your parents should be proud."

He shrugged. "Yes and no."

Okay, he didn't want to talk about his parents. She could respect that, but she still wanted to know more about him beyond that he was a badass, hot Green Beret. "Tell me about your hometown. Both Coho and the Kalahwamish Indian Reservation. I've heard a lot about Coho's living history museum, but I've only driven past that stretch of Discovery Bay, never had time to visit it."

"Discovery Bay, Coho, and the rez are beautiful, each in their own way." He smiled, and his eyes took on a distant stare, telling her he was visiting his home in his mind. "Growing up on the rez, with all those acres of forest, living at the edge of the bay, was…special. I mean, there was poverty—it's an Indian reservation, and Coho was a logging and sawmill town owned and ruled by a bigot for most of the twentieth century. As a tribe, we paid a huge price. But still, the rez was—is—*ours*. Our own nation. About fifteen years ago, we got the sawmill properties back, which changed our bottom line, but not our way of life. My mom is tribal chairwoman and has been since I was in my teens. So the Kalahwamish *really* felt like mine. My mom. My tribe. My whole world.

"It's hard to describe, how personal the reservation feels to an Indian. It's not like an old family farm for white people. We're talking about land that has been ours for thousands of years. Since the beginning of time."

He cocked his head. "I'm not the kind of Indian who doesn't believe in evolution. I get it—we *all* came from somewhere else. In fact, we came from here." He released her hand and spread his arms. "Or rather, Africa—fifty or so nautical miles to the west of us. Hell, I got to hold the Linus fossil in my hands last month— which was fucking mind-blowing—but still, I share my tribe's core beliefs. We respect our elders and the land. Our connection to our ancestors is intertwined with sacred sites, on and off the rez. That connection goes deeper for us, especially because we've had to fight so hard to keep it—our reservation, our language, the potlatch ceremony, our treaty rights. We've had to fight to keep every aspect of our culture. And now we have to fight to keep white people from appropriating the very thing we had to fight so hard to maintain to begin with."

She knew of all the atrocities tribes had faced: their language and the potlatch ceremony had been outlawed for many years. Children had been rounded up and sent to boarding schools to erase their connection to their native heritage. And this all came after the attempts at genocide that included smallpox blankets being given to natives by the British forces during the French and Indian War.

But knowledge wasn't the same as understanding.

She'd grown up white and wealthy and no amount of empathy could put her in his shoes.

All she could do was squeeze his hand. "You must miss it, being based out of Fort Campbell and then being sent for long deployments abroad."

He shrugged as if it was no big deal, yet he'd just made it clear it was a big deal. "Where did you grow up?" he asked. "You've mentioned Florida, but I thought your brothers live in New York?"

"We had half a dozen houses all over the world that we divided our time between, including New York and Florida. But none of them ever felt like a home." Really, none of them had been safe. She frowned, realizing he'd turned the conversation to her, when she really wanted to know about him. "When was the last time you were home?"

He grimaced. "Four years ago."

"Four years? Surely the Army gives you leave between deployments?" Given everything he said about how important his home was to him, that made no sense.

"They do. I haven't wanted to visit."

～⌇～

It occurred to Bastian when he asked about where she grew up that if he wanted her to talk about her family, he would need to open up about his. The more he shared, the more likely she was to do the same. But it had to be real, or she'd never open up.

This meant he'd have to talk about things he didn't share with anyone. Not even Cal and Espi. His friends on the rez knew, but they'd never *talked* about it. They understood without words why he didn't visit.

He held out hope that if she confided in him—without

sex as part of the equation—she wouldn't hate him when she learned the truth. He wouldn't feel like such a bastard.

He wouldn't *be* such a bastard.

"Why don't you want to visit?" she asked, her tone tentative.

For once, he welcomed the question. It was his opening. "My college girlfriend, Cece, grew up in the Skagit Valley. Her dad is Upper Skagit, her mom Kalahwamish. Ten years ago, right after we graduated college, she moved to Coho. She had big plans for us, but I'd been trying to break up with her for months. Technically, we *were* broken up. I'd ended it. She lived in Coho. I lived on the rez. I told her she shouldn't move to the peninsula for me. We were done.

"But my parents... They love Cece. My mom especially." His sister had died in a car accident just the year before, making his mom's attachment to Cece all the more intense. But he didn't tell Brie that. Talking about Lily was a different kind of pain and one he couldn't face in that moment.

He cleared his throat and continued. "Once Cece settled in Coho, my feelings were irrelevant. My mom told her I was going through a phase and would come around. When I found out she'd booked the Warren Cultural Center for our wedding, I couldn't take it anymore. I told Cece—*again*—we were never getting married, and I wanted her to leave Coho." He shook his head, back in the moment when his mother pulled him aside and told him not to be rash. He could take a break from Cece if he needed to think, but his mom had made it clear she hoped he would get his head on straight and marry her. She also reminded him it was Cece's tribe too, and she had as much right to live there as he did.

His mother was right about that, and he'd felt like a shit. Cece might not have grown up on Kalahwamish land, but she had the same deep connection to the place and people.

He told Brie this in halting words. He'd never verbalized it before. "But then, I found an escape. Cece wouldn't leave the rez, but I could. I joined the Army." He paced the small room. "My mom was devastated. She felt rejected. Like I was giving up the tribe. Betraying them. After all, I had a college degree—paid for with a tribal scholarship—and was supposed to use it for the good of my people." He dropped his gaze to the floor, reminding himself that only raw honesty would get him where he wanted to go. "I was glad my mom hurt. I'd hoped it meant she'd finally understand, because I felt rejected and betrayed too. Meanwhile, my dad was proud, but I don't think he really understood why I'd joined."

He lifted his head and met Brie's gaze. "And for my part...I *loved* the Army. It was a new family that kicked my ass on a daily basis. But they valued me. Honed me." He spread his arms wide. "I get to see the world and make a difference. Just ten days ago, I rescued a woman from a slave market while my team freed dozens of kids who were about to be sold."

He liked the way Brie smiled at that.

"I wasn't ROTC in college and didn't seek Officer Training School because I went the technical specialist route to become a warrant officer. My dad figured I'd get out as soon as I could, but once I made it through the Special Forces Qualification Course, I knew I was a lifer. This is the only job I want. It's who I am. I've been thinking of applying to OTS so I can make captain and run the team."

"You'd be great as captain." She cocked her head. "So you don't go home because your mom still resents you being in the Army instead of working for the tribe?"

He shook his head. "No. I don't go home because Cece is still there. Still at the heart of my family. She's on the tribal council now, my mother's protégé. She's a good steward, and I'm sure the tribe has benefited from all the work she does. She's not a bad person. But when I visit, I don't want to spend every minute with my ex who usurped my role in my family."

"And she doesn't respect your need for time alone with your parents?"

He shrugged. "I'm pretty sure my mom tells her it's okay. My mom is hoping I'll take one look at Cece and fall in love again. But that won't happen."

He'd actually tried on his last visit. He'd spent time with Cece, to see if the intervening years had made a difference. It would have been so easy to give his mother what she wanted if it meant having his home back. But in the end, his emotions were dead where Cece was concerned. He didn't love her. Didn't hate her. He was indifferent. So he'd left and never gone back.

"I'm sorry, Bastian."

"Cece is why I don't get involved. Relationships aren't worth it."

"I get that," she said, giving him an opening for probing questions of his own. But he missed his chance when she continued, "Have you ever tried bringing a woman home? To send the message loud and clear that you've moved on?"

"Are you volunteering?" He shook his head. "It

wouldn't work. My parents would hate you. They'd cling tighter to Cece." He closed his eyes and imagined his mom's shock and horror.

"Excuse me?" Brie's voice was soft. "Am I that awful?"

He opened his eyes, catching her stricken look. Shit. She'd taken it wrong. "No. I mean—you're Oil Company Barbie. And an anthropologist on top of that. They'd hate the idea of you. They'd never bother to get to know the real you."

"Oil Company Barbie?" Her words held an edge. "That's how you think of me?"

"Not anymore."

"But you just called me that."

Shit. He rubbed his hand across his face. "I'm fucking this up. I didn't mean it that way."

She rose from the bed and walked stiffly toward the door, opening it wide. "Even a pretty plastic toy has enough of a brain to discern your meaning. And this doll wants you to leave."

"Brie—"

"Just go. I need to be alone."

Bastian paused in the hall outside her closed door. A moment passed before he heard her sob.

Chapter Twenty-Two

S he'd held her breath, willing herself to keep it together until he left the room. The last thing Brie wanted was for Bastian to see her cry.

Oil Company Barbie? She'd busted her ass for five years as an aid worker. She'd been doing aid work in the midst of a civil war in South fucking Sudan for months, and he still saw her as Oil Company Barbie? It had rolled off his tongue too easily to not be a name he'd been calling her in his head.

It was one of the more condescending nicknames she'd ever heard. As if Princess Prime wasn't bad enough. Pretty much any other man could call her that name, and she'd feel the kick but be able to ignore it. But this wasn't any man. This was Bastian. And fuck, his words *hurt*.

It didn't help that today she'd have to don Princess Prime's makeup and clothes and be that fricking doll. She didn't want to put Brie Stewart in front of the media. Brie was private.

The truth was, Bastian was one of the rare few who got to know the real her.

As a teen, she'd learned to build walls around her heart and mind because so many people wanted to use her for something. They didn't actually give a fuck that she was a person with insecurities and needs. She was a bank account. A company. A daughter expected to use her body to close deals.

And yes, like a Barbie, she'd conducted negotiations while wearing four-inch high heels and perfect makeup. That was what women in her position had to do. Plus she'd smelled good while spearheading projects to skirt environmental regulations. She looked fuckable as she screwed over locals and fudged the facts on the effects of fracking.

She'd escaped from the business. Quit using drugs. Changed her name. Hid her past. And still she never let anyone in. She built even bigger walls.

Ezra, Jaali, and Alan didn't even know she was a Prime. Seven months of living and working together, with limited electricity and Wi-Fi. No TV. And in all those months of late-night talking, because that was the only entertainment to be had, she'd never once shared a detail of her life before grad school, never gave a hint to her background.

That hadn't been possible with Bastian. He'd known who she was. And at first he'd hated who she was. That was fine, because her walls were in place.

But then he'd saved her from a slave market, and her walls crumbled. They'd been stranded together for days and she had no defense. No hidden past.

So she'd been Brie Stewart and Gabriella Prime, combined. An aid worker from a wealthy family. For days in a row, she'd been free of secrets and completely herself. And still, even knowing the real her, Bastian had called her Oil Company Barbie without thought or hesitation.

She took a deep breath and wiped away her tears. She'd liked not having secrets. She'd enjoyed the fact that he knew her ugly but still respected her.

Or so she'd thought.

Another sob rose, and she swallowed it. Brie might care, but Gabriella didn't.

She pulled the magnified makeup mirror from the bag Savvy had sent, relieved to see her eyes weren't puffy. Brie was a crier, but Gabriella wasn't. Today, she'd armor herself with Gabriella's makeup and clothes. Brie had no place here anymore.

She glanced at the dress Savvy had sent. Simple. Classy. Cream and navy blue, it had a sleeveless striped bodice with a cinched waist and flared solid-blue skirt. An elegant throwback to the fifties. It would look better without the white cardigan.

She pulled cover-up from the makeup bag to hide the track marks on her arm. Savvy had sent the right colors, and Brie was an expert at blending. She opened the jar and grabbed a sponge, then stopped.

Gabriella hid all her faults and was as plastic as the doll Bastian had called her. Now that her identity had been revealed, she didn't have to revert all the way back.

To a certain degree, she could be her real self with everyone now, not just Bastian. That meant owning her past, even the ugly, shameful parts. She left her arm alone and started on her face.

B astian stood on the flight deck in clean ACUs and green beret, waiting for the key parties to assemble for the press conference. He hated this kind of event and wished his team was here to suffer with him, but SOCOM had wanted him to fly solo on this.

The senator stepped out on the flight deck with his entourage. The traveling press corps snapped photos of the man in a completely unnecessary flight suit, considering he'd arrived on a helicopter and would be leaving the same way.

These guys loved to play dress up. The sailor nearest to Bastian whispered, "That asshole avoided Vietnam. Tennis elbow or similar bullshit. It only flared up when it was exam time."

"Prick," Bastian muttered. The fact that Jackson was a creeper who'd groped Brie when she was fifteen made him want to deck the man, but that would be a fast ticket to the brig.

The senator waved and grinned at the press, then turned to the sailors and airmen who'd been assembled for this ceremony. Bastian was with a group of soldiers and sailors who would stand behind the senator as he faced the press and crew. Bastian was part of the backdrop to make Senator Jackson look important.

Standing several feet to Bastian's right was Captain Shaw, USS *Dahlgren*'s commanding officer, who shook the senator's hand. Next to him was Rear Admiral Howard, the commander of the carrier's strike group.

Smiles were stiff and perfunctory on all but Senator Jackson, who bore a wide grin. He looked like a kid on a field trip.

Senators were rarely honored with ceremonies like this. Usually they made stealthy, lower-cost trips to military bases in Afghanistan. Aircraft carriers were reserved for cabinet members and presidents—the big and sometimes regrettable *mission accomplished*-type ceremonies.

But this guy was tight with Brie's father and was taking advantage of that for political pomp. Barring big breaking news, this feel-good story of a USAID worker/American princess being rescued by Special Forces would lead the news at home tonight.

If SOCOM had their way, the op to rescue Brie would have been buried without headlines, but thanks to the senator's blabbing to the Prime family and Jeffery Prime Jr.'s leak to the media, here they were. Seeing an opportunity for positive PR, the Pentagon had caved to the senator's request for the dog-and-pony show.

If Jackson weren't on the Senate's Armed Services Committee, none of this would be happening, because the man wouldn't have been privy to the secret op to begin with. Bastian wondered if Jackson had been aiming for this PR show when he leaked the details to the Primes.

Heads turned, and the moment everyone—even, frankly, Bastian—had been waiting for arrived. Brie stepped onto the deck, leaning on her cane and accompanied by several members of the medical team.

Her appearance triggered a mix of lust and regret. Gone was his Brie. In her place was the polished, wealthy woman he'd met ten years ago. The years had added maturity, which only deepened her beauty. She exuded class and poise. But she wasn't the woman he'd gotten to know in South Sudan, which was where the regret came in.

Her short dark hair was styled in a way that sold the cut not as convenient for an aid worker in a country that lacked safe water, but as a fashion choice, similar to one of P!nk's shorter styles. She wore a simple dress that looked like something Audrey Hepburn might've worn. The wind swept across the deck, causing the hem of the skirt to ripple and reveal the lower edge of the bandage around her thigh.

Bastian felt a surge of possessiveness as the world was getting a glimpse of this brave, strong, fierce woman. This thing between them, it wasn't a fling, and it had nothing to do with Savvy's orders. It went far deeper, and for the first time since he broke Cece's heart, he wanted more than a sexual relationship.

But shit, right now she wasn't even talking to him. His thoughtless words had cut deep—because this was more than a fling for her too. His opinion mattered to her.

Her limp was pronounced in spite of her flat shoes as she walked without smiling, her gaze fixed in the distance, not on the senator, not on the press. Not on him.

She reached the microphone set up in front of the admiral, captain, and senator and nodded to the three men before turning to the press corps, sailors, and airmen. "It is with utmost gratitude that I thank Special Operations Command and the members of the Army Special Forces and Navy SEAL teams who rescued me and my coworkers who were kidnapped during the assault on our USAID facility in South Sudan twelve days ago. I'm told I can't name the soldiers who participated in my extraction, but I hope someday they will receive the recognition they deserve."

She nodded toward the senator in the slightest acknowledgment. "It is my understanding that Senator Jackson had been planning this trip for some time, but the date was moved up once he learned I was recovering here on *Dahlgren*, a kindness because he has been a friend of my father's for many years."

Bastian noticed she left out any reference to the man being her friend. She also didn't explicitly thank the senator for the visit.

"Finally, I need to thank the men and women serving aboard *Dahlgren*, for their kind treatment of me, excellent medical care, and their ongoing service to our country. I know how hard it is to be away from home for months at a time, and appreciate the sacrifices they make for our protection.

"I don't have a prepared statement from USAID about South Sudan and the work I did there. At this time, I will not discuss my abduction, rescue, or if my work for the organization will continue. I believe there has been some misreporting as to my role with the organization, and I wish to make it clear I am a federal employee. My work for USAID is not in any way associated with Prime Energy or its subsidiaries."

Standing behind her as he was, he could hear the edge in her voice as she included that dig, but the polish remained.

"I'm exceedingly proud to have worked for an organization devoted to helping people less fortunate across the world. USAID's work in South Sudan to stave off famine in the midst of civil war cannot be lauded enough. In the days since my rescue, dozens of children have died of hunger. Others were conscripted to fight, and still others were sold into slavery.

"While we don't yet have statistics to back up my words, I have seen those atrocities with my own eyes, and in one way or another, I intend to keep fighting for those children, to make sure they aren't forgotten. I want to see an end to famine. An end to Lost Boys. An end to slavery in all its forms.

"As the richest, most powerful nation on earth, it is within our ability to achieve this. To that end, I ask the senator, upon his return to Congress, to insist upon more funding for South Sudan aid and to fast-track refugee programs to find homes for these starving children orphaned by ongoing war. Thank you."

Reporters shouted questions, but Brie stepped back from the microphone. She turned and shook hands with the captain and the admiral, and briefly met Bastian's gaze before looking away.

The makeup made her eyes huge, and her skin had a warm glow. She was beautiful. So achingly perfect.

Jackson smoothly stepped up to the mic, while she was shaking the other men's hands, and Bastian wondered if that had been choreographed to allow her to avoid Senator Jackson.

Was Jackson somehow involved? Sure, this was a great opportunity for him to have a big photo op, but flying all the way to the Gulf of Aden… There had to be more to it than that.

The CIA couldn't monitor Jackson, meaning Savvy wouldn't have intel on the man unless the FBI was sharing—assuming the FBI was even investigating the senator's activities, which they probably weren't. Likewise, Savvy couldn't put the Prime men under surveillance, which had to be Savvy's justification for asking Bastian to get Brie to talk.

Brie was a back door to intel that was otherwise out of the CIA's reach.

Jackson was a powerful senator, sitting on a number of important committees, but to Brie, Senator Jackson was just creepy Uncle Al. Which also begged the question, what other men did she know, and what power did they wield?

S avvy sat in the club, watching the flight deck ceremony on a big-screen TV with Bastian's A-Team and the SEALs who'd been on the op. The men were ostensibly being honored in the ceremony, even if they weren't standing next to Bastian behind the podium.

"Holy crap. I forgot how hot Princess Prime was," a sailor said when Brie began her statement. "Think your buddy's hitting that?" he asked, looking at the assembled A-Team.

"Shut the fuck up and show some respect," Espinosa responded. The rest of the team glared at the sailor and his buddies, and it was clear that if the sailor didn't listen, things could get ugly, fast.

Thankfully, he wasn't so dumb as to further piss off an A-Team and SEALs.

Savvy watched Bastian's face, which gave the answer to the crass question. No, he wasn't hitting that, but his feelings for Brie were clear for all to see.

Guilt jabbed at Savvy, but she hadn't given Bastian his orders lightly. This was a high-stakes game and the Intelligence Community was limping—nearly shattered—by ongoing leaks and political corruption. Several Americans in high government offices, up to and including the former head of the Defense Intelligence Agency, had been compromised by Russia. The whole IC was scrambling and the net result was Savvy currently operated with a degree of autonomy. Her assets were safe as long as the intel she gathered wasn't reported all the way up the line.

But she only had a narrow window of time before Senator Jackson applied pressure to get Brie out of the region in an attempt to make it harder for the IC to connect the dots. He'd already asked to escort Brie back to the mainland, a request that had been flatly refused before Savvy was certain Brie would reject the offer.

Brie knew all the major players in the oil business, had been in the market, and had once met Lawiri in person. Savvy didn't believe that was an accident, especially considering a Russian mercenary had told her, *"My boss has been looking for you for some time."*

There was a power play happening in South Sudan, and somehow, Brie was part of it. Savvy knew it. She just needed all the pieces.

Pieces Senator Jackson didn't want her to have. Senator Jackson, former Texas oilman and current member of the Armed Services Committee. Senator Jackson, who'd groped Brie when she was a teen. Senator Jackson, who'd flown from DC to Djibouti the moment he learned where Brie was.

It only raised the question, could Senator Jackson have been looking for Brie for some time, or was he acting as someone's puppet?

Savvy couldn't rule anyone out.

Chapter Twenty-Three

B rie's phone rang the minute she was back in her
room in the medical ward. It could only be Savvy—
given that Savvy was the only one who had the number
to her new phone. "I stuck to the agreement," she said
defensively.

"I don't remember the line about Prime Energy having
nothing to do with your work for USAID, but I don't
really give a crap about that," Savvy said.

"Then why are you calling?"

"The doctor plans to release you tomorrow so you can
finish your recuperation at Camp Citron."

Brie frowned. The military base would be a welcome
break—she could walk outside without having to get
special permission to be on deck—but Savvy just wanted
her at Camp Citron so she could pick her brain for intel.
Brie had told her everything at least three times.

She wondered if Bastian was being released as well,
but then, she'd been surprised he'd remained on the
carrier, considering his concussion treatment seemed to
be simply to rest. He didn't need a massive aircraft carrier
for that.

"Why Camp Citron? Why not just send me home?"

"Where would that be?" Savvy asked.

"Seattle, I guess." The moment she said the words,
another option occurred to her: she could go to the villa

in Morocco. Her father had transferred the estate into a trust in his children's names before he divorced her mom when she was fourteen—presumably to keep her mother from getting it—and then hid the paperwork so she and her brothers didn't know they owned it.

Brie learned of the sketchy deal nearly a year and a half ago, when one of JJ's lawyers contacted her about the property. The trust included a stipulation that the house and its contents could not be sold or dispersed without the consent of all three siblings, and JJ wanted to sell.

Brie had immediately killed that deal for no reason other than spite. It was ironic that the estate was worth at least seventy-five million, and Brie couldn't tap any of that money. But she could live there.

The Casablanca villa was her favorite of all the family homes, partly because it was ridiculously over the top. A literal palace, fit for a princess. She'd spent the month of May there a year ago, a grand vacation before heading off to South Sudan in September.

"Seattle?" Savvy said. "Haven't you had enough rain to last you?"

"At least the roads are paved in the Pacific Northwest." She'd keep her Morocco plans to herself for now.

"Well, don't get too excited because it's going to take the State Department a few days to issue you a new passport. You'll be stuck at Camp Citron until then."

She should have known she wouldn't escape Savvy's brain picking that easily. "Fine," she said without hiding her sigh.

"You've already been assigned a private wet CLU," Savvy said.

The wet Containerized Living Units had an attached, shared bathroom. As if *that* was the worm that would entice her to bite. After living in South Sudan, she could handle a unit without a sink and toilet. Besides, the house in Morocco had twenty-two bathrooms. And two swimming pools—one an indoor Turkish bath, the other outside and surrounded by a lush garden. "I'll see you tomorrow," she said and hit the End button.

She didn't bother to wonder how the CIA knew her doctor's orders before she did. The woman had taken undue interest in Brie, which meant she wanted something from her. But damn if Brie knew what it was. She'd told her everything she knew about the market. *Three times.*

Months ago, she'd filed a report on the market with USAID. The report had eventually landed in Savvy's lap, and the woman had insisted Brie fly to Djibouti for a face-to-face briefing. Basically, Savvy had wanted to recruit Brie as an asset. Brie had shunned official involvement with the CIA—spying could harm USAID's mission—but she'd agreed to share what she learned through non-covert, non-deceptive means. Now that the market was destroyed and her employment with USAID likely over, she didn't see what use Savvy had for her.

Brie stepped out to the reception area, where a monitor was showing the ongoing ceremony on the deck to the staff stuck in the medical facility.

Bastian was in the background, behind the senator, just another face in the crowd. But not for her. Her eyes latched onto him and her stomach twisted.

Right now she was Oil Company Barbie except for the shoes. Barbie always wore high heels, but after being shot in the leg, high heels were out. Good riddance. She liked cute sandals with heels but had never been a fan of stilettos, especially after having to wear them five days a week for work.

The tire-tread sandals were a thousand times more comfortable and functional, even if they didn't force her into a posture that made her ass look good.

"Is the senator as big an asshole as he sounds?" the hospital corpsman working the desk asked.

"He's worse. Groped me when I was fifteen. Total creep." It was freeing to just speak the truth. This not-hiding-her-past thing would be good for her.

He curled his lip. "Figures. Asshole. What is it with politicians?"

The corpsman was handsome, with rich, deep mahogany skin, a nice smile, and friendly manner. He took his job seriously, and if he judged her for being Princess Prime once upon a time, he didn't show it.

The ceremony on the deck wound down, and she returned to her room, not eager to see Bastian again. Had she overreacted earlier?

Probably.

But damn. His words had come at her like a fist to the belly. She cared about his opinion of her more than anyone else in her life. Because she didn't have anyone else in her life—no one who really knew her, anyway.

She grabbed the makeup bag and slipped into the shared lavatory. Head? What term was used on an aircraft carrier? She stared into the mirror holding the makeup remover in one hand and a washcloth in the other.

She studied the stranger in the mirror. She hadn't looked like this since her month in Morocco, when she'd dated a wealthy Spaniard who moved in their neighborhood's social circles, and she'd accompanied him to several parties.

Part of her missed it. She'd enjoyed feeling pretty and wearing nice clothes. Did that make her shallow?

Or just human?

She warmed the washcloth, but at the last moment, turned off the faucet. Screw it. She'd face Bastian as the woman he believed her to be. After all, Gabriella Prime was part of her too. If he couldn't accept this part of her, then this thing between them was over before it started.

She looked down at her arm and the exposed track marks. No more secrets.

She pulled the lipstick from the bag and put on a fresh coat. At least she'd look pretty for the kiss-off.

B astian waited inside Brie's room. She might kick him out again, but he didn't want to face her with the entire staff of the medical ward watching.

She entered the room and came to a dead stop. She frowned, then turned and closed the door behind her. She paused with her back to him, hand on the door, and took a deep breath. "If you're here to insult me for looking like a Barbie, you can leave now."

He stepped up behind her, not touching her, but still trapping her against the door. "You're the most beautiful woman I've ever seen, with or without makeup. In a torn-up tobe or a designer dress. You're smart and dedicated and kind and nothing like the woman I saw at that meeting ten years ago. I'm sorry for referring to you in that way. Sorry I hurt you."

Her shoulders relaxed, and she let out a slow breath. "I

might have overreacted."

"No. I called you a shitty name I'd mentally given you ten years ago, which has nothing to do with the woman you are now."

"And what if...I like dressing up sometimes? What if I'm both Brie and Gabriella?"

He placed a hand on the door and leaned to whisper in her ear. "You look fucking hot right now. I want to hike up your dress and bury myself inside you."

She turned, her shoulder brushing his chest as she did so. With her back to the door, she leaned against it and looked up to meet his gaze.

A vibrant light lit her eyes. Her lashes were impossibly long, her lips a deep, full red.

"Apology accepted," she said and pressed a hand to his chest. For a moment, he thought she was going to push him away, but then her hand curled around the buttons just below his collar and pulled him closer. "You look hot in your uniform, yet all I want to do is tear it off you."

She kissed his neck, then moved upward to his lips. He took what she offered and slid his tongue in her mouth, telling her with slow, deep strokes how much he wanted her.

He scooped her up and braced her back to the door. Her skirt hiked up, and she wrapped her legs around his hips and let out a little pant as his erection pressed between her thighs. He held her in place with an arm under her ass, but pulled back to look into those luminous brown eyes. "Your leg? Does this hurt?"

Her lips trailed along his cheek; her teeth nipped at his chin. "A little, but it's worth it."

He dropped a kiss on her lips before lowering her to the floor again. "Anything that hurts you isn't worth it to me. We'll rain-check this." It might kill him, but he could wait. They'd do this right.

She kissed his neck. "Rumor has it I'm being sprung tomorrow, although the doc hasn't mentioned it to me yet."

"Are you being sent to Camp Citron?"

She nodded.

He smiled. "Well then, we can continue this in my CLU. As second-in-command of my team, I have a single." He kissed her brows, her cheek, her lips. He was eager to explore all of her with more privacy than the carrier hospital allowed.

"According to Savvy, so will I." She played with the buttons on his ACU. "Savvy said it will take a few days for the State Department to issue me a new passport. I haven't decided where I'm going to go once I'm free, but we can enjoy a fling before I disappear."

He stiffened. "Disappear?" But what he really wanted to question was the fling part. His hands rested on her hips, and he pulled her closer to him.

"I have no intention of becoming a Prime Energy PR tool, so I'll have to lay low."

That made sense. His hands relaxed their grip. "I have an apartment near Fort Campbell. You're welcome to use it."

She smiled, but he couldn't help but see the flicker of distress as she slipped from his arms and moved to the center of the room. "I thought...we were on the same page? I don't do relationships, and neither do you."

This was the first time he'd ever been on the receiving end of the relationship talk. And he didn't like it. He cocked his head. "I also don't get involved with women I meet on missions. Nothing is normal here."

"True. I just…Right now is all I can handle."

"Works for me." Right this moment, he wanted Brie naked in his bed. Right now was all that mattered.

A sharp knock sounded on the door. He stepped back and said, "Come in."

Brie's eyes widened. "Wait—"

The door opened, and their doctor stepped in. She raised an eyebrow at Bastian, her eyes lit with curiosity. Then her nostrils flared, and he had the distinct feeling she was holding back a snicker. "Sorry, I didn't know you were here, Chief Ford." She turned to Brie. "Ms. Stewart, I'm here to discuss your discharge tomorrow."

Brie covered her mouth, and a stifled laugh escaped. She cleared her throat, but he could still hear the laughter in her voice. "Glad to know I'm being sprung."

"I'll leave you to it," Bastian said as he slipped through the open door.

"I'll be in to see you next, Chief Ford," the doctor said. "You're also being released." Then the doctor did snicker. "It's good to see you're feeling better, but keep in mind *all* strenuous activity should be avoided until symptoms abate."

It wasn't until he was back in his room and saw his reflection in a mirror that he understood why both Brie and the doctor had been laughing.

Deep red lipstick smeared his neck and cheek.

B astian didn't return to Brie's room that evening, which was probably for the best considering the doctor's dire warnings about strenuous activity exacerbating his concussion. She did say that Brie's bullet wound was healing nicely, and, as long as she was careful, she didn't see any issues from sex.

She'd fixed Brie with a knowing smile and said, *"Just don't get too creative."* She frowned and added, *"And use a condom."*

"Do you know something I don't?"

The doctor laughed and said, *"No. Just an advocate for safe sex."* She'd then left the room and returned with a box of condoms.

After that, a physical therapist had met with Brie and showed her exercises she needed to do to rebuild strength in the mending muscle.

She wasn't ready for some of the moves yet, and a physical therapist on the base would check in with her in the coming days to guide her. For tonight, she was sore and tired. It had been a long and active day after being inactive for so long.

She crawled into her hospital bed, wishing Bastian would join her, even though the bed was too small and he snored. Even crappy sleep with Bastian was better than no Bastian.

Maybe she should reconsider her relationship ban.

Ahhh, but her situation was complicated, her family a wildcard. And now that she'd lost her anonymity, it was best to only think in the here and now.

A soft knock of warning was followed by Bastian slipping into her room and closing the door.

She turned on the light. "What's up?"

He smiled. "Get dressed."

"Why?"

"I've got a surprise for you."

She winced as her foot touched the floor. Bastian was by her side in a second. "You're hurting? We can skip this."

"I'm fine. Just had PT tonight, so I'm sore."

He waited in the hall while she changed. Ready, she stepped out of the room, and he offered his arm. She held him with one hand and her cane in the other as he led her out of her room, down the corridor, and out of the medical facility altogether.

"Is this even allowed?"

He grinned. "It is when you know the right people." He led her to the ramp she'd used to reach the flight deck earlier in the day.

"Where are we going?"

"You'll see."

She paused as they neared the outer door. "The flight deck is restricted."

"Relax. You won't get in trouble."

"But *you* will."

"Sweetheart, I'm Special Forces."

As if that answered everything.

But instead of leading her outside, he bypassed the exit and climbed a steep, narrow staircase she hadn't noticed before. Bastian helped her as she took the stairs slowly. "You ever see a jet take off from an aircraft carrier at night?" he asked.

She laughed. "Pretty sure that's a no."

They reached the top of the stairs, and he pushed open a door that led to a small open platform that overlooked the flight deck. Before stepping outside, Bastian grabbed headphones that hung on hooks just inside the door.

She stepped outside, crossed to the railing, and looked down on the operations going on below. Wind whipped around them and a cacophony of sounds rose from the massive deck.

"These aren't radios, ear protection only," Bastian

shouted to be heard over the noise. He placed the earmuffs over her ears. Unable to speak because of the noise and headphones, Bree held Bastian's hand as the deck crew worked in a magnificent choreography.

A jet was moved into position. Takeoff was like an explosion she felt in her legs, her chest, her fingertips.

Her heart pounded with exhilaration. Who knew this could be such an adrenaline rush?

She turned to the man at her side and pulled his head down for a deep kiss.

After a long moment, he lifted his head. He leaned down and pulled aside her headphone and said with laughter in his voice, "Good thing I'm not in uniform. PDAs in uniform would get me in trouble."

She pulled aside his ear protector. "But not sneaking me onto the observation deck during flight operations?"

He winked at her. "I cleared it with command."

She grinned. "Badass Special Forces maverick is not so maverick after all?"

"But I'm still badass."

She laughed and covered her ears again. Another jet was being positioned for takeoff.

They watched two more launches, then stepped back inside. After descending the stairs, Brie squeezed Bastian's hand. "Thank you. That was cool."

"It was for me too. I'm not on carriers often."

They returned to the medical wing, and Bastian paused outside her door. "This is where we say good night."

"You won't…?"

"Good night, Brie." He kissed her on the forehead and returned to his room.

Brie watched him go, then slipped into her room. She

was too pumped to sleep, but with nothing else to do, she put on the scrubs she'd been wearing as pajamas earlier and crawled between the covers. Tomorrow would probably be a long day with transport to the base, and tonight's PT had shown her how easily she tired.

She closed her eyes, remembering the feel of the rush of the jet engine, the rumble of the deck under her feet. The jet took off into the starry night. And Bastian held her hand, his fingers entwined with hers.

She was wide-awake. And aroused.

She threw the bedcovers aside.

They'd been circling each other since their second night in South Sudan. She wanted him, and there was zero reason not to go for it now.

She paused. Except his concussion. The doctor seemed concerned. And his head had hurt this morning. But massage had helped. If his head was bothering him, she'd give him another massage and leave.

She pulled on a robe and slipped the box of condoms the doctor had given her into her pocket. Just in case. Cane in hand, she headed down the hall to Bastian's room.

Chapter Twenty-Four

Anticipation coiled in Bastian's belly at the sound of footsteps outside his door.

It's about time.

He'd started to wonder if he'd read her wrong. But then the knob turned, and there she was, the beautiful woman who'd consumed his world for nearly two weeks.

She closed his door and leaned back against the panel. Her mouth curved in a slow, sexy smile. "You aren't surprised to see me."

"No." He rose from his chair and crossed the tiny room to stand before her. "Not surprised." He cupped her jaw with one hand and ran his thumb along her cheekbone. "Thankful. Exultant. Hard."

She rubbed his erection over his sweatpants. "Yes, you are." She slid her hand under the waistband and wrapped her fingers around his penis. Her eyes were liquid hot as she stroked his shaft. "It has taken way too long for me to get *here*." Her emphasis on the last word was punctuated by rubbing her thumb over the tip of his cock, followed by a slow stroke down his length.

Damn, that felt amazing. "Well, you were shot." He groaned at another slide of her hand. "I was being considerate."

Her lips brushed his. "Promise you'll never waste time being considerate again." She slipped her tongue in his mouth before he could answer.

He kissed her but needed to touch her like she touched him. He tugged at her robe sash and spread the garment wide at her shoulders. Hospital scrubs weren't the sexiest of pajamas, but he wasn't complaining. But then, all he wanted was for them to be gone.

She released his cock and her cane, allowing the robe to fall to the floor. He pulled the scrub top over her head and tossed it aside.

Her beautiful breasts were exposed to his gaze, his touch. He cupped one in each hand, then bent down and took a nipple into his mouth. It retracted against his tongue. She threaded her fingers through his hair and leaned against the door.

He moved to her other breast and sucked that one into a tight bud. He could play with her breasts for hours. He would play with them for hours. Later. In his CLU.

He was scheduled to remain on medical leave for a few more days and intended to take full advantage of it.

"Get naked," she said.

He pulled off his T-shirt, sweatpants, and boxer briefs. Naked, he tugged down her scrub pants and panties, then scooped her up and carried her to the bed. He laid her on top of the covers and stepped back to enjoy the view of her splayed on his bed, her only covering the thick bandage around her thigh.

"You're beautiful," he said as he ran a finger along her skin from her throat to her belly button. "Are you sure your wound can take this?"

She nodded. "The doctor just said not to get too creative."

He laughed. "We'll save creative for later."

She reached out and took his erection into her hand

and stroked the shaft. She licked her lips and said, "Raise the bed."

He needed no more encouragement and hit the button that brought the bed—and her mouth—to the perfect height. She pulled him to her and licked the length of him, then took the head into her mouth. She swirled her tongue around the tip, then took him deep.

Holy fuck.

She stroked him with hand and lips while her tongue slid along the underside and caressed as far down the length as she could take into her throat.

Seeing her lips wrapped around him, the feel of her mouth as she sucked... No fantasy from ten years ago or this week compared. He slid his fingers between her thighs and felt her wet heat. Slick and ready for him.

She moaned as she sucked, and the feel of her mouth, the sounds, the visuals made his balls tighten. She cupped them and kept sucking, and he was in heaven.

This wasn't just any blowjob. This was Brie. Sexy, funny, strong, perfect Brie, rocking his world, giving herself to him. He stroked her clit and ran his fingers around the opening of her vagina before slipping two inside her. She let out a soft groan and kept stroking and sucking. His thumb teased her clit as his fingers slid in her tight, slick body.

Christ. He had to taste her.

Now.

He slipped from her mouth, keeping his finger on her clit, and moved to the foot of the bed. It was too narrow a mattress for her to angle across it, so he climbed on from the bottom as she scooted up. He positioned himself between her bent knees and spread her thighs wider, careful of her injury.

He paused to stare down at her. Wet and ready, her pussy was fucking beautiful. He breathed in her musky scent. She was so aroused. His cock thickened even more.

He slid his tongue over her clit, and she let out a gasp. "Oh yes."

Another swipe of his tongue then another. He traced her lips, then thrust his tongue inside, stroking deep. God, she tasted good.

Why had he been considerate of her injury when he could have been taking care of her like this? He returned to her clit and sucked on it. Her body curled around him, thighs cradling his head, hands stroking his hair. "Bastian." Her voice was a breathy whisper. A plea.

He'd known she'd be this way. Open. Uninhibited. Eager. He slid two fingers inside her, wanting so badly to follow up with his cock, but they'd satisfy each other with oral. He didn't have condoms. Tonight, he'd make her come with his mouth and fingers and be content with that.

He licked and sucked, and her body tightened around him. He was rock hard and might come just listening to the sounds she made.

"Get inside me, Bastian," she whispered.

"No condoms. Come for me, Brie."

Her fingers twined in his hair. "In my robe...pocket."

He kept his fingers on her clit, holding her on the cusp. "You've got condoms?"

"Yes. The doc gave me a box after seeing you wearing my lipstick."

He laughed and climbed from the bed to grab the package. A moment later, he was back on the bed, between her thighs, his bare cock touching her tight curls. He handed her the condom. She stroked him several times, then rolled it down his length with exquisite slowness.

Sheathed at last, he positioned his penis at her opening, inserting himself a scant half inch. He kept his gaze on her face as she took the tip, loving the pleasure and need he saw there.

She grasped his hips in her hands and tried to pull him toward her, pressing her pelvis down to take him deeper. "More," she demanded.

Sex for him was often urgent, fast. Wild. Up against the wall. But with Brie, he wanted slow. Intense. They could do wild wall sex in his CLU, after her leg had healed more. Ever so slowly, he pushed inside her. She was so slick and hot, he could go balls-deep in one swift stroke, but he didn't. Instead, he enjoyed the exquisite torture of drawing out this first thrust of his cock inside her.

Once seated, he stayed deep. She clenched around him, so tight and hot, he let out a soft groan. Fuck, being inside her was all he ever wanted. Every fantasy come true.

He leaned down and kissed her. Slowly. Tenderly. Like he had in South Sudan. Only this time, they were joined, her pussy tight around him. He wanted to hold on to this, the feeling of perfection of being inside her. Part of her. Her strength. Her beauty. Her resilience.

The possessiveness he'd felt earlier returned, magnified by a thousand.

Brie Stewart was the woman of his dreams. Smart. Strong. Caring. Resourceful. Funny. Beautiful in every way.

As slowly as he'd entered her, he pulled back, determined to savor. She moaned softly, her thighs wrapped around his hips, hands gripping his shoulders, eyes closed, lost in sensation. He'd given that to her. He thrust again, faster this time. And he'd give it to her again. Another thrust. And again.

Her hands moved from his shoulders to cup his ass as he pumped into her, and it wasn't long before he lost all speed control. He supported his weight with a forearm on the mattress and slipped his free hand between their bodies to touch her clit. He stroked in time with his thrusts. His mouth covered hers as she came, capturing the sound she made with orgasm as her body quaked beneath his and her nails dug into his butt.

Her orgasm pushed him over the edge, and he groaned his own release into her mouth as he came. He came hard. Fast and intense. So fucking good.

He wondered if the release of endorphins would trigger a headache thanks to the concussion, but none came to diminish the moment. He lowered himself to her side, rolling them both to stay inside her. He made sure her injured thigh had no weight on it.

He kissed her lips, her brow, her cheeks. Soft, slow kisses as he gently thrust his hips. He stroked her clit with his thumb, causing her body to ripple with quakes.

"You're killing me, Bastian." Her eyes were closed, and she smiled as she clenched around him, triggering his own tremor.

He chuckled in her ear. Kissed her neck. "You feel so good, babe. How did we last this long without doing this?"

"I believe you said you were being considerate."

"Is that a synonym for stupid?"

She laughed and ran her lips over his throat. "It's time to admit I was right."

"About what? That we were fools not to do this sooner?"

"No. I warned you before we kissed the first time that I'm very good at sex."

He laughed and stroked her breast, ran his hand down her side. "You were right about everything."

Including the part about falling in love with her.

Chapter Twenty-Five

Savannah James was having a good week. The two children rescued from South Sudan had identified two individuals known to work for General Lawiri as the market's primary muscle. Now all she needed to know was who Lawiri's partner was, because the whole operation had been far too well managed for the likes of Lawiri. Add to that Etefu Desta had broken under CIA interrogation and they had a solid lead for bringing down the Djiboutian minister who'd conspired with him to steal water from Djibouti. And her friend—well, the closest thing she had to one here, anyway—archaeologist Morgan Adler, was on the base for a few days. Savvy would have a chance to pick her brain for insight into the growing problem of artifact smuggling in the region.

But best of all, Sergeant Cassius Callahan was in the gym, oblivious to Savvy's presence as he sparred with Pax.

Both men had pared down to simple exercise shorts and boxing gloves, and they both had sculpted, beautiful, sweaty bodies. Pax, slightly taller and broader, bore the dusky complexion of a southern European, while Cal was chestnut-skinned, hard-muscled perfection.

Their battle was friendly but still a competition. Like all Special Forces, they wanted to be the most alpha in the Army, and would happily take out their best buddy to prove it.

She enjoyed watching Cal when he didn't know she was there.

It was twisted, how she wanted him yet relished pissing him off. He never balked at letting her know how little he respected her, which of course meant she was determined to show him how much she didn't give a fuck.

But still, watching him as he battled his best friend was hot as hell. Sweat glistened on his brown skin.

She hated how attracted to him she was.

Yet she couldn't stop looking. Wanting.

She needed to get laid. It was that simple. But being CIA…made casual sex very complicated. Male undercover operators were encouraged to use prostitutes. For some reason, women weren't granted the same dubious license.

She knew the exact moment when her presence registered with Cal, because he dropped his guard and Pax nailed him in the jaw.

"Shit, Cal, what's wrong with you?" Pax said in lieu of apology.

Cal merely grunted and jabbed with his left. Game on. The two sparred and Savvy turned to the free weights. Maybe Morgan would spar with her later. Scratch that. Morgan was probably still in a cast. Savvy lost herself in the pain of her workout, forgetting Cal, Pax, and Morgan as she pushed herself to the limit and beyond.

She switched from weights to pull-up bars, then moved on to barbells. She was coated with sweat, muscles shaking with fatigue, when a shadow loomed over her, drawing her attention. She racked the barbell, knowing from the damn tingle in her neck exactly who stood behind her. Was it his scent? Whatever it was, it was unconscious.

And irritating.

"You shouldn't do that shit without a spotter."

Easier said than done. Most people disliked her. She was an unrepentant, manipulative spook. "Are you volunteering, Sergeant Callahan?"

"No."

"Then fuck off." But she said it sweetly, because she was nice that way. She lifted the bar again and resumed her bench presses. She grunted as she forced the bar upward, each press harder than the last even though the weight hadn't changed.

She hated bench pressing. Hated weight lifting. But it was better than ninety percent of her other options in that moment, so she forced the bar upward. She'd reward herself for this awful workout with ice cream tonight. A poor substitute for sex, but it would have to do.

Her arms shook, but she did it. Again and again. She knew her breaking point, and she was one press away. One more and she'd be done.

She held the bar an inch above her chest, gathering her strength, when hands swooped in and lifted and racked the bar.

Her muscles rejoiced, but her brain balked. She'd been coiled and ready to go—like a sneeze that never happened—and the denial of the last pain irked. "I didn't ask for your help, Sergeant Callahan."

"I don't give a fuck, Savvy. You were done."

There he was, using the nickname again. When Morgan insisted on calling her that, Savvy had fantasized about hearing Cal say it in a hot, breathless voice. This wasn't the same.

She bolted upright, her legs straddling the bench as she twisted to face him. "*No one* tells me when I'm done."

He circled around her, hovering above, his handsome face a hardened mask of dislike. He leaned down to her ear and whispered. "Sweetheart, you can't fake it with me. I *know* when you're done."

The innuendo ran across her nerves, and it took all her training in masking emotion to hold back a shiver.

Fuck, he was dangerous. Worse, he knew it.

He tossed her a towel. "Hit the shower."

Special Forces were all egotistical assholes, and Cal was the worst of the bunch. She scanned the room for Pax. He, at least, respected her. But she and Cal were alone.

"I'm not in your chain of command, Sergeant, and even if I were, I'd outrank you." As a SAD officer, her training matched his, but she worked alone, and her rank was...undefined. But then, he didn't even know she was in SAD. The only thing people here knew about her was that she didn't seem to be an analyst and wielded a strange amount of power for a case officer. But then, her position was unique, given that she'd been an analyst once upon a time, followed by case officer, before going through the equivalent of special forces training so she could join the ranks of the Special Activities Division.

She held Cal's gaze and caught the heat. He liked her asserting her secret rank. He was curious about her.

"Why are you messing with my boy Bastian?" he suddenly asked.

His boy? Bastian outranked him. She rolled her eyes. "I'm not messing with Bastian."

"You're fucking with his mind, manipulating him. Twisting the screws. I saw the way he looked at Brie

Stewart on the carrier deck. And she didn't look at him at all. People are going to get hurt."

"He's a grown man and a Special Forces officer. I think he can take care of himself. And if Gabriella Prime gets hurt, it's her own damn fault for not coming clean from the get-go."

"Her name is Brie Stewart. But all you see is a Prime, right?"

Fuck.

"I don't answer to you, Sergeant. And for the record, we're on the same damn side. If Brie Stewart has information that can explain what happened in South Sudan, I need to know what it is. Bastian understands that."

Cal just glared at her, holding her gaze.

She felt a charge as energy pulsed between them. Then he broke the spell by turning and leaving the gym.

B rie sat at a corner table in Barely North, the same place where she'd first met Bastian, her eyes fixed on the door, eagerly waiting for him. They'd been helicoptered to the base earlier in the day and separated upon arrival. Bastian had gone to meet with his team and SOCOM, and she'd been assigned a CLU, where she'd settled in before checking in at the medical clinic, then meeting with Savvy.

Day had faded into evening, and Bastian promised to meet her here as soon as he was free. She fiddled with the straw in her Coke, lost in memories of the night before.

The way he'd kissed her with aching slowness. Gently. Sweetly. He'd made her tremble with need, then delivered what she wanted, but on his terms. He'd employed a seductive tenderness that had been impossible to prevent or resist.

She was falling for him. Hard.

She doubted he'd been out of her thoughts for even a minute since she'd slipped from his bed at dawn after three rounds of making love over the course of the night.

The door opened and was held wide by the Green Beret she'd met on the carrier. Sergeant Blanchard. A blonde woman on crutches entered the club. She headed for a table, but Blanchard pointed in Brie's direction, and the blonde changed course and paused before Brie.

"Brie Stewart, I'd like you to meet Dr. Morgan Adler," Blanchard said.

The blonde held out her hand, "Morgan, please. Savvy has told me about you."

Brie received the handshake. "Call me Brie. It's nice to meet you. I've heard about you too, from Bastian. Are you going to be on base long?"

"Only a few days. I need to visit sites my crew recorded on the survey after I broke my ankle." She glanced down at her leg and frowned. "Then I'm heading back to the US."

Brie knew the woman's broken ankle had something to do with how she knew Bastian, but the mission—assuming that was what it was—was classified, so Bastian hadn't said anything beyond telling her about the Linus fossil and archaeological survey Morgan had completed for the Djiboutian government.

Morgan had been at Camp Citron when Brie was here in March, but they hadn't met. "Would you like to sit down?" Brie asked.

Blanchard's arm slipped around Morgan's waist. "No. Bastian will be here soon, and we'll grab another table."

"I just wanted to say hi because Savvy said you gave her information on artifact trafficking in South Sudan, and I was curious about what you've seen."

That had been a small part of the reason for her visit in March. The slave market was the primary reason, but artifact trafficking was also an issue there. After all, there'd been a hut devoted to antiquities in the market. "I'm afraid I don't know much. My work there wasn't archaeology related, but I know several sites were being actively looted and suspect Boko Haram was behind it. They're getting bolder as they move out of Nigeria."

"I'd love to see the site locations on a map. Archaeologists haven't been able to work in South Sudan since the civil war started, and we have no information on what damage has occurred at known sites. Next week, I'm meeting with a professor at William & Mary who is doing artifact analysis of the Djibouti tools. One of his students is creating a database to track sites that are disappearing or being looted due to war. The focus is primarily Syria, but any information you have on South Sudan would be welcome."

"I should have time tomorrow," Brie said. It would feel almost normal to discuss this with Morgan. "But fair warning, my specialty is cultural anthro, not archaeology, so I'm not the expert you might be hoping for."

"No problem. In grad school, I was even friends with some cultural students." Morgan winked at her.

Brie laughed, remembering the endless jockeying for superiority between the subdisciplines in the anthropology department. "And I even hung out with archaeologists—when the linguists were busy."

Morgan grinned. "At least the linguists are clean."

The door opened again, and Brie's heart rate kicked up

at the sight of Bastian. He looked good in jeans and a T-shirt as he crossed the room. She could swear he was even more handsome today than he was yesterday. She was officially addicted.

He reached Morgan's side and draped an arm around her shoulders, giving her a squeeze. "Morgan, good to see you again. How's the ankle?"

She kissed Bastian's cheek. "Healing, but not fast enough for my liking. How's the head?"

"Thick, as usual." Blanchard snickered.

"I'm fine, but SOCOM won't let me return to duty for another three days."

"Slacker," Blanchard said.

Bastian laughed and released Morgan. He circled the table to Brie. She looked up, and he dropped a kiss on her lips. "Hi, sweetheart."

His casual, boyfriend-like greeting surprised her, but it shouldn't have. He hadn't hidden their relationship on the carrier, so she wasn't sure why she suspected he would here. Maybe because she'd figured SOCOM would frown on them being involved.

"We'll talk tomorrow," Morgan said to Brie. "Enjoy your evening."

She hobbled to a table on the other side of the room, Blanchard at her side.

Bastian dropped into the seat at Brie's side. "How has your day been?" he asked as he signaled for the waiter.

"Boring, you?"

The waiter arrived, and Bastian ordered a soda. Brie stopped him. "Don't worry about me if you want to drink. I'm fine."

He shook his head. "Thanks, I'd love a beer, but the doc wants me to avoid alcohol for a few more days." The waiter left, and he draped an arm over her shoulder and settled into the bench seat next to her. His lips tickled her ear as he said softly, "I missed you today. I've gotten used to having you by my side twenty-four/seven."

She got a warm feeling in her chest. This wasn't good.

Withdrawal was going to hurt like a bitch.

They ordered dinner and chatted about their separate days. It felt almost normal, like this was a regular date. Which, Brie supposed, it was.

After dinner, he walked her back to her CLU. She was walking easier now and had gone without the cane since arriving on base, but it waited in her CLU, if she felt like she needed it.

He followed her inside her unit, closed the door, and leaned against it. He spread his feet apart and pulled her into his arms. Slouched as he was, they were face-to-face, lip-to-lip.

He did that thing where he kissed her so slowly, so sweetly, she was sure she was going to melt with the tenderness. The kiss was precious. Warm. Sincere.

Then it gained heat, turning hot and seductive. As her mouth clung to his, she tugged on his T-shirt. She leaned back and pulled it over his head, then ran the flat of her hand across his tattoo and down his abs.

"You have the most beautiful body. I love touching you." She slid her hand downward, into his pants, and touched him some more.

His erection was thick and ready for her. She wanted him to take her here, up against the door, but they both had some healing to do first. "When we're both better, I want you to fuck me against the wall."

His mouth took hers in a hot, deep kiss, then he raised his head and grinned. "Deal."

He scooped her up, and she protested. "You aren't supposed to—"

He silenced her with a kiss, which ended when he lowered her to the cot. "My head is fine. The docs are overly cautious. I could return to duty tomorrow, but I didn't fight them because I wanted time with you."

"I'll only be here for a few more days." Then she would go to Morocco. She'd decided that today.

He stretched out next to her. "Exactly. And I want to enjoy every moment we have." He unbuttoned her top, pulled aside a bra cup, and cradled her breast, then leaned down and licked her nipple. "For the record, I'm enjoying right now very much."

He freed her other breast from its cup and moved to straddle her, leaning down to take turns licking and sucking each. "God, how I love your tits," he said, then sucked on a nipple. She clenched her pelvic muscles as heat suffused her. His play with her breasts made her wet.

He reached beneath her and undid the bra. His knees pressed on her open shirt, and she giggled when he realized he couldn't get the bra off without removing the shirt he was kneeling on as he straddled her. "I seem to have created some kind of Gordian knot."

The giggle turned into a full laugh. Her left arm was also pinned by shirt pulled taut by his knee, so she couldn't help him extract her from the garment. "Whatever will we do?"

"Move lower," he said, scooting his knees down, kissing her belly as he went lower. He stopped and ran his tongue around her belly button, then moved on. Arms now freed, she could sit up and remove bra and top, but she liked the direction he was going and pretended she was still trapped.

He reached the waistband of her skirt, and instead of reaching around to unzip it, he rose on his knees and pulled the skirt up, bunching it in a band around her hips. He slid a finger beneath the crotch of her panties and stroked her clit.

Pleasure shot through her, and she let out a soft groan.

"You are so fucking hot," Bastian said, his gaze fixed on his hand and her center. He flicked her clitoris again. And again. And she wanted him inside her. Now.

"Get naked," she said.

He yanked off her underwear, only being careful as he pulled it over her bandaged thigh. Freed, she spread her legs wide, bending her knees. Opening herself to him. But he still wore his jeans.

"I was referring to you, not me," she said as she tried to reach for his fly.

He laughed and put his mouth on her. She let out a yell as pleasure jolted through her. He brought her to a fast orgasm with his stroking tongue. She came apart, her body curling to cradle his head as his mouth relentlessly licked and sucked.

She collapsed back, panting. "Okay. Get naked now?"

He unbuttoned his fly, freeing his erection, fished a condom from his pocket, rolled it on, and then, in one smooth stroke, slid deep inside her. Pleasure coursed through her on a sweet wave. He stretched her. Filled her. The delicious sensations made her shudder. His thrusts came hard and fast, and she clenched around him, loving the friction against her G-spot.

She came again, a sharp ripple of pleasure that triggered a sound that was more scream than moan. Bastian's hand covered her mouth—the unit walls were thin metal sheets—and he came in silence, his body quaking between her thighs.

He dropped beside her and pulled her to him so they were lying on their sides.

"Neither of us got naked," she said, glancing down at her skewed bra, open shirt, hiked-up skirt, and his open jeans.

He got up from the bed, removed the condom, and headed to the sink at the back of the unit. "Hey, I'm not wearing my shirt."

She laughed. "Because I pulled it off you."

"I was impatient. I needed to taste you."

She peeled off her shirt, bra, and skirt and tossed them on the floor. "I like it when you're impatient."

He returned a moment later, naked at last.

She shifted on the cot to make room for him. "The military really isn't interested in providing beds that accommodate two people," she said.

"Definitely not." He settled on the narrow bed, gathered her against him, and kissed her temple. "But it doesn't stop anyone. The no-fraternization rules on Navy vessels never stop anyone."

Neither of them served in the Navy, and they'd merely been patients in the medical facility, so maybe the rules hadn't applied to them. Regardless, it was clear—right down to the doctor giving her condoms—that no one cared if she and Bastian fooled around.

As far as the cot went, she liked the confined space, liked being pressed against him. Frankly, she didn't even mind if he snored and hogged the bed. She just wanted to be with him. Wanted every moment she could get of this.

"I Skyped with my parents today," he said. "They said the whole tribe gathered at the longhouse to watch the ceremony on the carrier on the big screen. My dad said everyone cheered the first time they recognized me standing behind you, then Dad leaned toward the computer camera and said, 'Your mother cried, seeing you in your uniform, wearing your green beret.' Then he added, 'We are so proud of you, son.'"

"Oh, Bastian. They must miss you so much."

"I told them I'd visit when this deployment is over, and my mom cried again. And then I felt like a shit."

She ran her hands over his bare shoulders, pulling him closer. "I understand the double-edged sword of hurting a mother's feelings out of self-protection." She knew that pain all too well. "The guilt is hard, but you were right to take care of yourself first these last years."

"She's my elder. And my mom. And I made her cry. That might make me the worst Indian ever. And fuck, I've *never* seen her cry before."

"Bastian, those were happy tears. She loves you. She wants to see you. And she cried when seeing you on the aircraft carrier because she's proud of the man you are and the soldier you became—even when she would have held you back from that path, she's proud."

He ran his fingers through her hair. "Maybe." His hand slid down to her cheek. "How long have you stayed away from your family?"

She stiffened. "My situation is a little different."

"I know. But how long? When was the last time you saw your father and brothers?"

"Eight years ago." The day she found out about Micah. The day everything changed.

"Tell me about it?" he asked softly.

"No."

"Why not?"

She rolled to her back, looked up at the ceiling. "This

is just a fling, Bastian. You don't need to know the ugly details."

"What if I don't want it to be just a fling? What if I want to know the ugly details?"

What if she didn't want it to be just a fling either?

It was too risky. "Please don't ask for more," she said. "This ends when I leave Djibouti."

"Why, Brie? I might not know where this is going, but I do know this is more than casual sex. I know flings. I've had dozens. So have you. This is different. Shit. I've never told anyone about Cece, about my parents."

And that was the problem. The talking. And the fact they'd slept together—without sex. This was…intimate.

And when he kissed her, she felt exquisite. Like he cared about more than just getting inside her physically. And when he was inside her, she felt a connection that went beyond friction hitting nerve endings built for pleasure.

The last time she'd felt anything remotely similar to this, the man had been Micah. "Relationships aren't in the cards for me. But we can enjoy now."

"*Why*, Brie?"

"Remember how my family wanted me to screw that guy when I was eighteen? Well, my father was pretty pissed I didn't live up to my end of a bargain I never agreed to." She grimaced, remembering when Alejandro had been sent back to Costa Rica because someone on the staff had spotted her slipping into his room.

She'd sold some of her jewelry and sent him money, which he'd used to pay for college and medical school, so in the long run, he'd come out fine, but her father's treatment of him had been wrong just the same.

And she had no more jewelry left to sell.

But what happened to Alejandro was the least of her concerns. "After that, my dad told me I could screw around all I wanted, but in the end, if I didn't marry Nikolai Drugov, he would dissolve my trust fund."

Bastian sat bolt upright. "The Russian oligarch? He was the man you were expected to screw?"

"He wasn't an oligarch then. He was a weaselly oligarch-in-training. My dad has wanted our families to align since I was a teen. My dad figures the best way to secure loyalty in business is shared grandkids or some other bullshit. All I know is I was expected to marry the creep, while no one insisted JJ or Rafe marry Lucya—Nikolai's little sister."

"Is that why you were disinherited? Because you refused Drugov?"

"No. That didn't happen until years later, because I—" *Shit*. She shouldn't have started this.

"Because you what?"

Her stomach churned. This would matter to Bastian. A lot. But the full truth was horrible, and there was no telling the first part without telling the last. She took a deep breath. "I made sure the Northwest oil pipeline project failed."

Bastian stiffened. "What do you mean? You were the advocate for construction. I sat in that meeting. I listened to all the PE bullshit. Most of which was said by you."

She closed her eyes. Every word he said was true. She'd been a shill. But once she'd learned about the Traditional Cultural Property and what it meant to the tribes, she'd done what she could to fix things. She crossed her arm over her chest, creating a barrier between her and Bastian as she rubbed her other arm. "I funneled information to the reporter who wrote all the articles that ended up killing the project. The information on the TCP. Prime Energy's illegal altering of the negative environmental impact data. Micah got the proof he needed to kill the project from me."

"*You* were the leak? You knew Micah Rogers?"

She wasn't surprised Bastian knew the reporter's name, especially given how closely he'd followed the oil pipeline project. Her fingers worried over a raised freckle on her right elbow, a spot she always rubbed in moments of stress. "Yes. We were lovers for several months."

Bastian sat up, scooting away from her. She missed his body heat. Hated how this would change his opinion of her. Micah's death was her fault.

She rolled over and stared at the thin metal CLU wall. "He didn't know I was using him. I left the papers out, where he would conveniently find them when I was in the shower. I always gave him enough time to take pictures."

In the end, it was one of those pictures that had killed him. Later, he'd been interviewed about the series of articles he wrote that took on Prime Energy and won, and included in the magazine spread were a few of the documents he'd obtained from an unnamed PE whistleblower. Several of the documents had been altered using a key only her father had known—a specific lowercase o had been filled in, looking like an ink misprint. She hadn't known that her copy was the only one with that particular solid o, hadn't known the pages had been altered at all. But then, she hadn't known her father suspected someone was leaking documents and she'd led them right to Micah.

From there, it had only required a search of her credit card bills—along with an illegal search of Micah's accounts, easy work for a man with Mafia ties—to see they'd concurrently visited the San Juan Islands on three different occasions.

She told Bastian this, then cleared her throat. "I was devastated when I heard about the helicopter crash that killed him. I was in grad school at Portland State, but home for the holidays when I heard the news. It was a tense visit to begin with, because I was clean and sober but hadn't parted ways with my family yet. I still figured I could do good for the company, that I could make sure PE followed environmental law and did real, ethical environmental justice evaluations. I made the mistake of sharing my thoughts with JJ and Rafe."

She pulled up the blanket, wishing she hadn't stripped after they had sex. Wishing she hadn't started this, because no way would Bastian let her stop talking now. "I'd heard about the news helicopter crash, but it was twenty-four hours before they released the pilot's and the reporter's names. When I heard Micah was on the helicopter, I lost it. Right there, in front of my brothers and father as we watched the news, I made it clear I'd cared about Micah. I couldn't hide it." She would never forget the smirk on her father's face.

"I fled to my room. After crying for an hour, I pulled myself together to try to figure out what I could do for Micah's family. The news said he had a wife and three-month-old baby."

"Was he married when you were sleeping with him?" Bastian's voice was stone cold.

"No. We'd broken up two years before—before he'd written the damning articles about the pipeline. He met his wife a few months later. He was a good man. He never would have cheated, and I don't poach. Ever." She gripped the edge of the blanket, pulling it higher. "I found a meal delivery service and tried to order gift certificates to provide meals for his wife and baby, but the order wouldn't go through. My credit card account had been closed.

"I called the bank and learned my accounts—all of them—had been shut down. I was broke—completely cut off. So I marched down to my father's study and demanded to know why. He presented the proof of the filled-in o, said he knew I'd been the leaker, and he'd seized my trust fund—which was under his control until I turned thirty—and was discontinuing my allowance, which had been set up when I quit working for the company to enroll in grad school. He said if I wanted back in the family fold, if I wanted my trust fund reinstated, all I had to do was withdraw from grad school and marry Nikolai Drugov. It was the only way I could prove my loyalty.

"I told him I was fine being broke, that I'd never marry Drugov or any man he chose. That my body wasn't part of his business deals." She cleared her throat. "He countered that I'd used my body to betray PE to a reporter, now I would use my body to make amends."

She wished she could read Bastian's reaction, but she could barely look at him. Her gaze shifted everywhere but his face, only catching him peripherally.

"The timing of Micah's death and my outing as the leaker couldn't have been a coincidence. I accused him of having Micah killed. He denied it. But I know he lied."

"That crash was investigated by the NTSB," Bastian said. "They determined the cause was mechanical combined with pilot error. It was all over the news."

She raised a brow. "You don't think my family could

arrange that? They're in bed with the Russian Mafia. They killed Micah because I betrayed them. I think they'd figured out that I cared about him, and my reaction upon learning the news only confirmed it." She cleared her throat. "Loyalty is the number one thing in my family. They didn't give a damn when I was using drugs, sleeping around, didn't care how I lived my life. But I betrayed them. So they went after a man I'd cared about and made his new wife a widow, his three-month-old child fatherless. The pilot was just collateral damage, and every bit as heartbreaking."

"You loved Micah?" Bastian asked quietly.

She shrugged. "Maybe. I broke things off when I started to care about him. I couldn't keep using him. I couldn't tell him how I felt. It was best just to walk away, so he could write the articles."

"He copied the papers. So he was using you too."

"It wasn't exactly a relationship based on trust." She finally met Bastian's gaze, and he didn't seem to hate her. But who knew how this would sit with him over time. "I talked to the FBI about the crash. They reviewed the NTSB findings and said there was no evidence of any tampering with the helicopter. The pilot might've had a medical emergency that compounded the mechanical failure. It was hard to tell given the condition of his remains."

She gripped the top edge of the blanket, rubbing the smooth edge against her palm. It was a sensory comfort as she saw in her mind that last confrontation with her family. The bile that rose as she finally saw that not only did her older brothers not give a damn about their baby sister, but that all three men were straight-up evil.

She'd fled to her room to pack a bag, grabbing her

jewelry and anything else she could sell. Her father had met her at the door, alone, ensuring there were no witnesses to his final words. *"Fuck around all you want, but remember what happens to people you care about."*

It was the closest he came to admitting he'd had Micah killed. She knew her father's ruthlessness well. He didn't bluff. And now he had a way to control her even without money.

She'd never gotten serious about a man again. It was too big a risk.

She met Bastian's gaze, and fear pulsed through her. She cared about him. If something happened to him because of her, she'd never be able to crawl out of the hole of self-loathing.

"I think you should go," she said.

Bastian's nostrils flared; his body went tense. "What the hell? What aren't you telling me?"

She gathered her haughtiest demeanor. "This is my CLU, and I'm telling you to leave."

"Is this because you think your family will come after me like they did Micah? Micah's articles crushed a billion-dollar project. Did you ever consider that's why they had him killed? That it has nothing to do with the fact that you'd cared about him?"

That might have been their motive at first, but her dad's final words still rang in her ears. "My dad isn't done with his revenge. He threatened anyone I care about."

"In case you haven't noticed, I can take care of myself."

Panic seized her. That was exactly the kind of attitude that would put him at risk. He didn't realize her family would never attempt a frontal assault. They'd use surrogates like Senator Jackson to undermine him with the military, or they'd go after his tribe. They'd strip him of everything that mattered to him before delivering a final killing blow that would look like an accident—or suicide. "Put your clothes on and get out."

He stared at her, his face tight with anger. His hands clenched and unclenched as his chest rose with heavy breaths. "Fine. I'll go now. But we aren't done here."

He jerked on his pants and donned the T-shirt, his movements angry, his eyes showing hurt.

This was for the best. He might think he was invincible, but she knew better. No one was invincible against the kind of pain her family would inflict.

Chapter Twenty-Six

B rie wasn't certain why she was called to a meeting in the Special Operations Command headquarters. She'd been debriefed several times by Savvy and SOCOM personnel. She dressed carefully for the meeting, applying makeup with the diligence of a former heiress.

The makeup was a kind of armor. It would show Bastian who she really was. She wanted him to see the world she could never escape. Not even in South Sudan. Not even in Djibouti.

Prime Energy would always find her. It terrified her to think the senator might already have told her father about meeting the Green Beret who'd saved her, that it might already be too late.

She entered the meeting room wearing the mantle of professionalism she'd always mentally donned before entering a business meeting. She wasn't intimidated by these men and women. She was a Prime, and as horrible as that was, it meant she'd grown up in a world where she'd learned how to work a room from age five. She knew when to be pretty and vacant, and when to twist balls.

Today, she'd crush some nuts if she had to. She was getting the hell out of here. She'd go to Morocco and present the vacant heiress to the world. She'd sleep with a half-dozen men and make it clear Chief Warrant Officer Sebastian Ford meant nothing to her.

She dropped into a seat near the head of the table as if it were her right. She avoided Bastian's gaze but met Savvy's, who nodded at her in approval. Apparently, the CIA wanted her to look the heiress part.

This world was as fucked up as her own.

Someone with stars on his chest entered the room, and everyone was called to stand. She did and nodded to the general before resuming her seat.

She rather liked the hierarchy of the military. It was spelled out and attainable. It wasn't like the hierarchy of her world, where a woman could be born into it, or fuck her way in, but there were few other entry points and no equality no matter how you got there.

The meeting began without ceremony or preamble. Brie wasn't introduced nor was she told who else was at the table. She'd met Bastian's CO and XO the day before, and the captain who was leader of his A-Team was also present, but no one else from the team was there.

Brie and Savvy were the only women in the room, and after a few minutes, it was clear Savannah James had called this meeting.

Savvy rapidly outlined the major players in South Sudan's ongoing civil war, starting with the president and opposing vice president, then moving on to describe other players who'd stepped in, finally coming to Lawiri.

His picture was projected on the big screen. He wore a military uniform and had dark skin with facial scarring indicative of one of the smaller tribes. "Erfan Lawiri split with the rebels over a year ago and is currently raising his own forces," Savvy said. "His main encampment was attacked six months ago, and we thought Lawiri had been taken until he showed up at Ms. Stewart's USAID facility demanding food for his soldiers about two months ago." She paused. "We have reason to believe he's backed by oil money."

More than just Savvy's eyes drifted in Brie's direction.

"Intel indicates it's highly probable the attack on the USAID facility was done to destabilize both sides and leave an opening for Lawiri to seize power in the vacuum. He's likely to have made deals—offering drilling rights in exchange for weapons to support his bid for power. HUMINT obtained after the market destruction indicates Lawiri's men provided security for the market."

Savvy clicked her mouse, and the slide changed. The next image caused Brie's stomach to churn. "Nikolai Drugov. As most of you are aware, he's a Russian oligarch with deep Mafia ties. He's in the Russian president's deepest inner circle and by all accounts is a sick motherfucker. We think Drugov is backing Lawiri, and the market was a joint venture between the two to fund Lawiri's bid for power. Drugov's oil company, Druneft, stands to gain a fortune in oil rights, while Prime Energy is in line to build a pipeline to transport the oil out of South Sudan. This would remove the current pipeline from operation, saving South Sudan from paying high transit fees charged by Sudan for using their pipeline—which South Sudan's Petroleum and Mining ministry says has led to the Upper Nile oil fields operating at a loss. Prime Energy has concessions with the Central African Republic and Cameroon ensuring that the transit fees will be much lower with the new pipeline."

Brie wasn't surprised to hear her family was in deep

with Druneft. They'd been working toward this kind of partnership since she was a teen.

Savvy fixed her gaze on Brie. "Ms. Stewart, it's my understanding that you're familiar with Nikolai Drugov and at one point he surfaced as a potential fiancé to cement your family's business dealings. What can you tell us about the man?"

Brie felt the blood drain from her face at Savvy's words. She couldn't stop herself and turned to Bastian. "You utter bastard."

His face was a hard stone mask, reminding her of the man she'd met that night in Barely North. Now she knew why his enemies called him Bastian the Bastard.

"That is irrelevant to this meeting, Ms. Stewart," Savvy said without a hint of remorse in her voice. "Please tell us what you know."

"Why? The last time I had any interaction with Nikolai was years ago. Your intel is far more accurate than my first-hand knowledge."

"But you *have* first-hand knowledge. We don't."

Brie flattened her hands on the table, to keep them from curling into fists. Finally she said, "He's ten years older than I am. Like me, he was raised in the business. Unlike some of the other oil company babies I grew up with, he knew the ins and outs of the actual work. He was also raised to be ruthless and has a nasty streak a mile deep. I was friends with his little sister, and she told me stories. Let's just say there was a reason she didn't have any pets. I was forced to date him when I was eighteen with the expectation that we'd marry at some point to join Druneft and PE in an unholy alliance. I refused to screw him or marry him. Later, when I was disinherited, my father told me I could have my trust fund back if I married Nikolai. Again I refused. That's pretty much all I know."

"Did you know several small companies have formed in the past five years that have both the Prime and Drugov names in the tax filings?" Savvy asked.

"No. It sounds like my father managed to secure the deals without using my vagina. Good for him."

Savvy's face remained blank, yet Brie picked up on her amusement at the frank word. "I'm sorry to say it appears Drugov's interest in you didn't stop when you refused his suit."

Suit. She hadn't heard archaic language like that since her dad tried to sell her to Drugov and called it an alliance.

"What do you mean?"

"Intel indicates Drugov intended to purchase you from the slave market. He was the 'special buyer'—after all, it was his market. He was just going to go through the motions of the auction to obscure the trail should the US discover what had happened to you. I agree with Mr. Ford's initial assessment that the slaver only sold Ms. Stewart to him because he intended to have her recaptured and resold to Drugov, thus doubling his take. Furthermore, intel indicates the Russian mercenary who found you in the abandoned village was one of Drugov's men."

"How can you know this?" Brie asked.

"Multiple sources collected from HUMINT and SIGINT."

Brie knew Savvy was referring to human intelligence—intelligence gathered through human contact, and signal intelligence—intercepted radio communications.

"That combined with intelligence provided by the children liberated by the A-Team, and we've had a lot of threads to connect."

It occurred to Brie that Bastian had provided some of the HUMINT—after getting her to talk in bed. Savvy's text message to Bastian came to mind: *Need answers, ASAP.*

Well. Now Brie understood what that had meant. Bastian was on a mission for the CIA. Tears burned behind her eyes, but she held them at bay with a deep breath. She called up her inner Gabriella. Gabriella had ice in her soul and had screwed a reporter so she could feed *him* intel.

Savvy clicked the mouse again, and again Brie recognized the image that appeared on the screen. Dread surfaced, only to be tamped down with icy reserve.

"This," Savvy said, "is the Prime siblings' estate in Casablanca, Morocco. Jeffery Prime divested the asset to his children to keep it from being lost to Ms. Stewart's mother in the divorce. Because it was not part of Ms. Stewart's trust fund, it was not taken away when the trust was dissolved. Apparently, even Ms. Stewart didn't know she was partial owner until several months before she arrived in South Sudan."

How the hell did Savvy know that? The details of trusts were confidential. But then, the woman was CIA, and had probably employed illegal methods to obtain information.

Sometimes she even convinced Special Forces operators to fuck unsuspecting women to get them to talk.

"As the rainy season intensifies, the famine is getting worse in South Sudan. With the destruction of the

USAID food reserves, residents in the east of the country are either fleeing into Ethiopia or dying. Every major city outside Juba is on the verge of collapse, and Juba could follow soon after. We believe Lawiri is currently residing at Drugov's estate in Morocco as he waits for both factions in South Sudan to fall."

Brie came to attention.

"Drugov's estate borders the Prime property, and Drugov is currently in residence. We know he's there because six days from now he's hosting a black tie party at his estate, which will be attended by Jeffery, Jr. and Rafe Prime."

Well, there went her plans of escaping to Morocco for a nice quiet recovery. Brie cleared her throat. "What is it you want from me, Savvy?"

"I want you to go to Morocco, find Lawiri, and expose Drugov."

"No!" The sharp word came from Bastian, who rose to his feet.

Brie glared at him and turned back to Savvy. "Bullshit. You want me to be bait for Drugov."

"That too. And sit down, Mr. Ford. You have a role in this op too."

Op?

Savvy nodded to Bastian's CO, Major Haverfeld, and resumed her seat.

"Mr. Ford," Major Haverfeld said, "we've gone over the logistics with Ms. James and believe this mission has the best chance of success if it's conducted as a covert operation."

"What?" Brie said. "I'm not exactly a trained spy. And I'm pretty sure Nikolai will recognize me."

"You aren't the one who will be covert, Ms. Stewart.

We would like to send Mr. Ford with you to Casablanca. He will pose as your boyfriend, but act as your bodyguard. All we need for you to do is locate Lawiri. Once we have proof he's in Morocco with Drugov, we can send in a team to seize him. Lawiri is wanted by authorities in South Sudan and Ethiopia."

"Plus, if we can get Lawiri to roll on Drugov," Savvy said, "we can expose the Russian for aiding the overthrow of a government to secure oil rights."

"And they're just going to magically accept me showing up out of the blue with my Special Forces boyfriend in tow?" She'd avoided her family for years—hadn't even wanted them to know where USAID sent her—and now the CIA and US military wanted her to visit her brothers as if nothing had happened?

"We believe Drugov's source—Senator Jackson—has informed the oligarch that Mr. Ford is the soldier who saved you in South Sudan," Savvy said. "I'm sure no one would find it hard to believe a relationship has developed, and after everything you've been through, you're due a break at your luxury estate. Officially, Mr. Ford is being granted R and R after a stressful week in South Sudan, which culminated in you both being injured."

"If Drugov was hoping to buy me for his sex slave, he won't be pleased to meet a boyfriend. Even a fake one." Because sure as hell their relationship was now in fictional territory.

"All the more reason to have him there," Major Haverfeld said. "You need protection, Ms. Prime."

"Stewart," she corrected. "And why should I go at all? Just send in a team and storm Nikolai's house."

"You know we can't do that. Not without risking war with Russia," Savvy said. She held Brie's gaze. "We believe these men are responsible for the destruction of the food in South Sudan. Food that would have fed thousands of starving people. People who very well may die now."

"We also believe," Haverfeld piled on, "they're responsible for the slave market. The one in which you were stripped naked, forced to wear a metal collar, and were to be auctioned off. The one where all those children were lined up, waiting to be sold. I think you have a lot of reasons to want to chase down this lead, Ms. Stewart. And there is no one in this room who has legal access to your family estate but you."

Goddamn, it sucked how they'd lined up their ammunition to corner her. She could deflect, but in the end, she'd be refusing to fight for a cause she believed in. "Fine. But I'll go alone."

"Hell no!" Bastian said.

At last, after avoiding him the entire meeting, she met his gaze. But she didn't see the man she'd made love with, the man she'd been falling for, the man she'd pushed away because it was the only way she could protect him. No. She saw the man who didn't do relationships. The one who'd seduced her on orders from the CIA.

She slowly rose from the table. "Make your plans, then. Let me know what you decide. For myself, I need a drink." She left the room without looking back.

Chapter Twenty-Seven

Bastian's already crushed heart sank at seeing Brie sitting at the bar. *Fuck*. Was he too late?

They'd kept him in the meeting, planning an op that would gut him emotionally if not physically. Still, he stayed, because sure as hell no one was going to Morocco with her but him. If he'd chased after her, he'd have lost his spot at her side. And it was likely only Savvy knew Brie was a recovering addict who hadn't had a drink in years.

Staying in the meeting, knowing she was here, had cut him. He'd done this to her, brought her this low.

His fault. He hadn't warned her that he needed to tell Savvy about Drugov. He'd been about to tell her last night, but she'd kicked him from her bed, out of her CLU.

He'd been angry and frustrated, and who did he run into but Savvy James? The woman had taken one look at him and knew he'd gotten Brie to talk. He'd done his duty and told Savvy everything.

Savvy had told him on *Dahlgren* that Drugov was a person of interest. The fact that Brie knew him personally was the piece that had been missing. Even after telling Savvy everything, he hadn't known until the meeting that Savvy had connected Drugov and Lawiri.

Now he knew the final piece, information that had

been shared after Brie left the room. Drugov had been after Brie for years—just like the mercenary in South Sudan had said. Lawiri's showing up at the USAID facility two months ago was likely to confirm that Brie Stewart was Gabriella Prime and the later attack had been twofold: snatch Brie and burn the food. Drugov would get the woman he wanted, and the country would further destabilize and fall into famine.

Now Brie sat at the bar, her back ramrod straight, facing the bottles of alcohol lined up on the shelves at the back of the bar.

He circled and saw there was no drink before her, just an empty counter and a woman facing her demons. He wanted to slide onto the seat beside her yet feared being the thing that would push her over the edge, cause her to lose the battle.

But inaction could be worse. What if she gave in because she was alone? Because she believed he didn't care about her?

He dropped onto the seat by her side, reminded of their first meeting on these very barstools.

And just like she had then, she rebuffed him before he had a chance to speak. "Go. The fuck. Away."

"I'm sorry."

"I don't give a fuck. Go away."

"No. I'm sorry, Brie. I was going to tell you that Savvy needed to know about Drugov, but you tossed me out."

"And you left because the only reason you fucked me was to get me to talk. Your job was done."

He couldn't lie, but knew she'd find the truth hard to believe. "Can we talk about this in private?" Someplace where drinks weren't being served and the bartender couldn't overhear.

"No. If you're just going to tell the fricking CIA everything I say, we may as well talk here."

She waved the bartender over. The man paused in front of her. "Have you decided?"

Her gaze fixed on the bar again, and Bastian held his breath. After a moment she said, "No." She nodded toward Bastian. "But he wants something."

Bastian did, but no way was he ordering a stiff drink now, not when she was fighting demons. "Coke. Please."

The bartender filled a glass, slid it across the bar, then moved to the corner—as far as he could go and remain behind the counter.

"I love you," Bastian said, desperate to breach her barricades.

Her body stiffened. Her eyes hardened and her nostrils flared, but she said nothing.

His heart pounded as her silence lengthened. Finally, she rose from her seat and left the club.

～◯～

Brie's entire body quaked with rage. He *loved* her? Right. If he loved her, he wouldn't have fucked her for information and then turned around and told the CIA everything. He wouldn't have let her be blindsided by that meeting.

He wouldn't have used her just like her family tried to use her.

Her father had wanted her to screw Drugov to seal a deal. Marry him to join empires. Her needs, her wants never factored into the equation. She was a vagina for male satisfaction and a womb to carry little Prime-Drugov heirs.

As if she'd bring children into that world. As if she'd perpetuate the horror that was her family on another generation.

Tears were falling before she made it to the door of the club. She could walk faster now that she'd ditched the cane, but she still couldn't run, which she desperately wanted to do. Her goal was her CLU, where she could lock her door against the man she'd kicked out of her bed because she cared too much, only to discover he was on a mission from the CIA.

Savvy must have arranged everything. That was why he was on the carrier even though he didn't require twenty-four-hour observation. He was there to get close to her.

And of course he'd gotten clearance to take her to the observation deck. Savvy had just run the meeting in a room full of SOCOM leaders. Brie had no doubt the woman could convince the entire fleet to assist her scheme. A field trip to watch jets take off was child's play.

No wonder medical center staff had looked the other way and the doctor had been free with condoms. Brie was dumb not to have seen it sooner.

She was halfway to her CLU when Bastian caught up to her.

"Brie. Please talk to me. Please."

She turned and fixed him with a teary glare. "I have nothing to say to you except I now understand why your parents would prefer someone else over you."

It was the most cutting thing she could think of to say, and it was effective. He stopped dead in his tracks, and she made it to her CLU without him following at her heels.

She closed the door behind her and finally let the tears flow. First she was assaulted by images of his body as he'd made love to her, waking feelings she didn't want. Emotions she feared.

Then she rewound to the first moment he'd stepped into the hut in South Sudan, when she stood before him naked but for a slave collar, and how her heart had surged at the sight of him.

Dancing under the stars in South Sudan. Kissing on the observation deck in the Gulf of Aden. Making love in this room. It was a vicious cycle of memories in which he'd elicited the most intense of her emotions.

And now here she was, adding another to the heap of memories.

She'd sat at that bar for thirty minutes, fighting the urge to order a drink. Now she wished she'd given in.

She'd give anything not to feel this, not to feel at all.

Chapter Twenty-Eight

Brie managed to avoid Bastian for all of thirty-six hours, but with their mission to Morocco scheduled for three days from now, she had to meet with him. They had to plan.

He was going to play her boyfriend, and they had to discuss their roles and form a strategy. He had to learn his part.

She stepped into the conference room in full Gabriella Prime makeup and clothing. She wore a pantsuit now, and her limp was nearly invisible. She walked with regal poise, and Bastian ached for her. Physically. Mentally.

He loved her. He knew that now with certainty. Somewhere between the slave market and Camp Citron, he'd fallen hard for her, and if he couldn't convince her to give him a second chance, he was pretty sure he would fall apart.

Was this how Cece had felt when he dumped her? He'd always assumed she'd loved the idea of them as a couple, and tolerated him as a partner, but maybe there really had been more to it for her. Maybe that was why she'd refused to let him go.

None of that mattered now, though.

Now they had a mission to plan. He was accompanying the woman he loved into the heart of a viper pit. There they'd face a Russian oligarch who'd planned to have her as a slave, a South Sudanese general who was selling out his people so he could profit from oil drilling, and her brothers who might have ordered a hit on the last man Brie had cared for.

Bastian would be her only protection, and right now, she hated him.

This might make South Sudan feel like a vacation.

Brie sat across from him at the table. "This is how we're going to do things. When we first arrive in Morocco, I'm taking you shopping. You need to look the part of Gabriella Prime's lover." Her gaze flicked over him, as if Gabriella wouldn't give him the time of day.

That was how she wanted to play this? He leaned back and smiled. Game on. "Gabriella gets off on my rugged good looks and the fact that I'm not a sadistic asshole like that oligarch guy."

"Rugged, maybe. Good looks? You wish."

He laughed.

"Children, please," Savvy said. "Save your flirting for later. We've got an op to plan."

"He's going to need clothes," Brie said flatly.

"I've ordered a dress uniform for him to wear to Drugov's party. You're going to need pick up a gown when you arrive."

"I'll get a few items, but I've got clothes, including gowns, there already from when I spent a month there last year."

"Good, because the clothing budget is going to be smaller than Gabriella is used to," Savvy said.

"Fortunately, Brie knows how to live on a budget," Brie said. "Next up, sleeping arrangements. The villa has twenty-two bedroom and bathroom suites. Bastian will sleep in the suite next to mine."

"Nope. I'm your boyfriend. I'm in your room."

"No one will know you aren't sleeping in my room. The house has over a hundred thousand square feet of living space. We'll take connecting suites."

"Still no," Bastian said. "You have servants. They'll *know*. They'll report to your brothers. And you won't be safe unless we're together twenty-four/seven. We sleep in the same bed. If a maid sees I've been sleeping on the couch, we're screwed. And when we're in front of your family, there will be public displays of affection. If your brothers get any hint there's something off between us, the game is over."

"I hate you," she said sweetly by way of agreeing.

"I know," he said, aiming for Han Solo nonchalant. He wished to hell Savvy wasn't in the room.

"Excellent," Savvy said. "Next item: Drugov. We want you to make contact with him as soon as possible after you arrive. I need a full report. His demeanor. How he's changed since you saw him last. Anything and everything you can tell me."

Brie smiled wickedly. "I could probably get him alone. I'm sure he'll be eager to talk to me without Bastian looming in the background."

"Fuck no," Bastian said. "The guy is a sadist, and his victims don't consent."

"Agreed," Savvy said. "You are not to be alone with Drugov, ever."

"And my brothers?"

"If you can avoid it. I don't recommend being alone with them either, but I know that will be trickier. They'll be eager to separate you from Bastian from the get-go. You're going to have to stick to your guns and keep him firmly by your side."

Savvy glanced at a metal briefcase on the table. "Which brings us to the next item. The CIA wants you both injected with subdermal trackers. Just in case you're separated."

He'd expected Brie to receive a tracker and fully supported taking that precaution, but wasn't so thrilled at the idea of being chipped himself. "Why me? That's a waste of expensive technology. I'm not the target here."

"Don't get your ego in a twist, Chief Ford, no one is casting aspersions on your badassness," Savvy said in an even voice. "You met Senator Jackson, and he was told you were part of Brie's rescue team."

Bastian nodded.

"Then they know you're a Green Beret and how you met. They will almost certainly want to separate you at the first opportunity and they might not keep it legal. Drugov's been after her for years. He's going to be pissed you're accompanying her. You're getting chipped, for Brie's safety and your own."

Savvy reached for the box and punched in the combination after swiping her thumb across the scanner. "You both know the drill, right? Once activated, the chip will transmit for up to four hours; however, it needs a working cell phone within ten feet. It hijacks the signal and transmits your location. If there is no cell coverage, no active phone, you'll end up draining the battery for nothing."

Bastian knew all the weaknesses of the trackers but also knew they were the best hope if Brie should be taken hostage. For himself, he had no intention of being taken but also wasn't so full of himself that he believed it was impossible.

After they went over the details of how to initiate the

trackers—massage the spot for five seconds, or sustained pressure on the spot for ten seconds—they then identified the best place to inject the tracker on each of them. Brie opted for her left arm above the elbow, while Bastian went for his right calf, because if they each had a wound in the same location, it might be noted.

The calf location would make it harder to trigger the tracker if Bastian's hands were tied above his head, but they all agreed it was more important that Brie's tracker be in the easiest-to-access spot.

Savvy glared at Bastian when he told Brie the story of Morgan Adler's abduction and how the tracker had saved her life, but she didn't stop him. As a CIA operator, she couldn't tell the story because it was classified on her end. Probably on Bastian's too, but he didn't give a damn. He wanted Brie to know why it mattered. If she needed to use the tracker, it would be a last resort but could damn well be the one thing that would save her life.

"Jesus, I swear, that hurt worse than getting shot," Brie said after the tracker was inserted and tested.

Bastian raised an eyebrow.

She pouted. "Fine, I'm exaggerating, but still, my arm hurts."

"While you're in residence at the villa, I expect you to be armed at all times, Chief Ford," Savvy said.

"I'm going to wear my Sig concealed, and I'll have backup on my ankle, plus a knife."

"Good."

He looked at Brie. "If you were better trained with firearms, I'd want you to wear one too, but at this point, you'd be in more danger if someone took it from you. This afternoon, we're going to resume the fighting lessons we began in South Sudan. We'll pick up where we left off."

Brie's face flushed, and he considered his words. Where they'd left off—they'd been damn close to screwing in the hot South Sudanese sun. "No," she said.

"You need to be prepared to fight, Brie," Savvy said. "I'd spar with you, but I don't have the time. And it's Bastian's job to teach fighting skills. So stop acting like a spoiled child and buck up."

Brie turned her glare on the other woman, and Bastian knew exactly which nerve Savvy had stepped on. If ever anyone was sensitive at being called spoiled, it was Brie. And he knew better than anyone that while Brie had grown up in wealth that ninety-nine percent of people could only dream of, she hadn't exactly been spoiled.

Sure, she'd had luxury items, but she'd been expected to maintain her stake in the family business with her body. "Back off, Savvy." He turned to Brie. "I'll keep it professional. Your safety is the most important thing here." Hell, he didn't give a fuck about anything other than her safety. If he had a say, she wouldn't be going to Casablanca at all.

But Brie had agreed to go, and he would take her. He'd protect her.

Hell, he'd die for her.

It was that simple.

Chapter Twenty-Nine

Because this was a covert operation, they flew commercial from Djibouti City to Cairo and from there caught a flight to Casablanca. Brie did her best to ignore her companion on the journey, but given the length of the flights—the first being over three hours and the second over five—it wasn't possible.

Not long after takeoff from Cairo, Bastian reached across the armrest and entwined his fingers through hers. She jerked her hand away, and he responded by pressing his palm to her knee. "We're going to have to touch a lot in front of your family. You'd better get used to it now, or we're going to fail."

She relented and took his hand, hating that the simple affectionate touch was comforting. Hating that just the smell of his skin did things to her, reminded her of how good it had felt when he'd methodically possessed every inch of her body. How safe she'd felt in his arms.

How her heart had opened and she'd gotten a glimpse of what it might feel like to fall in love. And even to be loved in return.

She hadn't slept well the night before and leaned back in her seat and tried to doze. She turned in the tight seat in an attempt to get comfortable, but sleep remained elusive.

Even though she was going to a twenty-two-bedroom estate of which she was one-third owner, she remained broke. The government had paid for these plane tickets, meaning they were crammed into coach. She didn't miss much about her family's money, but when flying, she did miss first class. Now in her cramped seat, she drifted toward the warm body at her side and settled against his shoulder, hoping he'd believe she was napping and unaware that she gravitated toward him.

He chuckled and pressed his lips to her temple. "Sleep, sweetheart."

She gave in to his offer and drifted off. She awoke with a jolt sometime later. A glance out the window showed they were just about to land. Extracting herself from Bastian's shoulder, she stretched to cover her flustered state. She'd been dreaming of Bastian—not surprising considering she'd been breathing his scent for hours— and in her dream, he'd been so sweet—like the night he'd crawled into her bed on the aircraft carrier.

She longed for the simplicity of that night, but of course, now she knew even that had been fake. Savvy had put him up to it. Nothing was ever simple. Except maybe the time they kissed while dancing in South Sudan.

Now she needed to act like touching him, being near him, didn't break her heart. She needed to look at him like she was in love with him, and more than anything she feared he'd see it wasn't entirely an act.

While he'd been working, she'd been…herself. She'd let him get to know both her Stewart and Prime halves, something she'd never dared with anyone else.

She turned to the window. They were low over the trees now, coming in to Mohamed V Airport. This had always been one of her favorite places—as a teen, she'd loved the sights, sounds, and smells of Casablanca and spent as much time as she could away from the villa, exploring the North African city.

She'd loved the souks, traditional marketplaces that were a maze of alleys and narrow streets where vendors sold spices, jewelry, food, and clothing. The colors, the scents, the language—she'd drunk it all in. It was in the souks that she'd begun to learn Arabic. She'd also spent as much time as she could on the public beaches and exploring the medina—the old walled city.

She'd last visited a year ago, not long after learning she owned one-third of the property. She'd financed the trip by ditching her Seattle apartment—using her rent money to buy her plane ticket—and upon her return, she'd crashed on a friend's couch as she made arrangements for the South Sudan job. It had been worth it for the month-long break.

The wheels of the airliner touched down.

She was home. Sort of.

⌒

Bastian wasn't thrilled to discover that Brie hadn't been teasing about taking him clothes shopping first thing. She took him to a fancy mall with a giant fish tank that featured small sharks along with thousands of other fish species. After buying clothes for herself at Dior, she dragged him outside to catch the musical fountain's hourly performance, then she took him to Armani to outfit him.

"My dress uniform will be enough."

"It's perfect for Nikolai's party, but you'll need suits to dress for dinner and other social functions."

"You don't really dress for dinner."

"When business is being conducted, always. And we will if Drugov comes to dinner. You need to look the part."

"The role I'm playing—the part I need to look—is your boyfriend, who is Army Special Forces, not some asshole who can't sit at a table without flaunting his wealth by wearing a two-thousand-dollar suit."

"I call the shots on this part of the op. I know my family, these people. This world. And to fit in here, you need overpriced clothes." She patted his cheek. "Think of yourself as Cinderella, cupcake."

The jab set his teeth on edge. "You think I'm not good enough for you, Brie? As I am? Kalahwamish soldier?"

She scowled at him. "Of course not. This isn't about *me* or what I think. If anything, you're too good for Gabriella Prime."

There she was wrong, but he wouldn't say it. She'd made it clear she didn't want to hear the truth and he wasn't one to try to shout down brick walls. To breach a brick wall, you take out the mortar, and that was what he would do with Brie. One brick at a time, he'd chip away at the surrounding grout. "Then why the hell do I need to play dress up when the point is I'm not from your world?"

"But you've got to act like you want a spot in my world. If you don't, if you play the part of the rugged soldier who has no fucks left to give, they'll fear you. But if you act like you want in, if you play by their stupid rules and pander to them, they'll think they have leverage, and their guard will drop.

"These aren't tech billionaires or others who've made their own fortunes. For the most part, everyone you'll meet here inherited their wealth. With this particular crowd, it's all about the money and letting everyone know where they rank in Forbes. I'm not saying everyone who inherits is this way. It's just true of my father's crowd. They have no time for or interest in the quietly wealthy. In this instance, they'll see you as just another guy who is fucking me for my money—and the last laugh is on you because I'm broke."

"You're one-third owner of a palatial estate in Morocco."

"But I can't sell it. I can't mortgage it. I can't turn it into cash in any way, and I'm maxing out my credit card buying us both clothes today."

"Which is why you shouldn't buy the damn clothes."

"No. It's exactly why I need to do it. For the same reason. If my brothers think I want back in the fold so badly I'll mortgage myself to fit in, they'll think they've got game when it comes to pushing me toward Drugov. As far as my brothers know, what I saw in South Sudan scared the shit out of me and I want the luxury and comfort of being a Prime again. I'll do whatever it takes to get back in the fold. *That's* the game we're playing here."

"No one is selling you to Drugov," he said quietly.

"No. But we want them to try. And they can't feel threatened by you or it won't happen."

He let out a sigh. "Okay." He stroked her cheek. "I'll do anything to protect you. Even follow you into hell and buy a pretty suit to wear when I get there."

She held his gaze, and for the first time, the sheen of hurt slipped away.

He'd loosened the first chunk of mortar.

"But I'm buying the damn suit," he said. "I'm not Cinderella, and you aren't going to bankrupt yourself for this op."

"They'll run a credit check. They'll know you paid for the suit."

"I'm counting on that, darling. That way they'll know how much I want to play their stupid game."

She smiled slowly, and he liked the look of respect in her eyes. "You're good at this."

"Honey, my people have been playing the white man's games for hundreds of years. Your brothers are fucking amateurs."

She rose on her toes and brushed her lips over his.

One brick down. A thousand more to go.

Bastian pulled the rental car—a basic Honda because he didn't intend to waste more money on a ridiculous façade—into the circular driveway. Before he could climb out to get Brie's door, the valet was on the job.

They had a full-time valet?

"Miss Stewart, it is a pleasure to see you again." The olive-skinned valet couldn't be more than twenty-one.

"Thank you, Tarek. It's good to be home."

Bastian was impressed she knew the guy's name, but then remembered she'd been here a year ago. He stopped at the trunk to grab their bags, but Brie gave him a slight shake of the head.

Right. The valet or the butler or one of the other servants could get it.

Servants. It wasn't even a dirty word here.

He met her under the arch of an elaborate entranceway and offered his arm. She looped hers through his, and they strode up twenty-five meters of red carpet that was flanked by columns and raised a step at five-meter intervals. An arched roof covered the long walkway, which ended in wide ebony double doors carved in bas-relief.

One column and step before they reached the finish line, the doors opened, and a dark-skinned middle-aged man who must be the butler greeted them. "Welcome home, Miss Prime."

"Thank you. I don't believe we've met?"

"Youssef, ma'am," he said with a slight bow.

"Nice to meet you, Youssef. You must call me Ms. Stewart."

"Of course, ma'am. Ms. Stewart."

"Are my brothers in residence, Youssef?"

"Yes, ma'am. But they are out for the day. Golfing, I believe."

"We will settle into my rooms, then. Please have our bags delivered and unpacked. We'll take tea in the pool garden in thirty minutes." She cocked her head toward Bastian. "Cognac for Chief Ford. Hennessy."

Bastian wasn't a fan of cognac, but she must have other motives for ordering the drink.

"Yes, ma'am. Which room shall we have readied for Chief Ford?" There was a disapproving tone in his voice.

She laughed as if his question was a delight. "Mine, of course."

With that, Bastian accompanied Brie into the most extravagant private home he'd ever seen. He couldn't hold back a low whistle. "Shit, babe," he said, intending for the butler to overhear. "We are *not* in South Sudan anymore."

Seriously, the idea that she'd gone from this marble-columned foyer with triple archways and—he glanced upward—carved ceilings, to pit toilets and thatched-roof huts was astonishing.

Her laugh was light and bright, like a new penny. He

doubted anyone else noticed it was fake. "Wait until you see our room."

He slid a hand over her ass and turned her toward him. He kissed her lightly as he squeezed her butt. "Youssef, make it forty-five minutes."

Brie had stiffened under his touch, but she recovered quickly and her body pressed to his, warm and sultry. Her tongue slid into his mouth, then withdrew, so fast he ached for a real taste. Her eyes were hooded and hot, but there was a hardness too that only he could see. Her voice was husky as she said, "Well then, we'd better hurry."

They climbed the wide curved stairway to the third floor, and he learned she hadn't been kidding about her room. It was at least eight hundred square feet with a curtained four-poster king-sized bed centered along the back wall. The room had three separate sitting areas with sofas and plush seats, a breakfast nook, and an office alcove. Double doors opened onto a large, lush private balcony that overlooked the Atlantic Ocean.

Brightly colored mosaic tiles decorated a deep sunken tub in the bathroom, which also had a separate shower with more masterful mosaic designs. He wanted to make love to Brie in that shower, in that tub, and on that bed. The sofas didn't look comfortable, so he'd skip those, but the balcony...yeah. There too.

He stepped back into the bedroom after gawking at the shower and said, "You know what this room needs?"

"What?"

"Help from Ikea."

Her laugh was genuine this time. "I think you're right. I can just see my dad, cursing because he can't find the hex key."

"Do you ever miss this?" he asked.

She shrugged. "Not really. The price was too high. And my ass doesn't care if the sofa is Ikea or something that was hand-stuffed by fairies in Belgium." She gave him a wry smile. "Although today on the plane, I'll admit I did miss first class."

"I've never flown first class," he said.

"It's disgusting how airlines have made coach so miserable to justify the outrageous prices for first class. It doesn't have to be that way, with a handful of people flying in comfort and the rest treated like garbage. Those were the things I didn't see before I escaped the family."

"Escaped? You sound like it was a cult."

"Isn't it, though? Worship of the almighty dollar? My father as the supreme leader?" She waved her hands to encompass the room. "I mean, who needs twenty-two rooms of this? No one actually lives here except the servants. There are ten servant rooms and a caretaker cottage. That's eleven people who live here full-time, waiting for my brothers and me to visit. The trust set aside a budget for the staff, food, and maintenance. I can't buy clothes, but I can order a four-thousand-dollar cognac to be delivered to you poolside."

Bastian practically choked. "Four *thousand* dollars?"

She shrugged. "Something like that. I reviewed the house budget the last time I was here. There's a cellar that holds at least half a million dollars' worth of wine. I wanted to sell some of the bottles to cover the cost of my trip, but there's a clause in the trust that prevents me from selling any of the house assets, and the liquor and wine is valuable enough to be listed on the assets and not just part of the food budget. Plus the staff knows I don't drink, so the missing bottles would have been noted. The cognac is JJ's favorite and hard to get in Morocco."

"I don't even like cognac." But he had to admit, he'd try it, just for the novelty of tasting something so ridiculously expensive.

Brie had changed into one of her Dior suits at the mall, and now she stripped it off, dropping the designer clothes on the floor. "Strip," she said. "The maid is going to be here with our bags to unpack in about thirty seconds. I gave instructions to unpack, but then you made it clear we were going to have sex. If we're caught going at it, it will be easier to convince everyone we're really a couple."

Brie turned to the bed and spread the sheer curtains.

"The curtains won't hide anything."

"That's why you need to strip. Keep your underwear on. We'll be under the covers, waist down." She dropped her bra to the floor.

Shit. Was this revenge on her part? A way to make him suffer?

But he was a good soldier and stripped, then followed her to bed. She lay on her back, and he settled between her thighs. His erection was all too real.

And as she predicted, the maid knocked a minute later.

Brie bade the woman enter in a husky voice.

The maid stepped inside, and her spine went ramrod straight when she spotted them. "I'm sorry, miss! I was told—"

"Unpack our bags," Brie said, letting out a slight panting sound.

Bastian stiffened—and not in a good way. He'd expected Brie to send the woman away once she caught an eyeful, not invite her in. "What are you doing?" he whispered in her ear.

"Chief Ford will use the closet on the right," she said,

not missing a beat as she pressed up against him. This was no act. The maid wasn't watching. The poor woman was studiously avoiding looking their way.

Which meant there was only one reason Brie was doing this. She was turned on and wanted to play.

He narrowed his gaze and leaned down and kissed her, filling her mouth with his tongue as he teased her clit with his cock. His briefs and her panties were all that was between them.

Oh damn, how he wanted to fuck her.

He released her mouth, then rolled over, pulling her on top of him. He grabbed the sheets to hide her panties. But at this point, they were just a thin and very wet barrier. Her breasts bounced as she smiled down at him, her eyes smoky with arousal. He licked his thumb, slid it inside her panties, and touched her clit.

She gasped and rocked into him. Seeking more.

The maid was in the closet, unpacking. This was for no one's benefit but Brie's.

He cupped the back of her neck with his other hand and pulled her down for a hot kiss, lifting his shoulders from the bed to meet her halfway. "I want to fuck you, Brie," he whispered against her lips. "I want to bury myself in your tight heat and feel your body quiver from the inside as I make you come."

She said nothing. She just closed her eyes against the stroke of his thumb, the pressure of his cock. He held her on the edge of orgasm.

"Please," she whispered. "Finish me."

"No."

He understood her now. She wanted him—every hard inch—but after his betrayal, she wasn't about to forgive and move on. No. She was going to get her needs met in other ways. Dress him up in pretty suits and fuck him like the boy toy he was, keeping her heart out of the mix. He'd been involved in enough no-strings liaisons to recognize the setup.

He gazed up at the woman he'd fallen in love with. The woman he'd betrayed. And for the first time since he'd told Savannah James everything Brie had revealed, he looked forward to the coming days.

Game on, baby.

He stroked her clit with his thumb, wishing he used his tongue. In due time. Maybe later in the sunken tub. Or in the Turkish bath. There would be plenty of opportunities.

Every time he felt her near the edge, he backed off and stopped thrusting his hips. From the look on her face, she was enjoying the prolonged ecstasy as much as she was fighting it.

He wasn't exactly sure when the maid left the room. There was just an awareness that the reason for the charade was gone.

He removed his hand from her panties and rolled to his side, not completely dislodging her as he held her close, but his erection no longer teased her.

"You're just going to leave me hanging?" she asked.

"Yep."

"Bastard."

"You know it."

She scowled, but he could see laughter in her eyes too. Finally, she sighed. "I guess I'll take a shower."

Remembering the shower massager, he said, "Can I watch?"

She leaned back. "Like when I bathed in South Sudan?"

"Exactly."

"No. You can't watch."

He laughed. He'd have been shocked if she said yes.
He'd mark this round as a draw.

Chapter Thirty

B astian didn't like four-thousand-dollar cognac any more than the cheaper brands. But he enjoyed watching Brie lounge in the pool area in a skimpy bikini. He'd opted to keep his suit on to conceal his weapons. He looked more like her bodyguard than her boyfriend, which was fine with him.

They'd done a solid job convincing the staff they were lovers, so he didn't have to try hard now.

It was early evening by the time they'd made it outside, and she wore the sultry evening like a sarong. The garden lights clung to her curves, and all he wanted was to touch, taste, and explore. But this was a long game, a battle of wills, and he was braced for all the darts she'd throw his way. And when it was all over, he'd drag her back to her room and fuck her brains out, let her know exactly how much he wanted her.

They'd both win. They'd both lose. But in the end, it would have been a hell of a journey.

He asked the waiter—or whatever a male attendant was called, footman?—for a beer, and the man produced a bucket full of ice with several bottles to choose from. He would never want to live like this—it was such a horrible waste of money that could do good elsewhere— but had to admit a short-term visit to the land of überwealth had its perks.

Bastian chose a local brew, Casablanca beer, and sat in a chaise next to Brie as she sipped tea. A glance around the garden and pool area, and it was hard to imagine that twelve days ago, they'd been stranded in South Sudan, talking about what she'd do if she got her period. She'd gained weight in the intervening days. Her skin had a healthier glow. A thin stripe of pink marked the blow she'd taken from the whip, and she now wore just a small bandage over the stitches in her thigh. The bruising had faded to a faint yellow.

He cocked his head. "Did you get your period? After South Sudan? You said it was due about a week ago." A week ago, they'd made love, and she'd been period-free.

"It started not long after we had sex the last time, probably right about the time you were telling Savvy everything. Ended yesterday."

"Savvy needed to know," he said softly, his first attempt at offering a defense. "Telling her was the right thing to do."

"I know that, Bastian. If I'd realized I knew something that *mattered*, I'd have told her myself. I'm upset that you didn't tell *me*. You led me to believe you wanted me—maybe even cared about me—but all you wanted was to get me to talk."

"I wanted you then. I want you now. Dammit, Brie, I'm in love with you." His last words were delivered louder, with a little more anger than he intended. But then, she'd walked away the first time he'd said those words. That rejection had cut deeper than he'd realized. Even if it was justified.

"How charming," a man said from behind him, and Bastian turned to see Jeffery Jr. standing several feet away, wearing his patented supercilious smirk. "Our baby sister is back, and she brought a...*plaything*." His gaze flicked over Bastian. "I see you went slumming in South Sudan."

Bastian stiffened, but it wouldn't do to break the guy's nose the first moment they met. They needed information from this asshole. After that, he'd break his nose. And a few other bones.

Brie stood and grabbed the four-thousand-dollar bottle of booze from the low table between the chaise lounges. She stepped in front of her brother, removed the stopper, and poured the liquor onto Junior's shoes and the concrete pool deck.

In a flash, Jeff Jr. struck her across the face. Bastian lunged from his seat, reaching him just as the bottle slipped from Brie's fingers. She reeled backward from the blow.

The bottle shattered, splattering alcohol and glass across the concrete as Bastian took the man by the throat and dangled him over the pool. "I've been trained to kill with every weapon imaginable and improvised. If you ever touch Brie again, I will cut off your balls and make you eat them with ketchup. Understand?"

The man's eyes were wide with alarm, but cold hate burned there as well. He didn't nod or say a word. He just hung stiff in midair, holding on to Bastian's wrist to relieve pressure on his neck, refusing to fight or surrender. Bastian dropped him in the pool.

He turned to Brie. "Babe, let's go inside. The pool area reeks of ass."

She glanced down at her bare feet. Her sandals remained by the chaise where she'd been relaxing. "The glass—"

Bastian scooped her in his arms and carried her into

the house as her brother quietly climbed from the pool.

~⟁~

B rie snuggled her face into Bastian's shoulder as he climbed the stairs, humiliated by the slap Bastian had witnessed. She'd forgotten how casually cruel her brother could be. Jeff Junior had always been coldly violent. Rafe was more calculating. Brie still didn't know if her oldest brother loved or hated her, but she had no illusions about JJ's affection.

What shocked her was that JJ didn't even attempt to play nice. She'd known he'd taunt Bastian with racial slurs, but she'd expected them to be veiled, or that he'd at least work up to blatant, once he felt secure. After all, Bastian might not be tall and hulking like Pax Blanchard, but he was still thick with muscles and intimidating. Few would discount him with a glance, and her brothers were soft. She doubted either of them had ever visited the gym on the second floor.

JJ's taunt was quick and deliberate. She was horrified for Bastian and felt degraded for herself. The strike to her face hurt less than the casual delivery of the blow. He hadn't feared repercussions from the blow because she wasn't worthy.

She'd never been worthy. It shouldn't hurt—it wasn't like JJ was a stellar guy—but still, the fact that her own brother couldn't muster even the faintest regard for her had always hurt.

And then Bastian had dispensed with JJ without even breaking a sweat. Never in her life had anyone stood up for her with her family. She'd never even known it was something to crave. But now she'd had a taste.

And it was delicious.

"Thank you," she said, then pressed her lips to his chest. She breathed in his scent. Musky, sexy. Hot. She was so utterly turned on by the way he'd not only defended her, but then he'd scooped her in his arms to protect her from broken glass.

She'd add it to her mental list of ways in which Bastian was heroic. The one she held up against the list of things he'd done to hurt her. It currently only had one line item, but it was the one that hurt the most.

"I'm sorry he hit you. I wish I'd reacted faster. Stopped him."

Her cheek still ached from the blow. "You're sorrier than he is."

"Oh, I'll make sure he's sorry." Bastian said as he set her down on one of the sofas in her bedroom. "This isn't over."

"He's going to be angry you got the better of him." She grabbed his hand as he rose. "He might try to blindside you."

Bastian shrugged. "No way can a little prick like him get the jump on me."

"He might hire help." She squeezed his fingers. Suddenly, she felt like they hadn't thought this mission through. Bastian was alone here. No team. She'd thought her brothers would be civil, but clearly, that had been a miscalculation.

The whole reason she'd pushed him away was to protect him, but now he was in the lion's den without a shield.

"He doesn't scare me."

"Maybe he should."

Bastian smiled, leaned down, and brushed his lips over hers. "You worried about me, sweetheart?" His lips left hers and trailed across her neck.

"Of course I am."

"So maybe you care about me a little bit?" His lips moved lower, following the strap of her bikini.

"A little... Maybe."

His tongue traced her nipple through the stretchy fabric. It puckered, and she wished the cloth wasn't in the way. He fulfilled her wish and she gasped as he cupped one breast in a hand and sucked on the other. Heat flooded her, and she clenched her pelvic muscles. Revising her wish, she mentally changed where she wanted him to put his mouth.

She was being greedy with her wishes, she knew.

All at once, he released her. "I will make love to you again—but not until you beg me."

"You don't ask much. Just absolute surrender."

He shrugged and offered a smile. "I'm worth it."

Yes, you are.

He held her gaze, and she was certain he could read her thoughts, but all he said was, "You need to change. I want a tour of the house and to meet all the servants. I need to know what I'm dealing with here."

❧

The house was insane. No one needed a palace like this. And that was exactly what it was—a modern Moroccan palace. The gym alone was...just that. A real gym, everything a Special Forces operator could want for a workout. "The only thing missing is a personal trainer," he said.

"I'm sure my brothers have one on retainer," Brie said. "Some guy who is ready to show up at the drop of a Ben Franklin, but neither Rafe nor JJ work out."

"Au contraire, baby sister."

Bastian turned to see Rafe Prime, Brie's half brother, the eldest of the Prime sons and the one everyone considered the brains of the family. The golden son, it was believed he would take over Prime Energy from his father someday.

"I've mended my ways. I work out five days a week. Eat right. I figure what's the use of having all this money if I'm not healthy enough to enjoy it?"

He stepped fully into the room and held out a hand. "Rafe Prime. You must be Chief Warrant Officer Sebastian Ford. Thank you for saving my sister in South Sudan."

Savvy was right about the senator bringing the family up-to-date. Rafe's congenial manner was in such sharp contrast to Junior that Bastian didn't know what to think. He shook his hand and said, "It was my mission to save her and the other hostages. I'm eternally grateful we were successful."

Rafe turned to Brie. "Welcome home, Gabby." He took her hand in his and leaned down to kiss her cheek. She remained stiff and didn't make an effort to kiss or hug him.

She cocked her head and gazed at him suspiciously. "Wow. You look a lot like Rafe Prime. How long have you been impersonating him, and has JJ figured it out yet?"

Rafe laughed. "No. He thinks I'm the real deal." He touched her cheek where she'd been slapped. She jerked away from him.

He dropped his hand. His brow furrowed at her quick rejection. "Youssef told me what happened. I'm sorry." He nodded toward Bastian. "Glad you had someone to defend you. I'll talk to him later. Right now, he's practically frothing at the mouth."

"Rafe, this would be easier for me if you wouldn't pretend we're chummy. JJ was horrible, but at least he was honest."

"And I don't see why we have to be enemies. You're my sister. I've missed you."

"Right. You probably cried for days when Dad cut me out of the family. And I noticed how many times you tried to reach out to me in the intervening years. I can count them on zero hands."

Rafe frowned, and Bastian really wished he could guess if the man was genuine or not. "I've always regretted not disobeying Dad and...hell, given you money, called. Did something. But you know how he is."

"I didn't want your damn money. I wanted justice for Micah."

"You don't still believe that crazy-assed conspiracy theory?" He looked to Bastian, and his eyes widened. "Shit. Have you been telling people you believe Dad hired a hit on your ex? It's crazy, Gabby. How can you even think it?"

"Because he did."

Rafe ran a hand through his hair. "Let's table that discussion for now. I freaked out when I heard you'd been abducted, and waiting to hear you were okay was the longest week of my life."

"I'm so sorry you had to suffer with worry while I was being sold as a slave and shot. It must've been horrible for you."

Rafe rolled his eyes and smiled. "There's the smartass sister I've missed so much. No matter how bitchy you are to me, I'm going to remain glad to see you. Grateful you're alive to give me a hard time." He crossed his arms over his chest. "I've done a lot of thinking and growing in the last eight years, about you and how Dad treated you. I'm sorry I didn't stand up for you. I want my sister back."

"You never wanted me as your sister when you had me."

"I was raised by an asshole to be an asshole." He reached out to touch Brie's shoulder, but she flinched and leaned toward Bastian. He complied by putting his arm around her. He knew absolutely nothing about Rafe Prime, but it was possible the guy was genuine.

"Can we take this conversation to some place more comfortable?" Rafe asked. "We need to talk. And not just about what happened eight years ago. We need to talk about Prime Energy."

"I don't see why I would care. I'm not a part of Prime Energy."

"Recent events could change that. Given all the press you've gotten these last weeks with the work you've been doing in South Sudan, the shareholders want you back. They're ready to reinstate you and make you the face of Prime Energy, head the PR and community outreach team again. It's why JJ's so pissed. They want you to have his job. If you'll take it."

"And what does Dad have to say about this?"

He cleared his throat. "You might be wondering why you haven't seen Dad on TV in the last few weeks—"

"You mean besides the fact that I haven't had a TV. Or given a fuck?"

He grimaced. "Yeah, aside from that. We've been keeping it on the down low as we reorganize, but Dad had a stroke six weeks ago. A big one."

Brie took a step back, her eyes wide. "Is he alive? Conscious?"

"Yes. But he can't speak. Can't walk. We've got the best doctors and physical therapists working with him, but...his prognosis isn't good." He frowned. "You can't be mad we didn't tell you. We tried to find you, but USAID wouldn't disclose your location because you gave instructions we were not to be told where you were. I only learned you were in South Sudan when Uncle Al called and said you'd been abducted."

"So, who's running Prime Energy?"

"I am."

Chapter Thirty-One

Dinner with Rafe—JJ didn't join them—was stilted, as Brie reeled from her brother's news. Her dad was dying? The board of directors wanted her back in the business?

And the question that nagged at her the most: did she want back in if her dad wasn't part of the deal?

When she walked away from Prime Energy, she'd believed it was final and had no regrets. But now—what if she could change things? What if she could make sure projects were done in ways that protected the environment? What if they gave more than lip service to environmental justice on the NEPA checklist?

The board had to know there was no way she'd ever rubber-stamp their climate-change-denying lies again.

If she took the job, she could steer the philanthropic budget. The money could buy sanitary underwear for girls in South Sudan and elsewhere, so they could get an education. She could build bathrooms at schools, so when girls had their period, it wouldn't keep them home.

She could do so much good with an annual budget of fifty million dollars—which was the minimum amount she'd demand from the board.

After dinner, she and Bastian finished the tour, including the Turkish bath on the lower level that led out to the pool area and gardens. Neither of them spoke about what Rafe had said until they returned to her bedroom. Inside with the door closed, Bastian said, "What are you going to do?"

She drifted around the room, her gaze landing on but not seeing the vases and artwork some decorator had picked for this room twenty years ago. "I don't know."

"I thought you hated your family. Hated the business." There was an edge to his voice. "And I thought you didn't give a fuck about the money."

"I do. I do. And I don't," she replied, answering his statements in order.

"But you'd go back at the first opportunity. You'd become Oil Company Barbie again. A Princess Prime reboot."

She turned to face him, hurt that he'd think she'd revert back to the woman she was ten years ago. "Why do you think I want to go back, Bastian?"

He spread his arms wide to encompass the room. "Gee. I don't know. Miss this much?" His gaze narrowed. "Admit it, you didn't take me shopping because you thought I needed an upgrade for the mission. You did it because you want to fit in. You want *me* to fit in. Are you ashamed of me, Brie? Am I too...*ethnic* for you? How much do you miss the pretty clothes?"

The disdain in his voice cut to her soft, pathetic core. "Fuck you, Bastian."

She made a beeline for the balcony. She needed air. She needed space. She hadn't figured she'd still have to explain herself to Bastian. The things she'd done to redeem herself in the last eight years meant nothing to him, and *he* actually knew her.

What about the people who didn't know her? People who'd seen the headlines ten years ago about her drug use, and nothing since then. They'd think her work in South Sudan was a ruse for good PR. For her reemergence into the spotlight.

As Bastian said, a Princess Prime Reboot.

She couldn't outrun her past. Couldn't redeem herself. Couldn't make up for the damage she'd done as a tool of Prime Energy. To all but a handful of people, she would always be nothing more than a vapid, selfish bitch of an heiress.

She'd thought Bastian was one of the handful. That he hadn't followed her onto the balcony proved he had no remorse for his words. Not that she expected him to.

But still, it would have been nice.

Clearly his "I love you" had just been a ploy. If he really loved her, he wouldn't assume the worst at the first opportunity.

The Atlantic breeze washed over her skin. Morocco had always been one of her favorite places. Sultry without being too hot. It was nothing like South Sudan or even Djibouti, although the country spilled into the Sahara. But the Djiboutian desert and the Sahara were vastly different.

Here, the Atlas Mountains separated the ocean from the desert, and on this May evening, it was a soft seventy-two degrees after reaching a high of seventy-nine. Straight ahead—to the northwest—she looked over palm trees to the Atlantic Ocean, but due west was Drugov's estate. She could only see a corner of his walled garden from her balcony. JJ's room had a view in that direction. With binoculars, she might be able to ascertain if any of his outbuildings were occupied. It might be worthwhile to invade JJ's quarters for that reason.

It wasn't like she could piss off her brother any more.

But still, sneaking and spying weren't exactly ideal. She shuddered at the thought, but she was going to have to reach out to Drugov tomorrow to get an invitation to his party. She rubbed her temples. What the hell was she *doing* here? She wasn't a spy. Why had Savvy been so gung-ho to send her into this Sarlacc pit?

B astian couldn't even look at Brie. He'd seen the frisson of excitement that ran through her when her brother said she could reclaim her inheritance, and his stomach had fallen. She wanted it. She wanted back in the fold, to return to her previous life.

Part of him couldn't blame her—facing being sold in a market had to change a person, and in her case, it probably made her wish for the security she'd once known. But still, it gutted him to see that the woman he'd stupidly fallen for might not be the real Brie after all.

She sat out on the balcony in the cooling evening for a long time. When she came inside, she washed the makeup from her face and changed into a silk nightgown—like the bikini, the garment was already in the wardrobe when they arrived—then without a word, she slipped into bed.

Jesus, even her pajamas probably cost a day's wages.

Where was the woman who'd talked about making underwear out of an old tarp? She'd been discarded somewhere between here and Djibouti, apparently.

He crawled into bed beside her, wearing an Army T-shirt and cheap pair of boxer briefs. The expensive sheets were probably cringing at his low-class sleepwear. He switched off the bedside light. This was not how he'd imagined their first night in this bed, but the last thing on his mind now was sex.

"Has it even occurred to you that I might take the job because of the good I could do?" she asked softly, her voice the only sensory interruption in the pitch-black and silent room.

"Of course it did. And if that's your reason for thinking you want it, you're deluding yourself."

"God, you're a judgmental ass." Her voice was more angry than hurt. "Pray tell how I'm deluding myself."

"I'm not judgmental. I'm honest. With myself and with you. And if you're telling yourself you can change a damn thing at Prime Energy, you're lying, to me and to yourself. You can't change corporate culture. You can't change the board of directors. They just want to use you for PR and spit you out again. And you're willing to let them. Why, Brie? Why on earth would you trust a board that only wants you back so they can use you? Why do you want to work for a company that has screwed over indigenous people all over the world? A company that denies climate change. A company that destroys lives and works with people like Drugov.

"Jesus, have you forgotten what you've told me your father did? He wanted you to fuck Drugov to seal a deal. JJ's clearly of the same mind, and you don't know if you can believe Rafe. But suddenly you're going to trust them? Because *now* they're going to listen to a woman they bought with a big salary and expense account? They see you as a fool they can manipulate. And if you take the job, that's exactly what you'll be."

⁓

Brie felt sucker punched by Bastian's harsh words. Not because they were mean, but because…he might be right.

In the hours since Rafe had first outlined the offer, she'd mentally spun a tale in which she was able to magically correct all the wrongs her father had committed and save the world…at least a little bit.

But why? Why had she created that fantasy?

Fantasy was all it could ever be. Deep in her gut, she knew that. A man who'd been willing to pimp out his own daughter to close a deal wasn't going to magically become a philanthropist. And even if he remained out of the picture, her brothers were all about the money. They always had been. Her dad had never had qualms about cheating people to increase his profit margins, even if it was only a negligible amount, and he'd raised his boys to be the same way.

He'd lived for the score, closing the big deal. And he was willing to associate with anyone—even Russian Mafioso—if it meant increasing his net worth. The company was hopelessly intertwined with Russian money and shady deals. And she couldn't forget that she knew deep in her soul her dad had killed Micah, and it was possible JJ and Rafe knew about it.

So why did she convince herself that she could do good work at Prime Energy?

She'd been searching for justification to take the job.

But why? Was it like Bastian believed, because she wanted to be rich again? Did she want her New York penthouse back? Did she miss the clothes and attention that came with being Gabriella Prime?

She didn't think so. Money was convenient and could be fun, but she'd been more content in the years after she was cast out. She'd been able to stay clean because, for the first time in her adult life, she didn't need to self-medicate. She'd managed to stop hating herself.

She'd had friends and a fulfilling academic life, and later work life.

So what did she want? What pathetic part of her wanted back in the family?

Was it the ache caused by Rafe, the good brother, actually being nice to her? She suspected that was the culprit more than a desire to wear stilettos and Dior every day.

She wanted to believe her brother really loved her. That she could find a place within her family. That she wouldn't be alone anymore.

She cleared her throat and spoke into the darkness that separated them across the large bed. "Do you have any siblings, Bastian?"

"I did. My younger sister died eleven years ago—we think she was texting and driving."

His answer made her ache with sympathy. "I'm so sorry."

"Lily's death was one of the reasons it was hard for me to break up with Cece. She was there for my parents when they needed her, and then they…glommed on to her. Not as a replacement—no one could replace Lily— but a comfort. A beautiful strong Indian girl with a bright future. Cece was hope for them. Hope they'd have a daughter-in-law to love. Hope I'd give them grandkids."

Unsaid was the fact that his parents would hate Brie. Especially if she returned to Prime Energy. That caused another mental ache.

If she and Bastian somehow found a way to ford the gulf between them, there wouldn't be a new family who would embrace and love her in the absence of her own. His parents would hate her. She would never live up to

Cece. And she'd just drive another wedge between him and the people who mattered most in his world.

She swiped at the tear that spilled down her cheek and hoped he wouldn't hear the pain in her voice. "If your family had cut you off for years and suddenly you had a chance to be loved by one of them again, would you be able to turn your back on the offer?"

"They aren't offering to love you again, Brie. It's a job. Nothing more."

"You don't get it. My family doesn't know how to love. This job offer is as close as it gets."

"And it was made by the board of directors. And JJ's pissed about it."

"I know that. And logically, I know my father—if he recovers—will still never love me, no matter what I do. I also know that I hate him and I never want to see him again, that I'm not grieving his illness. But still, deep down inside, I will always be that nine-year-old girl who wonders why her daddy doesn't love her. The girl who tried modeling at thirteen because then maybe her father would notice and be proud. The girl who started using drugs at fifteen, because the daily belittling remarks hurt too much without them. I can't change that about me any more than you can change the pain of having your parents appear to prefer your ex-girlfriend over you.

"Rafe was always my good brother. Still an asshole, but he...*seemed* to care. Do you have any idea how much it scared me to have Rafe talk to me like he missed me? Like he cared? It woke every vulnerable insecurity. What if I could have a brother? A family member who would maybe love me? I want it. And I hate myself for wanting it."

The tears were flowing freely now, and she just let

them. To hell with protecting herself from Bastian. She had no shields left to employ. "I don't get to be myself with people much. My coworkers in South Sudan didn't even know who I was. I hold myself at a distance because people will judge me, like you did the night we first met. Like you're judging me tonight. So I don't tell them. But if I had a brother at least he would *get* me. He knows how awful it is to grow up with Jeff Senior as a dad and JJ as a brother. If I had a brother again, then there would be one person on this planet who loved *me*. The real me. Even if it's only because he has to."

"*I* love you, Brie. I've told you that already. Twice. Three times now."

"Do you really? Because you sure were quick to assume I'm shallow tonight. And you were even faster to betray my confidence without so much as a heads-up."

He was silent for a long time.

Brie climbed from the bed and crossed to the bathroom to grab a box of tissues. She closed the door and turned on the light. A glance in the mirror showed she looked like hell, eyes puffy and red. Runny nose. Cheeks blotchy.

When she was Princess Prime she'd been too cold in her emotions to ever break down like this. But then, she'd also attempted to control her emotions with pharmaceuticals. She sat on the edge of the tub, blotted her cheeks, and blew her nose. She needed to get her shit together. She and Bastian had several days ahead of them and a job to do. Getting caught up in heartache would only hinder them.

She needed to be a coldhearted bitch like Princess Prime again, but this time without the alcohol and drugs. No more showing Bastian her vulnerable side, and she sure as hell couldn't let JJ or Rafe know they had the power to hurt her.

She was here to expose a general who pushed his people into famine so he could seize power, and to bring down the oligarch who sold children to line his pockets.

Nothing else mattered.

Chapter Thirty-Two

If it weren't for years of training as a Special Forces operator, Bastian would never have been able to sleep. As it was, he didn't sleep deeply. Beside him, Brie tossed and turned, but she managed to accumulate a few hours' rest.

Now the woman who faced him across the breakfast table—served in her private quarters—had a chilly demeanor, a new incarnation of Brie. She'd showered, dried and styled her short hair, and applied makeup. She'd dressed in an airy sundress that he guessed was vacation chic.

He'd heard her sobs as she sat in the bathroom last night, and he knew he'd hurt her—again—but at the same time, he wasn't ready to admit he was wrong in his assumption. She hadn't talked about her brothers prior to the planning of this op, and she certainly hadn't hinted that one of them could be less than pure evil. But even still, he should have guessed that there was more loneliness and hurt in her attitude toward her brothers than there was hate.

Right about now, he longed for the simplicity of training Djiboutians with his team. Or even better, dropping into a hot zone and kicking some al-Qaeda ass. This op was too muddled. He was the fake boyfriend of the woman he was in love with. Somehow, Savannah

James had convinced SOCOM to let her recruit him. Hell, even Brie was Savvy's asset now, her job to inform on her family and their associates.

For all intents and purposes, Savvy was their case officer, and they were spies. By definition, spies were traitors, and the truth was Bastian had betrayed Brie, and Brie would betray her family.

He stared at Brie as he sipped his coffee. Beautiful and coldly serene. She'd captivated him from the start. Hell, she'd captivated him ten years ago. He'd hated what Princess Prime did, but he'd been intrigued by the woman.

He hoped to hell Savvy was right about Drugov and Lawiri, or he'd thrown away something precious for nothing.

He wanted to go back to that night in her CLU. He wanted to stop her from pushing him away. He'd explain that Savvy needed to know everything, and then together they'd have told Savvy about her family.

That was what he should have done. But he'd let anger get the best of him. Like he did with Pax a year ago. Like he did every time he'd approached his parents about Cece. Anger and hurt won, and he was an asshole.

It was a miracle he'd made it to chief warrant officer and second-in-command of his A-Team, because he sure fucked up on the personal side of things. But he'd always been able to do the job when he kept his focus. Even when things were at their worst with Pax, they'd worked together fine. It was after hours when he'd been a dick.

With Brie, he'd just have to remember they were on the clock twenty-four/seven. Focus on the job and forget the woman.

Right.

She'd set her cell phone on the table next to her plate and it chimed with an incoming message. She picked it up and swiped across the screen. She smiled faintly, tapped out a reply, then set the phone down without a word.

"What was that?" he asked, irritated that he had to ask. They were supposed to be working together.

"A former lover has invited me to dine at his villa. I said yes."

Jealousy upended him like a rogue wave. "What the fuck?"

"I'm hoping he'll offer to make me his mistress. That way I can have the clothes, car, and palace, and all I have to do is fuck for it. He's a decent lover too, so it wouldn't be a chore."

The jealousy had blinded him, and it took him too long to catch on. "Dammit, Brie, I never suggested—"

"You may as well have. And you know what? If I did want to screw a guy so he'd take care of me, it's none of your damn business. My decisions, my body, my life. So you can keep your shitty judgments to yourself." She cocked her head. "In fact, how much would you give me for a blowjob? There's a Coach bag I've been eyeing."

He got it. He was an ass. The last dig was too much, though, so he just glared at her and said, "All eight inches."

She raised a brow. "Eight?" She snickered. "You wish."

His anger deflated, a slow seep he was pretty sure was leaking from his heart. "Aww, c'mon, if you want the Coach bag, you've got to humor me."

Her mouth twitched. "Oh, well, in that case, it felt like eight for sure."

He ran a hand over his face, not sure if he should laugh

or sigh. "I'm sorry, Brie. Again. It was wrong of me to assume you just wanted the money and status back. I wasn't wrong about you deluding yourself, but I was wrong about why."

"Fair."

"So who was the text from?"

"As I said, a former lover inviting me to dine."

Jesus. What had he done to deserve this assignment? He was going to pop a vessel before the day was over. Maybe even before he finished breakfast. "You'd better have RSVPed for two. And who is it? Savvy needs to run a check on the guy."

"I told him my boyfriend is with me, and we'd love to join him. We'll have to wait and see if he rescinds the invitation now that he knows you're here. His name is Armando Cardona. He's from Spain and is in the chemical industry—plastics and pharmachemistry. He lives in the neighborhood, and we met when I visited last year. I asked Youssef to notify him as well as a few others I know in the area that I'm home so the news would filter to Drugov without me contacting him directly."

He frowned. "When did you do this?"

"While you showered before dinner. I wanted Youssef to believe I was hiding it from you."

"Which you were."

"I'd planned to tell you after dinner."

But instead, they'd fought. Okay. He'd give her a pass on that one. "Savvy's going to have to run a background check on him."

"She already did. I told her about everyone I intended to contact here. There was no guarantee Armando would be here and not in Madrid, but I was hopeful because his company has a lab here. I actually reached out to him several months ago because I wanted to know if he would consider manufacturing reusable plastic-lined underwear. Having an Africa-based supplier might get past the aid blockades. So regardless of using him to get to Drugov, I wanted to see him."

Savvy hadn't told him any of this in the prep for the trip. But then Savvy always had her reasons for sharing and withholding information. "Any other lovers I should know about, or are you hoping to blindside me in public?"

"I don't think any others are here, but maybe we'll get lucky."

He stood, his jaw clenched. He circled the table and stood above her. "We're supposed to be working as a team, Brie."

She tilted her head back and met his gaze. "What do you want from me, Bastian? I can't help it that I slept with him. It was a fling and before I met you. You've slept around a lot too. I won't apologize for my past any more than I'd expect you to."

He didn't like standing above her for what he needed to say. He took her hand and gently pulled her to her feet. She rose and gazed up at him suspiciously.

"I don't give a damn that you screwed him in the past as long as it remains in the past while we're on this mission. Even if you don't give a fuck about me, my job is to protect you, which I can't do if you screw around with Mr. Pharmachemical. I've told you how I feel. I can take a lot of shit from you because of what I did, but if you want this guy, Savvy can send a different bodyguard, because I'm out. There are special operators in Rota who would be happy to take my place, and they can be here on a military flight in an hour. Even if you don't want the

Spaniard, if you want me replaced, I'll go. If we can't work together, you're in danger."

By the time he finished his speech, his heart pounded like he'd been doing double unders. A few choice words in this moment and she could take him out of the op and out of her life. And she'd have his balls as a souvenir.

"I don't want Armando."

Slowly, air entered his lungs, but he held himself in check. She still might want to replace him.

"There's only one man I want—as a lover or a bodyguard."

His restraint vanished. In a flash, he scooped her up and pinned her to the nearest wall. She wrapped her thighs around his hips. Before she could say another word, his mouth was on hers in a deep hot kiss. She sucked on his tongue and ground herself against his erection. He wanted to bury himself inside her, make her come so hard, she'd never think of another man.

He wanted her to be his, not just for today, for the op, but for all time. His. Always.

He raised his head and gazed down at her wet lips. She opened eyes that were smoky hot with arousal.

"I didn't give you a chance to say who you want."

She smiled. "You, Bastian. Always you. From the moment we first kissed, only you."

He dropped kisses onto her eyelids, lips, and neck. "Thank you." He'd needed to hear her unequivocal declaration more than he wanted to admit.

A knock sounded on the door.

"Damn," he said, setting her down.

"One moment." Brie projected her voice to the door. She then touched his lips. "You've got lipstick on you again."

"We're going to finish this later."

She nodded.

He left to clean up in the bathroom while she called to the maid to enter. It was time to get to work for the day. They could play tonight.

～♢

A rmando Cardona was as handsome and charming as Brie remembered, but she didn't regret that their fling was over. Bastian was handsome and charming and so much more. He'd saved her from a slave market and danced with her under the stars. He knew every ugly part of her and still wanted her.

Armando wasn't the least bit fazed that she had a boyfriend in tow, and he kissed both her cheeks warmly in greeting before turning his charm on Bastian as if Brie had delivered a potential new best friend. They settled down to a large lunch spread—the largest meal of the day in Morocco—the food was traditional Moroccan served on a central platter and accompanied with mint tea. They ate with their right hands, using flatbread as the only utensil.

Brie had missed meals like this in South Sudan. But then, she'd missed eating for pleasure in South Sudan.

Even though the invitation had been issued only hours before, Armando had invited a few others from the neighborhood, and she and Bastian found themselves in a cozy gathering that included a couple—husband-and-wife real estate developers who built high-end resorts— and the billionaire owner of an airline. Just a few people from the area, enjoying an intimate lunch.

"You will be at Nikolai's party tonight, won't you, dear?" Annette, the resort developer, asked.

"Nikolai?" Bastian asked, perfect in his role as tourist in the world of the walled estates of Casablanca.

"Nikolai Drugov. He's in oil, just like Brie's family," Annette said.

Because she'd met Armando a year ago, he knew her as Brie, not Gabby or Gabriella, making this luncheon feel more intimate than dinner with her brother last night had been.

But then again, Brie also liked Armando, while the verdict was still out on her brother.

"Nikolai is having a party?" Brie asked, showing just the right amount of interest.

"Yes. Black tie. He's celebrating securing oil rights in the Arctic. Huge reserves. I'm sure he'll want you there."

Annette's husband cleared his throat. "That might not be something to celebrate for Brie. I believe Prime Energy bid on the pipeline, but Nikolai chose a competitor."

Brie was more appalled at the idea of Russia drilling in the Arctic, but she didn't voice that. "I'm not really part of the company anymore. If PE didn't win the contract, it's not my problem. But it does explain why JJ is in such a bad mood."

"Well then, you must come!" Annette said. "These things are always so boring—the same middle-aged men talking about golf and football—er, soccer to you," she added with a nod to Bastian. "And business deals in China. I could carry on both sides of the conversation by myself at this point. Your Green Beret will liven things up."

As if Bastian was a pet or hired entertainment.

Annette clapped her hands. "Oh! You could tell the story about how you rescued Brie! And some of your other adventures!"

Right. Like the story of being purchased in a slave market was fodder to entertain party guests. And Bastian's missions likely involved a lot of bullets and blood. Not exactly an *adventure*.

Brie hid her grimace. At least she understood Annette. Once upon a time, she'd been just like her. Thoughtless, but not mean-spirited. Wealthy, white, and very, very privileged.

If Bastian was annoyed, he didn't show it. Instead, he said, showing a great deal of patience and grace, "My work isn't appropriate for party entertainment, and much of it is classified. As far as the mission to save Brie, that's her story to tell, and, I think, a painful one."

Annette's face flushed, and she touched Brie's hand. "Oh! I'm so sorry. That was thoughtless of me, dear." She seemed genuinely contrite, but Brie would bet good money she was now wondering if Brie had been raped.

Not that she blamed her. In reversed roles, Brie would wonder the same thing. Not in a salacious way, but in a way that tried to find the right words to express sympathy without being dumb, trite, or hurtful.

Annette's fingers squeezed Brie's to the point of pain, and her eyes had misted with tears. "I'm not usually so…dunderheaded."

Her husband snorted, taking away the tension from the moment.

The airline tycoon asked Armando a question about his plans for the coming weeks, and the moment passed. Annette leaned close to Brie and whispered, "I really hope you'll come to Nikolai's tonight. I promise to be more discreet."

"I'd love to, but I wouldn't want to distress Nikolai by

showing up uninvited. Our families go way back."

"Nonsense. I'll send him a note and let him know I invited you and insisted you attend or it would break my heart. We're breaking ground in Cuba next month on a new resort, and he wants the largest villa for himself. He won't dare say no to me."

Brie smiled. No. She didn't think he would. She suspected Nikolai Drugov was as eager to see her as she was to cross his path. That Annette made it possible only made it simpler for everyone.

Bastian gazed at her with concern, and she gave him a bright smile. He leaned over and kissed her cheek, grabbing her hand beneath the table. This wasn't affection for show, which somehow made it all the more special.

"How long do you plan to stay in Casablanca?" Armando asked.

"As long as the Army will allow," she said, giving the answer they'd agreed on in advance. "Bastian's on open-ended medical leave. Morocco seemed like the perfect place for us both to recuperate."

Armando cocked his head. "And what will you do, Brie, when Bastian returns to his unit? Dare I hope you'll stay with us in Morocco? Keep Annette from being bored with my party conversation?"

"I haven't decided. I doubt USAID would take me if I wanted to go back to South Sudan." She answered truthfully without thinking. Fantasies of saving the world through Prime Energy aside, from the moment she'd sat in the meeting at SOCOM, she hadn't given serious thought to what she would do after this was over. But the hard truth was that with her identity released to the world, further work for USAID was impossible.

Bastian's fingers tightened around hers. "I'm hoping Brie will want to visit Washington. My family is there."

She had a feeling he wasn't speaking as the character of her boyfriend, but as the real thing.

In typical Moroccan fashion, lunch lasted nearly three hours. After the other guests left, Armando stopped Brie and Bastian at the door. "I wanted to discuss something with you that wasn't appropriate for the table conversation." A slight blush darkened his olive complexion. "About the…underwear."

Brie smiled, understanding his discomfort. So many men had a difficult time talking about menstruation. Half the human population menstruated, and it was an essential part of human existence, but still, it made men squirm. She'd liked the fact that Bastian had asked her outright in South Sudan what she would do if she started to bleed while they were stranded.

She smiled up at Armando. "Did you talk to your engineers about designing a soft, flexible, reusable plastic liner?"

"I did. The women were excited by the project and offered to donate their time to the development, which meant we were able to fast-track it. I was delighted to hear of your visit because I'd planned to reach out to you. We have several different prototypes ready. Would you be interested in visiting the lab in the next few days? If you can't, I can bring them by your villa, but I'm sure the engineers would like to meet you."

Brie couldn't help but squeal and hugged Armando. "Of course we can go to the lab. I want to meet them too." She released him and enjoyed this rush of excitement. Good could come from her work in South Sudan and victories like this had been hard to come by lately. "Oh my goodness, Armando, do you have any idea what this could mean for girls in the developing world? A pair of underwear can change a girl's life. Her entire future."

He beamed, his blush gone. "That's what my engineers said. They are all women with higher education, some from Morocco, some from other African countries. They know the struggle. This project means a lot to them too. Thank you for bringing it to my attention. It will be a good tax break for our fabric-manufacturing branch and do some good for the world."

"Thank you for pursuing it. When can I visit the lab?"

"I'll set up a time and call you with the details."

"Perfect." She kissed him on the cheek again, then took Bastian's arm and left. For the first time in weeks, she felt a tiny buzz of hope. The world wasn't all evil. She couldn't change the past, but she could have a positive impact moving forward.

Chapter Thirty-Three

An invitation to Drugov's party arrived within an hour of them returning to Brie's villa. Brie proceeded to try on the three gowns that hung in her closet, asking for Bastian's opinion on which would be best for the evening. He didn't give a damn what she wore—she looked hot in all of them.

She was pumped and excited after the news from Armando, and he enjoyed seeing her light energy. They'd had precious little of that in the past few weeks.

She twirled before him. "What do you think of this one?"

He chucked her under the chin. "Here's looking at you, kid."

She groaned. "I suppose we were due for a *Casablanca* joke."

"I've been trying to figure out how to work in 'we'll always have Paris' for the last twenty-four hours."

She snickered. "More like South Sudan. Or USS *Dahlgren*."

He chuckled and rubbed the silky fabric of her dress between his fingers. "Where did you get this?" She wore a shimmery black number with a tight, low bodice that gave him a hard-on with each bounce of her breasts. "I thought you didn't have money for designer stuff?" And even his untrained eye could see this dress was quality.

Except for the items she'd bought at Dior and the things Savvy had acquired for her, he'd expected her wardrobe to be more casual. After all, she'd been just as broke last year when she visited.

"I purchased most of my clothes from a consignment shop in Seattle before I visited last time. Later, Armando bought me the gowns and a few other items because he wanted me to attend social events with him."

"So he knows of your estrangement from your family?"

"Yes. I didn't hide my strange financial situation of living in a palace but not being able to afford rent in Seattle. It was nothing to him to buy me clothes, and I let him because he wanted my company at events I couldn't attend otherwise."

Bastian smiled. Armando had been pleasant, and there'd been no tension between the two of them over Brie. "He's not really your type," he said.

She laughed. "Handsome and charming isn't my type?"

"No way. You fit better with men who are rugged. Ethnic. Maybe a bit of an asshole. Men who aren't afraid to get dirty. Not polished, pretty rich boys."

She grinned and pushed him onto the couch, then straddled him. The evening gown hiked up, almost to her hips. She draped her arms on his shoulders. "My preferred type is a man who fucks like a god and makes me feel alive. Beautiful. Exquisite."

"You are all of those things. Any man who doesn't make you feel that way has no business being inside your body."

"Make love to me now. Make me feel exquisite."

He thrust his hips upward, brushing her clit with his

ready but covered erection. "Oh no, sweetheart. You're going to wait for the next one. Tonight. After the party. We're going to have our own celebration."

"Promise?"

"Cross my heart." But then, because he was a masochist, he tugged down the shoulder strap of the gown, exposing her breast. She hadn't put on a bra for the fashion show. He sucked the tip into his mouth. She groaned and pressed her pussy harder against him.

Exquisite was the right word.

This was a dangerous game. They had to get ready for the party and bring Savvy up-to-date. She might have intel for him on the party guests. But all he wanted to do was suck on Brie's tits, lick her clit, and hope she'd return the favor and take him deep into her mouth.

He slid a hand under the skirt and cupped her ass. Maybe he could go down on her a little bit. An appetizer.

He felt a vibration against his chest, but not the good kind that was shaped like a bright-colored dick that he could play with, teasing her inside and out. No. This was his cell phone.

She glanced around the room. "Could the room be bugged so someone will always interrupt when things just start to get good?"

He laughed. "I sweep the room for bugs every time we return. So far nothing." He pulled out his phone. Savvy. She must've gotten his message that they were a go for the party. He had no choice but to answer.

"We're seriously taking a limousine to the house next door?" Bastian asked as they walked down the red carpet toward the circular drive where the family chauffeur waited by the open rear door of the stretch vehicle. Her brothers, she'd been informed by Youssef, were already inside and waiting.

"Yes," Brie said, smiling at his outrage. He was right. It was ridiculous, even if she was wearing three-inch heels. "Walking up a long driveway to arrive at a black tie event just isn't done."

"Rich people are so damn weird. We could climb the wall. Now that would be an entrance."

"I don't think I'm quite dressed for wall climbing." She smoothed the tight black silk gown. The dress was simple, with a low V-shaped neckline that hugged her breasts and set off a glittery bib necklace with over a hundred small-to-large teardrop rubies that came to a point with a flawless five-carat stone that rested between her breasts.

"Aww. I'd give you a boost." His hand cupped her ass.

She laughed. He was probably quite the skilled wall climber. She wanted to see that, but not in his evening dress uniform, which was hotter than any tux she'd ever seen.

She'd watched him dress earlier with the avid interest of a sailor at a strip club, except he'd gone in the wrong direction, covering his perfect muscles, but she approved of the end result.

"Why aren't you wearing your green beret?" she asked as they approached the limousine.

"No cover is worn with the blue mess uniform, or I would. I wish I could wear it. If I had cover, I'd have to keep it on inside because I'm carrying. I wouldn't mind letting Drugov know that not only am I Special Forces, but I'm locked and loaded. But...it isn't done. I can't wear cover tonight. If I did, anyone who knew protocol would know something is up and I'm flashing Special Forces status needlessly. Savvy said she thinks there might be other military there. Too risky for me to break protocol."

They neared the vehicle where her brothers waited. She didn't want to share Bastian with the world tonight. She wanted to keep him to herself and make love and show him exactly what his service meant to her. But they were on a mission—part of his service—and she wouldn't fail him now.

She had a role in this op. He couldn't do his job without her, the gateway into Drugov's world. And she wouldn't fail him or her country. She owed both so much.

They climbed into the limousine for the quarter-mile trip down one long driveway and up another. JJ glared at her and said nothing, wearing his usual sour expression as he took in the decorations on Bastian's uniform that proved the Native American was a thousand times the man JJ was. But then, JJ was an alt-right drone masquerading as pond scum, so even comparing the two was an insult to Bastian.

It took all of a minute to leave their driveway and roll up the next. At least when it was time to head home, she and Bastian could skip the limo and leave her brothers, but for this, it was best that the Primes arrived as a unit.

Drugov's entryway put the Prime red carpet to shame. The walkway was an abstract mosaic of bright colors. Stunning and a work of art worthy of a museum.

The inside of the house was even more beautiful. It was too bad the homeowner had a cruel, sadistic heart. Brie took a deep breath as she crossed the entryway on Bastian's arm, braced to face their host, a man she hadn't seen in at least eight years.

He hadn't changed. A few more lines around his eyes, but otherwise he remained the same Nikolai. Ten years her senior, he was forty-three but looked older. Hard drinking, a notorious playboy lifestyle, and living in the whirl of Russian Mafioso aged a man quickly. Some might consider him handsome, but she'd always been repulsed by the way he looked at her. His nature overrode his looks.

Piercing blue eyes fixed on her the moment she crossed his threshold, and the familiar unease settled in. She'd felt this since she was thirteen and he was twenty-three. No adult man should ever look at a child that way. But then, thanks to her modeling, she'd received that look a lot in her teens.

She came to a dead stop, and Bastian turned to her with a quizzical gaze. "You okay?" he whispered.

"Touch me. Every moment we're around Nikolai. Make it clear that I'm yours. Please?"

He dropped an intimate kiss to her neck, lingering longer than was acceptable in public. His lips teased her ear as he whispered, "Sure thing, babe. No hardship for me."

She smiled and brushed his lips with hers, fortifying herself. "Thank you."

Far too soon, she was presenting the creep of the hour with her hand. He squeezed her fingers and brought her hand to his lips. He kissed the back, holding her skin to his mouth too long. "Gabriella, my sweet. So good to have you back."

She tried to pull her hand away, but he wouldn't release her.

Bastian calmly extracted her hand from Drugov's. He

cradled her fingers against his chest. She felt the steady, hard beat of his heart.

"Nice to meet you, Drugov," he said, taking the oligarch's hand. "She's with me, and if you know what's good for you, you'll keep your hands and mouth to yourself."

From the look on Nikolai's face, Bastian was crushing his hand.

"Bastian, love," Brie said sweetly, "I think you're hurting him." To Nikolai she said, "So sorry, Nick. He doesn't know his own strength."

Nikolai's eyes glittered, but he said nothing, not even a soft grunt of pain. Bastian released him, and he flexed his fingers. Nothing broken. A shame.

"Your new toy lacks manners, Gabriella. Just what I would expect from a heathen."

"No, sir," Bastian said. "I know exactly how to behave. The question is, do you?"

Brie dragged Bastian away from the receiving line before their host could answer. She stopped short of the archway that led to the main ballroom. She pulled him to the side, next to a thick column, and said in a quiet voice, "You're going to get us booted from the party."

"So? The point was to make contact with Drugov, and we have. I'm game to go home now."

"We need to meet the other guests. It's possible Lawiri will be here." It was a long shot, but Drugov always behaved as if he were above the law, so he might openly host the exiled general.

"You're the one who wanted me to stake my claim," Bastian said.

She rose on her toes and kissed him. "And I love that you did. Unequivocally. But now we must behave."

Bastian kissed her, a soft, warm intimate caress. "Okay. Starting…now."

She wiped lipstick from his bottom lip with her thumb. "Now."

He leaned down and kissed her neck, then whispered. "Instead, why don't we shock all these lily-white rich folks with some heathen ways?"

She laughed as her skin tingled from his lips and breath. She wanted to lick his throat, rip off his bow tie, and slide her tongue along every inch of exposed skin. God, the uniform with all his medals and awards was such a turn-on.

"What the fuck is the deal with baiting Drugov, Gabby?" JJ asked, walking up behind her. "I thought we were here to play nice so we can get the pipeline project back on track."

She turned in Bastian's arms and flashed her teeth at her brother, feeling rather feral. "I don't give a damn about your pipeline project, and Nikolai was being creepy, as usual. So back off."

"If you don't help us here, there's no way you'll be reinstated," he said, his eyes hard and cold.

"By help you mean you want me to fuck him, right?"

"Don't be crude."

"Why not? That's what Prime Energy always wanted from me. You know how many smelly middle-aged assholes I had to fight off in my early twenties? I lost count. My answer remains no. Never."

"It's too late to pretend outrage. You screwed for the job. Repeatedly. I've heard all the stories."

The truth was, when she was using, she probably had slept with some of them. She couldn't be certain, and some of the men she'd rejected had certainly lied to save face.

"How many have you fucked for the business, JJ? You do that, then talk to me about taking one for the team. But remember this, I'm not on Team Prime anymore. I'm done being exploited by you and Dad and Rafe."

"Hey, don't include me in your list. I've never—" Rafe said before she cut him off.

"You looked the other way every single time, big bro. That makes you complicit. Silence favors the oppressor."

"Oppressor?" JJ scoffed. "What do you have to bitch about? You had everything a person could want."

"You think because we had money, I had no reason to complain when you and Dad tried to pimp me out? You think that just because we had a nice house and cars, I wasn't being exploited? Your sexism is just delightful."

She pivoted and crossed under the archway, entering the ballroom. She spotted the open bar at the side and made a beeline for it.

Bastian caught her arm, stopping her midway. "What do you think you're doing?"

She halted and shook her head. "Shit. That was ingrained. The bar was always my refuge when JJ baited me. I haven't been to one of these kinds of events with my brothers since I quit." She frowned. "I wouldn't have ordered a drink. I'm not that far gone. I'd have gotten a soda."

He looped her arm through his. "I know. But we should change your pattern so your instinct isn't to veer toward the bar. Develop a new coping technique."

She grinned. "I'm a big fan of sex as a coping mechanism."

Several of the tuxedoed men around them turned at her loud declaration. Bastian grinned. "Later," he said equally loud. "And I'll help you cope all you want."

A waiter appeared with a tray laden with champagne. Bastian waved him off. While Morocco was a Muslim country, alcohol was legal—although sometimes hard to get—and most of the guests tonight were either foreign or not religious, but there were waiters circulating with nonalcoholic beverages for those who didn't drink. Bastian grabbed two lemonades from a passing tray.

"You can drink, you know," she said. Her limits didn't apply to him, although she appreciated his support. "I'll be okay."

"No. I need to stay sharp tonight." He leaned down and whispered in her ear, "Besides, I plan to enjoy a different coping mechanism later."

This party couldn't be over fast enough.

Annette and her husband appeared, and she insisted on introducing Bastian around, cooing over his uniform. The medals and ribbons made Bastian stand out in a room full of gorgeously gowned women and tuxedoed men. The wealth at the party represented a sizable chunk of the world economy, and there was no doubt Brie and Bastian were the poorest guests at the event, but she had the best date in the room. He was by far the best man in the entire country.

No. Of all the men on the continent.

Screw it. All the men on the planet.

She enjoyed watching women fawn over him. How their eyes followed him and they lit with a warm glow when he gave them his full attention, engaging their interest. Did she do that? Light up when Bastian was near?

Probably. She definitely felt warmer. Safer. Energized.

She sipped her lemonade, standing back as he worked

the room, watching, enjoying. Chief Warrant Officer Sebastian Ford was all hers.

A man at a grand piano in the corner of the ballroom played accompaniment to a torch singer. Couples danced in the center of the room, and she looked forward to dancing with Bastian when he was done being paraded around by Annette. She nodded to Armando, who danced cheek-to-cheek with a gorgeous brown-skinned woman wearing an exquisite Indian sari.

Meanwhile, Bastian leaned down to hear the soft-voiced words of an elderly Moroccan woman. He clasped her hand in his and spoke to her in Arabic, causing Brie's heart to split wide open, allowing the emotions she'd been trying to hold back to flow freely.

She was crazy in love with him.

It didn't matter that he'd spoken to Savvy without warning her. None of her reasons for pushing him away mattered. At his core, he was a good man. The very best of men.

And he loved her. In spite of who she was, what she'd done in the past, he loved *her*. She'd never thought anyone would be able to love her—the real her. She had no money to entice him with, and she came with a crap ton of baggage. But still, he wanted her.

She felt an unpleasant tingle at the back of her neck a millisecond before Nikolai spoke in her ear. "Panting after a lowlife doesn't suit you, Gabriella." She could smell cigars and alcohol on his breath.

She wrinkled her nose. "Go away, Nick." He'd always hated being called Nick.

He pinched her elbow and pulled her to his side. "We need to talk." His hold on her elbow tightened as he tugged her away from Bastian, toward an archway that led to another hallway on her right.

Should she fight him? Or was this the opportunity they needed? He would say things to her that he'd never dare say in front of Bastian. But she wasn't supposed to be alone with him. Not even when there were two hundred people just thirty feet away.

In the end, she couldn't bring herself to cause a scene. If she did, they'd be forced to leave the party, and they'd have learned nothing about Lawiri. She'd use this opportunity to ask Nikolai about the general. It might be her only chance.

For this reason, she found herself at the far end of a long dark hall, alone with Nikolai Drugov and his gross cigar breath.

Chapter Thirty-Four

"It was unwise to bring a date, Gabriella."

"Wrong. Being with Bastian is the smartest thing I've ever done."

"You have made me angry. Again. You will be punished."

"You're insane. I am not an object. I don't belong to you."

"Oh, but you do. You always have. You owe me."

"What is *wrong* with you, Nick? I don't want you. I've never wanted you. You gross me out and have since I was thirteen. I don't owe you a damn thing."

"Oh, but you do. If it weren't for me, you wouldn't have the villa next door. My father sold it to your father at below market value, in exchange for you and your virginity. The house is now yours, but I never received full payment."

She took a step back as revulsion washed through her. "Your father sold the villa to my father when I was thirteen!"

He cupped his hand over her chin and squeezed. "You were so lovely at thirteen, those big, round eyes and long curtain of glossy brown hair. You posed for those cosmetic ads, with those sultry, fuck-me eyes at the camera. Your slender body. Tight little breasts. I would have fucked you then, but your father insisted I wait until you were eighteen. He was concerned your bitch of a mother would find out and pursue statutory rape."

"It would have been rape, statutory or not. And I was a *child*."

He released her chin. "You were never a child, Gabriella. No child poses like you did. You wanted to fuck. The pictures say it all."

It was this kind of sick bullshit that made her hate her mother for pushing for the photo shoot. She'd been a kid. Playing in front of a camera, not really understanding how men would interpret it. She'd had no concept of sexuality at thirteen. Had no clue what sucking on a popsicle would signal.

Modeling had been a lark.

"I would have married you," Nikolai said. "If you'd fulfilled the agreement. You'd have been my empress, my czarina. But you defied me. The only woman who ever dared. So I'll just take you. Use you. You aren't worthy of my name. You've soiled your body with too many men. You aren't that innocent girl you were at thirteen." He scanned her up and down. "You're still skinny with small tits, but I hate short hair. You will grow it long again."

He was insane, and she was done humoring him. She'd hoped to glean information here, but he was a lost cause. She took a step away, toward the ballroom. Bastian had to have noticed she was gone by now and would probably be pissed she'd broken their one agreed-upon rule.

Nikolai grabbed her arm. His touch wasn't gentle.

A man entered the hall, lit from behind she couldn't see his face, but he didn't have Bastian's build. He walked slowly down the long corridor, his footsteps soft on the tile. As he drew closer, she took in dark hair, brown eyes, and a handsome, tanned face with a thick beard. He gave Nikolai a hard look and said something in Russian, his tone commanding. Instantly, her arm was released.

She rubbed her bruised skin, wondering who the hell this man was and why Nikolai feared him.

The newcomer flashed a warm smile. "This must be the American I've heard so much about," he said in a heavy Russian accent. He held out a hand. "I'm an associate of Nikolai's and delighted to meet you."

She took his hand, and he pulled her to his side, away from Nikolai. Next thing she knew, her arm was looped through his and he was leading her back to the ballroom.

"Such a beautiful evening. You must dance with me." Once they were out of earshot, he added, "You shouldn't have gone off with Nikolai."

"I realize that now. Thank you."

"Your soldier is looking for you. I told him to let me extract you. I have...sway with Nikolai."

"I noticed. How did you do it? He obeyed you like a dog."

The man smiled. "He knows I can bring the world down on him like a hammer."

She had no doubt Russia had kompromat on Nikolai. It was how they controlled all their oligarchs. As rich and powerful as Drugov was, he couldn't outrun his government. This man must've been sent by the Kremlin to ensure their wealthy pawn stayed in line.

The Russian led her into the ballroom and past Bastian, taking her straight to the dance floor, where he took her in his arms as the singer crooned a song by Adele.

"Why are you here, Ms. Stewart?"

She was surprised he used her legal name. Everyone here was determined to brand her with Prime. "I'm on vacation. Recovering from an ordeal. Why are you here, Mister…?"

"I'm monitoring my boss's investment."

She noticed he didn't bother giving her a name. Again. "And who is your boss?"

He merely smiled and tightened his arm around her waist, pulling her closer. His secrecy—everything about him, really—should have her on edge, but for some reason, she didn't fear him. Maybe it was because he'd rescued her from Nikolai or maybe it was because his manner toward her wasn't the least bit threatening. But one thing she was certain of, the man was dangerous.

She hoped to hell he'd prove to be an ally.

B astian cut in on Brie's dance with the Russian who'd helpfully extracted her from Drugov without causing a scene. The Russian bowed to Bastian and Brie, said, "Stay out of trouble, Gabriella," and left them.

Bastian swept Brie into his arms, relieved but still a little angry she'd left with Drugov in the first place.

"Who is he?" she asked, glancing toward the retreating Russian's back.

"My best guess is he's GRU."

She leaned against Bastian, pressing her temple to his collarbone. "What is GRU?"

He tightened his arm around her waist, glad to have her safe against him. "Russia's largest intelligence agency. Like our CIA."

She raised her head and glanced in the direction of the mysterious Russian, then whispered, "I was dancing with a *Russian spy?*"

Bastian laughed. "And now you're dancing with an American Green Beret. Which is better?"

She grinned wickedly. "Wellll…" She kissed him. "He's not my type. What does it mean that he's here?"

She was three inches taller in heels, and he liked the way she fit against him as they danced. He spun her in a slow circle. "I think it means Russia knows Drugov's got a screw loose and they're shutting him down." He turned to see the probable GRU agent had disappeared into the crowd. Bastian wanted to get the man's fingerprints on a glass, but he wore white gloves with his tux. Not unusual at this party, but still worth noting.

"Nikolai is really crazy," Brie said. "Worse than he was a decade ago."

Bastian turned his gaze back to her. "Rumor has it he had his old man killed so he could take over the family business."

"Where did you hear that?"

"Savvy. She briefed SOCOM on him at length after you left the meeting." His gaze narrowed. "You promised you wouldn't go off alone with him."

"I know. I'm sorry. I won't be stupid like that again. I just…I hoped he'd say something he wouldn't say in front of you. He did, but it wasn't about Lawiri."

"You asked him about Lawiri?"

"I didn't have a chance. He was too busy telling me how he bought my virginity with the villa."

"*What?*"

She explained how the villa next door had belonged to Drugov's family, and they sold it after this house was built, apparently for below market value, because Brie's daddy had no problem including his daughter in the deal.

"Maybe he never really expected Drugov to try to collect payment," she said. "It could have been something verbal—a joke—that my dad laughed off. There were a lot of gross comments about me back then, thanks to the makeup ads. It's possible my dad didn't realize...but then when I turned eighteen, Nikolai insisted on collecting."

He heard the note of hope in her voice, that maybe her dad hadn't sold her all those years ago, long before she ever found herself in a slave market in South Sudan.

She met Bastian's gaze and stopped swaying to the music, her eyes wide with horror. "How many times have I been sold?" Her thoughts must've flowed down the same lines.

He tightened his arm around her. There were so many things he wanted to say to comfort her, but this wasn't the place. "Dance with me, sweetheart," he whispered in her ear. "Let me hold you."

She settled against him. One song ended and another began. Before he'd cut in, he'd made a song request, and with perfect timing, the singer's clear voice rang out with the sultry lyrics of "Kissing a Fool."

He held her tight and pretended they were in a muddy field in South Sudan, dancing under the stars, and hoped she was doing the same thing.

~⁓~

Dimitri Veselov watched the Americans dance. One thing was clear: the relationship between them wasn't a charade, as he'd initially thought. For his purposes, that was good, because he couldn't spend all his time trying to keep Drugov from the woman when he needed to get into the lab.

From Chief Ford's bearing, Dimitri could tell the sick bastard Drugov wouldn't get another shot at cornering Gabriella again.

Now…how to lead the couple to the truth without compromising himself? If he could get Chief Ford to destroy the contaminated stockpile, it would save the world a lot of grief, and Dimitri might be able to sleep at night.

If Drugov's orders from the Kremlin were what Dimitri believed, he would have to expose himself—putting his sister and her son in danger—to stop a genocide. But if Chief Ford swooped in and exposed Drugov and Lawiri and the atrocity they would commit to end South Sudan's civil war, then Dimitri could quietly return to his regular gig, and his sister and nephew would remain safe.

He rubbed his chin, glad he'd opted to wear the beard on this assignment. He hadn't expected to come into close contact with American Special Forces. The beard would disguise him if the Green Beret managed to get his photo. Combined with the darkened hair and colored contacts, he looked nothing like his picture in US government files.

His time was running short. He was expected back at his post in three days. He needed to finish this job and return home, hoping his handlers didn't guess he'd helped the Americans on this one.

If they figured it out, Sophia and Yulian were as good as dead. He wouldn't let that happen. And for once, he'd find out what it was like to be on the right side.

Chapter Thirty-Five

"We can't search the house." Bastian crossed his arms and stared at her, unable to believe she'd suggest something so ridiculous, especially after her scare with Drugov earlier.

"Why not?" Brie asked. "It's what we came here for." She fiddled with one of his pins and pursed her lips.

"Um, it's dangerous?" His brow furrowed. The problem had to be the uniform. Mess blue wasn't intimidating like his ACUs. No way would she be able to face him down if he was in full camo. Instead, she saw the bow tie and ribbons and figured he was like the other guys here, who she could manipulate with batted eyes.

Did her eyes have to be so beautiful? And when she wore that dark makeup, it turned them all smoky and hot. Thank God she hadn't had makeup in South Sudan, or he'd have been screwed.

He got a grip. He was telling her why they couldn't go off on a Lawiri hunt. "If one of Drugov's goons finds us, they won't be nice about it."

"There's a light meal being served in the teal dining room. We'll wander that way, like we plan to eat, then slip into the adjacent dining room and make our way upstairs. A door in the back wall of all the dining rooms leads to a servant hall, where we'll find a staircase."

"How do you know this?"

"When I was in my teens, we stayed at our villa a lot. My dad and Drugov's dad would meet and work out their price-fixing schemes along with a few other oil bigwigs—there was a Federal Trade Commission probe more than once, but they always managed to cover their tracks. Having adjacent properties in a foreign country helped." She glanced across the room toward the hall where Drugov had cornered her. "I was always desperately bored and creeped out by Nikolai, but when he wasn't here, I hung out with his sister, who was three years younger than me. She and I would play hide-and-seek for hours in both our houses. I know this house and all the back passages. Better to search now, while Nick is in the front room, entertaining two hundred people. We won't have a better opportunity later."

Shit. He didn't know if it was her big brown eyes or the logic of her argument, but he found himself saying, "We'll check out the hallway, but if it's not clear, forget it."

She shifted her fingers from his decorations to his bow tie, and tugged. "And, if it's clear?"

He caved to the pull on his tie—and her damn beautiful eyes—and kissed her, then said, "We'll scope out the second floor, but that's all."

Her grin widened and her eyes warmed like he'd just set off a sparkler. Damn, he was a sucker.

They wandered through the rooms on the way to the dining area. There they found a dozen round tables that sat ten apiece, set for dinner service. Half the tables were full, and waiters circulated with laden trays, some with appetizers, some with the main course, others with dessert.

It appeared guests could just wander in and sit down

for a multicourse meal served by waiters whenever they wished.

"Wouldn't a buffet make more sense?" he whispered in Brie's ear.

"That's so delightfully frugal of you."

He laughed. He'd traveled the world with the Army and visited both exotic and expensive places, but these houses with their armies of servants really took it to the next level. His mom wouldn't believe this story.

Until yesterday, he'd never been in a house that required a complete staff: cook, maid, butler, chauffeur, valet, gardener, and the still-undefined role of the guy who delivered drinks to the pool area. But now, day two in Morocco and he was on his third staffed estate. And he'd begun to believe it was passé to have only seven or eight domestics.

That's what they were called, right? Domestic servants.

The word servant still felt wrong. Like a slur. But it wasn't. It was just a job title, and the people who'd served in all three houses had been kind and strove for invisible efficiency.

They bypassed the dining room, appearing to wander aimlessly, striving for their own invisibility. Without so much as a glance left or right, Brie entered the adjacent, empty dining room and made her way to the back wall where there was an arched doorway. A servant was there, carrying a tray, and he startled when Brie stepped into his line of sight.

"Would it be possible to get a gluten-free meal?" she asked.

The waiter's eyes widened at her request, and Bastian guessed it was unusual in Morocco to deal with food allergies. But then, in many countries in Africa, food was scarce and people ate what was available, period. There was no accommodation for allergies, because there couldn't be.

The server went to the kitchen to check on her request, leaving them alone in the back hall. Brie took Bastian's hand and led him to a dark, narrow enclosed stairway. They were halfway up the flight when the snick of a knob being turned alerted them they were about to have company.

Bastian scooped Brie up and pressed her against the stairwell wall, as if they'd chosen this spot for a fast, private screw. He kissed her as if their lives depended on it, and she kissed him back with equal intensity.

He hiked up her skirt and lifted her. She wrapped her legs around his waist and sucked on his tongue. She reached for his belt buckle as the door opened fully, letting light spill up the stairs.

A voice with a heavy Russian accent came to them from the bottom of the stairs. "Aren't public displays of affection frowned upon when in uniform?"

Bastian set Brie down and tucked her behind him. He faced the man at the bottom of the stairs, hand on the pistol concealed by his jacket. Backlit as he was by the open door, Bastian couldn't see the man's face, but the voice matched the mysterious Russian who'd helped them earlier.

The door closed, and footsteps padded up the stairs. A red LED light flared. Bright enough to illuminate faces, but not white, which would blind them and ruin their night vision.

The man's gaze took in Bastian's disheveled uniform, and he made a clicking sound with his tongue. "I might've expected this from Ms. Stewart, but not from Special Forces."

"Just having a quickie," Bastian said. "Is that a problem?"

The man shook his head. "You were heading upstairs."

Bastian said nothing. It was a lose/lose kind of statement. Silence was the best defense. He didn't want to pull his weapon. Not now and not on this man.

Finally, the Russian said, "Keep your gun hidden, Chief Ford. I think we can help each other."

"I never caught your name," Bastian said in response.

"My name doesn't matter."

"Yes, but 'hey you' gets so tedious," Brie said, making Bastian smile.

"Call me Ivan, if you insist upon a name."

"Okay, Ivan," Brie said, "how can we help each other?"

"You want to know where Lawiri is?"

Bastian stiffened. Beside him, so did Brie. "Yes," he said.

"Is he here? In this house?" she asked.

"No. Drugov sent him away when he issued your invitation. Tomorrow, we will talk. I will lead you to him."

"When?"

"I will contact you in the morning with a time and place." He scanned them up and down and sighed. "I'll lead you out the front stairs. We'll make it look like I was giving you a tour. There's quite the trophy room at the end of the upper hall."

Brie shuddered. "I've seen it. It's disgusting." To Bastian, she said, "Big game. Cats of all types, everything with antlers imaginable, and at the center of it all, an elephant. Most are endangered species. And he doesn't eat the meat. It's just blood sport. He has them stuffed so he can show the world how small his dick is."

They reached the upper landing, and Ivan checked the hall before motioning for them to follow. "This is my second time rescuing you tonight, Ms. Stewart. There won't be a third time."

"I've been hanging out with Brie for a few weeks now," Bastian said, "and I've lost count of how many times I've had to rescue her. Welcome to the club."

Brie snorted. "They weren't all my fault. And I saved your ass at least once." She grabbed his butt and squeezed. "Worth it, I think."

Ivan rolled his eyes. "Come on, we need to get back in the ballroom before Nick the Prick notices we're all missing."

"We might not have found Lawiri, but we did find an ally," Brie said as they walked down the long driveway, skipping the limo ride to enjoy the breezy night. They'd rejoined the party, each dancing to several songs with different partners. Brie's dance card included an inebriated Armando and the airline tycoon, while Bastian had partnered Annette and several other women. Now, finally, they were escaping, done playing spies for the night.

"*If* we can trust Ivan," Bastian said. "I'm not sure."

"I'm not either, but for some reason, he doesn't scare me."

"He should. GRU operators are badass dudes."

"I'm sure he's as badass as they come—he scares

Nikolai, which I didn't think was possible—but I don't get that vibe from him. He can control Nikolai. We need him on our side."

"That's the problem, though—is he on our side? If he's GRU, he's team Nick the Prick all the way. You aren't going to find anyone in the GRU waffling in their loyalty."

Her heel landed on top of a small pebble, rolling her ankle—the same one that had finally healed from South Sudan. Bastian caught her before she went down and scooped her into his arms. "No more walking for you."

"See. Maybe the limo isn't so ridiculous after all."

"It's totally ridiculous. Especially when I can carry you."

She laughed and threaded her fingers through the hair at his nape. "And look, you've saved me again."

"I've already added it to the tally."

When they reached the carpeted entry path, Brie wiggled in his arms. "I can take off my heels and walk. My ankle isn't that bad."

His response was a simple "No."

Youssef's face was a careful blank mask when Bastian carried Brie across the threshold and breezed by him.

"At least take the elevator, not the stairs."

"Now I feel like you're challenging me." He headed toward the wide, curved staircase.

"Bastian! You've impressed me enough! Save your strength, because when we get to the bedroom, you're going to need it."

He laughed and turned toward the small lift. "I can't believe your house has an elevator."

"Only one, though. I think Armando's got two."

"He's such a show-off." Bastian hit the wrong call

button.

"Down?" she asked. "To the Turkish bath?"

"Yes."

With that single syllable, heat flooded her.

The door slid open, and he carried her into the lift. She untied his bow tie as they descended. She slid the cloth up to his nape and used it to pull his head down for a deep kiss.

The doors opened, and the kiss continued as he carried her through the lounge outside the bath to the ornate double doors. He ended the kiss so he could find the door handle.

He pushed open the panel and carried her inside, then shouldered the door closed. "I've imagined this from the moment you showed me the bath on the tour."

He lowered her to the floor. She scanned the room, trying to see it through his eyes, as if for the first time. It wasn't a traditional hammam. It was more of a grotto, with a serpentine tiled pool that wound like a river. Tucked into the first curve was a half-moon hot tub, set off with columns and arches. Along the back ledge of the tub were lit fragrant candles. A waterfall spilled from the tub into the main pool, which flowed down the room, ending at an enclosed steam room that appeared to be carved from bedrock. Another curve along the length of the pool was occupied by a tiled wet bar, where more lit candles glowed. Opposite the bar and hot tub, three half-dome alcoves filled the serpentine curves. Each alcove was padded with an oval-shaped velvet cushion the length and width of a queen-sized mattress, topped by thick pillows that lined the half-moon wall.

The Turkish bath was outrageous, extravagant, and her favorite room in the house. This had been her refuge as a teen, a place to hide from the world and find inner peace.

She turned and locked the door, then checked the security panel to make sure the door to the outdoor pool area on the other side of the steam room was also locked. No one was going to interrupt them tonight. She adjusted the lights, dimming the far half of the room, while lighting the chandelier in the nearest alcove, which emitted a soft, warm glow.

She'd felt guilty for missing this bath when she was in South Sudan and only had six cups of water with which to wash, but she had. The hammam was opulent in the extreme, and she was fortunate to get to enjoy it. Tonight she would do so without guilt.

She slipped off her heels and approached the hot tub, dipping her hand in to test the temperature. A perfect hundred and two Fahrenheit.

"When did you arrange this?" she asked as she swished her hand in the soothingly hot water. They didn't keep the hot tub at full temperature all the time, because it fed and heated the much larger pool. It took several hours to bring everything up to heat.

She turned to see Bastian taking a platter of olives, dates, grapes, cheeses, and breads from a small fridge mounted under the bar. "I told Youssef to set it up when we returned from lunch." He set the tray next to the hot tub, then returned to the bar to grab a bottle of sparkling pomegranate juice from a sweating ice bucket. He poured the bubbly liquid into two champagne flutes and placed them with the food platter next to the tub.

Finally, he turned to her and gave her a measured, sexy smile. Slowly, deliberately, he undressed, removing shoes and socks first, then moving up to cufflinks and the chain that held his jacket closed. He set them on the tiled bar top, then draped the jacket on a stool. He removed his suspenders and cummerbund and the small, hidden gun holster, before reaching for the shirt studs. She watched in rapt attention as each small stud dropped onto the bar, making a soft pinging sound.

He slipped off the shirt. At last he was bare from the waist up, and she took him in. Salmon tattoo and coppery tanned skin over hard, sleek muscles. Wide shoulders, narrow hips. Utterly beautiful. She remembered watching him write a message in the grass in South Sudan, taking in his perfect body and wanting to explore him then with her hands and mouth. Nothing had changed since then. She still itched to touch him, to lick him. And tonight she would. Every perfect inch.

They'd made love before, but somehow, this felt like a first time. But then, tonight she'd hold nothing back.

He met her gaze, watching her watch him as he removed his pants, followed by the knife sheathed to his thigh and gun with ankle holster. All that remained were boxer briefs that bulged with a thick erection.

She reached out to stroke him. She wanted to drop to her knees and take him in her mouth, but he stopped her. "Uh-uh. No touching until we're in the tub. I'm going to make love to you in the water, then again on that bed. And then maybe in the steam room, if I can last another round."

He pulled out her arm and pointed to the spot where she'd been chipped. A thin white line remained after the scab had disappeared. "You've got a tracker there, and mine is here." He circled the spot on his leg. "We'll leave those areas alone, but otherwise, I intend to touch you everywhere." He opened a cupboard under the bar and pulled out a box of condoms. "I remembered to put these here earlier."

She smiled and stepped up behind him, running a hand down his muscled back. She kissed his shoulder. "I was tested for everything when we were on the carrier. I'm clean." She slid a hand over his boxer-brief-clad ass, and added, "How about you?"

"I was tested again too. I'm clean." His voice had gone hoarse.

She laughed as she ran her lips down his spine. "Then we don't need those."

"What about birth control?"

"I have an arm implant, the kind that lasts for up to three years. They're recommended for all female aid workers—in case we're raped."

He made a sound low in his throat, and she knew what he was thinking. "That didn't happen to me. Thanks to you." She kissed his back, his shoulder, working her way around to his front as he turned toward her. "And tonight, we're going to make love and celebrate life and surviving and each other."

His hands circled her hips and he dropped soft kisses on her lips. "Well then, why are you still in this gown?"

She turned, presenting the zipper to him. "Because I can't reach the zipper."

He chuckled. "I planned everything about this op, but forgot about dress extraction." His lips followed the zipper down her back. The gown had a built-in bra, so when it dropped to the floor, she was left wearing the ruby necklace, silk panties, and nothing else. She slipped off the panties and raised her hands for the necklace.

"No," Bastian said. "Leave it on. It's sexy as hell."

She smiled and crossed to the hot tub, stepping into the

liquid heat, letting out a soft purr of pleasure as she sank into the steamy water. Bastian removed his briefs and settled in the tub next to her. He reached for the champagne flutes and handed one to her. They clinked glasses and then took a sip. She liked this pomegranate soda because it was tart and had a similar mouth feel to champagne.

She placed her glass on the rim of the tub and settled at Bastian's side, resting her cheek on his shoulder. She ran a hand down his thigh under the water. "This feels heavenly. I didn't realize how much I needed a soak after today. Or this week…or…er, weeks. Thank you. For setting it up. For thinking of everything."

"If you're tired, we don't have to make love. Just let me hold you."

She lifted her head and smiled up at him. He meant it, even though his erection made it clear his body wanted much more. She shifted, rising on her knees and then turning to straddle him on the submerged bench seat. She purred again as his erection rubbed against her clit and she settled on him, her breasts to his pecs, her mouth to his lips. "No way. You're going to make love to me in the tub, in an alcove, and in the steam room, just like you promised, Chief Ford."

He rocked his hips, causing his penis to stroke her clit. "I'm a man who knows how to take orders."

She took his bottom lip between her teeth and teased it. Then she released him and said, "I've never had sex in this room before."

His hands settled on her waist. He slid one down, over her ass. "Never?"

"Never."

"I'm curious why." His lips traced her shoulder. "The

first thing I thought when you showed me this room was how much I wanted to make love to you on one of those beds. To see you naked in the golden light as I thrust inside you."

She smiled. She'd thought the same thing when she gave him the tour, but hadn't been ready to let go of her anger at the time. "This is my favorite room in the villa. It always has been. It was my refuge. My safe space. This room is too special to share with just anyone."

His eyes lit with heat and something more. "Are you saying I'm special, Ms. Stewart?"

"I'm saying you're the most special."

"Well, I *am* Special Forces."

She laughed. "You certainly are a force. You're also the best man I've ever known. The only man I want to share this with." She stroked his cheek. "Because I'm in love with you."

His eyes widened. "Oh, Brie." The words were guttural. Full of emotion. He pulled her head down and kissed her, his tongue sliding deep in her mouth. The kiss was hot and intense and went on for a long perfect moment. His erection teased her clit, and she could melt from the sensation of being submerged in the hot water as he kissed her.

She released his mouth to catch her breath and opened her eyes to meet his hot stare. His hand cupped the back of her neck. "I love you too. You warned me before the first kiss. I didn't listen. You were right. One kiss and I was a goner."

She laughed. "I think it took more than one."

"Maybe. But I fell just the same."

She reached between their bodies and stroked his thick erection. "I think we should do something about it." She positioned his cock and slid down, taking him deep in one thrust. She kissed him as she rocked on her knees, loving the feel of him inside her while immersed in hot water.

She slid up, and her breasts rose from the water. Bastian sucked on her nipple, releasing it when it dropped to water level as she took him deep again. He cupped her hips and lifted and lowered her, sucking and licking her breasts at the peak of each thrust. She arched her back and moaned, the sound echoing off the tiles.

He was so hard, she was going to come fast. Too fast. And she still wanted to taste him. To prolong the moment. She rose up and he slipped from her body. "Sit on the edge of the tub. So I can go down on you without drowning."

He did know how to take orders. He moved two candles and planted himself on the ledge. She settled before him, kneeling on the bench. She stroked his cock from base to tip, then took him in her mouth, all the way to the back of her throat.

He groaned and cursed and whispered approval as she sucked and stroked and made his balls tighten in her cupped hand. His hands cradled her head as he rocked his hips. She loved the feel of his slick head against her tongue and the sound of his pleasure. She opened her eyes and held his gaze as he thrust into her mouth.

"Oh, fuck, sweetheart. That's so hot. You are so fucking beautiful."

She could tell he was close to coming. He slipped from her mouth and lifted her as he slid down into the water. "Your turn," he said, and rotated her to set her on the ledge, spreading her thighs wide. Then his mouth was on her, and she could no longer think. She couldn't even keep her eyes open as he licked her clit and slid fingers inside her.

He gently scraped her clit with his teeth, then sucked, and she bucked as pleasure jolted through her. Then he settled in with his tongue, stroking her to the edge, his thumb joining in as she quaked on the verge. He lifted his mouth as his thumb kept time, and he rose from the tub and thrust inside her in the same moment her body crested. The feel of his cock working in time with his thumb drew a sharp yell of pleasure from her.

With his thumb working her clit, he used his other arm to pull her back into the tub, all while still thrusting inside her. Her orgasm continued as he stroked her inside and out. She wrapped her legs around his hips and sat on the bench once again as he knelt before her and thrust hard and fast, water splashing around their shoulders. She clenched tight on his cock as the pleasure spiraled ever upward and her moans echoed off the tile walls.

Bastian's entire body tightened, and he came, his groan of release joining her sounds.

They sat together for a long moment afterward. Quiet. Breathing. Kissing. Him still inside her.

"That was amazing," she said, leaning languidly against him.

He slid from her body and rose to his feet, lifting her. She gripped his shoulders, amazed he had the strength for such a feat after that orgasm. He carried her from the hot tub, crossed the pool, and climbed the step to the padded alcove. He set her down on the oval bed and stretched out beside her, gathering her against him. "I love you," he said, his fingers trailing along her cheek.

She held his gaze. This moment was so perfect, it was hard to believe it was real. "I love you too, Bastian."

"This isn't temporary. This is the start of something.

The start of everything."

She nodded and fiddled with his hair. "We'll get my family to back off. I won't let them control me anymore and run from you. From us."

"I can take care of myself, but even so, after we take down Drugov, they'll have every reason to leave us alone." Bastian absently touched the rubies at her neck. "I want to reconcile with my parents, but if they can't accept you, I won't."

"Don't push too fast. Too hard. I don't want to be the reason you split from your family."

"You wouldn't be the reason. It's on them that they didn't want to let go of Cece, and I won't have them being rude to you while welcoming my ex into their home. They're *my* parents, and you're my…" His voice trailed off as he searched for a word. Finally he cleared his throat. "I don't want to jump too far ahead, but girlfriend sounds too…juvenile for what I think this is."

"Love, partner, friend with extreme benefits."

"I like what extreme implies." He grinned and grabbed her ass. "Does it mean I get to go where no man has gone before?"

"Oh, honey, you wouldn't be the first. But yes, you can go there as long as you bring lots of lube."

He laughed. "Fair enough." He nudged her to roll onto her belly, then massaged her butt before moving up to give her a proper shoulder massage.

She grabbed a pillow and tucked it under her chest as he worked magic with his fingers on her back, neck, and shoulder blades. His mouth joined his fingers and the massage took a sensual turn until sometime later she was on her back again and his mouth brought her to a second orgasm.

As her orgasm faded, she pushed him onto his back and straddled him, taking him deep inside, her body sparking with pleasure at the friction of each thrust. He cupped her breasts as she rode him, his black eyes smoky hot as he stared up at her.

"Is it like you imagined?" she asked as she rested her palms on his pecs and slid up and down his cock.

"A thousand times better."

He thrust upward at the hips, his orgasm overtaking him.

Afterward, they each cleaned up in the bathroom and returned to their alcove with sheets and blankets along with the platter of food and sparkling juice. They ate, feeding each other, teasing and playing with the food. Then they blew out the candles and talked until she couldn't keep her eyes open. They slept entwined, wrapped in a satin sheet, Brie feeling more content and happy than she'd ever felt in her life.

Chapter Thirty-Six

Bastian watched Brie sleep, knowing he should wake her but determined to give her a few more minutes of peace. He glanced around the darkened hammam. This wasn't just a luxurious Turkish bath, it had been an oasis, a break from the swirl of intrigue and chillingly real danger they faced in their task.

He was crazy about her, and last night, she'd given herself to him without holding back. The night had been the best of his life, and he'd give anything to have it extend another day, but they had a job to do so they could start their lives together and have more nights like the previous one.

He had a mission to finish. Then a deployment to finish. Then he and Brie would visit his family and decide their next steps.

He sighed and leaned down to kiss her awake. Her eyes fluttered open, and she smiled, then puckered her lips in a soft pout. "I suppose it's morning and time to face reality?"

"Yes. I used the intercom to request coffee be delivered to your room, and the maid told me Armando sent a message that we can tour the lab and meet the engineers in an hour, if you're up for it."

That they would meet with the engineers on a Sunday wasn't a surprise in a Muslim country where they observed Friday prayer, but he was surprised Armando had organized it, as he'd been quite drunk when they left him at the party last night.

Brie's face lit up at the invitation, and she sprang from the bed. "If it doesn't interfere with meeting Ivan, I'd love to go to the lab."

Excited, she grabbed the sheet and stepped into the pool to cross to the door. As she waded, she wrapped the sheet around her like a towel. The bottom of the long satin cloth dragged in the knee-deep water.

She emerged from the pool, and he chuckled at the sight of her wearing nothing but a ruby necklace and soaking-wet sheet. She regally exited the hammam, leaving her gown, underwear, and shoes behind.

She redefined the morning-after walk, making it proud and magnificent.

As she was. Always.

Bastian grabbed a towel, draped it around his hips, and plucked his guns and knife from the bar, then followed her out the door. She passed the elevator and headed for the stairway, leaving a water trail as she climbed the stairs and crossed the front hall to the main staircase. She grinned and said good morning to the butler as she passed him. They climbed the two remaining flights and arrived at her room to find the coffee delivered and curtains parted to admit the morning sun.

Brie dropped the wet sheet just inside the door, took Bastian's hand in hers, and continued into the bathroom. "We can shower together, to save time."

With the time saving that afforded, they were able to linger in the hot spray and play, but they didn't have enough time to make love. At least, not in the way he wanted. "Later," Bastian promised as he kissed her, the steamy water cascading down her back.

She stroked his erection and said, "Later, you're going to come in my mouth."

He grinned. "Yes, ma'am."

She kissed him one more time, then turned off the water and stepped from the shower.

One hour after he'd kissed her awake, they were on their way to the lab in the back of Armando's limousine. The Spaniard was cheerful and energetic in spite of his late night, making Bastian wonder if he either had a supermetabolism or had popped a pill.

From Brie's discomfort, she seemed to share his concern, and given that she knew Armando better than Bastian did, that didn't bode well. But she was excited about the excursion and maintained a determined, optimistic air.

"Nikolai has opted to meet us at the lab instead of sharing a ride," Armando said after they'd been on the road for ten minutes. Armando's accent was heavier this morning, and it took a moment for his words to register to Bastian.

Brie was quicker to question the statement. "Nikolai will be there? Why?"

"Because of his investment in the project," Armando said, as if Brie were slow.

"Nikolai has invested in the underwear project?" Brie's tone held alarm.

Armando cocked his head, confused. "Yes. Of course. I texted you about it."

"We didn't have cell coverage in South Sudan except when I traveled to some of the bigger towns. I didn't receive any texts from you after I asked you about the project last November."

"Oh. *Perdonar*. I thought you knew. *No importa*. Nikolai was pleased to contribute. He was looking for a charity project in South Sudan for his company. This was a perfect fit."

It was logical. Drugov wanted the drilling rights. But still, the arrangement didn't sit well with Bastian.

"There are any number of charities that provide food and other aid to ease the famine," Brie said.

Armando's brow furrowed. "I'm sure there are, but he is investing in this."

"I don't trust Nikolai," she said flatly.

Armando sat back and smiled. "You worry too much. There is no need for trust. My company is creating the product; his company will pay for manufacture; you and your family will raise money for distribution. Girls will get underwear for free. Everyone wins."

Bastian took Brie's hand and pressed her palm against his stomach. He understood her upset. Drugov had forced his way into the charity project of her heart.

The sick asshole had been obsessed with Brie since she was thirteen. How much of her life had been shaped by that photo shoot?

At two years younger than her, Bastian hadn't been aware of the buzz surrounding the ad campaign at the time. He'd been too busy playing laser tag and skateboarding to pay attention to inappropriate lust by men old enough to know better.

And why the hell had her parents allowed it? Her father was a shit bag. He knew that. But her mom? She should have protected Brie. Put the kibosh on allowing the campaign to publish once she saw the photos. Brie didn't talk about her mom any more than she'd spoken of her brothers, and Bastian figured the ill-advised modeling career had something to do with that.

Now, twenty years later, Brie was still paying the price, in the form of a sick Russian oligarch who'd fixated on her when she was a child and even purchased her virginity from an equally sick father.

Bastian cleared his throat. "Drugov is out."

Armando looked at him, confused. "What?"

"Drugov can't have anything to do with this deal. He's a sick motherfucker. He's after Brie."

Armando stiffened and sat up straighter. "I don't believe you have any say in this." His eyes flattened, and the congenial air disappeared. "Who the hell are you, besides her fuck of the week? You have no role here."

Bastian sat up to his full height. He wasn't tall, but he knew how to intimidate. He had Special Forces attitude and bearing. A pampered pretty boy like Armando Cardona didn't scare him in the least. "Drugov is out, and you will apologize to Brie for your disrespect."

Armando's eyes flared with hostility. "It is not her I disrespect. Just her choice of companions. You are a nobody. She will tire of you soon—"

Bastian snorted. "Like she tired of you? You fail to see I'm giving you good business advice here. Nikolai Drugov will be poison to your company."

Armando's gaze flicked over Bastian. "What do you know of business? A soldier. *El indio.* Go back to the reservation and drink your firewater and leave business to the men."

Bastian lunged for him at the same moment Brie shouted for the chauffeur to stop the car. Bastian gripped the man's shirt. "Of the two of us, you're the drunk who's been popping pills. You ever insult Brie or me again, and you'll be crapping into a colostomy bag for the rest of your fucking life."

"Brie, stop him!" Armando said, his eyes wide with fear now that reality made it through his drugged-up haze.

"Fuck you, Armando," Brie said. "Apologize. Now."

Bastian moved his grip to Armando's throat but didn't squeeze. The Spaniard looked like he was about to crap his pants already, and Bastian didn't want to deal with the smell.

Armando started weeping as the limousine finally pulled over. Interestingly, the driver said nothing. It appeared the chauffeur wasn't Team Armando either.

"*¡Lo siento! Mierda*. Are you fucking *loco*?" Armando said, his accent thicker than ever. "I had no choice. Nikolai will cut off my balls." His gaze flicked from Bastian to Brie. "No one says no to Mafioso."

Bastian released him. Armando's fear could explain his drugged state. He might be bracing himself to face Drugov, much like he'd gotten wasted at the oligarch's party the night before. The guy was a shit, a snob, and a racist, but this project was important to Brie and could be important to thousands of girls. Bastian would set aside his hostility for the good of the girls who would benefit. They'd figure out how to boot Drugov from the program later.

He turned to Brie. "Do you still want to see the lab?"

She sighed and glared at Armando. Finally, she said, "Yes. For the girls."

Bastian nodded and, in Arabic, commanded the chauffeur to drive.

Brie felt sick. Armando was high and had shown he was a sexist, racist pig. She wasn't one to judge on the self-medicating front, but his words to Bastian were unforgivable. And dammit, he'd brought Nikolai into the project that was closest to her heart, which meant blood money would pay for manufacture of underwear desperately needed by girls in developing countries.

Her stomach churned.

She simply couldn't do it. Drugov could have no part in this. He would get no benefit. No good PR. No tax write-off. She would raise money elsewhere—like she'd planned from the start. "Bastian is right, Armando. Drugov is out. His money is tainted. It would be stealing a life from one girl to give sanitary underwear to the next. It's twisted."

"There is no choice," Armando said. "The deal is done. Nikolai Drugov is owned by the Kremlin. People who say no to him are killed with mysterious poisons. I won't die because you don't approve of where the money comes from. We're talking about fucking *bragas*. Panties for poor *niñas*. No one cares."

"*I* care. These are people. Not *just* girls. Not *only* Africans. *People*. They count. They have as much value as you or I." Her stomach knotted at his casual dismissal. "They're poor and black and girls, so you think they don't matter? Are they somehow inhuman? Where is your empathy? Your humanity? They're Christian, Muslim, Animist, or they believe in nothing at all, and every single one of them is a fucking human being who has as much value as a sexist, racist piece of shit like you."

The girls she'd met in South Sudan had suffered so much. They deserved a life and education as much as any boy or girl in developed countries.

That the shallow, scared man before her couldn't see that was a reminder of everything she'd escaped from. She'd been a version of him once. Someone who made excuses for horrible actions. But she wasn't that person anymore. "Why did you even tell Nikolai about the underwear project?"

Armando crossed his arms and pouted. Seriously, how had she ever found him attractive?

"After he learned we'd been lovers, he threatened me. Said he'd cut off my balls if I touched you again." Armando glanced at Bastian and smirked. "Good luck, *amigo*."

Brie glared at Armando. "And how did he find out? Did you take out a fucking billboard? Blab at the neighborhood barbecue?"

He shrugged. "I might have said something to him. I don't remember."

"You're such a gentleman, Armando."

"I didn't know he wanted you for himself! That he already considered you his property." He cleared his throat. "He demanded I tell him if you contacted me. So I did."

Rage stole her breath. Finally, she managed to say, "I'm no one's property. *No one*."

"So what did you do?" Bastian asked. "You went to his house and said, 'Yo, Brie called me'?"

"Perhaps."

"Last November? Right after I contacted you?" Brie asked.

"Maybe. I didn't mark my calendar."

"Shit. Did you tell him I was in South Sudan and working for USAID?"

His brow furrowed. "I believe so. Yes."

Brie exchanged glances with Bastian. "Savvy said the first trickle of intel on the market forming came in in late December."

"Who is Savvy?" Armando asked, with far too much interest.

Shit. She was a crappy spy. Really, the very worst. "My cousin," she snapped.

A sickening thought hit her… Could *she* be the reason Drugov and Lawiri formed the market? Because Drugov knew she was there?

Surely he wasn't *that* obsessed and insane?

She met Bastian's gaze and knew he was thinking the same thing. It was nutty—and some would say egotistical—but she couldn't help but think the idea might have merit. Drugov wasn't normal, and it didn't have anything to do with her. It was all about his psychosis. Like John Hinckley's obsession with Jodie Foster. Hinckley's shooting of President Reagan had nothing to do with the actress and everything to do with unchecked mental illness.

Drugov could be very much the same, but he also had millions of dollars at his disposal, was a sociopath, and in deep with Russian organized crime and the Kremlin. There were few men in the world who were more dangerous.

And as he'd said last night, Brie had defied him and was the only woman who'd ever managed that feat.

At last they pulled up in front of an older building in the industrial part of Casablanca, to see that Nikolai had already arrived and was waiting in his silver Aston Martin.

At least he was alone. She wouldn't be comfortable

touring the lab if he had any of his henchmen with him. She clenched her jaw and climbed from the limousine. They'd meet the engineers, check out the prototypes, then get the hell out of here. She and Bastian would call a cab. She wouldn't get back in a car with Armando ever again.

Bastian slipped an arm around her waist and held her tight against his hip as they approached the front of the building. He pressed his lips to her temple and whispered, "We'll keep this quick."

She nodded, so grateful he was with her.

The building showed its age. Armando's grandfather had originally built this facility—a development lab fronting a large manufacturing plant—sometime in the sixties. It had been upgraded and expanded in the fifty-plus years since, but the façade remained the same. Blocky and modular in design, it looked like something from a 1950s movie predicting what the future would look like. White-painted concrete, it was composed of rectangular segments without a single arch or other feature that looked anything like present or past Morocco. But it did look industrial and retro-modern. If that was a thing.

The front lot was empty except for Armando's limousine, Nikolai's Aston Martin, and another vehicle that likely belonged to the security guard standing by the entrance. Morocco worked Monday through Thursday, with shorter hours on Fridays for prayer, but there was the rare business that operated Sunday to Thursday, which was what she'd expected to find here when Armando set the tour up, but clearly that wasn't the case.

Brie and Bastian passed Nikolai without greeting him, and entered the building to find a walk-through metal detector in the front vestibule.

"You will have to surrender your weapons, Bastian," Armando said.

"No," Bastian said.

"Then you will wait here while I escort Brie inside."

"No," Brie said in chorus with Bastian.

"You cannot enter the lab with weapons," Armando said. "We have strict security rules."

"Bullshit. And sure as fuck, Drugov is armed." Bastian nodded toward the Russian, who had followed them inside.

Armando glared at him.

"Forget it, Armando," Brie said. "Forget all of it. We're leaving." Brie turned back toward the door, her hand on Bastian's arm, to find the exit blocked by Nikolai and the security guard.

"But you just got here, my dear."

"Fuck off, Nikolai, and get out of my way."

"We're going to tour the lab. There is something here you will want to see."

Brie didn't like the way he said that.

A noise behind her caused her to turn, and two men entered the room from the back of the vestibule. They wore body armor and helmets like riot police, and their guns were trained on her and Bastian.

"What the fuck?" Armando asked, his voice laced with alarm. "Who are these guys?"

"Shut up," Nikolai said in an offhand manner. He turned to Bastian. "Get your filthy hands off Gabriella and put them behind your head."

Brie couldn't breathe. Her body felt like it had turned to liquid. In a flash, she knew giving in to the faint was exactly what she needed to do. She released all tension in her body and collapsed to the floor.

Bastian caught her on the way down, and she slid along his leg, keeping her body limp, her head flopped to the side like a rag doll. Her hand brushed Bastian's calf, not the one with the ankle holster, the one with the tracker. He shifted position, hopefully hiding her hand from Nikolai's view. She pressed on the tracker with her knuckles, so her hand appeared slack. Bastian leaned into the pressure, moving his leg to massage the spot for faster activation of the beacon.

"Get away from her!" Nikolai said.

"She's not breathing!"

This wasn't a lie. She held her breath, any excuse to keep Bastian by her side, to give them time to trigger the tracker. Plus he still had his weapons.

Had it been ten seconds? Was the tracker active? There were plenty of cell towers, and she and Bastian had working cell phones. A team could be mobilized from Rota in minutes. They would be here in less than an hour.

And Nikolai had no idea.

A thump and a bang, and Bastian was no longer above her. She let her hand fall to the floor and released a slow breath, feeling Nikolai above her.

Pain slammed across her cheek and jaw, an open-palm blow delivered with enough force to snap her head to the side. She sucked in a breath, and her eyes popped open.

"Wake up, Sleeping Beauty," Nikolai said with a sneer.

Bastian broke away from the guards and lunged for Nikolai, but he was caught, slammed to the ground, and stripped of his weapons. One of the guards punched him, a hard blow across the face, while another guard held his hands behind his back.

Bastian fought against the hold, and another blow came, a hard right to the cheek followed by a left to the belly. He dropped to his knees, blood trickling from his mouth.

Brie screamed. "Stop!"

Nikolai stepped forward and kicked Bastian in the groin, and he fell over, gasping for breath.

Brie crawled over to him, protecting him with her body. Nikolai would certainly hurt her, but he wouldn't kill her. That would defeat the point.

"Leave him alone, and I'll do what you want," she said, barely holding back the sob from her voice.

"No!" Bastian shouted even as he gasped for breath.

"Stop hurting him, and you can have me, Nikolai." Her voice was pleading.

Nikolai shrugged. "I get you anyway."

"If you kill him, I will fight you every second, and I guarantee, I will find a way to kill you, but first I will cut off your penis and feed it to your favorite dog. But if you leave him alone, I won't fight."

"Prove it." He ran a hand over her shoulder and down to her breast, then squeezed and twisted.

She held her breath against the pain. She let him hurt her, unchallenged.

He leaned toward her. She could smell the stale booze and smoke on his breath. He whispered in her ear. "But I like it when you scream." He twisted again, harder this time, pinching her nipple.

She grunted but didn't otherwise make a sound. Her eyes watered, but no tears fell. Control. Right now she needed to control every reaction. Every sound. She could only give him what she wanted to give. Not what he forced from her.

He released her nipple.

She took a moment to steady her breathing, then said, "I will give you nothing, not even my screams, if you hurt him more than you already have."

He slapped her. Hard. Fast. She didn't see the blow coming. Again, her head snapped to the side. This time, her lip split on her teeth. But she held in her grunt of pain, making only a small sound.

Blood dripped down her chin. She allowed her gaze to drop to Bastian. That was a mistake. The rage and pain on his face was almost her undoing. Instead, she looked to Armando and gave him a fierce glare.

His olive skin was now sickly green. Poor, stupid, weak Armando. He'd made a deal with the devil and had no idea what it really meant. Somewhere in the haze of drugs and horror, she saw his sorrow.

He knew now what he'd done.

Deep down, he'd probably known what was in store for her when he arranged this meeting. Hence the pills to see him through.

She turned to Nikolai. "You said there is something here that I want to see."

His slow smile made her skin crawl, but she held that reaction back too. She was an ice queen. Princess Prime in full regalia. She knew this drill. She'd spent years trying to unlearn the reserve but now was grateful her mother had served a daily lesson in ingrained cold-bitchery.

"I wish I could have seen you in the slave market," Nikolai said. "I bet you were magnificent. The regal princess, chained. I've been imagining breaking you for twenty years."

She wanted to spit on him, but he would take out his rage on Bastian, so she kept her face as blank as possible.

He circled her throat with his hand. "How did the metal collar feel against your skin? You will wear one again. You are mine. You have always been mine."

"Show me your surprise." She kept her voice even.

Don't give him the emotion he feeds on.

"This way, my love. I have a treat for you." To his men, he said, "Bring the soldier."

He needed Bastian to keep her in line. That would work for now, but there was no way he'd keep Bastian around for long. It would be too dangerous. Bastian was too well trained, and Nikolai was not.

After all, Nikolai needed henchmen.

And even now, a team of SEALs or Delta Force operators could be mobilizing in Rota. They needed to stay here as long as possible, to give them a chance to swoop in and take out Nikolai. The Russian and his three bots didn't stand a chance against a full team of special forces operators.

Chapter Thirty-Seven

After Bastian and Brie were stripped of cell phones and wallets, a guard slapped cuffs around Bastian's wrists. The guy didn't pay close attention to his tasks, and at least twice during the search, Bastian could have snapped his neck. But he allowed the search and cuffs, because Drugov would hurt Brie if Bastian seized an opportunity to escape.

It was the same reason Brie took Drugov's abuse without a word. She was protecting Bastian.

They just had to hold on for an hour or so. There wouldn't be time for a SOCOM team to plan the op. They'd come in blind, but they would come. Brilliant of Brie to trigger the tracker in those first moments without hesitating. And she still had hers in place, should Nikolai move her before the team arrived.

One hour. Two tops. And this Russian sonofabitch would pay for every red mark on Brie's body with interest.

He followed the unhappy entourage into the heart of the lab. Drugov's hand was on Brie's ass, and Bastian had to rein in the urge to rip the motherfucker's head off. In due time. They passed through stark rooms with long white tables, walls of cabinets, and massive air filtration systems. All workstations were empty and spotless. Computers and other more mysterious-looking equipment lined the walls. Glass vials, beakers, and test tubes filled racks and shelves.

They reached a doorway at the back, and Drugov pressed several buttons on a ten-key pad, then waved his hand in front of a shiny black box mounted beneath the number pad.

"What the fuck?" Armando whined. "Nikolai, you can't bring them—"

"Shut up or I will break your face."

"No one can see—"

Nikolai turned and punched Armando, a quick hard jab that dropped the Spaniard. Armando clutched his nose. Blood seeped between his fingers.

"Come with us, or go. I don't care. But I will cut out your tongue if you keep talking."

Armando got to his feet and left, retracing the route they'd just taken through the lab. The fact that Drugov let the man leave told Bastian a lot about Armando's complicity. This was more than a joint charity project. Drugov had full access to the lab. Either the Russian had kompromat on Armando, or they were full business partners. Either way, Drugov didn't fear Armando Cardona would tell tales.

How long had the Russian had access to this lab? What services was this lab providing to Russia? Russians were known for their assassination methods that employed chemicals and poisons developed just for that purpose, and this was a full-service chemical lab. Armando had even mentioned the assassination technique in the car on the way here, when he expressed fear of Drugov. Had he been naming a very specific fear because he knew what cocktails Drugov was making under his roof?

They descended a narrow staircase, entering a part of the building that Bastian would bet good money never saw government oversight or inspection. In the basement, they found a secondary lab. From the design of it, this lab was likely as old as the original building. So this company had always had side projects going on, invisible to stockholders and government agents.

Like the facilities above, the equipment had been upgraded over the years, and the tables were spotless and maintained. Conscientious scientists who dealt in death and chemical warfare.

It was in the back of the room they came to the gift Drugov had arranged for Brie. Her brother, JJ, bound, gagged, and stretched out on a lab table, his eyes wide with fear.

~⌒~

Savannah James stared at the map as people poured into SOCOM headquarters. Bastian's tracker had been triggered just five minutes ago, and less than half the team had gathered. This wasn't like when Morgan had initiated her tracker six days after she'd been abducted. At that time, after receiving the signal, this room had been full of special forces operators and SOCOM leadership within minutes.

But no one had expected Bastian's tracker to go off today. He'd called in his morning report an hour ago and things had been fine. This morning, he and Brie were going to the Spaniard's lab to see prototypes for Brie's charity project. It had all checked out.

Armando Cardona had checked out. The heir to a pharmachemical company, he wasn't a scientist, but he dutifully played his role in business management. Just enough to justify the large income. Cardona handled the Morocco branch of the company, with little oversight from his brother, the CEO who managed the business from the main headquarters in Madrid.

Savvy must have missed something in Cardona's background.

But what about the Russian Bastian mentioned? Ivan no last name, who Drugov feared. Was he GRU, as Bastian initially suspected, or had Ivan been sent by the Kremlin to keep Drugov in line?

He'd claimed to be an ally, but if he was GRU or Kremlin enforcer, he most certainly was not a friend to the US.

Bastian had promised to get a photo of the man today, but she hadn't received any emails or texts from him, and now his tracker was pinging and it was her job to determine what it meant.

"Zooming in on the location with real-time satellite images," the tech who'd been tracing the signal said.

Satellite photos appeared on the big screen, just as several members of Bastian's A-Team entered the room. Savvy studied the overview of Casablanca's industrial zone. "That's the chemical plant Bastian said they would visit."

"You think the tracker going off could be an accident?" Bastian's XO, Captain Oswald, asked.

"He'd have called to clear it if that were the case," Savvy said. "He's not sleeping. He'd know it had been triggered. His morning check-in today was routine."

"Why was he going to a chemical plant?" Cal asked. He was all business, his hostility toward her sidelined in his concern for his teammate.

"It was a charity project Brie initiated—plastic-lined

underwear for adolescent girls, so they could manage their periods and remain in school. Brie's neighbor owns the lab and plant. She asked him if he could develop a prototype."

"What do we know about the lab owner?" Cal asked.

"Not enough, apparently." She gave a rundown of what she knew about Armando Cardona and his pharmachemical company.

"Have you called Chief Ford, to see if it was an accidental trigger?" Pax asked.

Savvy nodded. "The call went straight to voice mail."

"Is a team being readied?" Cal asked.

"Yes," Captain Oswald answered. "A SEAL team is being scrambled out of Rota. They can be there in forty-five minutes, but they're going in blind."

Savvy stared at the aerial image, showing three cars in an otherwise empty parking lot and a static building. She'd fucked up. Why didn't she see this coming? What had she missed? There'd been no hint Cardona had business dealings with Drugov. They were neighbors in an exclusive, expensive neighborhood, nothing more.

But she hadn't started digging into Cardona's background until Brie listed him as a person she intended to contact in Casablanca. One week ago, Savvy had never heard of Armando Cardona. He'd never been on her radar.

"I need a list of what they make at that plant," she said. "This could be where Drugov gets some of his biological agents."

"I'm going through press releases now," a tech said. "I need a Spanish translator. Some of this is too technical for me."

Espinosa stepped up behind the man and leaned down

to read the screen. "Synthetic polymers—not the direct-to-consumer type. They supply other companies. Cellophane packaging, absorbent fill for diapers and sanitation products—that makes sense given Brie's charity project—they also develop and manufacture personal care products like binders and thickeners for hair conditioner, and structuring agents for cosmetics."

"What about pharmacology? Do they develop and test drugs?" she asked.

"If they do, it's not reported."

"I bet anything there's a drug lab there somewhere. That's probably why Cardona spends so much time in Morocco." Savvy stood next to Espinosa, staring at the computer monitor over the tech's shoulder. She couldn't read the list either, recognizing only a few of the Latin root words.

Cosméticos, of course, she understood.

She felt a prickle along her neck. "Who do they supply their cosmetics to? What's the brand name?"

The tech scrolled down to the bottom of the press release. "They supply several US and European companies. Their biggest client is a company called Carabella."

"Sonofabitch. That's the company Brie modeled for all those years ago. The ads that ended up being banned in the US because she was underage."

"I thought that company folded?" Captain Oswald said. "She wasn't the only kid to show up in their ads."

"They didn't fold, they sell under a different name in the US now. Peach Blossom Cosmetics or something else innocuous sounding. And you're correct about there being other minors in their explicit ads. Aside from Brie, all the other kids were Russian, because the parent company isn't in Spain, it's in Russia. Twenty years ago, when Brie was their cover girl, it was owned by Nikolai Drugov's father."

"Does Drugov still own the company?" Pax asked.

"No. That's probably why I didn't find the connection between Cardona and Drugov. But twenty years ago, the Drugovs and Cardonas were business partners, and it's possible that partnership didn't end when Drugov sold the cosmetic company." Savvy felt sick. "Odds are, when Bastian and Brie walked into that plant, they were walking into a trap."

"You fucked up, Savvy." Cal's voice was all hard edges, and she couldn't blame him.

"I know." Oh God. What had she done? She kept her voice even, devoid of the emotions that threatened to make her hurl. "Refresh the image," she instructed the satellite operator.

A moment later, a slightly different view of the same plant appeared on the screen, but with one important difference: the stretch limousine that had been parked in front was now gone.

~⌒~

B rie was on adrenaline overload. Being forced to hold herself together to limit her reactions for Nikolai was hard enough without seeing JJ trussed up. She didn't harbor much love for JJ, but he was her half brother, and she didn't relish seeing him in this position.

"What have you done, Nikolai?" she asked in as regal a voice as she could muster.

"Jeffery Junior has failed. Repeatedly. Most recently he failed to deliver you to me. It is time he pays for his incompetence."

JJ's eyes turned hard.

Brie stepped forward and removed the gag. If nothing else, this conversation would be interesting, and she had no doubt Nikolai wanted this confrontation. Anything to buy time for the SEALs to get here.

To her brother, she said, "Explain."

He glared at her and didn't say a word.

"My lady has bade you speak, Jeffery," Nikolai said.

His saccharine tone and overly formal words turned her stomach, but she would allow it. In Rota, the mission clock was ticking.

Special Forces are on their way. They have to be.

"What's going on, JJ?"

"You fucking whore. You ruin everything." Her brother spit on her.

She recoiled and wiped the spit from her face, then slapped her bound brother across the face. Behind her, she could hear Bastian struggling against the hold of his guards.

Nikolai laughed and said, "I should let the Green Beret loose so he can rip you apart. Because, you see, only *I* am allowed to hurt Gabriella." He twisted his fingers through her short hair, and yanked, jerking her head back, exposing her throat. "And you will hurt, my sweet," he whispered directly into her ear. "For making me wait so many years. For fucking dozens of men. For making me search for you in South Sudan. You have much to pay for."

Bile rose. She had no doubt he'd follow through with his threats.

He released her hair and said in a normal voice, "I offered your brother a deal. I would remove his father from Prime Energy so he could take his place, and he would deliver you to me, at long last. I did my part. He failed in his. Repeatedly."

Brie looked to JJ. "Is this true? Dad's stroke wasn't a stroke at all?"

"What do you care? You hate the asshole."

"I care because *I* was the payment for a hit on our father." She turned to Nikolai. "How did you make it look like a stroke?"

Nikolai spread his arms wide. "This lab provides many treasures to the Russian Federation. It didn't just *look* like a stroke. It was one."

Oh hell, if they had the power to off people with seemingly natural causes, the body count of the current regime in Russia was probably much higher than anyone guessed. Why throw people from windows when it was so obvious?

But then, the dictator of Russia didn't give a damn about obvious and preferred to scare by ordering blatant hits. Strokes were too subtle for him, but perfect for a man who wanted to take over the family empire.

"Isn't that how your father died, Nikolai?" she asked.

"You have always been clever."

"And you have always been a condescending shit bag. Why is JJ here, now?"

"Because he went behind my back to strike a deal with Lawiri for South Sudan's oil, and now you get to decide if he should live or die. You alone can save his life."

"Lawiri? The South Sudanese general? What does he have to do with this?"

"Don't play dumb, my dear. I know you came to Casablanca to find him."

She couldn't even keep her face blank at that.

"Don't be so surprised. American intelligence has been

compromised by Russia for some time. I even have my own pet in the DIA."

He couldn't be referring to Savannah James then, who was CIA. But then, Brie had no doubt about the woman's loyalty. She kept secrets; she manipulated. But Brie didn't question whose side Savvy was on. So how did Nikolai know why she was in Morocco?

There was only one possibility: someone in Savvy's chain of command was compromised.

"When we are done here," Nikolai continued, "I will bring you to Lawiri. You can meet the next president of South Sudan, and he will thank you for your service to his people. He is most excited about your sanitary underwear project, for it will be the final blow to both sides."

"You are batshit crazy, Nikolai."

He slapped her again. A fast, hard blow.

She shook her head, to try to regain her equilibrium. Okay. So being called crazy was a trigger. Best to file that away for use against him later.

"Tell me, my dear, should I spare your brother?"

"Screw you. Your actions are your own. I will not shoulder the atrocities you commit." She turned for the exit. So far she wasn't a prisoner. She would push that boundary now, because she sure as hell didn't want to witness what Nikolai might do to JJ.

Where was Rafe? Did he have a role in this ugly business?

One thing was certain: Bastian was on limited time. Their détente could last only so long, and she knew Nikolai had no intention of letting Bastian live. He'd said too much in front of both of them.

He would kill Brie too, but the sicko wanted to play

with her first, which gave her a little leverage. Being the object of his obsession meant there would be no quick or easy death for her. But it also gave her time and opportunities.

"Did you kill Micah?" she asked. She hadn't considered it until now, but it made sense. A quid pro quo with her father. All it would have taken was a toxin to trigger a stroke or something similar in the pilot, and down the helicopter would go.

Two good men dead, because Nikolai had fixated on her when she was thirteen and her father had fed his obsession with promises that weren't his to make.

"The reporter? The one you fucked? Yes."

She pivoted on her foot and punched Nikolai in the jaw, remembering everything Bastian had taught her about stance and swing during her fight lessons. Nikolai dropped, hitting his head on a metal table on his way to the concrete floor.

His guards grabbed her, yanking her arms behind her back. Metal cuffs clamped around her wrists.

Nikolai staggered to his feet, then backhanded her. She whirled, slamming into Bastian. She hit the floor, hard. Bastian lunged for Nikolai, head-butting him before planting a knee into his groin.

The guards pounced and dragged Bastian back, pummeling him with their batons until he dropped to the concrete.

Brie sobbed and scooted on her knees to his side, lying across his chest to protect him from the blows. A baton hit her shoulder and another her back. She couldn't hold back a scream.

"Stop!" Nikolai shouted. "Only I hit her."

Brie met Bastian's gaze. His eyes were angry but clear.

She mouthed *I love you* and turned to face Nikolai. She was nauseated, and her head throbbed. Pain coursed through her back and shoulders. "I don't give a fuck what you do to JJ. Take us to Lawiri. I want to spit on the asshole who burned food intended for starving people. Then I will submit to your sadistic games."

She still had her tracker, and SEALs were probably en route now. Once she laid eyes on Lawiri, she'd trigger it.

They'd get Lawiri and Nikolai. It would end here.

No matter what happened to her, it would end here.

Chapter Thirty-Eight

Bastian watched as Drugov and his security guard shoved Brie up the stairs. Despite her protests, he was leaving Bastian behind with the two guards in riot gear and her shitty brother. He hated that she'd be out of his sight, but at least this way, he could take out the guards and go after her.

And he'd have a team of SEALs to back him up.

But they needed to get here fucking fast, because the moment he was free, he was going after her. The psycho asshole had been waiting twenty years to torture and rape her.

The door slammed closed at the top of the stairs. Bastian smiled meekly at the two henchmen and said in Arabic, "So, who do you have orders to kill first, me or the asshole on the table?"

"You."

Bastian sprang to his feet and took the guy down with one kick to the throat. Before guard number one hit the floor, he kicked number two in the balls and elbowed him in the face as he fell. The goons were amateurs who believed their body armor would protect them, while Bastian had trained for hours on how to fight with hands bound. Plus these shits had pain coming after they way they'd hit Brie with their chickenshit batons.

One was out cold. Bastian planted his knee on the

other man's neck and asked in Arabic, "Where did the fucker take Brie?"

"I don't know," the man said.

"What are you saying?" JJ asked. "Untie me. I'll help you go after Brie."

No way in hell did Bastian trust Brie's brother, and he wouldn't waste more time with the guard. A kick to the head and the guy was out cold. Bastian found the cuff keys in his utility belt. In a flash, he was free and had his weapons back. He searched for a cell phone but came up empty.

Fuck. A call to SOCOM would be really helpful about now. There would be a phone upstairs, and if not, he'd steal a car and go after Brie. He headed across the room.

"Where are you going?" JJ asked. "You can't leave me here! They'll kill me!" His voice broke.

"Like I give a fuck." He'd let the SEALs deal with JJ and the guards. He had to find Brie.

He reached the staircase as the door at the top opened. He dove to the side, gun ready.

Footsteps descended. Ivan—or whatever the hell his name was—came into view. He met Bastian's gaze without flinching at the gun pointed to his head. He was unarmed but carried a leather satchel. He held up his hands—which, Bastian noted, were gloved—in surrender. "I know where he's taken her."

Bastian kept the gun trained on Ivan's left eye. "Where?"

"I'm the best hope you've got, Chief Ford, and you need me alive if you want to save her."

Ivan didn't know about the tracker. Bastian had options. But his gut said he needed Ivan's help.

He lowered the gun. "Let's go."

B rie had been shoved into the backseat of Nikolai's car. Nikolai was in the driver's seat, and the security guard sat in the back with her.

She was scared for herself, but terrified for Bastian. She had no doubt Nikolai had ordered the goons to kill him as soon as she was out of the room.

Bastian can take them. He'll strike before they have a chance to shoot.

His training outdistanced theirs by miles. As long as there were no other surprises in the lab, Bastian would be fine.

They wound through the industrial part of town. She didn't know this area, had never really had a reason to explore it. She'd studied maps with Savvy but hadn't expected to visit this part of town. It had never occurred to her that Armando would have moved forward with her idea, or that he'd suggest a factory tour.

But then, the tour had merely been a way to take her and Bastian by surprise. Nikolai knew Bastian's training. He knew Brie would never agree to enter his house outside of a party with hundreds of witnesses. The lab tour had been inspired. And Armando had been a fine actor, mentioning it before she'd even seen Nikolai again.

"Is there a prototype?" she asked Nikolai. "Or was it all a lie?"

"Poor Gabriella. We left before we could show you." Nikolai met her gaze in the rearview mirror.

She was glad he was too much of a control freak to relinquish driving. It meant he was up front and she shared the backseat with a goon who wouldn't dare touch her in front of his nut-job boss. "Show me?"

"The underwear is ugly and not to my liking. A waste. But yes, Armando did make the underwear. And it will be dutifully given to girls in South Sudan, just like you wanted. In fact, they will deliver South Sudan from the war. Little did you know, your period panties would bring peace and Lawiri."

"What the fuck is that supposed to mean, Nikolai?"

"I have prepared something special for the girls. Each pair will come with a starter pack of pads."

Only Nikolai could make something like that sound ominous. "The point of the underwear is that girls can fill it with anything absorbent. They don't need maxi pads."

"Don't need, but still, I am a generous man."

"What are you planning, Nikolai?"

He held her gaze in the mirror, making her hope he'd crash the car so she could escape. "I will let Lawiri tell you. He is most eager to meet you again."

"I need a phone," Bastian said as Ivan led him down another flight of stairs, then down a corridor.

"Cell phones don't work in the lowest level of the lab," Ivan said as he dialed a code into a security pad.

"Then we need to go up. Out."

"No."

The door opened to reveal a corridor that appeared to be a dead end. Bastian turned and decked Ivan. He dropped, and Bastian followed him down and pinned him to the floor. "You said we're going after Brie."

"This first. Then Brie."

Bastian's hand closed on his throat. Beneath him, he felt Ivan's muscles coil. The guy was a snake, and Bastian had no doubt he was a deadly variety. "No. Brie first."

"One minute. Just give me one minute. You'll see."

"No."

The man was ready to strike. If he was GRU, he had training equal to or even surpassing Bastian's. They could fight to a draw, but it wouldn't help Brie.

"This is more important than Brie or either of us," Ivan said. "And Brie would agree."

That Ivan could strike but chose not to gave Bastian pause. "What is it?"

"The surprise Lawiri and Drugov have been cooking up to end the civil war in South Sudan. We need to destroy it."

Bastian released his throat and lifted his weight from Ivan's frame, rising to his knees. "What's the surprise?"

"Brie's project—the girls' underwear will be distributed with sanitary napkins to get the girls started."

"So?"

"The pads have been infected with Ebola."

Bastian's entire body went cold. "Infected? Like smallpox blankets given to Indian tribes in the seventeen hundreds?"

"Exactly."

"I thought Ebola couldn't be weaponized?"

"Russian scientists have been working toward weaponizing Ebola since it was discovered." Ivan scooted backward to lean against the wall. "The Soviets experimented with chemical and biological agents all throughout the Cold War, so they had the expertise required. The Drugov family had billions to throw at the problem. The other main issue was having a decent lab." He spread his arms, indicating the building around them. "The Cordova family provided that."

Bastian was no expert, but the Army had covered the

risks of Ebola before his team deployed to Africa. "But Ebola doesn't last long outside the host."

"Natural Ebola doesn't. This strain isn't natural."

Another wave of dread spread through him. "But heat kills it," he insisted.

Ivan's jaw tightened. "Not anymore. Listen, the biggest roadblock was always the fragility of the virus." His tone gained urgency as his speech turned rapid. "It's an 'enveloped virus'—so the core virus is surrounded by a lipoprotein layer. Recent developments in gene splicing allowed them to hybridize it with a more stable virus and knock out the part that denatures with heat. Then they created microcapsules that hold the virus in stasis when dry, so it can survive for long periods outside a host. As far as I've been able to learn, they mixed those microcapsules in with the superabsorbent polymers that fill maxipads. The problem is, when the microcapsules get wet, the outer membranes break down, activating and releasing the virus."

"Gets wet. As in menstrual blood."

"Yes. Once released, the Ebola virus attaches to mucosal tissue—such as vaginal walls. Girls will get sick anywhere from two to twenty-one days after exposure. Starvation is taking too long. Lawiri is impatient for the country to collapse."

"So he made a deal with Drugov for genocide." Bastian stood and extended a hand to Ivan. He took it, and Bastian pulled him to his feet.

"Yes. Genocide. Starting with adolescent girls."

Much as his brain screamed to go after Brie, Ivan's words had trapped him here more than restraints could.

Ebola.

Biological warfare.

Genocide.

Everything was crystal clear now. This had never been a simple plastics factory. This was one of Russia's chemical labs. Owned by a Spaniard—who must fear kompromat or be otherwise beholden to Russia—and run by a twisted oligarch who was tight with the Russian dictator. Nothing was off-limits. Nothing too horrible.

The only surprise was that the lab wasn't in Moscow. But then, that was where the CIA had been looking for decades. And an accident there would endanger the oligarchs and government officials.

It made sense the lab was here, where no one thought to look. A chemical spill or mistake with Ebola wouldn't hurt Mother Russia and they were close enough to Sierra Leone and Liberia that it could look like the outbreak was natural and caused by a visitor from either West African country. And given the popularity of white supremacist ideology in Russia, the fact that most of the victims would be Muslim wouldn't engender tears from anyone inside the Kremlin.

There was another keypad and shiny black box mounted next to the door at the end of the corridor. "I don't have access past this point," Ivan said.

Before Bastian could ask how Ivan planned to breach the security, the man pulled a severed hand from his satchel.

Bastian stumbled back. "What the fuck!"

"It was faster than dragging Armando down here." He typed in a number, then waved the hand in front of the black box.

Bastian was glad the door didn't have a retina scanner. He did not want to see the sonofabitch pull an eye from his pocket. "I thought palm readers didn't work with severed hands."

"It's not a palm reader. It's RFID, embedded in the palm between thumb and index finger. Everyone with access to the secret lab has an embedded chip. That way they can be tracked all around the building, always, and every minute they spend inside the lab is logged. I was afraid I'd damage the chip if I tried to dig it out."

Ivan waved the hand again, closer to the box, and the door slid open.

"How did you manage it? Getting to Armando, I mean."

Ivan gave him a slight smile. "I played chauffeur." He stepped into the small room and opened one of several lockers.

Bastian hadn't paid attention to the man behind the wheel of the limousine, but he was certain Ivan hadn't been the man who'd opened the door for Brie in Armando's driveway. "How—?"

"I paid off the regular driver. I was already in the driver's seat when he got the door. Then it was a simple matter of him circling the car and slipping away as I opened the driver's door and sat up in the seat." He grabbed thick plastic coveralls from the locker. "Armando was pleasingly forthcoming with the door code."

Before or after his hand was cut off? Bastian couldn't find it in him to pity the bastard. He'd knowingly housed a biological weapon lab, and he'd set up Brie's abduction. "Is he dead?"

"Not yet. I used a tourniquet. He might survive, but someone from the Kremlin will probably take care of him."

"Not you?" Bastian asked.

Ivan shook his head. "My orders weren't to kill Cardona." He opened an upper locker and pulled out a mask and gloves. "Put these on." He handed Bastian coveralls, mask, and gloves, then located a second set for himself.

"Who were you ordered to kill?" Bastian asked as he donned the safety suit.

"Drugov."

Bastian was surprised the Russian gave a straightforward answer. "Why?"

"They never tell me why."

"If those were your orders, why is he still alive?"

"Because I found out about the Ebola, and was trying to figure out how to destroy it without revealing that action to my employers."

"You aren't following orders now?"

"If anyone discovers I helped you, I'm a dead man."

"If Cardona lives—"

"I wore a mask, and he's wacked on drugs. I dosed him to get him to talk." Ivan dropped his filtered mask in place and turned to the door on the other side of the small room. A sign, written in Arabic and posted on that door, warned that masks were required and all exposed skin needed to be covered beyond this point.

Sweat beaded on Bastian's brow. Ivan was right, this was more important than going after Brie, but fuck, it killed him to know this delay in finding her likely meant she would suffer. He pushed open the door, wondering what horrors in addition to Ebola they'd find in this room.

Stark stainless steel tables lined the room. There were sinks and shelves and equipment, and everything was completely empty.

There was nothing here.

Ivan stopped in his tracks. After a moment of hesitation, he kicked a table, sending it careening into the wall. "Motherfucker. We're too late. The Ebola is on the move."

Chapter Thirty-Nine

Brie's hands were bound behind her back, but she could still reach the tracker. Savvy had made sure of this when they'd selected the spot for the chip to be inserted. Should she initiate it now? Or wait until they'd reached wherever it was that Nikolai was taking her? It would transmit for up to four hours.

What if Nikolai was taking her on a longer drive? The tracker could be spent before they reached their destination. Much as she itched to send out her SOS, she had to wait.

It had been too much to hope Nikolai was taking her to his villa. She knew his villa as well as she knew her own. But he drove the other direction.

It slowly dawned on her that she knew where they were headed, and the realization made her stomach cramp. There was a small airport in the city—closer than the new international airport she and Bastian had flown into. When she'd flown to Morocco with her father on his private jet, they'd always used this airport.

Nikolai was taking her to his private jet. Where they would go from there was anyone's guess.

Bastian ran for the stairs. They had to get to the upper floors, where a cell phone would work. Ivan said he'd planted a tracker on Drugov's car. They'd get Brie's current location, and Bastian would call SOCOM. The team could reroute and save her.

She would be safe.

They reached the main floor and Ivan directed him the back of the building and into the warehouse with a four bay loading dock. Parked on a ramp just inside was Cardona's limousine.

Bastian set off for the vehicle at a dead run. Cardona had a phone Bastian could use while Ivan used his to track Drugov's location. It had been at least forty minutes since the tracker had been initiated. It was possible a team of SEALs was only minutes away.

Inside the limousine, a drugged-out Cardona was curled in a ball, cradling his bloody wrist, out cold but breathing. Bastian grabbed his cell phone, which had bloody streaks on the screen. Apparently, Cardona had tried to make a call but hadn't connected before passing out.

Bastian wiped off the screen and dialed Savannah James as he jumped into the front passenger seat of the limousine. Ivan would drive while Bastian contacted SOCOM.

~⟋⟍~

Savvy signaled the incoming call with a hand motion, and the room went silent as she answered. Her cell had already been patched into the console, knowing her number would be the one most likely dialed if Bastian got to a phone.

"What's going on, Chief Ford?" she said.

"Drugov's taken Brie. We're going after her now. The lab is a Russian death factory. Drugov has a stockpile of sanitary napkins infected with Ebola that he plans to distribute to the largest UN refugee camp in South Sudan."

The words had the effect of a bombshell across the room full of SOCOM commanders and special forces operators. The men visibly flinched and emitted sounds of shock and horror.

Ebola in a refugee camp could lead to an outbreak unlike any seen before. Over a hundred thousand people were in the Upper Nile refugee camp, which was already stressed beyond capacity, dealing with famine, cholera, and malaria. The sick would be cared for by family and friends, not medically trained aid workers. The virus would spread.

But this information changed things. Forewarned, they could stop it. She'd known sending Bastian and Brie to Morocco was the right thing to do, but she'd had no idea the threat Drugov posed was this big.

"Where is Drugov?" Captain Oswald asked.

"There's a tracker on his car." Bastian read off the coordinates, which a tech typed into the system. "I'm on my way there now."

This agreed with the data from his tracker, which was on one of the large screens. He was on the road and moving fast. Whoever was driving was ignoring all speed limits.

A second screen showed the coordinates Bastian had just relayed, and Savvy blanched. "Bastian, Drugov is at a small airport in the heart of Casablanca. Does he have the Ebola-infected pads with him?"

"I don't know. Maybe. Probably. The lab was cleaned out. It would make sense he'd move it before grabbing Brie. He could be taking Brie and Lawiri back to South Sudan, with the intent to deliver the infected supplies. He believes his plan to cause an Ebola outbreak remains a secret. He has no reason to think his donation won't be accepted."

Chatter in the room rose, and Savvy muted her end of the call. She didn't want Bastian to hear commanders suggesting that they let Drugov deliver the goods and apprehend the oligarch and the general then. She cleared her throat. "You're talking about leaving Brie Stewart with Drugov for what would be at least a six-hour flight—longer if he doesn't go directly to South Sudan and we can't find him."

"How far out is the SEAL team?" Bastian asked. "Please tell me there's a SEAL team on their way."

"There is," Savvy said after unmuting her phone. "They're ten minutes out."

"Reroute them to the airport. We'll probably arrive about the same time."

A SOCOM commander gave her a nod, and she said, "Done," to Bastian.

She met Cal's gaze, and for the first time in days, his eyes didn't hold hostility. Had he expected her to argue for sacrificing Brie?

But in another situation, that might be exactly what she did. In this instance, they had a better opportunity to grab Drugov, which happened to include saving Brie from hours of rape and torture.

But if the plane took off before the SEALs could get there, all bets were off.

If the plane took off, they'd have to face the decision of whether or not to shoot it down. In the first minutes of flight, it might circle over the ocean, providing the perfect opportunity to stop a genocide and an oligarch with one shot.

Brie's heart raced in overdrive as Nikolai forced her at gunpoint to march onto the cargo plane.

Cargo plane?

That wasn't his usual mode of travel.

She debated initiating her tracker. But the flight would almost certainly last longer than four hours. She had to be patient. She needed information. "What's going on, Nikolai?"

"I wanted to show you your present. It would be my wedding gift to you, but I no longer wish to take you as my bride now that your body has been defiled by so many men."

"Fuck off, Nikolai. I'm not ashamed of my past. I'm just glad your tiny prick is the one I've never let near me."

He backhanded her again, and her genuine reaction was to laugh, in spite of the pain. "Oh, did that hit a nerve? I bet your dick is so tiny, I won't even be able to tell when you're erect."

Another blow came, but she didn't let up. "That's why you beat instead of fuck, isn't it? Because you hope I'll be in so much pain, I won't notice you have no penis."

His hand closed on her throat, silencing her.

She closed her eyes, refusing to give him the satisfaction of seeing her fear. He wouldn't kill her. Not yet. But the world was beginning to tunnel. She could pass out.

He released her throat, and she took a deep, gasping breath.

"Come see your present," he said, dragging her with him.

Inside the cargo hold, she came face-to-face with Lawiri. He grinned the same gap-tooth smile she remembered from their first meeting.

"It is a pleasure to meet again," he said in heavily accented English. "You have served my people well."

"They're not *your* people. You are one of them, not above them. If anything, you are beneath them."

His lip curled. "They are pawns. Animists. Children. I will be their king."

Nikolai pinched her arm. She refused to react, holding herself still as ice as his fingers tightened like a vise.

When he got no reaction, he took his burning cigarette and pressed it into her shoulder. She couldn't stop herself and whimpered at the searing pain.

"Breaking you will be exquisite," Nikolai said, his cigarette breath mingling with the scent of her burned flesh.

She swallowed bile and said nothing.

"Your precious girls will all die, you know," Nikolai added. "And it will be your fault. Your underwear. It will make them sick." He spread his hand to encompass the boxes lined up in the cargo hold. "Ten thousand pairs of underwear. Ten thousand lucky girls."

Nikolai's nasty hints became clear. She didn't know *what* was in the underwear, but it was something deadly. Biological warfare. Genocide.

She broke. She head-butted Nikolai, then twisted to kick the exiled general in the nuts. Just like Bastian taught her. Her action wouldn't save anyone, but at least the blows would cause both men pain.

Nikolai fell back, then came at her again. His hands closed around her neck. She bucked and kicked but couldn't get a good angle.

The world slowly dimmed.

⟳

The limousine raced down the Casablanca streets without a care for traffic law, for which Bastian was grateful. Ivan was like a ninja behind the wheel.

They reached the airport, and he barreled through barriers, driving slalom through cars, guardrails, signs, and medians.

They careened past several parked planes and pulled out to the front of the long airstrip. At the far end was a cargo plane, circling around to begin its takeoff run. "Motherfucker," Ivan said. "That's Drugov's plane. We can't let it take off."

"No shit," Bastian said.

"No. I mean, we can't let it take off with Brie on it. Or she's dead." Ivan hit the gas, and the limousine shot forward, heading straight for the oncoming plane.

"Yeah. No fucking shit." Drugov would have Brie in his clutches for hours in the air. He would rape her. Torture her. There was no guarantee he wouldn't kill her before they landed in South Sudan.

"No. I mean the cargo plane was my failsafe. In case Nikolai tried to escape before I could get to him."

They sped forward as the airplane did the same, limousine and cargo plane playing chicken on the runway.

"What does that—" Bastian braced himself as they closed the distance, the giant tires of the oncoming plane on a collision course with the nose of the car.

The airplane lifted a heartbeat before impact. The tire bumped the top of the windshield, shattering the glass and sending the speeding limousine into a spin.

Ivan hit the brakes as he turned into the spin. Glass rained down as they came to a stop a hundred and eighty degrees from their starting direction.

"There's a bomb on the plane," Ivan said. "It will blow when it—"

A fireball erupted in the sky. The cargo plane shattered, and debris rained down, pelting the hood of the car and burning Bastian's skin.

Chapter Forty

B astian stared at the smoldering debris in horror.
Brie.

No. Fucking God. No.

He was frozen in agony. In shock.

Brie.

In three weeks, he'd fallen crazy in love with her. Her wit. Her strength. Her passion. She was everything he hadn't known he wanted, hadn't known he needed.

She was gone. One instant. One flash of orange, and she was gone.

He hadn't protected her.

One minute, maybe two minutes more, and he'd have found a way to stop the jet from taking off. She'd be alive.

With a primal roar of pain and rage, he turned on the man in the driver's seat. The man who'd caused this. He had Ivan by the throat, and he would squeeze his life out. He would tear him apart.

Brie.

The look on her face as she'd straddled him in the hot tub last night and taken him deep. The way she'd kissed him as she told him she loved him, then showed him with her body exactly what those words meant to her.

She'd been regal. Beautiful. Passionate.

He'd wanted to give her children, a true family to love.

To spend the rest of his life with her. To share her joy and her sorrow.

Gone.

Ivan gripped his fists, his face turning red, then blue. With leverage from his knee, he shifted Bastian's weight and broke the grip on his throat. In a flash, Bastian was shoved through the shattered windshield, and they grappled on the hood of the car.

They rolled off the front, and Ivan pinned him to the tarmac.

The fight left Bastian. Ivan wasn't the enemy here. Drugov was. But Drugov was dead. Killed with Brie and the pilot.

Brie.

"Sorry for this, but you leave me no choice," Ivan said. A zip tie closed around Bastian's wrists. "I didn't know she'd be on the plane. If Drugov had the Ebola in the cargo hold, her death isn't in vain. Odds are Lawiri was with them too."

"Do you think I give a fuck about any of that?"

And in that moment, he didn't. The big picture no longer mattered. He hadn't been here to fight for his country, to stop a mad Russian oligarch. No, he'd signed on to this mission so he could protect Brie. He didn't care about anything except the fact that the person who mattered to him most in the world had just ceased to exist.

In the worst moment of his life, he was stripped of everything that had previously defined him. He wasn't a soldier. He wasn't a Kalahwamish Indian. He wasn't even a man.

He was a shattered shell that used to be human.

Brie was gone. Irrevocably gone.

He closed his eyes and relived their first kiss. And the second. The first time he'd made love to her. And the last. The moment she'd pleaded with him to ensure no opioids would be administered to ease her pain. The look on her face as she gripped his hand and watched jets take off from the aircraft carrier. The defiance in her eyes as she confessed she'd leaked information to her lover to crush the pipeline project that threatened air and water.

The shock and fear on her face when he walked into the hut in South Sudan and saw her chained by the throat.

He'd told her he loved her, but it wasn't enough. Had she known how deep his feelings ran? That she'd become part of his soul, his reason for breathing? In three weeks, she'd upended his life to the degree that he now couldn't fathom how to move forward from this moment.

The noise of a helicopter invaded his agonized thoughts.

"I can't be here," Ivan said. "I'm sorry, Bastian."

And then he was alone in front of the shattered limousine. No fight in him for the chase. He let Ivan go. Part of him knew the Russian had been smart to ensure the virus didn't leave Morocco, but he couldn't face that basic truth just yet.

Bastian had no fucks left to give.

The helicopter landed on the airstrip and SEALs in full gear poured out. A small force circled Bastian, pummeling him with questions. He shook his head, mutely crying as he stared at the burning wreckage that was scattered across the runway and adjacent grassy field.

He was pulled to his feet. The zip tie around his wrists was cut.

"You're certain she was on the plane?" a SEAL repeated, his words penetrating the fog and muted hearing that had followed the explosion.

"Where is the man you called Ivan?" another asked.

He shook his head. He hadn't watched Ivan leave the scene. Didn't know if he was on foot or if he'd taken a vehicle. He'd seen nothing but the embers of the jet.

Cardona was pulled from the back of the limousine. A medic checked over his wound. "Who did this, Chief Ford?" the man asked when Cardona was too drugged up to answer.

A layer of fog lifted, and Bastian answered. "Ivan. I think he's GRU. But there's no point in trying to get the prints Savvy wanted. He wore gloves. Always." He looked toward the plane. "He was sent here to take out Drugov. He set the explosive as a failsafe should Drugov try to flee with his stockpile of Ebola."

Cardona's cell phone rang, and Bastian turned to see it on the hood of the limousine. He'd forgotten he'd tucked it in his breast pocket as they raced across town. It must've fallen out as he fought with Ivan. He glanced at the screen. Savvy's number. The SEALs would have told SOCOM everything they found here. He flicked his thumb across the surface, but the voice he heard wasn't the CIA operative. "Fuck, Bas," was all Cal said.

Somehow, this was the voice Bastian had needed to hear. A friend. He took a deep breath. "I shouldn't have let Drugov take her. It's my fault."

"No, man. This isn't on you. Blame Drugov. Blame Lawiri. Blame SOCOM and Savvy for sending a civilian in in the first place."

Bastian searched for white-hot anger he could direct at SOCOM or Savvy, but that well was dry. "No. everyone was just doing their jobs. Going after Drugov was the right thing. He weaponized fucking Ebola."

Sirens surrounded the runway. A fire truck came careening across the tarmac.

Strange that he couldn't muster anger at Savvy or his commanders. But the truth was the only person he blamed was himself.

He never should have let Brie go.

He never should have delved deeper into the basement lab with Ivan.

He never should have agreed to the lab excursion at all.

So many nevers.

So many mistakes.

All his. And Brie was gone.

"What the—?" Cal's voice cut off, and Bastian knew he'd hit the mute button.

A moment later, the phone was unmuted, and Savvy's voice came on the line. "Bastian, Brie's tracker went off a few minutes ago, it took some time to be certain it wasn't somehow triggered in the explosion. But we're certain it's her, and it's red hot and moving fast across Casablanca."

"What?" Bastian couldn't breathe through the surge of hope.

"Brie triggered her tracker. She wasn't on the jet. She's alive and in trouble."

B rie kept her face blank as she feverishly rubbed at the tracker embedded in her arm. She'd passed out after Nikolai choked her, and woke who knew how long later, rocking with the motion of... It had taken her a moment to recognize she was inside a helicopter, and a loud noise had roused her. Her brain was foggy as she'd tried to figure out how she got there.

Next to her, Lawiri screamed something, his words lost to the noise of the copter.

She took in the situation. This was Nikolai's helicopter. She was crammed in the tiny rear seat with Lawiri while Nicolai was up front with the pilot. The helicopter meant his megayacht must be nearby. That had to be where they were headed, because there was no helipad at his villa.

He was taking her away from Casablanca. To his yacht.

As soon as this became clear, she'd pressed on the tracker. SEALs were nearby. Her best hope was to trigger the tracker now. They would find her quickly, before the yacht could set out to sea. Nikolai couldn't expect them to arrive so fast. He'd be caught off guard.

Lawiri cursed as he stared at something on the ground behind him, but the noise of the helicopter drowned out his words. Only Nikolai wore headphones. There would be no conversation until they landed.

They sped over the top of the city, passing the marina and heading out over the Atlantic.

Fuck.

The boat was already at sea? Would the tracker work on the yacht? She could only hope Nikolai had installed the system that extended cellular service to thirty miles from land, or she was dead.

And if the yacht was more than thirty miles out?

Then she'd submit to his torture and find a way to kill him in his sleep.

This was the same choice she'd faced in the market. There was no shame in not fighting. She would bide her time.

Thank goodness she'd initiated the tracker while they

were still over land. If she'd waited...she couldn't think about that. She had triggered it. She would be rescued.

And just like he had in the market, Bastian would come.

She knew in her gut he'd escaped from the chemical plant. He would find her.

A dot in the ocean up ahead became clear, and the helicopter began its descent. The boat couldn't be more than three miles from shore.

They landed on the deck, and Brie twisted to open the door with her bound hands, but Lawiri grabbed her, preventing her easy escape. Nikolai exited from his seat, then snatched her from Lawiri, pulling her out onto the deck as the rotor blades slowed.

Nikolai dragged her toward stairs leading to a lower deck. She was gratified when he took out his cell phone and began speaking in Russian.

They still had cell service.

Lawiri chased after them, following as Nikolai pushed her through a door that led to the upper salon.

"You fool!" Lawiri shouted as he yanked on Nikolai, breaking the oligarch's hold on her arm. She scooted back and away, twisting to watch the confrontation.

What the hell?

"The Ebola is gone! You idiot!"

Ebola?

That was what he'd infected the pads with?

The man wasn't just crazy, his heart was pure evil. She'd never believed in evil before. But this was so much more than a lack of empathy combined with greed and avarice.

And what did Lawiri mean it was gone? What had happened while she was unconscious?

"You crazy shit!" Lawiri continued. "You stupid—"

Nikolai backhanded Lawiri. Underscoring that he *really* didn't like being called crazy.

Lawiri struck back, nailing Nikolai in the face and pinning him to the wall, his forearm across the oligarch's neck. "Don't fuck with me, Drugov. I'm not a soft little man like your Russian friends. You don't scare me."

Nikolai's eyes hardened, but he looked at Lawiri with fear he couldn't quite hide. "The crates were full of diapers. Nothing more. They were on the cargo plane to fool Ivan. The real supply is being trucked to the White Nile refugee camp along with aid generously donated by Prime Energy."

"Why did you need to fool your accountant?" Lawiri asked, leaning into Nikolai, maintaining the power position.

"He's not my accountant." Nicolai's voice was thin as Lawiri controlled his air supply. "He was sent by the Kremlin to check up on me. I think he's an assassin known as the Hammer, and his true purpose was to kill me."

Lawiri leaned back, allowing Nikolai more air.

"He put a tracker in my car, so I led him to the plane full of diapers. No one fucks with me or my enterprise, not even the Kremlin."

Lawiri stepped back, fully releasing him.

Nikolai straightened his collar, then held up his phone, reminding Brie of the call he'd made a minute ago. "I just got word the man who ordered the hit against me has collapsed." He flashed a feral smile. "My pilot was a spy for the Kremlin, and now the Hammer has eliminated him for me."

Ivan wasn't GRU? He was an assassin? Her head was

spinning. From the blows she'd taken, the fast, bouncy flight, and everything else that had happened today. It was all too much.

"Ivan rigged the plane to explode. I made sure it would go off and he'd believe his job was done."

The cargo plane had exploded?

She felt the blood drain from her face. That must have been the sound that jolted her to consciousness.

Nikolai gave her a nasty grin. "Yes, my sweet. If anyone knew you were with me, they now believe you are dead. Which means no one will come looking for us."

She wobbled on her feet. If the tracker hadn't worked, then Nikolai's words were certainly true. Bastian—and everyone—would believe she was dead. "They'll realize when they don't find my remains."

"I'm afraid the hold was packed with C4. The Hammer is nothing if not thorough. They won't guess none of us were on the plane until it's far too late."

The tracker is working. They know I'm still alive. They're already planning a mission to save me.

The engines on the giant boat came to life. They were leaving. How long would it take a boat this size to go thirty miles? How long would they be in tracker range?

"Bastian knows I'm with you. As does Armando."

"Armando will never talk, and Bastian is dead. My man just confirmed it."

She felt the blood drain from her body as she stared at the phone in his hand. He'd been speaking in Russian. She hadn't understood his words. Could he be lying?

She wobbled on her feet.

He had to be lying.

Bastian couldn't be dead. She covered her mouth with the back of her hand, holding back a heave. She glared at the monster before her. "If the Kremlin wants you dead, nothing will save you."

"Oh no, my dear. I have taken on the Hammer and won. I have even bested a Green Beret. My power is solidified. The traitor who ordered my death has been taken care of. I have multiple US senators in my pocket, including your 'Uncle' Al, who intends to run for president. We will ensure he wins. I also have an alliance with the CEO of Prime Energy. I'm a gateway to the US economy and government. Next to the Russian president, I'm the most powerful man in my country. No Russian will dare cross me again."

"Rafe isn't in your pocket." She believed that. She had to.

But beneath it all, her heart pounded as she inwardly sobbed.

Bastian.

"Rafe is of no consequence. He will be dead within the week, and JJ will seize control."

"But you were going to kill JJ."

"I only gave the order to kill your lover. Your brother was to be freed once you and I escaped to the boat." Again he held up his phone. "He's being released as we speak. He will convince Rafe that the men who abducted you in South Sudan followed you here. They took you hostage and tried to escape on a stolen cargo jet. Alas, there were no survivors."

He flashed his teeth. "You and I can enjoy many months together on my boat, and no one will ever look for you. *That* was the deal I made with your brother. He will cover up your disappearance, and your family business will get sympathetic press. The poor family suffering the loss of father and Good Samaritan daughter in the same week. When Rafe goes, it will be all the more shocking."

She cleared her dry throat. "What do you have on him? On JJ? What did he do?"

Nikolai smiled. "When we're in my stateroom I can show you the recording of him fucking a whore in a Moscow hotel room."

"So?" Getting caught with a prostitute wasn't enough to buy someone's soul, especially not someone like JJ, who probably arranged for prostitutes to share his hotel room on every business trip.

"Your brother wanted a special kind of whore. One who allowed autoerotic asphyxiation."

Oh shit.

"Unfortunately, we pumped your brother full of drugs, so he wasn't…as careful as he should have been. The poor girl died. She was fourteen. He then paid my men to dispose of the body."

Her heart cracked. Her brother had raped and murdered a child. Odds were the girl had been sold into sexual slavery like the girls at the market in South Sudan.

She leaned forward like she was going to puke, but then she kicked Nikolai in the balls.

He doubled over, then staggered forward and took a swing, but she was ready for him this time and blocked it. She spun and made a break for the door. In a flash, she was on the deck, Nikolai on her heels.

She'd have to kick him harder next time.

She ran for stairs that led down. If she could get to the rail, she could jump into the ocean.

Could the tracker transmit from the water? Definitely not if the boat was speeding away, taking the booster antenna with it. Plus, with her hands bound, she'd likely drown.

Nikolai had been one step ahead all along. He'd manipulated everyone and even evaded a hit ordered by the Kremlin. He really might be invincible.

She nearly tripped on the steep steps several times but managed to catch the rail with her bound hands before she pitched forward. She made it all the way to the lowest deck before Nikolai caught her by the throat and pulled her back to his chest.

"Leaving so soon, my sweet? But you haven't even seen my stateroom yet. I've been preparing it for you for months. One might even say for years."

Chapter Forty-One

Bastian planted himself in the Blackhawk with the SEAL team and geared up—weapons, Kevlar helmet, protective eyewear, body armor, earpiece, and more weapons. He didn't have his uniform, but that wouldn't stop him from participating in this takedown. SOCOM objected, but the SEALs were on his side. None of them dared deny him.

With an earpiece, Bastian was now a part of the conversation with SOCOM headquarters in both Rota and at Camp Citron. "Given the speed and trajectory, she's on a helicopter," Savvy said. "They're over the Atlantic now. Drugov's boat must be at sea."

"Any chance we'll lose her signal?" Bastian asked.

"Some of the megayachts have cellular boosters, extending the range for miles. Given how much business Drugov does from his boat, it's likely he has that. But without that, yes. We'll lose her signal."

"Why aren't we airborne, then?" This from a SEAL seated not far from Bastian. "We can have eyes on them in minutes. Otherwise, we might lose her."

Other SEALs chimed in supporting this, and without further debate, the Blackhawk lifted. They didn't have time to dick around and discuss options.

"What intel do you have on Drugov's boat?" someone in Rota asked.

"It's massive—over two hundred feet," Savvy said. "Minimum crew of five, but more likely closer to ten. It can probably do fifty knots without trouble." She paused. "It looks like the copter landed." She gave the coordinates. "It's about five klicks out. Nothing but blue water all around."

There would be no hiding a Blackhawk. With more time to prepare, the SEALs could've gone in underwater, taking off from a boat positioned a half mile away. But by the time they arranged that, the yacht could be long gone. Fifty knots per hour was fast for a boat that size.

"Any guess as to whether or not Drugov's got heavy weaponry?" someone asked.

"I have no intel in that area. But knowing Drugov, expect anything and everything. Including biologicals. But he won't use anything that might contaminate him. Nothing airborne or easily transmitted."

"He'll use Brie as a shield," Bastian said.

"He will," Savvy confirmed.

"Any Navy assets in the area we can use?" Bastian thought he recognized Cal's voice, but it was hard to tell through the headphones with the noise of the Blackhawk.

"Nothing close enough to do us any good," answered the SEAL team leader.

"I've found pictures of the boat. Profile and aerial view," Savvy said. "Sending now."

A moment later, the leader of the SEAL team leaned forward, holding a large tablet out for all nine men in the bird to see. There was a second Blackhawk with the other half of the sixteen-man platoon, where Bastian imagined they were doing the same thing as the commander outlined a plan of attack.

Nothing quite like planning a mission just minutes

before executing it, but in this instance, they had no choice. Aside from the potential of losing the boat, the longer Brie was alone with Drugov, the more likely she was to be raped and tortured.

It was either go in now, or risk losing Brie forever.

N ikolai's cabin was a playhouse of horrors, and he'd been preparing this nightmare for her. Years ago, she'd thought BDSM might be fun. She'd learned right away that she liked bondage, but the rest—not so much. The result was she knew what several of the items were, and they all terrified her—especially knowing Nikolai would be wielding them.

Whips, chains, and assorted tools for inflicting pain were lined up on a shelf. The furniture included a St. Andrew's Cross, a spanking bench, and some items that looked medieval.

He'd bound her to the spanking bench and— fortunately—left her alone as he spoke with the boat captain.

Shaped like a short, one-step staircase, the spanking bench interior was a barred cage—just large enough for her to fit inside, should Nikolai desire to crate her. But instead, he'd cuffed her wrists on the floor on the outside, forcing her to lie over the top with her ass in the air. Her knees tucked into the step with her ankles cuffed to the base.

Her range of motion was zero, and the blood was flowing to her head with the forced downward-dog-with-bent-knee pose. There was minimal padding over the metal cage bars. This bench wasn't designed for comfort and consensual play.

When Nikolai came back, he intended to use the lineup of whips to punish her for denying him all these years. For defying him when she was eighteen.

Shit. Shit. Shit.

And she'd thought the metal collar in the slave market was bad.

Is Bastian really dead?

No. She didn't believe it.

Nikolai's goon had lied. Or Nikolai himself had lied, knowing the words would break her.

SEALs were coming, and Bastian would be with them. She just needed to figure out how she could help.

Not that she could help, bound as she was.

The team wouldn't be able to sneak up on the yacht, not on a bright sunny day like today. Not if they were in a Blackhawk or an Osprey. This meant Nikolai would want to use her as a shield. She worked at the cuffs that held her wrists. If she could hide, he wouldn't be able to use her.

But this wasn't for consensual beginner play, where the sub could escape if things got too rough or scary. This was the real deal and so were the cuffs.

She thought she heard the whirr of an engine over the boat noise.

Shit!

She pulled at the cuffs, trying to make her hand as small as possible by tucking in her thumb and pulling. The cuffs were metal covered in satin. The satin provided lubrication, but the binding was too tight.

The metal edge split the satin, and broke her skin. Blood provided more lubrication, but her lowest thumb knuckle would have to break to pass through the narrow opening. She pulled, trying to break her knuckle with sheer pressure.

Tears rolled down her cheeks. She couldn't do it.

The doorknob turned.

No! No! No!

Nikolai stalked into the room, his face a mask of anger. He pulled his arm back and slapped her across the cheek with twice the force of all his earlier blows. But she was tied, and her body couldn't absorb any of the impact. Her head snapped to the side as pain radiated down her neck.

"What the fuck have you done?" he shouted, then slapped the other cheek with his other hand.

Her brain sloshed around in her skull, and her lip split in a different spot.

A voice cut through the noise of helicopter and boat engine. "Nikolai Drugov, release your hostage and surrender."

He grabbed one of his whips. Pain exploded across her back. "You bitch!" Another blow. "How did you do it?"

She couldn't breathe. Couldn't move. Fire shot along her shoulders.

He released the ankle cuffs, then her hands, yanking her to her feet by her hair before she could gather herself to strike him. She fell against him, her knees jelly, her head swimming from both pain and from being suddenly upright after being tied head down for several minutes.

She didn't wait to get her equilibrium. She kneed him in the balls and used momentum from the blow to lunge for the crop that sat next to the whips on the shelf. She struck him in the face with the crop.

She charged him, knocking him flat and running for the French doors. He caught her at the doors, wrapping an arm around her and pulling her back to his chest, his grip tight.

He grabbed something from his pocket with his free hand and held it in front of her. A syringe. He used his teeth to yank off the orange cover, revealing the needle.

"Fight me again, and you get half of this. Ask yourself, Gabriella, how much do you want it?"

"Fuck you."

"The second time you fight me, I'll hit the plunger to the bottom. You might overdose at that point, but it's a risk I'm willing to take." He moved the needle to her neck. "Don't start thinking you're about to be rescued. My men will shoot the Blackhawk out of the sky."

He pulled her back, away from the French doors. She didn't fight, but she didn't exactly walk either. "If you take down a team of SEALs, you'll never be safe. Russia will hand you over to the US in a heartbeat."

"A Blackhawk that was attacking me? No. Your military attacked my vessel as I was vacationing in Morocco. It is an outrage. My government will stand behind me."

Shots sounded in rapid succession. Were they on the upper deck already?

"You *abducted* me. Let me go, and they'll leave you alone."

"You came willingly with me. You said as much at the lab. I own you, Gabriella. You will tell the SEALs to leave, or you will get the needle."

He was crazy if he thought she could or would be able to convince the military to leave her with him. But then, she'd known he was insane for years. She just hadn't quite realized how warped he'd gotten.

He pulled her back to the St. Andrew's Cross, a large X in the center of the room. "Put your hands in the cuffs." He waved the needle in her face.

She obeyed, placing her wrists at the top of the X. He tightened the cuffs around her wrists, one at a time, keeping the needle at her throat. Next he bound her ankles.

Footsteps pounded on the deck above them. He moved to stand behind her, again placing the needle at her neck.

The SEALs moved quickly, before Drugov's men could ready any shoulder-fired rocket launchers, should they have them. The first feet hit the deck before the announcement was done. The pilot brought them low enough for them to jump from the copter, allowing for a quicker exit than a ladder required. Because he wasn't a member of the team and hadn't trained with the men, Bastian was last out. He wouldn't mess with their timing.

A rifle barrel appeared in a window to Bastian's right. He and the SEAL next to him reacted in the same moment, dropping to their knees and spraying the window with bullets. A bullet zinged by Bastian's shoulder, close enough that he felt the air shift, then the shots went upward as the gunman dropped.

Glass, unless it was bulletproof, was a shitty shield, making Bastian wonder where Drugov found his goons.

A similar scene played out on the other side of the deck. Another dipshit down.

The team broke apart in groups of three as planned. They would search for Brie while the second Blackhawk circled, taking out henchmen if they dared show their faces on the deck.

There'd been no time for a buy-off on the mission, no time to set rules of engagement, but an American woman—an aid worker—had been abducted by a twisted, biological-weapons-making Russian oligarch. The team was on board to use lethal force. They'd explain themselves after the fact. Stockpiles of Ebola-laced panty liners would only seal the deal.

Drugov would fry. Diplomacy with Russia could fuck off.

Bastian's group took the middle deck. Aerial photos had shown a private deck off a room at the back, probably the master suite, and the most likely place for Drugov to have Brie. Bastian had called dibs. No one objected.

These guys might not be US Army Special Forces, but they were okay.

They dropped from the upper deck straight into the sectioned-off deck. The French doors were tinted glass. They flanked the doors, and a SEAL popped the lock. The doors opened inward.

And there was Brie, spread eagle on a giant fucking X. Drugov hid behind her, like the pathetic asshole he was. He held a needle to Brie's neck.

Chapter Forty-Two

B rie's heart was ready to explode at seeing Bastian. It was so much like when he'd stepped into the hut. Like then, his face was a mask of controlled emotion. And here she was, tied up.

She was clothed this time, but the silk blouse and pencil skirt hadn't faired well in the last few hours. The whip had shredded the top, while the skirt had split along one side.

But there was Bastian, beautiful Bastian. Alive. Here. For her. Again. This time he had Kevlar and a rifle. He might not be in uniform, but he was geared up and ready to fight for her.

The needle pressed against her throat. If she moved her head forward, it would pierce the skin. "Send them away, Gabriella." Nikolai's voice was low, his head right behind hers in the middle of the V formed by the top half of the X as he ducked down to hide behind her.

She was terrified of the needle. Her battle with addiction hadn't been won the first, the second, or even the fifth time she'd tried to go clean. It had taken years and multiple attempts and with one jab, she could be right back in the thick of it.

But one thing she knew, if Nikolai shot her up, she'd suffer, but she'd survive.

She could beat it, even if it meant crawling her way

back.

Because that was what she did.

She was a master at starting over, and believed in herself now in a way she hadn't when she'd tried and failed.

And this time, she wouldn't be alone in her battle. Bastian would help her.

He'd hold her hand and love her.

She stared at his face. Protective glasses covered his eyes, but she could sense he was staring right back at her. He and the two SEALs with him held their rifles at the ready. They were just waiting for an opening.

She turned her eyes up and toward the right, directing his gaze to her hand, where she held up four fingers.

She took a deep breath and counted down with her fingers. At zero, she jerked her head forward, and the needle pierced her skin. She rammed backward with her head, a hard jab that probably landed on the bridge of Nikolai's nose.

He dropped from the unexpected blow. Gunfire zinged between her spread legs, bullets from three rifles, pelting Nikolai in the legs. He dropped lower, and the bullets hit his chest.

She stood there, breathing heavily, syringe protruding from her neck. Her legs had turned to mush but the bindings on wrists and ankles prevented her from falling and catching a bullet. In a weird way, the St. Andrew's Cross had saved her, keeping her out of the line of fire.

Her whole body shook as she watched the needle with her peripheral vision.

All three men lowered their rifles and charged into the room. The SEALs grabbed Nikolai, pulling him through the frame of the cross, between her legs, while Bastian came for her.

He gently removed the needle, set it aside, and probed her neck. "It wasn't in a vein, and the plunger wasn't pressed. If you got any, it was just a drop." He leaned down and sucked on her neck as if he were removing venom.

He then swished his mouth with water from his hydration pack and spit it on the floor. He released her feet, then her hands, and caught her when she would've collapsed. He scooped her against him.

"I've got you, Brie. As soon as we get the all clear, I'm taking you to the Blackhawk."

From the shouts of the SEALs, she gathered they were reporting in that they had her. Drugov was alive. Barely.

She buried her face against Bastian's armored chest and breathed him in. Gunpowder, sweat, and Bastian. Tears returned to her eyes. "Thank you." She lifted her head and met his gaze. Beautiful Bastian. She stroked his chin. "He told me you were dead. I didn't believe him, but still, I was so scared I might've lost you."

"I was sure I'd lost you." His arms tightened around her.

"The last crew member has been rounded up," one of the SEALs said. "And Lawiri is in custody."

"Are you impounding this boat?" she asked.

"That will be for the Moroccan police to decide, ma'am," the SEAL replied.

"You're going to want to take any computers or USB drives you can find. Nikolai told me he has kompromat on my brother. If he has that here, there could be more. Plus he probably has information on his plans for Ebola-laced pads. This room is probably a treasure trove for intelligence." She wondered if they'd also find kompromat on Uncle Al. It would be fitting if Nikolai's actions brought the senator down as well.

The SEAL repeated her words into the radio, and she gathered that word came down from SOCOM to collect any digital media they could find. Like the bin Laden raid, they'd take what they could quickly grab and leave the rest behind. Morocco could decide what to do with the boat and the rest of its contents. Bastian carried her out through the double doors.

The midday sun was blinding and the ocean was a crisp blue.

How was it only noon? It felt like a lifetime ago that she and Bastian had shared a shower together.

Bastian reached the stairs that would take them to the upper deck, and she insisted on climbing the steep ship ladder herself. He cursed when he saw the stripes on her back from the whipping and the burn on her shoulder from the cigarette.

The moment they were on the upper deck, he scooped her up again. She protested, pointing out that she'd have to climb a rope ladder into the Blackhawk, but then she saw the litter they'd arranged to hoist her and Bastian together.

They'd just settled into the helicopter, where she sat facing out the side opening, her gaze fixed on nothing, when one of the men radioed the news that Nikolai had died.

The man who'd been obsessed with her since she was thirteen would never hurt her or anyone she loved again.

Chapter Forty-Three

They were flown to a US Navy ship at Naval Station Rota, where a doctor examined Brie's injuries while Bastian was debriefed. Her wounds were cleaned, and she refused all painkillers stronger than ibuprofen. She had ugly bruises on her back, throat, and cheeks to go with the burn on her shoulder and stripes from the whip. The cuts on her wrist from trying to escape the cuffs weren't deep, thankfully. She was told she should expect to be sore for several days, but there shouldn't be any complications in her recovery as long as her wounds didn't get infected.

A young woman sailor led her from the medical facility to the room where Bastian and the SEAL team were answering questions. She took her place at the table and repeated everything Nikolai had told her about the shipment of Ebola-laced underwear.

All UN camps in South Sudan had been notified not to accept any shipments of supplies until they could be searched by a hazmat team—something that would likely delay food distribution for a large population already suffering.

The debriefing lasted for hours, during which time Brie learned that her brother and the guards had all been rounded up at the chemical lab by Casablanca police officers, who'd been called by the US military. No one knew whom Nikolai had spoken with when she arrived on his yacht, but it was likely a Russian contact who knew nothing about the arrests at the lab. It appeared Nikolai had lied about Bastian's death simply to strip Brie of hope.

Brie also learned that Russian news carried a story of a Russian politician very publicly succumbing to poison during his daughter's wedding reception. Brie didn't know if it was more *Game of Thrones* or *The Godfather*, but odds were, the dead man had ordered the hit on Nikolai, leading to questions as to the identity of the mysterious Ivan.

Bastian questioned Ivan's loyalty to the Kremlin, suggesting that the US could have an ally in the GRU— if that was what the man was—and it might not be in America's best interest to vigorously pursue his identity. It was agreed to limit inquiries with Kremlin sources. No one wished to expose how Ivan had aided Bastian and Brie. Questions were likely to get the man killed.

Nikolai's guards were arrested, but until they had evidence of JJ's complicity with Nikolai, there were no grounds to detain him. He was expected to return to the Prime family's villa once he was released.

The RFID chip was retrieved from Armando's severed hand, and Moroccan police, FBI, and Interpol would likely work together to get access to the data recorded in the lab system for all the RFID chips with access to the basement part of the facility. With that data they could determine how many scientists had worked in the secret lab. Identifying the scientists should be easy— they'd either have the RFID chip still implanted, or a deep cut from removing it.

After much back and forth, it was decided that Bastian

and Brie would be flown back to Camp Citron, where Brie could recover for the next several days and be available for questions. The FBI would be brought in to examine the electronic data collected from Nikolai's boat in hopes they could find evidence to arrest JJ—before he fled to Russia.

It was late that evening when they boarded a military jet and departed Spain for Djibouti, accompanied by several Delta Force operators who would be working with Savvy on unraveling the mess that was South Sudan.

The flight would take eight hours. Exhausted, Brie leaned against Bastian as the jet took off. She closed her eyes and thought of her brothers. She'd had a brief conversation with Rafe, in which she told him what Drugov had said. It only felt fair to warn him that JJ had planned to have the oligarch kill Rafe so JJ could take over the business.

Rafe was skeptical, but he promised to be cautious. He'd just received word that their father had taken a turn for the worse, and he intended to fly back to the US the following day.

The timing of the turn in Jeffery Senior's condition only confirmed Nikolai's words for Brie. One thing about Nikolai, he was sick and vicious and deeply rotten, but he generally spoke the truth.

Deep down, she believed Rafe wasn't complicit with JJ, and she hoped to have a chance to reconcile with him and be siblings, but she would never work for Prime Energy again.

Bastian draped an arm around her. "How's the pain?" he asked.

"I think every part of me aches, but it's manageable." Her voice held a slight rasp. She was warned to watch for signs of swelling in her throat increasing, and one of the men flying with them was a medic who'd been briefed on her condition.

Bastian's lips touched her forehead. "It's a long flight. You should sleep."

"I don't know if I can."

"Try. For me?"

She smiled up at him, this man who'd come after her and helped save her from torture that would have resulted in an agonizing death. She'd been told he watched the cargo plane explode, believing she'd been aboard, and could only imagine how awful that had been for him, given how much it had hurt to be told he was dead.

She, at least, had reason to doubt Nikolai's words.

"I love you," she whispered, aching for the blows he'd taken. All because of her. Because Nikolai had been obsessed with her since she was a child. How many people had been harmed because of one man's depraved fixation?

Had the cosmetic ads been the cause, or the result? She hadn't known Nikolai's father owned Carabella. Had she been offered the gig because Nikolai had wanted to see her vamping for a camera? But none of that mattered now.

Instead, she had the horror of knowing the slave market had formed in part because of her—that it served other goals of Nikolai's was merely a bonus for him. The food destruction would kill hundreds in the famine. Again, it served Nikolai and Lawiri's other goals, but the facility had been selected because of her.

And if they couldn't locate the Ebola-laced pads, thousands could die. What if they weren't going to South

Sudan? What if Nikolai had shipped them elsewhere to bide his time? What if they couldn't find them? There was a lot of territory between Morocco and South Sudan. One truck wouldn't be hard to hide.

"I love you too," Bastian said, smoothing her furrowed brow with an index finger.

She closed her eyes again and was pelted with images from their nightmarish day. She shoved those aside and instead chose to focus on the previous night, when they'd made love in the hammam. For a few hours, they'd escaped into each other and the world had been perfect. And it would be again. She had to believe that.

F ifty-six hours later, word came down that the truck had been located in Nigeria. Bastian was in the gym working out with several of the guys on his team when Savvy came charging in to share the news. Bastian abandoned his workout to tell Brie, who was still asleep in her CLU.

He let himself in and paused to stare at her as she slept. The bruises on her face and neck had gotten worse and were now in the purple-fading-to-green stage. But no amount of bruising and swelling would diminish her beauty to him. She could be Brie Stewart or Princess Prime and he didn't care, because no matter what she wore on the outside, she was the most beautiful woman he'd ever known on the inside.

Her dedication to her work was only one thing he loved about her. He was also pretty crazy about the way she faced challenges, owned her past, and was passionate about making the world a better place for those in desperate need, no matter the risk to herself. And the way he felt when he was with her... He imagined it was similar to a drug high but without the steep price.

He sat on the cot beside her and leaned down to kiss her lips. "Wake up, sweetheart."

"Don't wanna," she murmured without opening her eyes, but she smiled.

He kissed her neck, her lips, her cheek. "You sure?"

She let out a soft purr. "Well, maybe." She opened one eye, then glanced at the clock. "It's not even seven yet. What are you doing here? I thought you were working out with your team this morning?"

"I was. But Savvy interrupted us with news I thought you'd want to hear. A UN team found the truck."

Brie sat up, both eyes open, fully awake now. "They did? And the pads weren't distributed yet?"

"Everything is sealed tight. They found it in Nigeria as it was crossing into Chad. The team collected samples, which are being sent to the CDC for testing." There was still hope that the scientists had lied to Drugov about their success in bioengineering the virus, and Russia didn't have weaponized Ebola in their arsenal. "But out of caution, they're moving the truck to a remote area, where they will remove, then burn the contents."

She threw her arms around Bastian's shoulders. "I'm so relieved."

He held her against him, breathing in her scent. Truly, deeply, and undeniably happy. South Sudan's civil war would continue. People would starve. The situation there would remain horrific. But thousands of young girls wouldn't contract and spread Ebola simply because they'd gotten their period.

He'd take this as a win, pathetic as it was.

The embrace ended, and Brie relaxed against his chest.

"You should try to go back to sleep," he said, stroking her hair. He knew she hadn't slept well the last two nights.

"I should get dressed and talk to Savvy. I want more details. Hell, I wish I could see the pads burn with my own eyes."

He understood that need. He released her and rose from the bed, clearing a path for her to get up. She grabbed clothes from the locker and pulled them on. They'd left everything behind in Casablanca, so she was back to wearing T-shirts purchased at the base store.

"Savvy also told me our suitcases will arrive today." At the Army's request, yesterday a maid had packed their belongings under the watchful eye of an FBI investigator, who'd shipped the bags to Camp Citron. "You'll have your new passport back."

She bit her lip. "I guess that means I'll be heading home soon. I'm a distraction for you, and you need to get back to training Djiboutians."

He nodded. "Yeah. Tomorrow I'm back to my regular duties." He frowned. "You won't go back to Morocco, will you?"

"Not while JJ's at large."

"Good."

"I made a decision when I was tossing and turning last night. Today I'm going to talk to Rafe about breaking the trust and selling the Casablanca house. I'm going to use my share as seed money for a charitable foundation focused on menstruation underwear for adolescent girls. I'm going to suggest Rafe donate his share too. I want JJ's portion too, but odds are he'll have to be convicted of conspiring with Nikolai in my abduction before he'll give it up. Donating the money to my foundation is the least they owe me, considering Dad used my virginity to buy the place."

"I think that's a great idea. But damn, I'll miss that Turkish bath."

Her smile lit her eyes. "Me too. Maybe we can visit again before the house sells. How long are you going to be stuck here?"

He stepped forward, crooked a finger in the front of her jeans, and pulled her to him. "This deployment is all kinds of screwed up, but another A-Team is coming in a month. Even if our trainees aren't ready, we'll go home. They'll need our CLUs for the new team, and they can wrap up the training with the Djiboutians before they start with a new set of trainees."

She rested her forehead on his chest. "I can wait a month." She lifted her head and met his gaze. "But I'm going to have to get used to you being gone on long deployments, aren't I?"

He nodded. This was the hard part of being in the Army and a relationship, and something he'd managed to avoid for nearly a decade. "This is my job. And when it doesn't suck, I love it."

"Don't worry. I'm in, Bastian. A hundred percent. If I only get you six months out of the year, I'll take it and be happy. If USAID were still a possibility for me, I'd seek short deployments while you're gone, but at this point, I'm too much of a kidnapping risk. So maybe I'll set up my foundation near Fort Campbell, Kentucky."

Bastian's heart expanded. "You're going to stay in my apartment?" He'd offered his home to her several times, but she hadn't been ready to make a decision.

She nodded. "Pax told me yesterday that Morgan's heading to Fort Campbell in a week. I don't really know her, but…I don't know…the idea of having an almost-friend there to help me settle in is appealing. Plus she'll be missing Pax as much as I'm missing you. We can commiserate."

He kissed her nose. "You should know my apartment is nothing like your home in Casablanca. There's a lot more Ikea going on than hand-stuffed by fairies."

"As long as it doesn't have a pit toilet, I'm good."

"Um—" He winked at her.

She laughed and stepped back, turning to the sink where she brushed her teeth, then studied the bruises on her neck in the mirror. "Damn, I look like hell."

"You're beautiful. You look like you've been *through* hell. There's a difference."

He stepped up behind her. "I'd like to Skype my parents today and introduce you to them."

In the mirror, her eyes widened. "Are you sure? Maybe you should mend your relationship with them before you throw me into the mix."

He planted his hands on her hips and turned her to face him. "You are the most important person in my life. I want them to meet you. To know what you mean to me. I'm proud that we're together, that you love *me*. Hell, I want a do-over of the flight deck ceremony so I can step up to the microphone and tell the whole world Brie Stewart is *mine*. And if you were still Gabriella Prime, that wouldn't change how I feel. I don't love you for your name, your money—or lack of it—or any façade the world sees. I love *you* with everything I am." He paused. "When I watched that plane explode—" He cleared his throat as his eyes teared. "I—I—" He shook his head. "There aren't words for the feeling."

Her eyes filled with tears that didn't fall.

He pressed his lips to her forehead and took a deep breath, then said, "I'm not going to waste another moment of my life on hurt and anger. I'm not going to spend another day pissed because my parents chose Cece over me. I left instead of fighting, but I'm not going to run anymore. I love them. I love you. If they don't see that inside you were never the person the world believed you to be, then they aren't giving you a chance."

She cupped his face between her palms. "I love you so much. I'm scared you'll be hurt in this. I don't want to be the cause of more pain between you and your parents."

He took her arm and ran his fingers over the needle scars. "You've owned your past, and you've busted your ass to make amends. Hell, you were the reason the pipeline failed in the first place. If they can't see who you are, it's on them. And in that situation, *you* wouldn't be the cause of my pain. They would. But that's not going to happen, because I have a feeling I've underestimated them in my hurt and anger. They love me. I know they want me to be happy. And when I'm with you, I'm happier than I've ever been in my life."

She pressed her forehead to his chest. "In the Turkish bath—I couldn't believe how happy I was, in spite of our crazy situation. I was happy because I was with you. Even being stranded in South Sudan was fun in the strangest way." She let out a soft laugh and lifted her head to meet his gaze. "We'll always have South Sudan."

He laughed. "Damn. You beat me to it. That was supposed to be my line."

She stroked the stubble on his cheek. "So, your enemies call you asshole. Lovers call you bastard. What do friends with extreme benefits call you?"

"I don't know. I've never had one of those before.

What do you want to call me?"

She draped her arms around his neck and kissed him. "Mine," she said. "All mine."

Author's Note

Readers of my Evidence Series will recognize a certain Russian character in this book and might wonder about the timeline differences between the two series. Where possible, I avoid identifying the exact year in the books, but I will say that *Catalyst*—set in the "nebulous now" that happens to be spring 2017—takes place about six months before *Cold Evidence*. If you haven't read the Evidence series but want to know more, you can start with *Cold Evidence*, where the Russian makes his first appearance.

I couldn't resist connecting this series to another one of my books, *Grave Danger*. Set in Bastian's hometown of Coho, Washington, in the year 2002, *Grave Danger* is the story of the Kalahwamish Tribe's treatment by the owners of the historic sawmill town. A romantic mystery, *Grave Danger* features an archaeologist who digs up an old murder victim, and a police chief who battles both attraction and suspicion from the moment they first meet. You won't find fifteen-year-old Bastian in the story, but you'll probably meet him as a teen when I write the sequel.

The issue of girls in the developing world dropping out of school because they have no way to manage their period is real, as is the crisis of famine and civil war in South Sudan. If any part of this story has touched you, and if you can afford to give to those in desperate need, please join me in donating to a charity that sends reusable menstrual panties to the developing world, and/or food aid to South Sudan.

Some suggestions are:
Days For Girls - www.daysforgirls.org
Pads4Girls - www.lunapads.com/pads4girls
World Food Programme - www1.wfp.org/south-sudan-emergency
Oxfam - www.oxfamamerica.org

Thank you for reading *Catalyst*. I hope you enjoyed it.

If you'd like to know when my next book is available, you can sign up for my VIP list at www.Rachel-Grant.net.

Acknowledgements

Thank you to Centers for Disease Control and Prevention Infectious Disease Specialist Jennifer McQuiston for answering my questions about Ebola. Her opinions do not represent the opinion of the CDC. Inaccuracies due to error or fictional license are all on me.

Thank you to Vicki Lowe, descendant and involved community member of the Jamestown S'Klallam Tribe, who read this manuscript with an eye for sensitivity in writing a character with a different ethnic background from myself. Any mistakes in this area are my own.

Thank you to Darcy Burke and Elisabeth Naughton for endless (and patient) plotting help with this book (that would not end). Thank you to Gwen Hernandez, Gwen Hayes, and Toni Anderson for both their plotting wisdom and for critiquing this manuscript.

Thank you to all the authors who are there for me online—using Twitter, Facebook, or private messages—who keep this from being a lonely profession.

To my readers, thank you for all the wonderful emails, Tweets, and posts. It means so much to me to know my work brings you joy, something I greatly need during this difficult time.

Thank you to my children for accepting the chore of making dinner more often without complaint. I write better when I eat healthy, home cooked meals.

Thank you to my husband for his support and patience as I struggle with characters and scenes, but mostly thank you for sharing this wonderful life with me.

About the Author

Four-time Golden Heart® finalist Rachel Grant worked for over a decade as a professional archaeologist and mines her experiences for storylines and settings, which are as diverse as excavating a cemetery underneath an historic art museum in San Francisco, survey and excavation of many prehistoric Native American sites in the Pacific Northwest, researching an historic concrete house in Virginia, and mapping a seventeenth century Spanish and Dutch fort on the island of Sint Maarten in the Netherlands Antilles.

She lives in the Pacific Northwest with her husband and children and can be found on the web at www.Rachel-Grant.net.